Other books on Trafford and Amazon by Author are "How Green was Our Wave" and "The Republic of Paradise." kevin.cavey@gmail.com

BRAY FOR THE BRAVE

QUIET BEGINNINGS WITH A BIZARRE ENDING

KEVIN CAVEY

Order this book online at www.trafford.com
or email orders@trafford.com

Most Trafford titles are also available at major online book retailers.

Print information available on the last page.

ISBN: 978-1-6987-0844-7 (sc)
ISBN: 978-1-6987-0845-4 (e)

Trafford rev. 01/30/24

www.trafford.com

North America & international
toll-free: 844-688-6899 (USA & Canada)
fax: 812 355 4082

The Author was born in Dublin in 1941 and holds both Irish and Canadian citizenships. His great grandmother on his father's side was from Cincinnati Ohio but moved to Ireland when in her twenties. The Author married Ann Marie Kelly in 1969 and they had one fine son Paul and two beautiful daughters Carolyn and Georgina. His early years were in the hotel and restaurant business and finally hospital catering. During free time from work and also in retirement he studied Theology, Physics, Mathematics and Art leading to the eventual study of Architecture in University College Dublin. His sports are surfing, skiing, painting, and mountain hiking.

For this book, as for two others, I received help from family and friends. Also, Kathleen Carney from Bray's public library who gave me a copy of Albert Einstein's Theories on relativity which I struggled to understand and never did! In later years, a lot of these studies came together indicating various ways forward. Also, thanks to the good Lord above and to my wife and family who gave me support despite many obstacles.

One of my friends asked me about what was behind the thinking when I wrote the first section of this book. I said it was to recall the controversial days of living and working with my Dad, Bill Cavey. Caution was required in the science section, but I carried on in the hope that I was not the victim of being fossilized in my own certainties! Unfortunately, I think I was. The experiences of the hotel business are real, then physics is kept to a minimum, and the third section is an exciting dream! It is up to you to make it come true!

PART 1

BILL CAVEY'S ROYAL HOTEL
(A True Story)

William Henry Cavey

T he story, I am about to tell, can happen once upon a light wave. It traces its origin, to that innocent, and helicon times of the late forties. This was a time, when the world population began to relax, after years of war and destruction. My first consciousness must have been close to the moment of birth because I remember being very comfortable and then suddenly being reluctantly awakened. The result was a feeling like everything began to move a new feeling that I was now experiencing. There was no looking back and as luck had it, I was blessed with a nice home. My dad was William Henry Cavey and my mother, Vera (Smyth) Cavey. Our family lived in number 17 Cowper Drive, on a peaceful cul-de-sac in Ranelagh, South Dublin. The home was a two-story flat roofed dwelling on a short cul-de-sac lined with Georgian and Tudor style homes. Their house was positioned at the end of the road close to an electric supply generator and a large unused field which on which a small bungalow was situated. All this was to the south side of their house while on the west there was a railway connecting Dublin with the coastal towns of Bray and Wicklow. Bray was a fascinating because while it had at the time population of 13,000 this almost doubled in the summer when the British and North of Ireland tourists descended. It became a sort of Brighton and a great place to go for fun and relaxation.

Meanwhile back in Ranelagh one could argue that the Cavey house was a little out of place in such an old-style neighbourhood because of its very modern design and art deco profile. It had smooth concrete walls painted white, and the roof parapet was topped with a line of red brick. There was an internal stair that made its flat roof accessible. However, it was rarely used yet this was a feature that made the house, very special, to the occupants. On the downside, it had single pane iron framed windows, the sort that was common during that era as there was nothing else available at a modest price, so had to put up with continued condensation. Nevertheless, the house had a sort of classic design, reminiscent of 'Villa Savoye Poissy by Le Corbusier.' The foreign visage was made all the more convincing as there was an abundance of semi tropical vegetation in front of the house. For example, close to the hall door there was large Trachycarpus Fortune with its very oriental looking fan leaves. Cleverly positioned close by a Japanese lantern climbing plant (lantern columbine) with bright orange lantern shaped flowers bringing a splash of pleasant colour as one enters the home. As well as some castor oil plants, there were several Cordylines Australis with their long green spikes that rattle in the wind. Then there was the controversial aspect for consideration. The Harcourt Street to Bray train line passed behind our back garden. To some people this would be a nuisance, but our family were unperturbed.

Though the country had been neutral during the second world war, thousands of youths became soldiers on the side of the allies. Some joined the American Armed Forces, but many more joined the British Armed Services some as Doctors and flyers, but the majority joined the infantry. In many instances joining-up was done to gain employment. As a result, when the war was over there were lots returned soldiers, with tales of valor. I was, of course a typical youth of medium height for my age with fairish hair and I am told I had a very open and trusting face. I spoke with a good articulate accent; this was inherited directly from my Dad who was a generation closer to being American and my south Belfast mother. As they often chastised me, I developed a polite demeanor with adults, but I was a dare devil amongst my peers. However, from a commercial point of view I was not a smart kid and was also only mediocre in school. I always seemed to miss out on what was being said and therefore was constantly one step behind the posse. The folks often left me home alone and I did not mind because I had an electric train and a newfound hobby of collecting soldiers. But if they were not home before dark, I got frightened. To remedy this, I reckoned I should be aggressive. This meant standing the hall and bellowing at the ghosts, telling them that I was coming to get them, they were to get lost, or I would mince them. It worked wonders.

My Dad was called Bill, William or Willie depending on how long people had known him. He was not tall but because of his sport of rowing, had developed very broad shoulders. His mother was called Annie O'Brien who was from Cincinnati Ohio, but at the age of sixteen she became blind. The story goes that the nuns in the convent where she went to school prayed constantly for her recovery. Alas, her sight was restored without surgery some four years later. Annie vowed in gratitude to God that from that time onwards she would never look in a mirror again. Bill said that his mother kept that promise till the very end. Later her family who were originally of Irish decent returned to Ireland. Annie eventually married a man who was a dairy farmer from Hollywood West Wicklow and raised Bill and a family of six. Bill was therefore part American but as a child in Dublin that was not identifiable. He remembered going to school in Sing Street where he met the late Gay Byrne and others of that era who by now are dead and gone.

BILL'S SHOP

In 1939 Bill noticed a grocery store for sale at 39 lower Camden Street Dublin. Without hesitation he approached the Allied Irish Bank on south Richmond Street about getting a loan to purchase the shop.

Martin, Bill's Assistant at his Wine and Spirits shop

A Mr. Watson the then manager identified Bill's honesty and determination, a quality worth an investment. Bill worked hard in his early life and had now become the proud owner of a store called William H Cavey Grocer. Interestingly enough, Bill's earlier home was near the five lamps Clontarf on the north strand. Alarmingly, it was bombed during the second world war but by then it had a new owner and there was no loss of life. The bomber had been mistaken Dublin for London. Bill also remembered that when he was a boy and still lived in the north strand their house was taken over by the Black and Tans and used as a machine gun post. He was of course way too young to have joined up.

HIS ROMANCE

As Bill was a person with a charming manner his customer increased and so did his trading profits. Now it was time to share his life with another. Before he met Vera Smyth from Belfast, Bill had a crush on a fine lass whose father owned Cunnium's Pub at Christ Church Place in Dublin. This relationship did not develop, and time was passing. His close friends called Perter Curry who was a newspaper correspondent in Dublin knew that a charming daughter of James Smyth from Belfast, would be attending a dinner dance at Shanganagh Hotel and invited Bill as a possible suitor. Little more need be said because Bill and Vera became engaged weeks later and Bill began a series of journeys to visit her home in Myrtle field Park and her parents, James, and Sarah Smyth. It was love at first sight and soon Bill was travelling to 15 Myrtlefield Park in Belfast with sides of bacon that was much appreciated by the Vera's family when their war coupons were often spent. Soon they were married most likely in Saint Brigid's Parish Church Derryvolgie. Following that they went on a spectacular honeymoon around the Irish coastline. It started in Donegal, and when in Galway they stayed in the beautiful Ashford Castle which in those days had peacocks wandering free in the extensive grounds. Vera had two brothers and a sister. Her father was James Smyth a salesperson for Douglas and Greens Linen company in Belfast. James was a top-class salesperson, and this was evident because he was often sent to New York selling their product. He was a tall lean man with a long face, horn rim glasses and receding hair. On his return from trips on the Cunard Queen ships he usually gave me a few pencils or a notebook – I was delighted. However, as he liked whiskey, and a good smoke he was very entertaining when with adults. Some of his actions entertained me. I liked how he drew a senior service or a player's cigarette from his silver cigarette case, then tap it on the metal cover to firm it up before lighting it. Then he gripped it in two brown fingers and took up where he had left off talking. Vera's mother was very small, plump and with on lame lag. She wore the cloths in keeping with her gender, long dark coats, dull pattern dresses with a broach and a hat with some floral decoration. She was from a farm in Co Down and was full of old sayings. "It's a weary world," Ach ani, ani." or "Have some bread and butter with tith, tith, tith."

THE ROYAL HOTEL BRAY

The Quin's hotel stood high and overlooked the bridge at the entry to the town from the north. It was built in 1776 and owned by John Quin Senior. In 1800 he gave it to his son and for a brief time it was called the Meath Hotel. In those days both Charles Dickens, Sir Arthur Conan Doyle and William Thackery are alleged to have stayed. Then in 1845 Daniel O'Connell also joined the list of dignitaries who graced the hotel with their presence. The hotel was re designed by the architect John Mc Curdy who also designed the Gresham in Dublin and the Royal Marine Hotel Dun Laoghaire.

QUIN'S HOTEL
Bray

In 1946 it was to have a new owner, and that was Bill Cavey. The hotel had been on sale for quite a while It had about forty rooms and it consisted of three building linked together. It was on the main street with a commanding view of traffic entering the town. In no time, Bill bought an adjoining building making the hotel much larger. This purchase was just in time to catch the tourist trade that began after the war. Also, as the hotel was more than ten miles from Dublin therefore by law people could travel from the city and get an extra hour drinking time because this was County Wicklow and not County Dublin. Needless to say, trade was enormous, and this sorted Bill's finances and led him to plan for a bright future. He had bought 17 Cowper Drive, Ranelagh but now faced having to travel as often as possible between 39 Camden Street and Bray, some twelve miles away. In those days he often used the train. As there were also many social engagements and he now needed my mother at his side. She was inevitably brought to bray on weekends and that meant I was also dragged along. Now Vera as said was a home bird by nature, but she could be very charming with guests. On several occasions in the hotel gentlemen pulled me aside and said that my mum was very pretty and that I was lucky she was so nice. I guess they wanted me to repeat their compliments to her, which I did. She just rolled her eyes to heaven.

BIKE AND TRAIN

Before buying a car, my dad had a bicycle to get around and had a tiny saddle fitted to the cross bar for me. I was about four at the time and in my estimation, he was the greatest and in him I felt the essence of almighty god. He could do anything, my hero. Bill was generous and I saw him leave home with tools to help a local poor person with their broken windows and doors. This made a lasting impression. He also had a saying – one had to be cruel to be kind and as time went on, I found this was true. Nevertheless, I felt I was a lucky kid, because my home was at the end if a cul-de-sac, no traffic, plenty of play space, roller skating at will. The rear of the house was also endowed with a nice L shaped garden. There was a high wall behind which the already mentioned, steam-trains passed on their way to and from town Bray or further. There was another person living with us and that was my parent's home help, a girl called Kathleen from Wexford. Kathleen and I became so attached that she was like a second mother and often filled in to keep me happy when my folks were elsewhere. She was the unlucky one, because on one occasion she witnessed my falling while playing on a heap of logs, one of which had a rusty nail protruding that cut my face just above the right eye. There were screams and lots of blood. So, Kathleen dragged me on the local bus to Doctor Nightingale's on the south circular road who put in three stitches. Over the years the scar remained. Around the same time, I fell at the same place and badly cut my right-hand thumb. Now, the wound was not properly cared for and after several months I was taken by my parents to a Doctor Mc Mahon, who lanced the suppurating wound. After another three months the thumb was in worse condition and it seems that the Doc had damaged the bone when he lanced it. Therefore, I found my life governed by a sore the thumb that would not bend and grew in a disfigured shape. This meant no more school rugby and the avoidance of any impact that would make it sore and tingling. I also recall an original event that occurred on my fourth birthday. My Dad and my grandfather James Smyth from Belfast (Glander, as he was called) had a surprise for me and my partying friends. My Mom and her friends came out to the garden where we were playing and said for us to look up at the roof. Just then there was an enormous crashing sound (tin cans rattling). They said Santa Clause must have crashed, and with that Santa dressed in red and with a white beard looked down on us and waved while showering us with candies. We went berserk but no one questioned what was Santa doing here in May!

Bill had also been successful in the production of KV (Kevin Vera) Mayonnaise and Salad Cream. He successfully supplied Aer Lingus the National Airlines during the Second war years. Then when the war ended Cross, and Blackwell's returned to the market and Bill got out. He then became a wine shipper, one of the first of its kind in Ireland. The manager of the wine shop was Eddie Gilmartin, and his assistant were Alfie Byrne. Eddie was a member of the Rathgar and Rathmines choral society- a man of great fiber. He was a walking connoisseur of wines and on quickly locating where each precious box was located when shelves were needed to be replenished in the store. Alfie always made the tea and loved talking to old ladies and at the least provocation was the source of loud laughter. There was a Miss Mulvey who was Bill's bookkeeper. She was positioned on a highchair and desk with a big ledger in front of her. The book had multicolored edges and her writing was very neat. When I grew older, at Christmas it was expected that I would go in to help in the shop. I was given many tasks to perform but one stuck in my mind. Dad taught me how he cut bacon on his manual slicing machine. First, he laid pieces of grease proof paper beside the slicer and told me to make packets of twelve slices. To every third slice of good back bacon, I was to insert a slice of collar, which is cheaper. "They are paying for the Back bacon but how else can we make a profit? Now away you go." That little exercise encapsulated what business is all about, but it frightened me and what if someone complained, I would be so embarrassed.

Bill's brother Frank was also an entrepreneur and a very successful one at that. He was married to Billie who was a woman of character who loved a drink and a laugh. They had four children, Morris, Noleen, Angela and Sheila. Frank secured the Jaguar Car agency for Ireland and had premises was almost opposite Bill's shop. Now, this was no small venture and soon, he was delivering new Jaguars all over Ireland. The Irish Jaguar Club had to say that delivery in the Republic was complicated by enormous rates of duty on imported cars. To circumvent this most manufacturers supplied 'Complete Knocked Down' kits for the Irish agent to assemble locally and using locally sourced components. The said that historically Frank Cavey & Sons were appointed as official Jaguar agents in 1937. They assembled SS saloons, and MkV11's and this was made easier because Frank had a close relationship with William Lyons the owner of Jaguar. In 1951 six roadsters were assembled and sold and in 1952 another 20 XK's were imported fully assembled. Morris Frank's son joined the company and became a racing driver. In 1950 he did a mechanical check on a D type mark V3.5 Liter saloon ZE 7445. Then he joined the owner, Cecil Vard to enter the Monto Carlo rally. Both he and Vard drove together for some years and won other races around Ireland. As a result, when I went to school some guys called me sauce because of Dad's mayonnaise, and others asked if I could get their Dad's name on the waiting list for a car. This was in the days when I was at St Mary's college Rathmines, a school that I loved.

HALLOWEEN

I recall when I was four or five and it was Halloween, and at 4 pm as promised, my dad came home from work with a box of fireworks. I had never experienced such excitement before - I could feel my heart pound with expectation. By 5pm it was a pitch-dark evening with a clear sky. The crowd of neighborhood children gathered for the show. Bill was the one to manage the evening. He had the fireworks, the matches, and the responsibility, which he handled with professionalism. Then he spoke out loudly requesting that everyone must stand well back, while he did the lighting of the fuses. The show commenced with a display of Catherine wheels and bouncing Betties. This was followed by Roman Candles followed by the climax of the entertainment- sky rockets. It was at this point that I felt my first curiosity about physics. As I stood aghast, Dad selected the largest Rocket from the box. With great care he ignited it, running immediately back to where my mother and I were standing. With an almighty swish the rocket shot upwards into the black inky sky. A magnificent shower of sparks erupted in a multicolored plume and at the same time there was a deafening boom. The onlookers gasped while I was so overcome just wanted to be everywhere at once. My legs were just not good enough for the task, I needed wings. I thought that I must run and find the burned-out rocket - but where was Paddy who was known as Padser, my next-door buddy and the others? I felt weighed down by his human inability to move where and when I wanted. Unknown to me I was the victim of the first force of nature, that of Gravity. I was not the only victim of this invisible force, because the beautiful rocket, also a victim, turned at its zenith and came crashing to the ground. Yes, a great invisible kill-joy force, was at work in our midst.

From that evening onwards my mind was spurred on to wonder about the universe, what is it? I pondered. I was still too young for reading and studying the subject of physics and the forces of nature. So, it would have to wait till a later stage in my life. However, there was nothing to stop me pondering eternity. - in simple child logic I questioned? If space goes on forever as I was told and if God who is eternal also goes on forever then the two must have something of a common bond, a denominator and must surely meet at some point in time! Even the physical Universe must be a highway to a higher dimension. Padser told me that if God stopped thinking about us, we would not exist! In later years that point struck me as being something to do with the possibilities our having a quantum Creator. So that thought was laid to rest for future consideration! From then on, I used my dad's binoculars to look at the moon on clear nights. I could see the craters quite easily and was astonished.

THE NEIGHBOURHOOD

On a more down to earth subject, my life was affected by a train that that ran behind our house. I got to know the schedule and used to climb up on the back wall and wave to the engine driver though he or she never noticed my presence. Then to add to the excitement my Dad was sometimes a passenger because of his hotel in Bray that he visited quite often. My greatest moment was when as the train passed, he would open the window and chuck a packet of biscuits or sweets into the garden. What a calamity, and who else had such a Dad! However, the train belched lots of smoke that dirtied any fresh washing on the cloths line. Therefore, they had to be taken in before the train arrived. My Mum was a wonderful cook and had recipes for cinnamon biscuits and cakes with lots of marzipan, but she could also do more than that. Most of her recipes were from her early days in Belfast and some from her school days in Bally Castle.

To recap, our home was number 17 while in number 16 there was a family from Wexford. Paddy Carroll their young son my pal was the one I referred to earlier to as Padser because my Dad used to call him that name. He had an elder brother called Milo and two sisters, Una and Mella. In later years Mella became Ireland first lady high court judge. His Father was a chief superintendent in the police and manager of the Irish International Boxing team in the 40's. Then I noticed that he was driven to work daily in a Ford 8 by a detective named Johnny Walker. Johnny was a tall trim man with neat well-oiled hair who always arrived bright and early every morning at 8.30 a.m. He would back the car out of the Carroll's garage. Then he would proceed to give it a polish before taking Chief Superintendent Carroll to the Phoenix Park his place of work. One day when Padser and I were hanging around, we asked the detective if he carried a gun, and then began pestering him to show it to us. Eventually he drew out from inside his neat double-breasted suit a rather bulky Wesley automatic. We were astounded not only with the shape of the gun, but with its weigh. When he and the Superintendent were leaving, they often allowed us stand on the running boards of the car travelling at about five m.p.h. Walker would rev the engine and it would seem like it was really going fast, another a thrill. This was like being a gangster in Chicago except that we knew nothing of them darn places.

Dad on the other hand had a Jaguar but then moved over to own a cream colored '47 Chrysler, license number ZD 9963. (Our phone number was 91331.) I think he became conscious that he should support his brother. He then began buying Jaguars but had trouble getting servicing, but he stuck with it. A feature of the Jaguar was a boost button you pressed a minute or so before pressing the starter button. This was a lot better than having to crank the engine with an iron bar, as did most cars in the 50's. It also had an openable sunroof. Often times Padser and I were let stand up with our head and shoulders out through the opening. This happened when the car was moving quite fast perhaps taking us for a day at the beach. The 'Super' next door never complained about danger, he just trusted, that was the good old days. There was a rather posh (meaning the best cabins on a trans-Atlantic liner are **p**ort going **o**ut **s**tarboard coming **h**ome - **posh**) young fellow whose family lived opposite our house. He often came out his gate and surveyed what was going on. Then if he saw us, he would look in disgust and call us isosceles triangles. This was hardly an insult, but we felt it was because of the way he said it! One day his parents took delivery of an extraordinary car. It was American and perhaps the beginning of USA's new trend in automobile profiles. This one was a Studebaker, and it had a long boot or trunk that was the same length as the hood or bonnet. Everyone kidded that you would not know if it was going or coming. On the twenty second of May 1947 my baby brother Colm was born. From then on, I was not the most important being in our family and I had to learn how to share. However, as he was six years younger than me, I could push him around but that came to an end when he got older.

At the top of the cul de sac and beside our home there was a large electricity generating station that had a terracotta tile roof long church like windows and the building was constructed of silvery granite and white concrete. There was a row of tall poplar trees lining the building, and on sunny days with a blue sky, the scene, conjured a feeling of ancient Greece. I felt like I was dreaming or that I had visited such a place before! It seemed unreal, quite of out of character, in fact like a place where someone like Plato or Aristotle might have lived. Of course, I had never heard of them at that early stage. There was a nice family called the Shaw's living in a bungalow there. It was on the ESB Electricity Supply Board property site and the parents were the caretakers. They had two daughters Eileen and Joan who was my age but being a girl Padser and I did not bother with her at first. They went to Sanford Park School in Ranelagh. The gates to her home filled the end of the cul-de-sac and she would often hang on them looking at us like she wanted to play. Her garden was very large filled with vegetables, and stretched to meet the railway line, divided by a low wall. All this was adjacent to our house and in view of my bedroom. One day she said through the gate that she had a secret and would tell us if we came in. We did so and messed around a bit, playing hospital with her dolls. She never told us the secret, but I reckon it was to do with where babies come from. As the railway line was so accessible from her garden lots of the neighborhood gangs traipsed through her land to put stones on the train tracks so as to make gunpowder they thought. This dangerous pastime came to a head one day when all of us arrived at the same time and lined the tracks for about twenty feet. We hid behind the wall and as the train came the cracking was like gunfire. To our horror the train slowed down and then stopped while a guard began to run towards us. We bolted in all directions and in my case, it was upstairs and under my bed. I never tried that sort of fun again.

Yet, our naughtiness never went away. One day Padser and I were discovered green faced and ill from smoking my dad's pipe filled with crushed Cuban cigar. Padser also invented the toothpaste sandwich. The paste was spread between two Marietta biscuits and squeezed together till it oozed out the holes. The result of this transgression was stomach pains, and some domestic internment - not worth it! The folks could be tough when necessary and, in those claim free days an adult could punish one by giving a whack that would make a boxer jealous. It was the way of life, it was everywhere. The teachers in school would slap a lad for any reason they wished and even the bus man was likely to give one a clip on the ear for not having enough money for the fare or for giving lip. Then there were one's peers, who could corner you and land a few punches because you just were not part of their gang though you would sometimes do the same back! Then there was the dog at the end of the cul de sac who savaged anyone who walked by his house. He was known as the bowler, and I was terrified of him. Later when I got to ride my bike to school, I was beaten up on the way home if I happened to take the wrong route. The offending guys in question would run out of their houses and threw any and everything after you. Surviving life in those days one felt like being in a pin ball machine crashing from one rebound to another. Finally, I was shot on the bare leg by a pellet from a pellet gun. The sting was enormous, and the villain was a lad shooting out his bedroom window. It's a wonderful world!

Bill had three sports that he practiced. One used to be rowing but now replaced by swimming. The second was golf and the third was lake and river fishing with his friends. He rarely came home without a good catch. As he liked the west of Ireland, and also appreciate good hotels, sometimes he took me along. The trips were usually in spring, and we always went to Ashford Castel in Cong. After a winter of school and cross teachers and feeling sorry for myself, visiting the fresh greenery and the lake was a relief. I felt like after all life was worth it. A Mr. Gibbons from the village was the local ghillie and Bill availed of his services on each trip. The hotel was true to the term castle. There were battlements and fortified wall spread around the property and it all looked out on Lough Corrib at the point where the river Corrib entered the lake. We went trolling for trout every day and visited at least ten of the 365 islands that were in the lake. The Castel was originally owned by the Guinness family and later by Lady Oranmore and Brown. Despite the splendor, I think at the time I was mentally mixed up. I told myself that it was my fault and just to grin and bear it. However, I learned over time that by staying positive and filling my mind with loads of new thoughts and observation, I could control the phobia. At Ashford Castel I felt a wave of relief derived from the magnificent exploding nature all around. At every island where we landed, I always headed off to explore. I was looking out for enemy snipers or Apache scouts, all very exciting. I think I used to pray or recite a mantra about my being intimated by life as I went, but this did not detract from the fun. On one such adventure I climbed an Ash tree and wailed to the sky. Then to my surprise, while the weather was bone dry, I found the main stem had streams of water running down its surface. In an instant I believed that the tree was crying for me. The thought that some object in nature or super nature could pity me was of immense consolation. This brought about a ray of hope that was to grow in time. On one trip we landed on a U-shaped Island called either inchagill or innchmahon, not sure which. There were some tourists there before us and their ghillie had wrapped their fresh caught salmon in wet newspaper and cast it into the embers of their fire. After twenty minutes he retrieved the salmon and cut away the paper to reveal succulent pink fish which they shared with us on slices of buttered bread. This and other memories will live forever. In later years I related the story to a well-known lady, who ran a cookery school. She wrote a book of recipes and related my story but said a fisherman told her! So much for me. Bill also was a golfer, and he found that I was too impatient for the sport. However, he had plenty of friends in the Bray Golf Club where he played often and became a member of a team competing in Prestatyn in Wales. This got a lot of media interest.

In the summer we stayed in the Bray hotel. We resided in room number 15 on the second floor that overlooked Bray main street. So, after a day at the seaside my folks were glad to shunt me and young Colm off to bed early so they could get down to have dinner. Left to our own devices, we would jump and dive from the sideboard onto the beds as if still in the ocean. Then as darkness fell, we would listen to the sounds of happy throngs of people singing and having a jolly good time. Many were, Welsh or English or Scotts and in those days the emphasis was happiness. At least by midnight we would be asleep.

One day I saw in a newspaper a picture of Pearl Harbor in flames. I asked my Dad what was that all about. Somehow it was then that my American gene came to the fore. I was shocked to the core by the thought of such a terrible thing happening to my beloved America. I could not believe that such a great power could have been hit by such a calamity and I almost cried. Later I came across a pile of National Geographic Magazines in the back porch of Padser's home. He said they were belonging to his Dad, so I flicked the pages and settled on some graphic pictures painted in oils by a war corresponded. They were vivid renderings of the war in the Pacific. Some were of Arial battles with US Navy hellcats in a cloudless sky over an ink blue ocean with fleets of battle cruisers ploughing up the sea below. But other pictures were of Marines fighting under the green canopy of the jungles in Guadalcanal, Bougainville, and New Britain in the South Pacific. There were pictures of tanks plowing through the jungle, some covered in flowers and of landing craft dispelling their cargo of troops into the surf as they dashed ashore. My mind was illuminated with this discovery. Parallel with this interest in the drama of war, my mum happened to enjoy a selected part of American history. She read 'Gone with the Wind' several times and told me all about it. She favored the Confederacy over the Union regardless of reason, I think she liked the lifestyle they portrayed. Thus, I became a supporter of Robert E Lee and the grey uniforms. Wednesday was my school half day for playing rugby. This was St Mary's in Rathmines and as I had a broken thumb I could not play. Therefore, she began taking me and my brother to the movies on Wednesday afternoons. To my delight, very often the films were of warfare. Two that stuck in my mind were the sands of Iowa Jima, and the Shores of Tripoli. They seemed to evoke some palatable shadows in my mind.

The combination of Marines splashing through blue water on to white sandy beaches just took over. I began to collect toy soldiers and military equipment, mostly made by the Brittain Company. Christmas and every birthday brought on boxes of mainly first world war lead painted soldiers, howitzer guns and ambulance wagons just to name a few. I discovered a brand of US soldiers available in toy stores. These green soldiers had the proper bowl-shaped Mark 1 helmets and in addition to rifle men some bore Bazookas and Flame throwers. In no time the army grew, and I began to find other lads who were also collectors, so a battle was inevitable. Padser was not interested in soldier games but there was a chap called Alan Johnson, Andy Gill and Paddy Hart from nearby all who became war buddies. One other buddy was my brother Colm who sometimes joined into my fun and other times charged around and knocked everything down. Regardless of all this euphoria let it be known that I would never have been a soldier other than joining their medical corps.

2

The Game

The imaginary warfare gathered momentum, and in summer we were often found on our knees in the back garden surrounded with 'Tri-ang Tanks' and military regiments. Then because our armed forces had grown so large, the garden became the only suitable battlefield - the grass represented the ocean, and the flower beds were land. The climax came in an invasion that took a whole Friday to set up and a day to perform. To explain it you will have to allow your imagination to go with the flow. Scale down your size and imagination as you often have to when playing with children's toys. This was long before 'Toy Story' but the idea was the same. There was an armada of ships, some were wooden, and some were just cardboard and used as troop carriers. The wooden boats were battle ships their guns made of blocks of wood with six-inch nails as gun barrels. These guns could rotate and looked quite real to the boys. There was also a large sheet of plywood attached to blocks of wood. The wood represented a hull and the attached plywood a landing deck of an aircraft carrier. The aim was for one side to land a landing force on a flower bed, which was said to be an enemy held coral island defended by the other team. For ammunition corks and chunks of dry clay were used. The four of us loved what we were doing because this game was as close to a real war that any of us would experience! The rules were as follows, there were four dices which each side rolled to find out how many shots they could take. Each side took it in turn and moved forward or any direction and fired, but then had to remain static while the other did likewise. With air attacks it was different. It was a free for all and the excitement was enormous.

On the agreed Saturday and under the command of Johnson and myself, the flotilla of attack transport ships (ATP) made their way towards an enemy island. Generals Patrick Hart and Andy Gill were on the defensive. They each had a section of a long-curved island, baked dry in the summer sunshine. The island was filled with wallflowers, better described as tall waving Coconut Palms that grew right down to fringe the shore. Apart from looking attractive, these trees provided a deep and shadowy protection for three hundred and fifty of the Imperial Army and that included cunningly concealed artillery and some tanks dug in for defensive purposes. The stage was now set, there was no escape, conflict at Saipan was inevitable! The approaching ATP/s were riding low in the grass, because they were carrying a precious cargo of troops and heavy equipment. There were also several boats with front ramps from which tanks could alight (LST/s or Landing Ship Tank). In all there were over four hundred troops in the attacking force, attacking in two waves and backed up by a hundred floating reserve. Some of the soldiers were made of lead and others of plastic. Some of the invaders were more up to the minute as they were wearing battle dress, with spotted camouflage helmets (hand-painted). The others were a mixture of red coated busby guards, first world war kaki clads and many other types. The defenders had odd soldiers to make up their ranks. Some were missing arms or even heads, but they carried on regardless.

The first conflict occurred after a given command, from Admiral Spruance. With that, Navy's 'Hellcats' roared into life on board the plywood carrier. The planes laden with corks were whisked into the air to begin strafing the island. Each time a fighter dived to the attack it was met with a rising wall of deadly hail fired up by Hart and Gill. Within minutes almost half the squadron were destroyed while the remainder limped back to the awaiting 'Flat Top'. It now transpired that the only air support remaining available, was from land-based army air corps situated far back, at the rear end of the garden. At last, the battle ships joined in and began pounding the island crushing the pretty wall flowers without respite. Like the aircraft, the ammunition used consisted of wine bottle corks, or chunks of dry clay.

Defending Generals, Hart and Gill now threw the dice and achieved three sixes and a four. Their hidden artillery boomed into action. They had twenty-two shots between them, and so, the two closest battle ships became targeted, and seriously damaged. Delighted with their achievement, they laughed and shouted, "your turn." At this stage, the land-based Army fighter-bombers arrived with the thunderous delivery of supposedly thousand-pound bombs. In the excitement many more wallflowers were trampled and broken, and the island began to look the worst for ware! It was a stroke of luck that my parents were gone to town taking my little brother along and that I was left in the care of Kathleen, our home help.

Now, we the attackers, threw the dices and managed an eighteen. We knew that the time had come, for the landing to proceed. Therefore, the command was given to head for shore. The landing crafts instantly turned their prows towards the beach and jolted forward towards shore at full speed. Now the barrage was lifted, and the planes departed. There was a hush, only broken by our high-pitched voices, while at the same time hurriedly pushing the boats towards shore while keeping our precious shots until they landed. The green lawn glistened in the sun and a gentle breeze bent its short blades like ripples on a real ocean. The air was perfumed with the scent of broken flowers and of laburnum and cordyline blooms. Despite the beauty of the moment, all was about to change as three hundred and fifty defenders prepared to counter the impending onslaught.

By now the concentration of fire and bombings had weakened the defenders thus enabled the first wave to get ashore. They were followed directly by a much-required delivery of tanks. Now the eighteen shots must be taken, and they were focused on the defending bunkers and gun emplacements. Having done that, they must now sit and take whatever punishment was coming. It was the defenders turn and with almost defiant determination General Hart flicked the dices and landed a 21. With deadly accuracy they destroyed our three tanks, several mortars, a dozen attackers and with a few remaining long shots hit the second wave of attackers as they came into range on their way towards the shore. One of the marines in the first wave later reported his experience.

"After blindly storming the beach in the first wave, and diving for cover while under fire, it took some time before I regained my senses. I found myself lying just inside the tree line and could hear lots of noise and the voice of the sergeant barking orders while the calm voice of our lieutenant kept reporting to Combat Command by radio. This gave me some consolation and re assurance. I looked back on hearing the pitiful cry from others on the beach who were badly wounded and calling for a corpsman. There was a dazzling panorama of green sea and blue sky in stark contrast to the billows of grey smoke casting hideous shadows. Out in the bay I could see the second wave on its way, but from the crossfire it was receiving I knew they were in a lot of trouble, being "bracketed" by the enemy gunners who were firing over our

heads. Then I realized that our guys were also shooting' at something. There was an awful din, and smell of cordite. Somewhere in front of me some of our group was moving towards a large bunker in the undergrowth. One of them had a fuel tank on his back which was marked with marine camouflage. It was a flame thrower, one of our more formidable weapons. As he shuffled forward, he was given a volley of supporting fire, enough to enable him to get in position. He stepped into the open, seemed to lean forward and then let fly. There was a high pitched wee'yah sound, and a billow of orange flame engulfed the damned bunker. The enemy's shooting abruptly stooped, and the only sound was of burning. Just then the heavy voice of our Sargent ordered, "Up and at em' let's make some room on this island". I rose with the others and began moving forward, but this time, with fixed bayonet."

With the attackers now feeling the heat Johnson and I became a bit reckless and, in our haste, tipped over a boat with the last of our tanks and guns on board. I shouted to Hart that that was just an accident, but he and Gill said it was too bad for us, and so all the equipment was lost. With our next dice, a miserable twelve, we managed to land the second wave and our precious floating reserves. With a much-enlarged beachhead we dug in. The defenders then scored a fifteen and with that Gill let out a loud cry shouting,

"Kamikaze, Attack, Kill zee Malines," Then Hart shouted even louder, "Shush, Andy you're wrong, it's a Banzai Attack".

There was a howl of laughter, and Gill looked shy. We braced for the action but instead of picking targets and weakening us, they gathered all their manpower together and charged. Then they fired the full fifteen shots in a concentrated area and milled forward. They punched right through our line, traveling the entire way to the beach. On-route they over ran a command post and a field hospital, and only stopped when they ran into a wall of fire. It was from sailors, who activated guns on two of their landing craft, and from an MGB that roared in to assist us. Just then an Army plane in the vicinity landed a couple of bombs into the remaining enemy. Alas, the Banzai had now been finally countered and the attack dissolved. The battle for the flowerbed now ended but only after the imaginary, commander of the island died as a result of either using his own hara-kiri knife on himself or being killed by Naval fire. Reports were quit conflicting.

The boys stood in silence, amidst the scene of destruction. The first to speak was the defending general Patrick Hart who said,

"That was a 'swizz', you had way more troops than us, and we had no aircraft."

Johnson replied – "We had much more to do than you guys," Hart grunted – "Well, next time, we get to do the landing," Johnson and I retorted, - "O. K, but we get to defend that large rocky area at the other end of the garden." Hart and Gill froze, - "That's also not fair, that would be impossible for us to take!" Johnson chuckled in response, - "Hard luck, you wanted a swap so next time we're defending the rock we call it, Iwo Jima - Ha, Ha!"

Suddenly there was the sound of distant rumbling. All eyes looked up, had the enemy found a secret weapon? The sound grew louder. People on ships and those in the jungle could feel an increasing vibration, what could it be! There was a shout from within our house,

"It's the train, the Harcourt Street train!"

The kitchen door was thrown open and Kathleen came tearing out jumping wildly over the battle zone. She was intent on getting the washing gathered in before it was destroyed by those deadly black smuts. The scene was so comical that the boys began to roar with laughter, but at the same time running to assist. With that the 'Iron Horse' was upon them, its smoke was everywhere. The war zone turned gray, and the ground vibrated like Krakatoa was about to erupt. Just in the nick of time the cloths were retrieved and saved from the smuts. Kathleen then surveyed the war zone and exclaimed,

"Kevin, what will your mother say to all this? Oh, what will she say?" Then she also began to laugh, "You silly omadhauns" (fools)"- look at the mess you made, and the flowers are destroyed, your parents will 'kill' you when they get home."

That is almost what happened! However, many wars and battles such as this were yet to take place in Cavey's back yard. However, none were to surpass the immensity and grandeur of the Saipan attack, nor the dedication of the players. As you may know in those days there was little or no detailed media coverage of events. However, at the time unless one a National Geographic Magazine or some psychic perception of conditions, the Saipan re-enactment could not have taken place. These wars were however a sort of metaphor of the real world one lived in at the time, a type of transcendental experience, played out in micro-proportions through the small hands of eager youths.

3

Belfast

In 1946 following the second world war, one of the features of the staying in 26 Myrtle field Park in Belfast was the sight and the sound of British Army Armored cars, Bren-gun carriers and trucks of all sorts pounding up and down the Lisburn Road. The drivers wore khaki and various coloured berets and if I was lucky there might be a few steel helmets in the mix. Their officers always stood high up controlling the flow. I could hear the strange engine sounds early in the morning and last thing at night. Through a child's eyes, this was most impressive, whereas the adults did not seem to notice. Each year we visited the military activity diminished till it was completely nonexistent, and thus I missed the excitement.

There were two boys living next door, Teddy, and John Hannah. Hannah was the sheriff of Belfast and the boys invited me to string along with them in their games. This was either playing as the three musketeers using bamboo canes as swords or just regular cricket. The boys were dedicated to Eric Compton and showed me how they treated their bats with linseed oil. I later got a Hammond bat and copied their instructions. We had good fun year after year, but they never reframed from reminding me I was from dirty Dublin.

My grandparent had four children, Vera, Molly, Jimmy, and Willie. They lived as said, in a very nice Tudor style house in Myrtelfield Park. It had grey gravel walls with wide dark brown boards quite in keeping with the Tudor period. In July, my grandfather who was very strict, always hung a Union Jack out their front window. Later I learned that Glander (grandfather) worked for a northern non catholic firm and felt obliged to fly the flag. One day I discovered where the flag was kept, and I was found walking around the garden with the flag wrapped around my tiny body. This event had no political significance whatsoever – just funny. The house had a creaking staircase and a large grandfather clock in the hall, which seemed to say, "Tick, I make time, and tock, I have plenty of it." To insulate from the cold, it must have been the custom at the time, but they had three very thick dark, maroon-colored curtains on brass bars draped across doors. One for the front door, one for the dining room, and one across the bay window in the drawing room. They were easily swung aside when entering either room or looking out the bay window. My mother told me her favorite pass time as a child was to read a good book and eat an apple while cocooned behind the big curtain in the bay window. Their cocker spaniel, Rory, was my best pal and he would sit with me on the reclining couch in the dining room while I read. The books were housed in a cabinet with lattice glass and were pictorial encyclopedia books depicting wars from over the centuries. There were pictures of Waterloo with red clad dragoons charging towards the French lines while riding magnificent white horses. There was Hercules fighting a monster and lots of first world war trench scenes. Plenty to entertain a young lad. All this and the hum of the military vehicles on the Lisburn Road and the fife and drums as it approached the twelfth of July added up to my growing understanding society.

When it was time to visit my Grandparents, my dad would drive us there and then return to Dublin. Not being used to long journeys I used to get car sick. After trying different ideas such as letting a wire trail behind the car to reduce static, it was finally overcome by wrapping brown paper around my middle. I guess it was all psychological. There were always the fear of the customs checks by both north and south customs authorities. At a certain time, the borders closed for the night so one had better be there before 10 pm. Then there was a Trip-tuque (three folded document) which permitted a certain number of visits and it had to be kept up to date. My Dad had to stay an extra day when he missed the 10 pm closure on one occasion. This was because of a typical family gathering at which there was copious amounts of whiskey and brandy consumed. The delay was also because of entertaining arguments between my grandfather and a fellow called Gerard Keogh who used in typical north of Ireland fashion made his point by punching the sideboard with his forefinger while saying, "listen to me.......".

Granny Smyth was small and lame in one leg. She was wonderful at baking potato and soda bread, just in time for one of her delicious breakfasts. When I got out of bed, I had to wash in cold water in a washing dish like most people in the 50s. Then with my mother we would descend to the old-fashioned dining room to the odor of fresh Ormo bakery toast. My grandfather would have a fried kipper with soda bread as an accompaniment and there was always Tate and Lyles golden syrup for the toast. Other than that, I was not interested in food and only took it to survive. Then it was time for me to go and call on Teddy and John next door and play three musketeers or cricket. Eventually they began to talk very rough, so I ran away and gave them up as friends. However, there was my cousin Denis Cremin who lived in Cranmore Gardens. His Dad was an accountant from Co Kerry who married my Mum's sister, Molly. One of the Cremin's became the head of Philosophy in Maynooth College and Con Cremin became the Irish Ambassador to USA in the 50's. The other Cremin was married to a Crushel who owned a shop in Kenmare and one at the Gap in Killarney. Then there was uncle Jimmy and Aunt Marie who had six children and one of the eldest was Brendan. He was younger than me and later became a good friend of my brother. I had lots of fun visiting Brendan but also liked going to visit Denis. We were a bit noisy but if we did so on a weekend, one of the neighbors would come out and tell us not to make noise on the sabbath. At the top end of Cranmore, the boys school known as Inst Marlow. At lunch time the boys came out on the fields playing Cops and robbers. The robbers were being chased and could be identified as they had their school caps on back to front. At the time I thought that I would love to go to that school. The best I got was an invitation to Denis's St Brigid's Parish School. It was quite a novelty at first but soon I was out of my depth and had to sit and listen while feeling very shy. I found consolation in reading Rupert books. All in good spirit.

BILLS FIRST AND SECOND DEVELOPMENTS

Soon after that Bill enlarged his hotel by buying an adjoining property. His builder was Mc Loughlin and Harvey, and they were used also for further developments. This was in the late 40's and it enabled him to open a luxurious dining room and an adjoining ballroom. For months before he drew and painted pictures of what is might look like. His art was wonderful, and I was fascinated. When the extension was built and with ideas given by the architect, they ended with Edwardian style dining room and ballroom all coloured in tones of maroon and magenta and with lots of mirrors and ornate rope embellishments. There were three large chandeliers made of pale pink glass and a well-appointed band stand under and acoustic canopy. The dining room was at a slightly higher level from the ballroom and when not in use was divided off by a huge maroon heavy Curtin. It was with these rooms that he ran his dinner dances and made his name for good dining and wedding receptions. As there was only the Gresham hotel in Dublin running dinner dances at the time, the Royal became a wonderful second choice for many. Also, as mentioned, in those days people requiring a drink after 11pm could go beyond the city limits to Bray and get an extra hour and all they had to say to the doorman that they were bonified. Needless to say, this generated enormous night trade and a great revenue earner.

It seems that Bills very good friend Bill Gleeson who owned Sunbeam Fashions and Jeff Smurfit who was in carboard containers, offered him an opportunity to join them in their expansions. This would have probably meant an investment, that I do not know. Vera said that she had discouraged it saying you are better to invest in yourself. In future years Gleeson and Smurfit became millionaires twice over. Then around 1958, dad made his second major alteration to the hotel. He re-employed the Architect called Bill Dwyer to design a rooftop room to be used for serving breakfasts and small functions. Dad said this way they get a fresh room with a welcome in the mornings and a view of the Wicklow surroundings. He also wanted twenty-four new rooms with bathroom and an elevator. The elevator machinery was housed in a new tower above the rooftop room to which the Architect added a decorative capping like a schoolteacher's mortar board. He added mosaic to the roof cap in the colours he had chosen for the building. He used the latest mustard yellow- and maroon-coloured bricks, so the building would be impressive. However, none of our family liked the material because it was different from the older part of the hotel and thus, the bricks were plastered over and painted in to match the cream of the building.

London

Bill and Vera had holidays in Spain and once they went to the Canaries with old friends Frank and Daisey Buckley of FX Buckley Butchers. They went to Barbados and stayed in the Sandy Lane Hotel. There they met two people from Boston who invited them to visit. They did that but when there saw an Army and Navy store with M1 US Army helmets for sale. They brought one home for me – the very best gift I ever received. They also went to Spain and Greece on other occasions. There was one trip they always took in January and that was to London. When there, Bill would visit the Hotel and Catering Exhibition and also celebrate Vera's birthday that fell about that time. They stayed in the Dorchester and dined in all the best hotels, Royal Garden, The Savoy, Claridge's and so on. This was his reward for all the hard work he and Vera had done. Then on several occasions they took me as well. I was already quite used to English people and English Psyche. This was from the Belfast relations and the tourists in the hotel. However, I was taken aback by the amazing army of bowler hat and striped pants brigades of London men. It was the standard of the times and as I remember, I had seen some of that in Belfast. Then there were the large numbers of Indians notably working in Gatwick Airport. All this and the politeness of the hotel employees created a great childhood impression. The aftermath of the war was evident in a sad way because there were very many fellows who were evidently shellshocked who paraded on the footpaths, saluting and shouting orders into the thin air. Those who were healthy were usually doormen delighted to be in uniform. The standard of catering was exciting. Though very young I loved the toast melba, the hors d'oeuvre trollies and above all the crepe suzettes. Spoilt. Naturally, we saw the changing of the guards and visited the popular sights. Also, because I loved diving, they took Colm and me to Morecombe where there was a magnificent pool, 199 ft long by 90 ft wide. The water was clear blue and there was live organ music played in the mornings. On the earlier occasions we travelled from Dublin by B and I Steamer. I was fascinated by the third-class section at the stern of the boat because it was wild. There was singing and empty porter bottles being regularly tossed into the sea as we went. Dad said they were emigrants going to live in England and this made me sad and ashamed that we could not provide enough work for our own.

One day when back in Ireland, there was a commotion in the hotel. Word had it that a DC3 had crashed on the top of Djouce mountain, the date was the 12th of august 1946. We went there with locals and had a huge climb to reach the summit. The occupants were gone but the plane remained with pieces of it scattered over a large distance. It seems it was carrying refugee children from Germany, going to America. There were fatalities, but the majority survived to be housed in Glencree Sanatorium.

This by coincidence was opposite to a very sad German Army first world war graveyard. These were people who had been interned during that war. However eventually some of the children settled in Ireland some went back to Germany and some finally got to America.

Bill had quite a devoted group of associates working for him. Dan was his head barman, and he was a great asset. He had the knack of attracting a lot of customers to the amber room and public bar on the corner of the Queensborough road. Essay was the head of housekeeping and Jack Carville his Cocktail barman in the French bar adjacent to the dining room. Jack eventually bought bill's shop from the receivers. The head chef was Noel Black a man who stayed cool and could turn out vast numbers of well-prepared dinners. In later years he became head chef in the Pasadena Golf Club California. The dispense bar to the dining room was run solely by the very dedicated Miss Jones. Kathleen Giffney was the pastry cook and she had a flair for making hot deserts like bread-and-butter pudding, queen of puddings or even frozen cassata and individual baked Alaska's. The head waiter was Bill, and his assistant was Lilly who was well capable of taking over. She came from Wexford, otherwise all the others were local. John Cave was the lounge waiter whose wife was an abbey actor. The management team comprised of Mary Sheehan, Helen O'Brien 'Hobi' and a miss Imelda Gilchrist 'Gilie'as they were affectionately known. Miss Duggan was the linen lady who sewed and mended torn linen when necessary. They were all country ladies and were very good organisers and they had a good way with customers and knew the way to keep the associates in line. It did not take long for me to become impressed with two of the hotel's lower echelon. One was kitchen porter, Tommy Ebbs who created a constant bad impression, yet he always turned up for work, scruffy though he was. The other was very sad yet jolly fellow who was devoted and sought perfection at the job, and that was John Mc Cabe better known as 'Chicken'. He had been reared in an institution but ran away and was found in the open with his head in a wet hoodie. The outcome was that he suffered serious hearing loss and seemed often seemed like a simpleton, but he was not. Now he had a good job, and the hotel was his new family. 'Chicken' had a great sense of humour and loved teasing Kathleen Giffney or any of the young cooks or waitresses that came his way. All this was harmless, and laughter was the main ingredient of the day. The pay master was Ms Kathleen Warren, a small thin lady with glasses and a serious expression. She always wore very thick stockings and tweed clothing and came and went from work on a strong looking bike. No one would argue with Ms Warren and in a few years from that she would be paying me and my brother's salaries! I originally had 5 punt a week nett, later 10, and after being married it went up to 35 per week. It did not seem to matter because everything was in a good cause and this was to have been our future! Bill was a born economist because one day we discovered that he removed toilet paper from the toilet, beside the public Bar. Instead, he replaced the toilet paper with used paragon machine dockets. These were the third copy from lounge sales and not needed. This brought on consternation amongst us, but he prevailed. He and Vera were charitable in their own way. They invited relatives from the north to come and stay in the hotel thus giving the Smyth family a very happy two weeks' vacation. They also invited the Nolan children who were from a broken home to stay. Uncle Bill to them was a hero. Not with standing, when Bill could be very angry if one worked for him but when you were away from the hotel, he was friendly and often called me and Colm by the old Dublin name, 'Jemser or Jockser'. If he met a person who had plenty of true Country wit, Bill would laugh like he was just a boy. He loved a good story. We enjoyed that but Bill was also friendly with the people who mattered to his business, such as Mr Hipwell the local auctioneer, who negotiated properties for his new expansions. As there was partially empty land, but with some housing at the back of the hotel, Hipwell's skills were needed. Over the years he engineers for Tennent's to move and the land to be bought by Bill. Then there was the Bray Chamber of Commerce all which he handled with care.

4

A Seismic Shift

Sometimes there was lots of fun at home. Every Tuesday evening Dad went to the Bohemians social club for men. Therefore, on Wednesday mornings he was full of jokes and laughter. This often digressed into his chasing us around the house with his false teeth in his hands covered in a towel while barking like a dog. The sheer horror let us to laughing convulsions. As mentioned, on the serious side, he ran dinner dances every Saturday night in the recently named Royal hotel. His was the only dinner dance in Dublin other than the Gresham Hotel and was therefore very busy. When we attended my mother often got me out on the dance floor and taught him how to waltz and foxtrot. I might have been ten at the time. Then during the summer evenings while we were waiting to go home, I got to hear the talented piano player called Chris Power entertained at sing songs in the lounges. I noticed that many of the guests seemed to get sillier as the night went on. Then many of them would get up and sing a song while some fell asleep and were wakened so as to leave or go to their rooms! That was old fashioned politeness – them were the days! When I was twelve, the fun stopped. They announced finally that they would sell our home and we were to move to a new house in Bray. We would live there so my Dad could be nearer to his ever-improving business in the Hotel. This came as a shock and it took a long time for me to settle in Bray. Then in a flash I remembered on many occasions they had visited large homes in the local area but never thought it meant that we would move. One outstanding property for sale was called Ardmore which later was to become a film studio. This monstrous Georgian house stood alone in the middle of fields and a line of trees that marked the cliff running behind it and overlooking the Dargle river. On the dull November Sunday that we were taken there for a visited my brother Colm and I looked on the experience as a ghost hunt. There were huge empty rooms, and the entrance hall was very large and had only raw floorboards as did all of the rooms. There was a sort of stables or coach house at the rear. It looked like it was once a great residence for a very large family, and one could imagine people horse riding around its large demesne. However, it seems they did not attempt to buy Ardmore.

When it happened, the intended move was a dose of bad medicine for me because I loved our home in the suburbs and had Padser next door as a friend. I was doing well at school in Saint Mary's College Rathmines but now would have to leave both it and my school pals. I asked if Kathleen would come along and was told she would. Despite that chink of good news, I was literally dragged to Bray screaming kicking. All this had a marked effect on my formative years and seemed to stunt my self-confidence. At the age of thirteen this move devastated me and left me wallowing with Phobias that I had to learn to control. I resigned myself that this is that life is all about. I reckon this is what millions of young migrants go through when they are on the move to a new settlement. In an effort to stay committed, I taught myself how to overcome the neurosis. In effect it felt like everything was closing in on me at the one time. To ward it off, I learned to keep active and to let one's mind flit from thought to thought so that the phobia becomes forgotten. The solution was also to live in compartments and concentrating on the immediate job in hand. Then as I had the hobby of collecting toy soldiers and was the fascination with the Military activities and all this helped concentrate and illuminate my imagination. One such venture was to make an 8mm war movie with pals in the woods behind our new home. Dad was commissioned to shoot the film with his 8mm Kodak movie camera. This was in the grounds of our newly purchased Georgian house called Mount Herbert. The house overlooked the Dargle river and Little Bray as it stood on the edge of a steep cliff to the rear. It also had a beautiful front garden and a wooded area to the back which sloped down to meet a millrace from a mill further upstream. Now there was a great amount to explore, so I got busy. Soon I got back into a better disposition and began to forget all about my phobia. A school friend called Herve De Quillen, Herve Renard and my brother Colm took part in the film. Herve Renard's dad was a freedom fighter in Brittany and then came to Ireland and opened an art school. De Quillen was a school friend. Our Dad as said, kindly shot the film. After about six months I decided home was now very different than it had been in our smaller house in Rathmines. Now there was too much space and too many lonely moments. Also, the family seemed to be cross, and the hotel dominated our thinking. Unfortunately, I now had to change schools. I was enrolled in Willow Park Holy Ghost Fathers college in Blackrock. This meant a long bus journey often in a steamed-up bus to and frow daily. Then, an event lifted my spirits and that was the vulnerability of Bray seafront to being flooded in winter storms. In 1950 two events were of note, first there was a great storm that destroyed the lighthouse at the mouth of the harbour. It was exciting to see it lying while covered in waves before it slipped permanently into the depths. Secondly on the 24th of September in the same year a giant reinforced concrete cross built by a Christopher Dodd a local builder. He employed a hundred crafts people to complete the task. It was erected on top of Bray Head for what was names as the Marion year. In those days, the north end had no beach once the tide rose. As a result, waves often clashed over the promenade. It was a local pastime to dodge the deluges. In later years, the council organised mountains of shale to be taken from the shallow banks on the east coast and dumped along the whole length of the seafront, creating a protective beach from end to end.

In Mount Herbert the only good thing from a kid's point of view was the wilderness of trees and a river that lay within the grounds. Living in such a large house made me feel like a spoilt brat, which I was fast becoming. On the positive side there were lines of laurel trees bordering the driveway to the house. As these were old, they tended to tip forward and as a result their stems were curved and very inviting to be exploited. Colm and I got long wooden sections cut from other trees and laid them on top thus making a treetop path. We could scramble like monkeys for quite a distance and at very good pace. As it turned out, Kathleen did not settle and in a short time gave notice and emigrated to Vancouver. I was still young enough to miss her very badly. From then on for years to come she mailed me rolls of Canadian comics and Dollars with every pack. I saved them so I could visit her in the future. Unfortunately, that was not till she was in her eighties and ill in hospital. On the glamorous side of life Ardmore Film Studios was in full swing and many movie stars stayed in the area and particularly in the Royal hotel. One evening when Colm and I were in bed at ten o'clock as usual. We were awakened by a commotion. The film stars, Peggy Cummins and Terrance Morgan were visiting our house and Bill brought them up to our bedroom to meet us. Peggy tucked us in and bade us goodnight with a kiss each and her autograph. She said now you will be the envy of your pals. Then they left. Now naturally my pals did not believe the story and it occurred to me that the incident this was a bad omen because it might mean that I might always start at the top and gradually work my way down! The I put that out of mind hoping it not happen, but in time it did.

During the course of events, many celebrities came to either stay or dine in the Royal. In addition to Terrance Morgan and Peggy Cummins, there were other celebrities such as, Gary Player, Nicole Berger, Donald Sindon, John Cassavetes, Ann Haywood, Roney Delaney, Lawrence Harvey, Brendan Boyer, Brian Poole, Constance Smith, Richard Todd, Aldo Ray, Robert Mitchem, Betsy Blair, Diana Wynter, Katherine Hepburn, Peter Cushing, Michael Wilding, Sarah Miles, Peter O'Toole. There will be more to say about Peter O'Toole later.

Mount Herbert.

5

The Ocean

Just to show how much my dad loved the sea as sometimes he would interrupt his visiting accountant at work and say, "Jim I'm going for a swim, do come along with me, go on!" Then my folks would take me on their backs and swim out into the deep. Soon I cut loose and became a dedicated swimmer and expert diver at that very same spot. This 'magic club' as I saw it, was positioned centre ways along Bray promenade and featured two gantries protruding out into the sea from which you could dive or swim. There was a high diving tower at the end of one of the walkways from which Bill once jumped while dressed as a baby with an inflated tyre around his waist for a fancy-dress contest. Christie was the club attendant in those days, and he kept the club spotless. Quite regularly on a summer's afternoon Bill would take the family down the coast. This was because he had worked all morning and at about 3pm there was always lull in the activity before it reared up again at six o'clock. He usually used the lull to go back into his shop in Dublin but if the weather was very good, he took us to Brittas Bay or Greystones. Both were perfect summer places. Greystones Harbour with its old, battered wall was facing west and therefore sunbathing was very popular. In the east it is difficult to find a west facing perch. Naturally, I also loved Greystone's harbour and its people. One diving trick was to lie back on the diving board with your legs in the air. Then to roll forward so as to go headfirst into a dive. This was very easy as it delivered you accurately into the water and impressed the on lookers. One other trick was to take a smaller person on piggie back, then dive in having told then to lean backwards. This was also easier than it looked. The harbor was a picture post card old world place. It was great for fishing or as we use to do, just sunbath and swim. I joined the local swimming club and competed in swimming races but also, I was amongst teenagers many of them very pretty girls. One of them was Evernia a very Tammy sort like you expect to find in the deep south. She took a good suntan and got on well with my parents. She hardly noticed me, but my parents liked her. One of the excitements was to dive or jump off the back of the harbour at high tide. Some duds did dive but they were the brave ones, but I only jumped. Later that area became my favorite snorkeling zone with clear deep water and easy access.

In the summer, Vera would take us to Bray beach. I would have to walk but Colm was too young and was therefore in a pram. She always chose the sunny side of the street and as a result used to sing a popular song at the time: *'Just direct my feet to the sunny side of the street. I used to walk in the shade with my blues on parade, but I'm not afraid I'm a rover crossed over...'* Another song by Max Bygrave *'You've got to have heart, all you really need is heart and if one says that you'll never win, that's when the grin should start...'* There was also; *Once there was a silly old ant that couldn't move the rubber tree plant, but anyone knows an ant can't move a rubber tree pant, but he had high hopes...'* These songs gave me and many others some hope over the years. They helped calm mental anxiety.

Around the northeast side of Bray Head there was a second great swimming spot called the cove. This was a series of three outdoor swimming pools which were created by the simple insertion of a sea wall and only two divisions as the cliffs formed barriers at either end. This was the home of the Bray Cove Swimming Club which was chaired by Joe Groom a wonderful larger than life person who was a senior member of the Fianne Fail Government Party in power at the time. The largest pool was called the men's and it had three metre diving boars and a ramp for starting races. The next pool was - you guess – the ladies and it was smaller and not suitable for competitive swimming. There was the children's pool which was smaller again but just as deep and unfortunately full of seaweed and absolutely no sand. As you can guess it was never used for swimming, but it was a Mecca for catching crabs and minnows. One day I saw a poor crab that had fallen victim to a young red headed boy with angry eyes who cut off its legs and launched it into the middle of the pool floating on a piece of driftwood with its stumps wriggling as it went – eek!

There was a concrete club house and several bathing boxes, with balconies and flat concrete roof most of which were accessible from back because being an inlet the ground rose sharply behind. Teenagers used to stretch out on the roofs and catch the summer rays, some with radios and all looking fit and strong. Larry the attendant found that he could not uphold the rules as so many would be up on top. It was my dream to try and sit up with those superior lads but usually I was made stay with the family by the pool. One day I learned a hard lesson. As there was a long sprawling steps descending into the cove my mother said to me as we stood looking down on the scene blow,

"Kevin, I am parking the pram (with my little one-year old brother) right here and jamming it into the fence so it cannot move. You are to stand by and mind it until I come back."

"Okay Mum but where are you going? "I said dreamily.

"I see Patty Groom down there and I want to tell her something, I will only be a minute, now stay put, don't move."

In here large, patterned dress, she trotted down the steps with an air of urgency. Just then my baby brother Colm began to cry. The first thing I did was to pull out the pram and begin to rock it side to side. At that moment one of two friends shouted hey look over here I see a nest in the cliff face. I immediately said to the other fellow who was nearer.

"Jimmy, hold the pram for a second and I ran to look".

Then I turned back and to my horror Jimmy Martel was standing beside me and the Pram was careering at high speed down the steps. It made a sickening jump and bump, and another jump this time even bigger and a Man on his way up put up his hand to stop it. The pram bounced off his path and fell over on its side. The jolt dislodged the baby who rolled like ball and miraculously came to a stop on grassy hollow. At that moment, my Mum arrived and we both examined the screeching child. Apart from on scratch he was intact. The pram was retrieved, and I became a little more obedient from then on. So, enough about the origins and let's see how the teen age years progressed!

When in Greystones, my claim to fame was a diving adventure with a guy called Peter O'Neill. He persuaded me to follow him in a dive beneath the end of the harbour! At this point much of the structure had collapsed leaving an accessible cavern, but from under water! So, at low tide he led me in a dive into the cavity and to my surprise it was filled with sunlight and sand. We only stayed a few seconds and then he led the way out by a different exit. "Phew, that really was a unique experience" I said. Peter agreed. One day we went to Brittas Bay in County Wicklow. I had not been there before and at first sight I saw a wide bay stretching for three miles. I could not believe my eyes. Here was an almost real version of a pacific paradise - miles of sand dunes, and the ocean under a blazing blue sky. The only inhabitants were curlews or seagulls, and, in those days, there was open access and lots of grass areas to park a car. The south end had an enormous dun that one could see from a distance. Climbing it was harrowing and the decent was narrow and very steep, but all fun. In later years I was astounded to discover it had been erased to make room for one little corner of a paved car park. What a shame. Despite that, Brittas Bay was a dream come true and all just an hour from home. From that moment on it was my greatest pleasure to get there and to add to the enjoyment there were waves. Now if only I had a plank or a surfboard! But as I did 'not have such, I used our inflatable Lilo or air mattress and road the swell to shore while screaming with joy.

My two pals in Bray also went to Blackrock College. One was Eddie Lloyd whose Dad was the manager of the local Bank of Ireland. The second was Jurek Delimata whose grand uncle the famous James Joyce of world renown. They made studies a bearable commodity with their flashes of humor, usually when needed most. I was now sixteen with a sore thumb and beginning to get to know local youths and invited to their homes and at Christmas to at least eighteen parties always with the same gang. Regardless of this joviality, I managed to pass the Intermediate Certificate examination which was a crucial step in one's education. Nevertheless, to my surprise I was taken out of school and persuaded to forget about science, art and architecture, my favorite subjects. Instead, I was to go to Hotel School, train and then to join Dad and work in his hotel. I fought back and insisted that I wanted to finish school and then do Architecture as first choice. They said I was not clever enough and at the time they were probably right, but that was to do with maturity. One further argument was that university is going out of fashion and one should learn a trade instead. I never agreed but their plans went ahead.

6

Hotel School And Zurich

On a grey September morning I entered the Hotel School of catering and domestic science, on Cathal Brugh Street in Dublin 1. There, I met a fine bunch of students bent on learning hotel business. I think they thought that I was a mother's boy not street wise like them. It was usual that I bought a monthly bus travel ticket from the CIE offices in Dublin. One day I was late getting there, and the office was closing, and a Mr. Goggin said I was too late. I realized that I could not face home telling them that there was no ticket. Therefore, in a fit of panic I pleaded with him. He relented and signed up a ticket for me. Then he asked if I was anything to do with the hotel in Bray. He then said for my Dad to call him as he was looking for a conference venue. As a result, this large CIE conference came to our hotel for five or six years following.

At first, I had difficulty getting to know my class. Jerry Rubin always made fun of whatever I said and Neil Fitzpatrick seemed to take on the roll of class leader but when we had night classes, he invited me to his house for tea. Amongst the girls there was Peg Kennedy who was a sort of Calamity Jane and I learned early on not to cross her. Eventually, I made friends with most of my class and after the second year went to Switzerland for experience. My buddy was a fellow called Brendan Donnelly whose father owned the Anchor Hotel at Parnell Square near the college. Brendan and I went by boat and train to Paris where we immediately took a cab to the Folles Berger and enjoyed the high kicking girls and the flow of Champagne. We left the following day with sore heads and arrived in Zurich's Bohnhoff. In moments we were mixed in a throng of baggage porters all wearing washed out blue smocks, pulling bags and smoking Rossli Stumpa cigars. The aroma told one how liberated the average workers in Switzerland really were. We were employed by a fine hotel owned by Casper Mantz. It was called the Hotel St Gotthard on Bohnhoff Strasse. I trained as commis-cook, chefs-d'oeuvre followed by garde manger, and Poisoner. Brendan had different duties. We were shy in the face of a team of thirty chefs, all speaking German or Switzer Deutsch. They tended to stare at us, and few spoke or laughed. We began our shifts at 7am the breakfast was great – large jugs of strong coffee, peasant bread with salt less butter and mountain berry jam. However, lunch was a disaster. It was served at 10am, too early for us to eat and what we got was miserable. One example was gruyere cheese, and boiled potatoes, as much as you like. Also, there was the day we got spätzli a sort of fried noodle with apple sauce. Herr Vonnox was our direct supervisor, and he was extra strict. He told me to break at two o' clock and come back to work at 'halb sex'. To my horror, I was an hour late returning as 'halb sex' in Swiss terms meant half five, in other word half before six. Oops, I died of embarrassment. Then one day we had a surprise. We were sent to collect an item from the Bohnhoff which was within sight of the hotel. When we got there the item was a frozen Deer. We carried the stiff across the main street to the waiting arms of Herr Vonnox and Herr Earnie the sue chef. It was worth noting that the Swiss public did not turn a head, it seemed this was not an unusual occurrence.

Bill and Vera came out to visit and took me to Lucern. They enjoyed their Swiss experience and I felt very important being their guide. From the beginning of my working time, I got friendly with Jurg Kuhn a Swiss trainee cook. He was doing his apprenticeship and eventually did a final exam under his tutor Herr Bourgie. He was seen boning meat and cooking fish and finally lining up every herb that ever was and naming them for the examiner. Jurg spoke good English and invited me to his home for cheese fondue followed by kirsch soaked in sugar lumps and tea. His mother was charming and when the meal was through Jurg took out his scuba tank and we walked across the adjoining field to Katzensee, a tiny lake where he demonstrated his skill. I declined getting in as visibility was zilch. Then there was an Israeli fellow called Marin Drucker who could be called up to military service at any moment. He was good fun and he clued me in about how what made the Swiss and the Israelis tick. He also spoke slow distinct German which was a great help to me learning the lingo. Jurgen Lindler was a Bavarian, very tall and very friendly he adapted our gang and was always around. In the afternoon when on a break about five of us would go to Hallenbad swimming pool on Limmattalstrasse. This was an indoor Olympic Pool and most the times it was very quiet. We always had enormous fun because despite the guards watching we played tag, running up the high diving board to escape being touched and by jumping wildly into the air and landing in the pool. Amazingly the guards did not stop us. Jurg once decided to try and swim the length of the pool under water. He got three quarters way and then came to the surface unconscious. The nearest fellow to him raised the alarm and we got him out of the water. By then he had recovered.

Brendan was on different shifts and different days off than me. Therefore, as the winter set in I planned to take the bus to local ski resorts to learn how. This only cost four rappen and the ski pass was for almost nothing. On the first trip Jurgen Lindler and his Swiss Air girlfriend came along. The resort was called Stoos and it was about an hour and a half away. The snowcapped alps were daunting, and we entered a deep chasm and stopped at a funicular station between snow laden cliffs. From there we were taken up a very steep cable car to the top where the skiing happened. I hired my first skis, and they were wooden with straps of leather with buckles. Going up by lift was easy but coming down was the challenge. I learned to launch for a target or bump on the slope and then stop. Turn and go for the next safe place. However, the system let me down because halfway down I missed my stopping point and swished into the next adjoining valley which was tiny. Doing a snow plough stance, I began gliding downwards and decided as it was too late to stop, I would continue to the bottom. At the bottom I stopped and fell over. To my dismay the snow was extra deep there, and I felt trapped. Now I could not even hear the skiers on piste, just my pounding heart while I was locked in isolation. So, I tried taking off my skis. When this was done, things got worse because now I sank even deeper. The skis had to be re fitted and eventually I managed to climb upright myself. This was achieved after a dozen attempts. Then I had to trudge ever upwards till I reached the top. The episode meant that I was missing for half an hour and Jurgen had got really worried. A week later at Einsiedeln I accidently fell at the end of the main slope right by the village graveyard. I could not release my skis because my leg was forced up and over my head with the nose deep in the snow. Help! I thought and to my delight a local man dashed forward, and quickly undid my bootstraps and this saved me getting a nasty sprain. It was there that I realized how much I liked glazed Swiss gingerbread with marzipan filling after a hard day's activity.

The St Gotthard hotel was commissioned to do some Stadt Service which meant outdoor catering for the hotel. I did four. One was to a vineyard in Neuchatel where we laid out a buffet for wealthy clients. The second was near Flumserberg where we served champagne with wild strawberries and canopies. Another was serving dinner in Mr Mantz's home on Lac leman. Then there was an enormous undertaking a function in a castle at Bodensee. This is situated in the north east corner of Switzerland with views of both Germany and Austria. We loaded two vans with equipment and food which included suckling pigs and a side of beef. The castle was on top of a steep hill and the road up was spiral and difficult. In the courtyard we erected a spit over a large charcoal fire. The chef then took over and began to cook the pork and beef. We the waiters, began to set places for a eighty people throughout the various rooms, some small and others large. All the time we could see the village, the lake and Austria through lattice windows. Now without a break, we were decked out in medieval attire. We wore tights and dress-like belted smocks and a flat hat with a feather. How zat! Ugh! I hope my friends do not see me, I thought. Soon the people arrived, and they were also in medieval attire and what is more the President of Switzerland was among the throng. We brought trays of wine and drinks around the castle, climbing small winding staircases or wide-open stairs where the guests were gathering. Soon there was the sound of merriment and the odor of roast beef and pork. The fare was then loaded on large boards and to the sound of trumpets played from a tower, we carried the food around the entire castle for the gests to see. Then it was time to boost the temperature of the meat, divide it onto platters and distribute as fast as possible. From the courtyard one could see in the dark the black shape of the turreted castle and the bright yellow light form the windows like in a fairy story. There was traditional alpine music and played by a group who toured from room to room and the atmosphere was electric. By the time the party ended at four in the morning and by the time we packed up it was 6am and 9am before we arrived back in Zurich. I starved and worn out and therefore delved into a Café Complete in the Bahnhof Café. I gave a sigh of relief satisfied that we had provided an extraordinary service.

After a year, my time was up, as this had been the final year of my college practical training and I was scheduled to work for a Major Rialle of Borrie-Manoux in his Bordeaux vineyards in a month's time. Then I got a message to say it had to be cancelled because your Dad is ill. So, the long journey home began. Jurgen invited me to stay with him on route. I took the train from Zurich to Bon which is by way of the Rhine. I had secured an ancient book just like Portillo was to do in later years. Armed with this and while reading about the locale, I enjoyed a bowl of soup and read the history of wine making and of Koblenz. Jurgen had a moped and took me for a tour of Munich and around Bon and into the Bundestag. By now I had a good smattering of German and this was a great finale to a year of catering, cooking, and skiing in Europe. In some ways I had accomplished a lot and in others I had much to learn.

7

Hotel Responsibilities

I learned the details of what happened to Dad when I got home. He had had a heart attack brought on by his falling sleep in the Forty Foot an outdoor swimming area in Dun Laoghaire, and not awaking when rain fell, and his temperature dropped. This state of mind and subsequent exhaustion was brought on by local efforts to unionize the hotel. It seems he took it very personally, hence the attack. He was now back at home and able to tell me to take charge as manager and to be paid 10 punt per week and to live at home as usual. He gave me my mother's Ford Anglia and bought her a new one. At this stage he was bed ridden and said I should look in for instruction every day, but that faded out, as he became more active. The hotel as explained, had a very fine team of associates and I knew that I must learn to work with them. Being temporary manager of the hotel had its good and bad points. On the good side I had a pleasant personality and could make people smile and feel relaxed. However, I was a slow learner and underneath it all I was quite shy and self-conscious. To cover up I played on my distant American connection but also worked very hard and did so for long hours. Worked from 8am to 3pm and back 5.30 pm to about 11pm or later. I only took an odd day off. I found that by being there I had a lot more control and nothing ever went wrong because of my presence and Swiss know how! We had a good function business and that included conferences and weddings. On a few occasions we had conferences that lasted three or four days and, in these instances, I worked from dawn to late, late, late. Then the Irish Management Institute had a block booking for twenty people Monday to Fridays all winter over several years. This was ideal for us. As Mount Herbert had a large garden with flowers, Vera arranged that Breen the gardener would have enough fresh flowers to decorate the hotel on important occasions. Vera had tomatoes growing in the large glass house and also grape vines, that were planted outside and brought into the glass house through ducts at ground level. It seems the roots have no difficulty with the cold, but the upper branches need the heat. On some occasions Bill cut golden private or small flowers for table posies and brought them with him to the hotel in the mornings. Despite his ego Bill was religious, as he had a picture of the Sacred Heart at the top of the hotel stairs, and he maintained fresh flowers in water on its shelf. This made the good lord part of the family and it was also a welcome for visitors who in those days were respectful regardless of their faith or beliefs. However throughout it all we never gave up going to mass. Seats were difficult to secure on a Sunday and on one occasion I said to myself I was fed up standing up and giving my seat to women in the aisles. I was determined to stay put regardless. Just then another woman arrived that had no seat. I could not see her but said to myself 'not again'. Then with a second thought I said to myself, 'I better give it away, it could even be my own mother' and promptly stood up. It turned out that it was my mother!

I noticed that my dad was only happy when he knew I was on the premises, cleaning ashtrays, clearing dining tables or even helping to do the washup. I could never complain because Bill had often been seen with his white cuffs turned up helping to work the Stains electric washing machine. He also scraped plates but above all he would pour the gravy on outgoing function main course before they left the kitchen. He expected me to be managing the entrance to the dining areas, taking visitors names, smiling a lot and seating them at a suitable table, that is when the pressure was on. I really enjoyed performing those duties, but it was rough when he got angry over something small. The hotel industry is like that because everyone is keyed up and a misplaced word can cause a storm. One very regular luncheon guest was Kathleen Carney the chief librarian. Ms Carney always read a thick book during lunch thus, making full use of her down time. While Bill was artistic himself, he was also glad of my artistic touch, writing notices or drawing pictures of poultry or vegetables on the dinner menus, but he did not take me into his confidence to the extent of explaining how his finances worked. I knew our trading figures but nothing about his loans and liabilities many of which did not show on the balance sheets. It shows how the family hierarchy can be bad for healthy business relations. He did make use of the balance sheets by saying they were not as good as he would like, and I should try harder. From a social point of view. I was the sort of small-town celebrity who could get to befriend many girls with ease. Most of the girls I knew were from around, but they gathered for dances in the local tennis club on Saturday and Sunday nights. Therefore, I would go there when the bars closed in the hotel. Usually, I just caught the last hour. Alternatively, sometimes a pretty girl would arrive in the hotel to stay with her parents. I usually tried to impress and be a guide to showed her around or even the parents if they were interested. One of the frequenters of the Tennis Club socials was my friend Jurek Delimata whom I mentioned and who was born in Scotland but educated in Ireland at the same school as me. Jurek's mother was Italian and his Dad Polish. Jurek had a tremendous imagination a knowledge of literature, and he loved talking about outer space. As Jurek was special as a result he was not very popular amongst the rank and file of our classmates. His wisdom and aptitude were wasted on them. Had they known, but that the famous James Joyce was a grand uncle of his. It came from his mother's side as her mother was Mrs Sherrick and hailed from Trieste.

Bill's three female management supervisors were skilled at keeping the hotel up to standard. My mother had the habit of calling in to chat with them and I often found this un-business like but had to accept it because this was Ireland, not Switzerland. People here are happiest and do their best when someone has an interest in them. My first task was to revise the menus with the Chef and head waiter. I was striving for a continental sort of presentation of the food. Some dinner examples were, steak tartar, a hors'douvres trolley in which all tomatoes had to be skinned and their butt end removed. They cooked at table dishes like minute steak Dianne flambe and beef stroganoff. Other dishes were salmon or file de boef en-crout or Escalope of veal Viennoise with as Spätzli, Rusti Potatoes, and heart of lettuce salad. For variety there was chicken curry served with an enormous curry board consisting of, poppadum, Bombay duck, sliced banana, raisins, desiccated coconut, and mango chutney. Then there was a desert trolley and some delights also cooked at table, such as creep suzette, and pineapple flambe. Our pastry cook was an old timer, and her hot puddings were a must with luncheon guests. Coffee if in the lounge, was served on an individual tray with miniature cream jug on the side. As there was a substantial function trade now all cold buffets were displayed on mirrors. So as not to neglect the associates, they were given new uniforms. However, the locker room facilities were not adequate and for that we did not do well. I think in today's world we would have been questioned. Because I had such a hard time in college and in Switzerland, it never occurred to me that our staff might be feeling that too. We did not enquire if some might have been living in poor circumstances or what their family needs might be. As there was a shortage of work generally it seems they were very patient and just kept smiling and doing their best without complaining. However, the hotel was semi unionized but as we were well outside the city, there was little or no interference.

8

Twenty First Birthday Gift, USA

When I was twenty-one my folks offered me a sports car. I immediately thanked them but declined the offer. I did not want to be a type cast spoilt boy of a wealthy family. So, I just had a dozen friends to a disco instead. I had a nice girlfriend called Yvonne and she lived in Bray. The funny thing was when I went to night class and then called in to see her on the way home, my good friend Jurek Delimata would already be there, and it was like we were changing shifts. Yvonne was polite but thought the whole episode as ever so funny. Sometime later as if an answer to a prayer mum said that dad had booked to go to the USA on the Queen Elizabeth from South Hampton. The tour was for hoteliers to visit hotels on the east coast and promote their own. Now being ill, he could not go and offered the trip to me. This was unbelievable and it was impossible for me to refuse. I have always been an admirer of American ways. Their approach to business and how they turned failure into success. On the surface, they always seemed to be fifty steps ahead in style and fashion. All the way from high school sweaters and jeans up to inveigh league and sharp business suits, paper thin, and loose fitting. Furthermore, their large cars were like space craft on wheels, I did not care that they were gas guzzlers. In the sixties none of their paraphernalia was available in Ireland and that also goes for our attempts to produce a good cup of coffee. Now I was about to be immersed in that world.

Boarding the Queen Elizabeth at Southampton was a momentous experience. It was October and there I was in a silver-grey tweed coat feeling very clumsy and non-American. Coming up the gangway was a great mixture of young and old. The older people seemed to find deck beds and promptly wrapped themselves in rugs and lay out. As one of the youngsters, I was out of my depth and concentrated on watching all the activity on deck. The having met a young bunch in our group and a few American lads I came to life. After dinner at night, the bars came alive, and the dancing began. In no time I had a swiss dance partner come girlfriend called Karin Kowbiak (I think) who was emigrating to USA with her parents. We usually danced for a while and then went up on deck. I enjoyed her company had so much fun but once stayed too long up on deck and got a very sore throat from the cold air and the steam from the funnels. From then on, I drank Grog, a sailor's rum drink good for nautical ailments. At dinner, I got friendly with to two girls from Florida, Ann and Maddy Oppel. Ann was the eldest, tall thin and very Italian looking. She had a slow sincere way of talking and was very interested in Italian and Irish history. Their Dad was second generation Irish, and their mom was New York Italian. When they heard that I loved diving and also going to Miami with the hotel group, they insisted that I visit them in Largo, in Clearwater on the west coast. I realized that I could jump the tour and learn all about American living. On the night of our arrival off the coast of New Jersey it was nighttime. Ann told us to go look to see the lights of Manhattan on the horizon. Our group just stood riveted watching the city rise from the depths. The lights were amazing and left us with a lasting impression. When we got closer, Ann gave us a running commentary telling which building was which. She pointed out the Maxwell Coffee add that claimed, 'Good to the last Drop'. She said people now as what is wrong with the last drop? We docked and went our ways. I bade Karin adios, but she did not know their New York address, other then1200 5th Ave, not enough to locate so that was the last I saw of her and her rather stern parents.

After touring all the important sites and being brought to see hotels with our group, we ended up on the train to Miami. We shared the bar with a platoon of troops, either the 82nd or the 101 st Airbourne. I cannot remember. We drank together and had a sing song where I sang Dixie but with the wrong words. PFC Tower was a very friendly trainee officer who later wrote from Vietnam. However, at this stage the boys thought they were going to war for sure against Fidel Castro and so they drank themselves silly. When the train stopped at fort Bragg, we had to hunt for all the lost uniform hats and helped lower some unconscious fellows off the train. If they lost their gear, they would suffer penalty. We were booked into the Casablanca Hotel in Miami. It was very impressive and had a selection of swimming pools. The following day I got to dive in one of the pools. You see, I booked a diving lesson and to begin the instructor threw the aqua lung and gear into the deep end of the pool. I was told to dive in and put it on underwater. I think he was being smart. However, on the second attempt I actually did it. The trick was to first grab the weight belt and then take a breath from the lung then clear your mask. The rest was then easy. So, he just said, "that's it, you did well, your lessons finished".

As promise I cut loose and went to visit the Oppels in Clearwater. I re booked my passage home two weeks later than anticipated. I hired a ford Galaxy and as per their direction, drove west on the Tamiami trail. I was delighted to be driving an automatic large American car and to be on the open road. I stopped halfway and took an airboat trip in the glades. Then I continued till I got to Tampa Bay and phoned them. They said not to bother wasting time going through Tampa but to take the new Skyway bridge instead. I located the Skyway bridge leading directly to Clearwater. This took half an hour instead of a two-hour roundabout. The Oppel's met me in Clearwater and directed me to their home at sun heights in Largo. On first sight I nearly had a seizure because they had an eighteen-year-old daughter called Patty. This was a girl that looked as if from the south seas, Hawaii, Brazil, or Italy. She was magnificent. I settled into their home with the greatest of ease. Gus their father was retired and he and Carm, both played the stock market but also helped in the local catholic church. I felt like I was a returning member of their family and to confirm the fantasy, I was able to wear chinos, sneakers, and button-down oxford material shirts galore.

CRYSTAL RIVER

Sun Heights brought me nothing but pleasant memories. One of the guys living there was a local cop and he dressed me in his uniform for a photograph. Then he took me on a night round of duty, lots of radio work and 10- 4 over and outs. We heard a group was gathering in the local swamp and so three cars made a coordinated swoop only to find that they were parents burying treasure for Halloween the following day. On his off duty he took me to a local Bar for a few beers and a broiler maker. A friend he met told me he had been on Omaha beach on D Day. I was agog. The Oppel's house was surrounded with exotic plants and fruits, such as papaya and guavas. To make it all the more exciting it backed onto a grapefruit grove from where, the sound of bumps in the night as the ripe grapefruit fell to the ground. I was advised to take a stick or to roll grapefruits before me if walking in the grove so as to frighten away snakes. This I did with dedication. One occasion remained in my mind and that was the day we went to Crystal River. Ann got her 57 Chevy ready for the road, Patty and Maddie piled in and she drove to pick up two boys at their homes. Greg was a laugh a minute with his cracker mode of speech synonymous with the southern states. Next was Ray who it turned out to my dismay, was Patty's boyfriend. I was ever so jealous. Not only was he her special but he cuddled her on the trip and I just had to look the other way and pretend I was so happy. They rented a boat and scuba gear and followed a map of the lake, to a spot that was marked as the spring. At this point the murky water gave way for a large patch of clear water that was immerging from deep caverns some fifty feet below. All one had to do was anchor the boat at the rim of the hole and gear up and then dive downwards. I quickly put on the scuba tank and carefully lowered myself over the side of the boat. It was eerie standing in brown water and walking towards the crystal spring with a view downwards of over fifty feet to the bottom. I took the plunge. All at once I was in a water world like the South Pacific. The visibility was excellent, and I could see small fish circling and feeding from plankton growing on the luminous walls of the hole. The entire chamber was tinted with blue and the sunlight penetrated down into every corner. At the very bottom it narrowed down to a crack through which the Aquafer replenished its precious liquid. I was down about twelve feet and as there was no pinch area on my mask it was necessary to take it off and hold my nose and blow to adjust ear resistance. That done I replaced the mask and blew the water out from it. Then I descended another twelve feet. Now I was three times deeper than in the pool in Miami. This was getting serious. This time all did not go according to plan and when I blew, my mask did not clear, and I made for the surface in a sort of panic. As soon as they saw me, they shouted get out quick, your nose is bleeding. Why, I had nearly done myself an injury, but I was lucky on this occasion. It was a warning not to dive deep without pre instruction. The merry group, then had a barbecue under some trees laden with Spanish moss, on what was known as banana Island. They downed a few Schlitz's each and sang a few songs and then headed back to Largo in Ann's good old 57 Chevy.

The following day Ann said we would camp overnight in Hillsborough state park. There were two cars, one for the girls to sleep in and I got the other to myself. As well as the girls there was Patricia Fash, who was planning to become a Nun. They did not take their baby sister Claire as she was too young. The Park was a mass of tropical palms and there was a chest high river of dark brown swamp water flowing through the middle. This was filled with teenagers swinging and dropping and swimming all over the place. We joined in the fun but collapsed in the cars by about nine o clock. Next day it was finding a coffee and head home but not before we got to watch lots of Armadillos parading in the carpark. Then there was the trip to Weeki Wachee, to see the underwater cabaret. It was quite new at the time and quite an impressive experience. The theatre was built about five feet below the surface of a gigantic spring. There was a wall of glass some stretching for some fifty feet. resulting in a clear under view of the complete spring. It was so large that they had even sited an underwater Spanish galleon at the bottom, and this was used for part of the show. The actors were mare maids with fish tails, and the men were pirates, all breathing air from tubes while performing their act. On another occasion we all went to the hop! Yes, a real hi school dance in the local auditorium. Most the guys wore candy coloured button down shirts and some of the afro types did some incredible dancing. I got to dance with the girls and that included Patty as Ray was not there. Then Gene Pitney the renowned entertainer came on stage and sang CC Ryder. Finally, there was that evening on clearwater beach when Pat and her sisters Ann and Maddy and me, strode in the sugar white sand singing "we're off to see the wizard, the wonderful wizard of oz." Now many years later how strange it is, because I am on the same quest, as Dorothy and her friends. I am indirectly attempting to break the universal code and to find Oz even if it is on a scale unimaginable. The quest is daunting, and the path could lead eventually to a macro or micro, conclusion or both! This interlude in western Florida kept me back from returning on the Queen Elizabeth but instead I had a berth on the famous Queen Mary.

Three years later once again in New York I had an amazing experience of being in their first ever blackout. *"The power failure was all the way from Canada to Washington DC. Since then, there have been two more but nothing on the scale of this one. It hit about 5pm November 9th, 1965, as people were coming out of work. There was a crowd around a lad on the pavement who had a radio to his ear and told us all what was happening. I reckoned if I did not get grub quickly, the restaurants could be forced to close early. I went to the nearest dining room to the hotel it was called Rays, and they featured venison. After a good meal I retired to the hotel, but I got a call from the Irish Tourist Board office as they knew I was visiting. Some lads asked if they could stay in my room as they could not get home due to the chaos. I made them welcome as I had a spare bed and a couch."* Now back to 1962, I was scheduled to go home and when I arrival at the docks, was asked for my passport. Like a buffoon, I had packed it in my case, and it was already on board. A poor old customs officer with an "Erin Go Breagh" flag on his desk, rolled his eyes to heaven and led me on board to try and find my luggage. Thanks to my silent prayers we found it and I retrieved the Passport. This was another paramount experience, and I had an interesting time on the return comparing the two ships. Now it might sound fussy, but I preferred the Elizabeth. It was built in 1939 five years later than the Mary and was used like the Mary to ferry troops to war but did not go into service with Cunard Line till 1946. It was an honor to have travelled on either. I did not make so many friends on the return and after all the sunshine and Americana, going home was a very dull experience.

9

Bills Final Development

Things were different in the hotel on my return. By now my Dad was working fulltime and had immediately asserted his presence. He proposed changing the name to the Royal Starlight whereas I asked for it to be called the Wood book Arms. This would be in keeping with the local Golf Club and surrounding area. Bill won out because he wanted to feature the rooftop aspect of the property. He planned for a large roof top neon sign on the tower, but this was yet to happen. He also was not overly impressed by all my talk about the new world or with the improvements I had attempted. To trump my blarney, he gave me a shock when he announced that he intended enlarging the property even more. We already had 80 bedrooms, just some were with bathroom. We had as said - a large dining room and ballroom and a rooftop breakfast room. There was a bar with entry from the main street and we were fully booked from May to September and for all rugby week ends, Easter and. Christmas. Now I could appreciate the adjoining bathroom shortage but could not agree to his proposals but had little choice. I said I thought we should invest in cash control machinery as a priority. Looking back, it seems that in the back of his mind he was going to make the property big enough for me and my brother Colm. That only came to light later on. One must bear in mind how naive I was because I did not have a share in the business, and we never had family business meetings I trusted that it would all work out! Despite Bills apparent disappointment in me and some of the staff as he roamed the hotel, he also enjoyed the regal life. He often shared a table with Vera for the Saturday night Dinner Dance. Before going in they would sit in the front lounge and Bill would drink several La Ina dry sherries or Tio Pepe's. He often jumped to his feet and went to deal with small issues he remembered or observed. They often got talking to guests and invited them to join in for a drink. A very nice touch. Guests could also enjoy piano music in the mode of the famous Charley Kunz, Bill's favorite composer. Then they were escorted to their table on which there was bottle of Claret, usually Chateau Margaux or St Julienne sitting in a basket ready for their meal. He had the habit of calling me over at regular intervals to tip me off about failures in the general service etc. I did not hold any of this against him, but it was hard to take. One memory was how he dressed in the summer wearing a light linen dust coat with a rose, a sprig of heather or lavender in the lapel and vera would wear something equally lovely. Bill always looked and acted like today's detective Herculin Poirot. He had the same physique and constantly referred to his little pocketbook where he recorded everything. When finished dinner he always lit up a Cuban cigar and carried on his supervision of the hotel in that mode. His brother called him "Puffin Billy". On a comical note, just a few years later when my wife and I were expecting our first child, she suddenly went into labor at home which was Mount Herbert at the time. I left the hotel and tore back by car to collect her, but we ran into Bill with his notebook. Though we were at wits end, he nevertheless went through the pages, one at a time to see what might be there for me. However, all was well, and we got on our way and arrived at the hospital on time. We ended with a beautiful girl as reward for our patience. We called her Carolyn Maria.

My brother was near to finishing school and indicated that he would also like to go to the hotel school in Cathal Brugha Street where I had gone. Colm was a very good looking fellow and he had grown taller than me and had a great build. He had his own friends from school days and from around Bray, but they were all six years younger than me, so I rarely crossed paths with them. Vera decided to take Colm and I with her to Lough Derg. This is a penitential island in a lake in County Donegal. Bill had made the same pilgrimage thus setting an example. This island dates its services back to the 5th century and was a penitentiary for Saint Patrick. It's a very tough station because does not eat or sleep for twenty-four hours and prays. I continued to do that trip biannually ever since. Therefore, in the spirit of goodness and true to his intensions, Bill attempted to buy the Kilcroney hotel, which was near to the village of Enniskerry (Now made famous in a fairytale movie, Disenchanted). It had been a convent with large swarths of land and a good purchase. However, though he made a good offer, he was gazumped by another client and the deal fell through. So, as he had already bought some adjoining properties, he now hurried to expand and build a new block raising the hotel capacity to 130 rooms with bathrooms. He probably thought that it would then be big enough for two of us. There was to be a new kitchen with basement for storage and an additional dining room. A new elevator and an enlargement of the roof top room to accommodate a restaurant come function room. He said that there were grants being issued by the tourist board and they should not be missed. I said as before that I thought we were doing fine as we were and maybe just to improve the rooms, along with a modern control system for food and beverage. He dismissed my bleat, and the show went on.

By now the hotel was well known for its well-run Christmas Program. It began on Christmas Eve with a reception in the Roof Top Room followed by a sumptuous dinner with several choices among them was always Smoked Salmon and Partridge and Veal. We also had Starlight Frost Cake among the deserts. This was a multi layered Cassata with cherries and angelica and a hint of rum on a sponge base. This was a specialty of the cook named, Kathleen Giffney. Christmas day was a feast and finished with a dinner dance and cabaret. Bill had a spotlight that could change colours, and he liked to work it while he watched the goings on. By now most guests were getting into the swing of things. On the first night they were mostly unhappy after travelling along with general Christmas pressures mixed with guilt. By Christmas Day they were thawed out and by St Stephens day they were very friendly, and the humor was high. We had hired two busses and took those who wanted, for a trip around Wicklow with a stop at a pub and a dance around a bonfire. There were always two accordion players playing old time tunes. A friend of mine, Bernard Rogan was hired as an entertainer and did a great job, but this was after we had been let down badly by Billy Quinn. Billy was very effeminate but very funny. His favorite act was to dress as a woman and join the cabaret. We had him for two Christmases but on the second occasion he asked Bill for pay in advance as he had a family difficulty to deal with and when he got the cash he disappeared.

Though Bill never told us where he got his funds, I guessed it was from our net profits after tax. He still had a good friend in Mr Watson of Anglo-Irish Bank in Richmond Street. I trusted that he knew what he was doing, but I knew it must need a large loan. His plans at any rate, were going ahead regardless of my reserve. Bill and vera decided to take some advice from someone therefore told Noel Dooley their surveyor to book the builders on a time and material arrangement. This was as opposed to a signed contract or several contracts as the job materialized. As a result, this decision had a major mal effect on progress. Noel Dooley was a very interesting character, and I can see how he impressed Bill and Vera. Both he and his wife were very British sorts. Noel sported a mustache and gold rimmed glasses. He always wore a double-breasted navy blazer with gold buttons and drove a Bentley. He only met and discussed the building program with Bill. Yet I always attended meetings with the Architect, Patrick Campbell as Bill knew that I had a good eye for reading plans and had an understanding of the layout. I also had done many drawings of how the hotel might appear. Bill appreciated this but barely needed it because he himself had an amazing imagination. Bill's influence and attitudes took its toll on me for I had become like mafia, win, win, win at any cost, but if you are nice to me, I will be nice to you (horrid). Expand and give more and more employment but do not let anyone stand in your way (horrid). All this was in contrast to my good intensions when in Lough Derg. Bill was a hub of activity and full of ideas. In his "modus operandi", when he had an idea, he would set the ball rolling immediately and work on the details later. He said that is the best way to get the idea moving. I have used that approach ever since on many selected occasions. In later years when I did not have my dad's budget at my favor and was an employee not an owner, that philosophy was derelict. However, back then I had lots of ideas about the new development, and some were kick started using his methods. For the catering, I envisaged all trays and containers to be to the same module and had racks made to facilitate this strategy. I wanted the cooking to be in a straight line rather than an island. Also, I was hoping for a Market Forge oven and ranges and refrigeration at positions close to the cooking. As the Hotel and Catering Exhibition was on in London at the time, he took me there and that is where we place most of our orders. As said, it was important that we had good refrigeration near to the cooking areas. This meant importing units from America via Johnny Whitlow of 'Recold Refrigeration' in Dublin. I knew Johnny in school. I also told him that I hoped we could have a sunken bar in our new rooftop restaurant and Johnny's equipment might be used. However, it turned out beyond Bill's budget and never happened. Therefore, I had a lot to do with the decor and of course menu design to go with it. Then one day on visiting the new basement in its early stages I noted that there were a dozen places with steel rods protruding upwards. I asked the foreman if they would be pillars and would they travel all the way up to the roof. He said they would! Now, as we had planned a roof top dining and function room the pillars would obstruct the room enormously. I informed Bill and he called the Architect who worked his magic and twelve of the pillars were eliminated by redistributing the weight. Phew, a disaster had been avoided.

ROMANCE

Regardless of my challenges at work my social life continued. My first girlfriend was Yvonne Gillan from little Bray. She was quite continental looking and slim and we got on very well. Comically apart from a date or two, as often I called in to her house when I finished night classes and was greeted by my friend Jurek departing. Obviously, he had a shine on her also. Her mother was very amused and so was Yvonne. After about a year Yvonne finished the relationship, and I very sadly went my way. Then, I hit it off with Mary Mc Gloin whose aunt owned the Lake Hotel Killarney. We attended lots of parties and had a wild time. I had by now began jogging and playing rugby with Greystones RFC. My sore thumb had become bearable though completely deformed and it would not bend. Then as a late starter I did not fully understand the game. I got pushed out to the wings, to become wing three quarter and enjoyed the position because all the action came from one side only. I trained on Tuesday nights, asking Dad to cover my shift, and he did. At this point Bill had secured more land for a car park and the builder Mc Laughlin and Harvey had commenced development but in a short time a giant crane that was installed in the center of the newly intended block stopped rotating and we discovered it was broken, it just stopped working. There was a dispute about who was responsible. The result was that the redundant crane remained, and the building program slowed down badly. Bill and the surveyor dealt with the problem and yet we had to bear the costs accruing. It was now too late, and the show had to go on regardless.

FIRST IRISH SURFING

For two years I played for Greystones Rugby Club, but found that I had another interest brewing. In 1964 when the idea of surfing got into my head it became a passion. Despite the demanding hours I worked there was always the afternoon free. I decided to put the time to good use. I read the reader's digest about surfing in Hawaii and decided as the sport did not exist in Ireland I would try and make it happen! I built a wooden surfboard and launched it in Bray with the help of my bother. It worked and I got to stand up and become very excited with that good result. The first promotion I undertook was to advertise in the Irish Independent special notices that surfing had arrived. I rallied my friends, and we formed the Bray Ireland Surf Club because there was surf there in storms. Now in keeping with the do or die family attitude I spotted an opportunity to promote our new surf club. I wrote to John Seaverson and Pat Mc Nulty of Surfing Magazine in California, and they gave us great support by writing and displaying the photos I sent him. In 1965 I returned to USA and got to Hawaii, but more about that in the next chapter. In March 1966, our club mounted a stand in the Royal Dublin Society, boat show to advertise surfing. We had a free slot on the balcony, and I showed movies I had brought back from Hawaii and had our first old surfboards on show, all this to Hawaiian and Beachboy background music. The show went on for five days and was a major draw for young people. Just then I had an ally to the cause – it came in the form of Roger Steadman from London. He was moving to Ireland and already was a surfer. He and I formed a company called C@S Surfboards and secured the Bilbo agency as envisaged. A trip was organized to the north west to learn about the coastline and to put surfing on the map. We surfed in Strandhill, Bundoran and Rossnowlagh, Loughrossbeg Bay and eventually Portrush. When in Rossnowlagh we called into the Sandhouse Hotel where the owners welcomed us and at the same time ordered two surfboards for their family and guests. As well as surfing, I joined the Bray Junior Chamber of Commerce. May Dad was in the senior Chamber and was quite influential. His style was to make notes in the meeting and then relate them back with all his criticisms and to drive home his opinions. I tried this in the Junior Chamber, but it did not work for me. Then it was announced that the chamber would organize the first ever Bray Sea festival. There would be a boat race and some other events. I volunteered immediately but spotted another opportunity to show off surfing. I contacted the Dun Laoghaire Lifeboat and asked would they visit the seafront for the festival. They agreed and I asked would they make a movie of my surfing behind the wake of the lifeboat? They agreed. So, I delivered the fully loaded 8 mm movie camera to the cox and also a tow rope. On the day of the sea festival in July it was bright and sunny, I paddled out on my ten-foot board to meet the Lifeboat. They cast me the rope and I was towed the length of the seafront. As the wake was enormous, I was soon able to let go of the rope and free surf behind them. One of the crew filmed the event. In later years I gave the DLB a copy of the film. My concern for Bray made me take an interest in the Bray Seafront and so I drew up a proposal for its development. It included making a breakwater come docking area at the harbour end. Also, to build a groin down the middle of the harbour so the river flows to the sea without circulating and also to widening its mouth. Laying a track for a children's train to run the length of the beach and also an open-air swimming pool. The local paper called it a pie in the sky project and a councillor named Costello of Sein Fein campaigned against it. Then some years later and for other reasons this same poor fellow was shot dead by his political enemies. Oddly enough, without any of my doing, some elements of the plan were pursued at the harbour end. Then there was the addition of a mammoth delivery of sand and shale taken from the outer banks, to fortify the beach. This was a great idea put forward by Michael Ledwidge and agreed with the county council which was somewhat an achievement – a great idea, too good to be true, but it was true.

USA Again

In 1965, and before the hotel building program was completed, I made the planned return trip to USA. I had saved for three years and procured a special Greyhound 99-day ticket from for the total of $99 and it was only for tourists. I would make the trip semi business as I again got some financial support from the Irish Tourist Board because the trip was part sales related. This time I flew to Boston and in upper New York State I stayed in the home of friends of the family, Dr Cannon. After a nice time in Cazenovia, I took the greyhound to Cleveland and stayed with John Grey an intern in the Cleveland Clinic. John said that he would take me to see the Cleveland Clinic and be ready at 5 am. We all dressed in white coats and began touring the wards. I had to look the other way on quite a few occasions. Then at about 8 am the group gathered at an x ray board at which the surgeon asked me a question. John explained I was a visitor. I was embarrassed but also quite hungry for some breakfast, but that would have to wait! Eventually at 10 am John took me to the canteen, which was now closed, except for a stale cup of coffee. We went home about 4 pm and later we went out on the town.

Next stop was Chicago, Cheyanne Wyoming Reno Nevada, Las Vegas and to San Francisco. Somewhere near Chayanne a fellow called Alle Gillette got on board. He sat opposite to me and went on all about how cool he was. He hinted that his family were wealthy from razor blades. Guess what razor blades! He did not look the part but wore army khaki and cowboy boots and he also said he had a six shooter and showed it to me. I was not sure what to do but soon after that the bus stopped, and he was taken away. There was a stop in before Reno Nevada by a lonely night club. We went in for coffee, half asleep. What did we find but a bar with dancing girls, feathers, and loud music? We went through

Reno and eventually got to Las Vegas where I got a cab to the Stardust Hotel. This hotel featured a big dinner and cabaret, and gambling was its main attraction. I bought a post card of the hotel with the Stardust written in huge star like letters above the property and thought maybe Dad would be interested. I visited downtown and heard the big artificial cowboy say out loud, "Howdy Cowboy". I rented a car and drove to Boulder Dam and prepared to leave the following day. Now with all my curiosity satisfied I boarded the bus for California. As we approached the Californian border the driver said we could not bring fruit into the state, I liked the sound of that, it was sort of special. Earlier he had smelt my Galois tobacco and said no smoking cigars and then he sniffed again and finished off by saying or foreign tobaccer. It was time to wind up the sales and promotion, so in San Francisco I phoned all the talk shows and told them about Ireland and our Royal Starlight Hotel. Then I took a tram to the beach. This was near Fleishhacker, on the main beach south of Kelly's Cove. There were young lads with surfboards, and I asked if I could borrow on. To my amazement they said yep. So, I paddled out in three-foot swell and caught a ride. Then contrary to inclinations I got out and thanked them. This way I looked cool. Actually, this was my first time on a proper fiberglass board. Up to this I only had a homemade balsa board. It would be later that year before my glass boards began to arrive from Cornwall.

HAWAII OR BUST

Out of curiosity, I went to a travel agent and asked about a flight to Oahu. It cost 200 dollars return and I reckoned I might never be this way again, so I booked. I arrived as if hypnotized by setting foot on the territory that had been bombed in 1944. I was agog at the military personnel socializing everywhere and of course the Polynesian shirts that so many wore. I stayed in the YMCA and met a guy from New York who was with Pan Am and had won a world tour he claimed. He said we should team up and hire a car. We got a mustang convertible and he often got me to drive while he shouted instructions as we went. In the end I realized how to stay safely in one's lane and how to handle four way stops. We went downtown to hotel street where there were hundreds of marines and navy personnel filling the bars. It was a sea of khaki and white and the din was enormous. Then we went to a strip club in the middle of

Waikiki and the next day he bade me farewell and continued his world tour. That left me with a super car on a hypnotic island. Therefore, I hired a twelve-foot surfboard and jammed it upright into the back of the car and off I went. The first stop was two miles after Makapuu where I turned down a lane and joined in with mainly natives surfing a reef. One guy was so proficient that rode on half a surfboard. Then on to Sunset beach where I paddle out to discover the tiny waves I saw, were actually over twelve feet. Sitting in fear I also watched while the planes took off from wheeler field no doubt, filled with troops for Vietnam. They were probably the guys in hotel street the night before! Then, I saw a set of waves approaching and without hesitation paddled towards shore at the same time catching a wave and surviving the drop and the rush. I could not believe there I was hanging to the right and flying across the face of a big wave. On my next attempt I caught a smaller less aggressive wave, had a good ride and then decided to finish up for the day. In the meantime, I missed other waves and was buried in white water struggling to survive. Then I paddled in and went back to Waikiki but on the way, I got to visit the Banzai Pipeline. This can be big and dangerous but that day it was almost flat. After that I had to bid Hawaii a sweet aloha and departed. I did not have a pretty "whine" to kiss me goodbye and put a garland around my neck, but even without that I vowed to return.

I rejoined the greyhound bus and got as far as El Paso. A taxi driver of Scottish ancestry took me to see Juarez on the US Mexican border. There I saw a cop back a line of traffic of twenty cars, back because he wanted to let other traffic through. At this point I was spun out and a trip across Texas would be too slow and too costly so to remedy that, I flew to Tampa in an almost empty plane. I was collected at the airport by the Oppel's and was take to their new home in Clearwater though sorry not to be in Sun Heights. Yet all was well because I met the old gang. Amazingly, the Opple's had just gotten a phone call from the Irish Embassy to say I was invited to visit Cape Canaveral. I had made a request from Ireland before I left and somehow NASA agreed. This was the coming together of a great adventure particularly as the Cape was never open to the public. Gus and Carm, both insisted that I borrow their car and to take Patty along with me. I could hardly argue. In fact, I made a pass by trying to hold her hand on an occasion, but she would have none of it. Just as well. We set off with Patty directing me as we headed back east and through a small town with pink and white stucco homes called Orlando. Today that image has disappeared. At the Cape we were met by security guys who showed us around and seemed to think we were physicists. The giant Titan was in its 100-foot house being pumped with hydrogen fuel and was scheduled to be transported up a gentle in cline to its gantry at top from where it would be launched. There were four large lakes around the site in case of an accident resulting in and a deluge of fuel falling from above. Then we went to one of the outlying observations pods. There we looked back at the launch pad with a periscope that could enlarged the image. If one revolved the scope, there was a nice view of Coco Beach and the surf. I guess I blew it when I exclaimed, "Surf's Up". Yes, my immaturity had taken over! Forgetting that, the visit was a great success and remined us that humans will have to travel outwards for the human race to survive its ever-increasing numbers. It was early evening and Patty, and I had a meal in a diner and returned to Clearwater. I found the roads great and had no trouble with driving.

Ann said that she was moving up to New York. All the young boys here were in Vietnam and her future would be up north. Originally that is where Gus and Carm had come from, and she still had relatives in the area. So, I was to accompany her in her old 57 Chevy packed with her belongings. Sadly, we left her family, her folks with Maddy, Patty and Claire all waving furiously as we went on our way. Ann was a secretary and knew what discipline would mean. She said we would stop at 7pm but start always before 8am. On the first night in South Carolina, we could not get separate Motel rooms because we were not married and were not trusted and were told to go. We therefore tried the next motel as if we were married and that worked ending up in the same room. As you can guess, hanky-panky as Ann called it, was out of the question it would have been all wrong, but we laughed ourselves to sleep as there was nowhere to go in the area. Next day brought us to a place called South of the Border, which was a massive trading post for food and souvenirs and a big tourist attraction. Soon after that we avoided Atlanta and eventually ended up in Boston in a three-story house with siding and a porch. This was owned by a friend of Ann's and I then heard Patty was flying up to stay and visit a specialist for her own reasons. This would be in Newport and therefore, we picked up Patty and drove her to Newport. When all that was over, we visited the local bar used by Yale students, then I had a nice chat with Patty while sitting on a park bench and surveying Newport Harbour from on high. Later in Boston I bought a beige tweed Iveagh League jacket and kept it forever. Then it was time for me to say merci, adios amigo, and fly home to Ireland. On my return I showed my dad and the Architect the post card from the Stardust Hotel in Las Vegas and they both agreed that it could be copied to read Royal Starlight Hotel. This was done and the enormous letters were mounted on the hotel tower for all to see. I was so proud but hoped the locals would not object. They did not but many of them called it the Zhivago sign!

THIRD TRIP TO USA - SAN DIEGO

By now my boards had arrived it was June 1966, and I made a trip to Tramore on the south coast. We had made a video of the first surfari in March to the northwest but now added to it with this trip. On arrival the local lifeguards crowded around with curiosity. They whooped with delight when they realized what I had on the roof of the car. I passed out the boards for them to try. This was the first moment that proper surfboards were used on Tramore strand. They had been using a fourteen-foot lifesaving board but now they were to ride ten-foot fiberglass models. Those fellows were, Hugh O Brien Moran, Derek Musgrave, Eamon Matthews, Dave Kenny and a few more, all who became hooked for life. The following October I got a great surprise. It was an invitation to come to San Diego next October to compete in the world surfing championships 1966. This bowled me over. It all happened because I had written so often to Pat Mc Nulty of Surfer Magazine. Word had got to Monseigneur Clarkin and he asked from the pulpit for support for Ireland to compete. Larry Gordon of Gordon and Smith Surfboards was the main sponsor. San Diego was amazingly surf conscious and we were given rooms in a nice motel called The Half Moon Inn on shelter island. Teams were given the use of the latest Ford Camero sports cars, four to a car – share it around. I shared my car with England (Rodney Sumpter who had surfed with me in Ireland), also India and Mexico. So that meant each of us could have the car for about four hours each. On our first morning's brief over breakfast a college student arrived writing up the event for her college magazine. I got to talk to her, her name was Sandy Reni. So, I said I would like to take her for dinner. To my surprise, she agreed and gave me her address at El Cajon. I bet she was thinking, gee free food. As luck had it, I managed to get use of the car from three pm till seven. This was just enough time for me to collect Sandy and take her to the Tiki Tiki Restaurant on Shelter Island and deliver her home. It was all a novelty and I hope she enjoyed it! Next day the cars were taken back because several had been driven into the sea by some irresponsible surfers, I was lucky to have got the car early. Putting all the bad news aside, we surfed in groups around the area for five days taking in La Jolla, Mission Beach and finishing with Ocean Beach for the Semifinals and finals. I got to the semis and just enjoyed watching the finals on a sunny beach filled with colourful people and a great atmosphere. The whole event concluded I went to Newport Beach and stayed with Jim Duane. We surfed Huntington and the next day he dropped me to the local airport where I got a flight to New York. On the flight, which was almost empty, and as we passed over the Grand Canyon, one of the stewardesses came over and invited me to join them, up front for a game of cards. Wow, that was a fun invitation, and I accepted. After a half hour of jokes and poker the girls went back to their chores. That capped a great experience, and I could not wait to report on the event as soon as possible when I got home. As a priority I got our club together and explained how the event was run. This meant that we had the know how to mount an Irish contest. Our committee agreed that we should go for it and run an event in Tramore. We got wonderful help from the boys and from Dr O'Brien Moran who was on the local council. Also, some of their parents joined in and the event went ahead. It was Ireland's first ever Surfing Championships held on September 3rd, 1967. The event was a great success and was held annually ever since. Now at last, surfing was Irish sport and an Irish reality, my ambition had fulfilled. Now Ireland was a new Hawaii.

True Love 1967

Once again when trying to be a good manager, I received a group of students from my old Hotel School. Bill told me I was to show them around our hotel. I noticed one girl with fair hair, sallow skin and with a very continental look. She had a good figure and was a very friendly. In no time I got all of their phone numbers and wished them well. The next day I phoned Ann Kelly, the girl that I fancied. We became friend and I got to visit her family, then Bill suggested that he would employ her in the shop coming up to Christmas. Ann says that it was a great experience, particularly as she had to serve small brandies and snipes of Guinness to the old ladies of the inner city. She also was delighted to be invited with me to attend a reception in Dublin Castel for the world hotelier meeting hosted by the Irish Hotel's Federation. So, by now She was my girlfriend and a year later we were engaged to be married. The wedding was in Donnybrook Church followed by the reception in the rooftop room of the Royal Starlight Hotel and honeymoon in the Canaries. The Kelly Family lived in 55 Nutley Road Ballsbridge. Ann was the eldest and had a sister called Patricia and two brothers Gerard and David. All were to marry and be great successes in business and also live close to one another and to us. In the meantime, the hotel development was nearly finished. The issue over the crane had not been settled and it looked like we would have to pay for its presence. We began expanding our wedding and conference trade to the point that I was working from dawn to dusk and always feeling like the less I was paid the more the hotel would prosper and that someday it would all balance out. The roof top opened and became popular for functions and diner dances. In the summers Colm and his cousin Brendan Smyth from Belfast worked as lounge waiters and made lots of money from tips. Colm had now graduated from hotel school, and it was time for him enter the family business. They now told me to work opposite Colm, which meant every second morning every second evening and we could give each other a day off. I was appalled, as now I would lose control. However, I had to swallow my pride, yet the rebuke was sweet, now I could have time for Ann and to get our home organized. My Dad came to the fore, he offered me his vegetable garden with access to the Herbert Road if I could get a mortgage and build a bungalow. I applied to the Irish Permanent Building Society and after an enormous delay it was finally granted. With much appreciation the process went ahead. It was my call to draw up a plan, and need I say that once again I was influenced by American psych. The plan, though compact and simple, had the profile of an Arizona ranch with a low-pitched roof that overhung the entrance creating a porch. Our neighbors Tim Healy the town engineer produced the drawings, and a builder was engaged. Ann and I named the house Susswald which should mean sweet wood, but it is not correct German, but we liked it anyway. After lots of formalities

Susswald before it was demolished by a developer.

finally the Irish Permanent Building Society agreed our mortgage. Our first baby was a girl, called Carolyn Maria born in St Michael's hospital Dun Laoghaire on the 9th of November 1969. Later Paul William born in Canada and finally Georgina Maria born in Dublin. These events were to give us great happiness.

To promote Irish Hotels Bord Failte organized a series of travel agents' workshops. These were held in London and Frankfurt. Ann and I did the London venue and later Colm, and I went to two workshops in Frankfurt. This was a most successful way to secure business as there was no question of buying drinks or food for agents. The agents just sat in at one's display table and talked shop. We got a few good tours from this process which included Sean O'Shea's Emerald Isle tours from northern England. The hotel was now improving in standard and in keeping with this, one day a South African man of Indian descent came for interview. His name was Freddy Naidoo and he wanted to be our wine waiter. We advertised the position as per immigration regulations, but got no response, clearing the way for Freddy. He came to Bray with his wife and told me his son Chris Naidoo would open a lady's hair dresses in Dublin. Dressed in a royal blue jacket and white shirt he cut a fine figure cruising around the dining area as he dispensed chateau wines to the visitors. On weekends the trade was enormous with dancing in two areas, two bars, a restaurant, a grill room and at least a wedding celebration or a dinner dance. Bill was often in the thick of things when he should have left it to us. One night I got a call from the front desk to say there was a fellow with a knife in the lobby. I went there, post haste, and to my horror, Dad was there blocking his entry and with his arms outstretched. The villain had the knife now hidden in his coat. I bolted over and pushed Dad away and took over his position. Then I looked for help but the lounge had emptied. There was a frozen moment while he glared at me. Then to my horror he drew out the knife. It was long, and he began waving it at me. I needed protection and therefore grabbed a chair and raised it and went towards him raising my voice and warning him to go and that the police were coming. For a brief moment he waivered and just then I heard the loud rumble of Colm coming down from the roof top room in support. With that the knife man ran out the door. One week later in the middle of the day, a derelict fellow stumbled in the door of the hotel and fell on the ground choking. His tongue was clenched in his gums as he had no teeth, and he was foaming. I pulled open his mouth, but his tongue slipped back down his throat. All I could do was try and grab his tongue and pull it up allowing air to breath. Within half a minute he sat up, pushed me out of the way, and was gone. It seems he had no idea how close he was to the pearly gates. In quieter moments one could have a nice celebration in the rooftop room, and that's just what we did. We were delighted to be fully open and running so it was champagne time. Our cousin Geraldine Cremin was there but Vera had stepped out when the shot was taken.

1969 Celebrating the hotel extension. Bill Cavey first left, Cousin Geraldine, Kevin, Wine Agent, Colm with Champagne and Ann Cavey sitting on the counter.

PETER O'TOOLE

One day the famous film star Peter O'Toole booked in to our hotel. He was making the Lion and The Winter in Ardmore studios. He, being originally Irish was a relation of the Driscoll's in Bray and they ran a guest house called Ulysses. It was going to be a long stay and we had one of the best rooms allocated for him and it had access to the stairs to the Rooftop Restaurant. Before his arrival I went to the local tobacconist and bought over a dozen Galois cigarettes. These were put in his drawer as we knew they were his favorite. One evening, Sarah Miles who was also filming came to see Peter and thy both came up for dinner in the Rooftop Restaurant. They made a pretty picture sitting in the extreme corner of the room overlooking the river and black silhouette of the distant mountains. Their beauty was also enhanced by the golden drapes and the hidden lighting surrounding them as they dined and consumed the best of wines and Galois cigarettes. They looked to be a romantic couple and it was late before they decided to leave, but it was great that they choose the rooftop for their booking. As we were delighted with the ambiance of the rooftop room, we had a quiet family celebration on one occasion. Not to be forgotten, the only remaining part of the hotel that had never been improved was the public bar that opened out to the main street. Bill had decided to have this renovated in keeping with the rest of the hotel. Once again Peter O'Toole became the pivotal personality in an event that was soon to follow. As a custom he enjoyed coming in with his team at about 7 pm from filming. He liked the public bar old-world atmosphere. However, none of us had the good sense to tell him that on such a day it would be closed for alterations. At about 7pm on the first evening of its closure I got a call to go the bar, an emergency. As suspected, the bar was in darkness and the power had been cut off by the builders and the chandelier was now lowered to flower level. In the middle of all this stood Peter O'Toole shouting that he wanted the bar opened. I told him the plight we were in, but he still insisted while screaming his demands. As politely as possible I apologized and pointed out that the bar could not be opened but instead, there were lounges with service at his disposal. He shrieked in defiance and I shouted back that there was nothing that could be done. Raising my voice was a mistake because he darted up behind me and pushed me against the wall at reception with a firm grip on my upper body. There was a moment of standoff and then one of his team pulled him away and they left. That night he checked out of the hotel. Just a blimp to be forgotten, and no hard feelings.

We ran into some trouble that was not of our making. One day, the Springboks rugby team booked to stay with us, because we were known as the English Rugby teams always used our place for accommodation. Some months later, three members of the west wicklow anti-apartheid committee came to see us. They said we were to cancel the Springboks or there would be trouble. I responded that we were impartial to politics and we had made a commitment in good faith, therefore we would not cancel. I took the matter to Bill and this time for a change the family agreed, and we stood firm. From that moment on we met trouble that involved pickets and even a serious incident. Ann while at home with baby Carlolyn was startled to hear the earsplitting boom of an explosion at the end of Bill's garden and close to ours. It was intended to cause us alarm, and it did. The Police said it was meant to hit our home but went off prematurely. We put the incident out of mind and eventually welcomed the team to the hotel. We valued their business, but they were not very appreciative of our service and support and really not worth all the trouble. As a result of our stance several other hotels followed suit and accommodation was now available for them around the country.

12

Distant Drums

There were sounds of a civil rights revolt in Northern Ireland during 1969. To everyone's horror, there was the eruption of violent and civil disturbance resulting a massive reduction of business from both Northern Ireland and the UK. Tourism in the Republic of Ireland went into a downward spiral and remained there for the following five years and only slowly returned to normal. All this meant that the good life of being the town's most prominent business would come to an end. In fact, due to the large loan it was likely that the Hotel could get into financial difficulties. We would wait to see what would happen or maybe we could stop it happening! In no time, Bill, Colm, and I were called into the AIB bank to see Mr Franklin the new bank Manager. Bill's friend Watson had retired. This new man did not know us but was driven by the latest disastrous results. He told us that our loan was so large that the interest was not being paid back and if that continued, we would face receivership. He said that spending was to be capped and he would watch our progress. Bill did not appear in the hotel quite so often at this stage but after a few months called a meeting with Colm and I and said that he was retiring, and we were to take the reins. Unfortunately, there were no reins to take, as he had always held them, and the debts had already been accumulated. We did not have any choices, just a slim hope. The slim hope was as Colm and I discussed. If we can let the hotel carry on at 112,000 gross profit per annum, and not to drop below that perhaps Franklin will be satisfied. Then if he and I can generate new income from new ventures and use that income to develop, we might outride the trouble. Was it worth a try?

We agreed, and Ann backed what we were proposing. Colm had a good connection with some fellow in Trinity College who proposed making our Rooftop into a Disco with entry by a rear staircase. Once up, there was a fine bar, cloakroom and washroom facilities plus fire exits. It ran three nights a week and generated massive publicity among young people without any advertising. We included an egg mayonnaise and a roll and butter. This was to legitimize their drinking for an extra hour. Ann helped in the very big task of making up the salads. Using cash from the disco, we now could afford to renovate our ground floor disused kitchen. With a small investment we could open a grill room with a separate entrance from Queensborough road. We named it the Dargle Grill and it was based on good value informal dining with lots of decor relating to the local river and surroundings. This also became a hit with middle-aged clientele. Now we were becoming the darling of the local population. The hotel was no longer just for tourists it was theirs.

One day I climbed up on the hotel lift tower and painted some worn parts that could be seen from the road below. Then Ann and I repainted the lady's room on the ground floor. Colm and I moved out of our back-room office and converted it into a chart room for all sorts of bookings. One could see at a glance what lay ahead, and it was close to the reception. We moved our offices to an unused bedroom. Ann suggested, we apply the BBC because their serial the Oniden Line could be used as the theme for our ground floor restaurant. We wrote to the BBC and received their permission. This meant having artwork produced that portrayed the 1880's Liverpool steamboat and schooners as they traded around the world. Portraits of the characters in the series and a menu to match. The room would have these pictures placed above banquette seating and tables and lit with picture lighting. This was also not a very heavy expense as we located a local artist who did a very good job quite cheaply. We had one of the old iron fireplaces removed from the basement of Mount Herbert and fitted in the lounge adjoining the Oniden Room and over this we had a model ship in a large bottle. The stage was set.

The Hotel at its prime during the early 70's. Left to right,
Roof Top Restaurant, Lounge bar and Breakfast Room.

Staying away from the hotel was impossible. Bill continued to work and potter around during this period. His favorite haunt was at 11am he would have a la Ina sherry in the public bar known as the Amber room. He always invited the handyman Joe Mc Grain to join him for a pint, while Bill would have a sherry. He would open his notebook and give Joe a list of things to be mended. He always had lunch with us at about 2pm when the rush was over, and Colm and I, usually joined him. On these occasions we eat lightly often soup and a salad. However, despite the normality he kept his cards to his chest. We had been watching our audit figures returned monthly to us from Conor Ran and Co Auditors. We were now due the annual audit figures and were looking forward to their arrival, but they did not come! Jim Monks arrived in the hotel and we asked him where the returns were? He said, "The audit went to your Dad." This came as a surprise because we were becoming result conscious and the audits helped. The hotel was by now showing a turnover of 220,000 punt gross profit per annum, double that it had been two years before. We asked him about the audit but never got to see it. On the surface the hotel looked like it found the formula for success. The rooftop which was a restaurant and a lounge, and a breakfast room was lit from end to end and very busy. The Oniden room and entrance lounge was bathed in soft lighting and the massive Royal Starlight sign in ruby red shone out over the town and countryside. We had been cruising along, had suffered no interference and with fingers crossed, thought that we just might make the cut. I went immediately to see Dad, but he brushed off the issue saying that it was now too late to do anything.

There were two more meetings with Franklin at which he emphasized that were not to spend anything and to heed his word. At this stage we did not intend any more spending it had all been done. Therefore, we aligned with his advice and gained at least another nine months. It was amazing how slow they were in calling us in. There was no such thing as a being in administration in those days. If there was it would have been a help. We had asked Bill if there was any way out of the mess and he had suggested for us to see PV Doyle a massive hotelier whom he knew. Colm and I went to see him, but it all came to nothing, and he did not point to any financial wizardry. I just felt a bit cheated because we had given him inside information for free. So, we had done the very best we could do in our circumstances. We had not run away; we had stayed the course and for the first time ever we would have to look out for ourselves and not to do everything for the good of the hotel only. In a bid to draw some profit from the sinking ship, the family agreed to put the hotel for auction. I was listed at 500,000 including carpark. On the auction day as hotels were not seen as profitable in the impaired market, there were few bidders, and it was withdrawn at 200.000 punts.

THE FALL OF CAMELOT

Then in 1973 the final letter arrived. It was to announce that were being put into receivership, but it was another three months more before the receivers from Donald Hampson walked in. He took our keys and took inventory of the whole hotel. He saw a mark in the wall where the Sacred heart picture had resided and demanded to know what had been there. When explained about the Sacred Heart Picture, he said no more. To this day I still keep that picture. We decided to stay in the job for as long as possible and for me that meant three months with pay leading up to Ann and my emigration. We had applied for a visa to go to Canada as Ann had relations in Vancouver. As the Vietnam war was at its height, we reckoned that I would be drafted if we had applied for USA. Our competitor was the local International Hotel. It had 200 rooms and large function facilities. It was built in 1862, but in June 1974 we were alerted to black smoke and the sight of the hotel burning. Its owner was pacing outside smoking a large cigar while the fire brigade struggled to find a source of water to spray – there was difficulty with the mains and the tide also had gone way out. It was rubble by day two. However, we were still going to Canada but despite this plan I went to the shop to see Dad alone. It was interesting that over the years while the hotel was spared no expense, the shop had been neglected yet it was a profit maker. I found him in his office and asked him if I could buy the shop and going to Canada would be cancelled. He dismissed me saying the shop was already too encumbered. This was true because later I found out that the shop had been given as collateral against the hotel debt. In no time Bills Solicitor, Kevin Smith gave me papers to sign revoking any ownership of the shop. I presume Colm got the same. In the long run the banks agreed to take Bill's house but permit his purchase of a smaller home. In like manner we put our Susswald for sale, it was mortgaged with the Irish Permanent Building Society, but it had not sold by the time of our emigration. Gerard, Ann's brother managed the sale in our absence. Since those bygone days, one third of the original Royal Starlight Hotel has been sold off and that included some of the roof top breakfast room. The remainder of the rooftop has been converted into bedrooms. Interestingly the first new owners were friends of PV Doyle and the current owner's son was in school with my son Paul. Now the hotel has developed in another direction with a swimming pool and Gymnasium. Susswald has since been demolished and replaced with four compact houses. Bill and Vera came to the Airport to see us off. He gave me a bear hug and I could hear the sound of his rapid breathing and the thump of his heart as he must have been feeling strong emotions. Certainly, I was. This was the last I saw of him because we were in Canada when he died. We returned from Calgary in 1980 after my being the Room Service Manager looking after Prince Charles and Prince Andrew during their six day stay in the Four Seasons Hotel during the Stampede. Also having spent many happy times skiing the Rockies and having had the thrill of being a sole surfer, surfing on Vancouver Island's west coast. On our return to Ireland I re connected with the surfing world and lived happily with my wife Ann. Our grown Children Carolyn and Paul are both married with families and Georgina our last, is married and living in London. Also, on our return from Canada though six years later, we found things had not changed in Ireland since we left. However, within a few years the pace increased, and the economy improve. I again worked in hotels but also studied art and physics and, Architectural Science. My mind was challenged to the end degree.

Sadly, Bill had died in December 1979 after returning from a walk. Vera died of dementia, very quietly in a nursing home in March 1998 and we were with her till the very end. Kathleen died in April 2011. My Brother successfully ran his own business but in October 2020 he died at home of natural causes. May they rest in Peace. R.I.P.

More Of The Brave

In our time living in Bray, we encountered the friendliest and braves of people. Under Bill's direction each and every one of his associates were dedicated to the job. Indeed, their pay was never that great, but the persevered while winning the hearts of our customers.

Today, the brave includes others such as Ger and Linda Byrne took a great chance and moved to the wilds of Sligo in the eighties, and at Enniscrone set up a surf school called The Seventh Wave. This business has and is thriving and the surfing keeps them healthy and great examples to their community in Co Mayo.

Not to be forgotten, there is John and Aoife Mc Nulty who took a chance and eventually had success. They opened a school called Bray Adventures and are constantly inundated with young people or corporates wanting to Surf, Paddleboard, Coasteering, Hill walking or kayaking and more. Their Facebook tells their story and their adventures can be seen and booked on line.

It should be remembered that the infamous, Sinead O'Connor lived in Bray for fifteen years until her passing on the 26th of July 2023 RIP.

Alas, another special person is Katie Taylor who is the holder of World Female Boxing Champion. Katie has fought her way to the top and a credit to her home town of Bray and current Irish home which is in a house built on what used to be part of Bill's land.

These are but a few.

PART 2

PHYSICS AND COSMOLGY
(A Dream)

University

In my dream a fellow called Larry Coughlin originally from Bray related this story. He said that in the beginning I gained entry to the physics program in Trinity College Dublin. This was just a start and if successful I will still have to work towards getting a master's degree in science technology, engineering, and math's. Because of my lofty ambition I will still have to get a degree in biological science and computer science and when that is through the final challenge will be to pass the long duration flight astronaut physical test provided by Nasa. All this will take at least seven years so that I can join a flight in space. On arrival in Trinity College, I hit it off with a fellow from Japan. He had applied for the same space program as me and was prepared to wade through all the requirements. His name was Heroshi Akari. Heroshi was unusually tall, very slim and a smiling face. Together we shared this adventure in Physics. We learned that one can measure the speed of galaxies moving apart and that our galaxy, the Milky Way is traveling at 400 – 600 km per second outwards. That there are 100 billion stars in our galaxy and that there are 100 billion galaxies in the Universe. They know that matter as we know it only makes up 9% of universal material and the remainder is dark matter or matter, they cannot see. It is established that in the early stages there was only one force, and it divided into four. Gravity, Strong and weak Nuclear and finally electromagnetism. It struck me that geometry was the basis of existence and guessed that in the beginning there was nothing other than pure motion and geometrical shaping's. From that all this evolved – quite extraordinary! These simply axioms were to be the fuse that ignited my scientific lift off. I was unaware that I had touched on a conflicting area of argument between the Peripatetic theory of infinity and the Christian

Dogma of omnipotence. But this was of no concern, yet it spawned a dream about discovering a unification between science and the metaphysics or spiritual world. I wanted to unlock a secret of the universe; any old secret as long as I was involved in the discovery! If there is to be a secret, it might be something like what Spinoza of 1632-1677 AD had deducted centuries before but with a considerable difference. Benedict de Spinoza held that there can only be one substance that can reproduce and rely on itself and that is the creator who is therefore immanent but also transcendent. This simple belief is the difference between having a universe or not having any universe at all. However, this takes us away from the physics that is being discussed though there is a connection. Then as if being scolded, Maimonides, who was a Jewish philosopher, said that one must not attempt to delve into areas beyond ones understanding, it is like someone who cannot swim trying to become a pearl diver. It is also known that knowledge from the divine seeps down slowly and is administered drop by drop to those who deserve. The average person does not have enough time to wait around for their share and instead get on with their lives. Therefore, knowledge of the divine is left to the religious who have a capability to perceive far in excess of any others. To progress in the accumulation of knowledge people must find that they may spend their lives in confused contemplation. This can be remedied if certain assumptions are accepted as a firm base from which to build one's beliefs. This sound Cartesian, which it is, but also it is good advice. One is therefore conscious of one own's frailty, feebleness of mind, a minuscule being in the face of the many scientific giants. We know that we are mere 'pip squeak' grappling with a cosmos larger than life. Therefore, to cope with what lay ahead, students learned of the methods to deal with the vast mathematical calculations necessary for students. I, like others would have to calculate in tens. For example, if one were to question how many atoms there in the universe? it would be illustrated this way 10^{78} to 10^{82}. This means 10x 78 zeros or 82 depending. The diameter of the earth would be 10 x10 whereas the diameter of an atom would be 10 $-x$ This technique enables unmanageably large or small numbers be calculated easily, while at the same time dwelling within one's understanding. I wondered what basic principles dictate the type and makeup of the particles in nature and also what caused them to have various strengths. I had heard about field theories and tried to learn what I could about them.

Mr Eldron, our physics teacher was about thirty-five, sandy hair and steely gray eyes, entered the lecture theater and looked firmly at the students. His penetrating stare caused many of the audience to turn their eyes from his gaze, it was not that they were guilty of any wrongdoing but, no one wanted to attract attention especially in the first lecture. He began with a getting to know the people and asked them to tell their short histories. He began to lecture on the subject of the Atom. I sat upright, feeling comfortable and eager to learn! He told us about Father Georges Lemaitre's theory of the Primordial Atom that existed before the proverbial Big Bang when the universe was formed. He held this was a unified quantum globule from which the whole universe was spawned. I therefore said to myself that there must be at least four ultimate particles of which all others are either branched from rather like clones.

GRANUALITY

The Atom, explained Eldon, the minuscule building block of the universe, the most sought-after object of our time, is the perfect parameter on which to compare scale. The Greek philosophers, Democritus, and Leucippus in 400 B.C. were the first to devise the concept. They called it the Atom but incorrectly thought that there were different types of atoms making up various elements. Nevertheless, they had at least hit on a scientific truth. It was not until 1808 that a Lancashire schoolteacher named John Dalton made some experiments that confirmed the atomic reality. E Rutherford in the beginning of the twentieth century put the atom finally in true perspective. He proved that all the positive charge and nearly all the mass of an atom is in the nucleus. The rest of the atom is composed free space and electrons that equal in number to the atomic number making the atom electrically neutral. In other words, our mysterious little friend has a nucleus made up of tightly bound positively charged protons and neutrally charged neutrons, both which are orbited by a swarm of neutrally charged electrons, whizzing around at enormous speed. However, in some cases electrons are free agents and are not connected to any nucleus. Remember the electron has a dual nature which has a bearing on quantum theories. Through the eyes of quantum mechanics, electron fields can be described as both particles and at the same time waves. Heisenberg's Uncertainty Principle dictates that it is impossible to know simultaneously both momentum and position of a micro-particle with any degree of certainty. The more we know about where a particle is, the less we know about its motion and visa-versa. Quantum mechanics show that energy is packaged in bundles or quanta, but that also particles can be exhibited in the form of waves. This revolutionary way of looking at nature was invented by Louis De Brogie, when in 1924 he stated that electrons have wavelike properties. Listening to Eldron caused me to see the electron as a feminine entity not because it seemed to unite with others forming a family but co incidentally because it shares space with the next closest electron belonging to the nearest atom thus creating a binding called the covalent bond which enabled matter to form. "Bond Street", I punned this to himself.

At this point I wondered if the whole universe might be wave-like if observed by a giant onlooker? I was not to have any answer to this question as you may have guessed, at least not at the time! I listened again to Eldron who had been saying that the Electron possesses a negative electrical charge (Ref; Wordsworth Dictionary of Science & Technology W&R Chambers Ltd,) of 1.602×10^{-19} coulombs and as you will find out, its mass amounts to 9.109×10^{-31}. Now if one descends deeper into the atom there is an even smaller scale exposed. First there are the Hadrons, Baryons and Mesons that make up the Protons and the Neutrons and their interiors in turn are composed of the finest granules identifiable and they are called Quarks. Quarks come in four varieties Up, Down, Strange and Charmed. These fundamental particles are the "ball bearings" of the nucleons. Within this domain there are strict rules that cannot be broken and one such rule is that the quarks are attached by string like attractors that keep them contained within the nucleons regardless of circumstances. In recent years, the construction of giant particle accelerators and electronuclear machines high speed particle collisions have been created and the results observed. Physicists have produced energies of high order resulting in an ever-clearing picture of atomic structure. Proton and Electron accelerators consist of underground tunnels of perhaps up to 8 kilometers in diameter. The reason for this size is to enable them to be drawn along by magnets without the electrons losing energy as they would if the track were too curved. To create a proton an electron, anti-electron (or positron) collision is required so as to obtain energy of; 1 GeV which is equal to 1 thousand million electron volts. That was then but today they have progressed to have a massive

Hadron accelerator in an effort to produce Higgs Bosons almost the final step in producing a master theory of everything.

Undaunted Eldron carried on saying that many of the physicists who observe the atom say that somehow it resembles its monolithic offspring, the Universe. Though this is but an analogy nevertheless it is comparable because the main mass of the atom is concentrated in the atomic nucleus exactly like that of the planetary systems, the main mass content being found in its sun. Also, the radius of the central nucleus is only a tiny fraction of the radius of the outermost orbiting electron, thus bearing a direct comparison with our own solar system. Eldron stopped speaking and moved to the blackboard where he marked a dot with white chalk. He then paced across the room, taking two large steps and one tiny one, bringing him to the nearest desk where he placed the piece of chalk. He said that if one is to increase the size of our little atom by one hundred million, then a dot, the size of the one he marked on the black board, would represent a nucleus, while the outermost electron would be located in an orbit approximately seven and a half feet away just about where he had left a piece of chalk laid on a desk at the back of the classroom. I was very impressed. Then Eldron said that the antithesis of this is evident if we reduce the stellar universe to the same extent as we did the atom the mathematics hold true. The nearest star to our planetary system will be 10/3 cm, just as our outermost electron did appear in the scaled-up atom that we just spoke about. It seems now appropriate to meet other constituents that make up the atom. We must attempt to give them some meaning through their rather meaningless micro haze of activity that is indefinable to the naked eye. We look towards the famous covalent bond, the catalyst of material. Invisible though these tiny structures maybe it turns out that physical and chemical behavior of matter depends upon the ways in which they bond and interact with each other. These interactions are a threshold where physics and chemistry meet in their continued quests to advance their respective fields. Let me carefully repeat some important information that I already mentioned. The proton has a positive charge and shares the nucleus with the neutron. The neutron acts as a balancing agent in the atom. Since a whole atom carries no net electrical charge, the number of protons in the nucleus known as the atomic number, must equal its surrounding electrons. Although the electron is the catalyst of all elements and is negatively charged at the same time atoms remain neutral. This is because the proton is positively charged, that is to say the nucleus is positively charged and the number of electrons is such that their total charge exactly balances with the nucleus. Now just how can there be such perfect symmetry with one always being equal to the other? The answer to this question came in 1932, when James Chadwick identified that what was thought to be high energy y rays emitted from bombarded light elements was in fact that particles were neutral or without charge and they were naturally named neutrons. Following this discovery, one could calculate the change and mass of the nucleus quite easily. For example, if one were to take oxygen, one need only assume that it contains 8 protons and 8 neutrons. In this case the total mass is taken as 16, while the charge is only 8. Since a whole atom carries no electric charge, the number of protons in the nucleus must be equal to the number of electrons in the extra nuclear region.

ELECTROMAGNETISM

He then said that we must now peer into the Atom again. He began with the Electron calling it the busy bee of the universe. All electrons are the same, though not aware that in future years there would be an alternative view. It would be claimed by (G Feyman of the California institute of technology that there is only one electron, and all others are but a reflection) However, Eldron pointed out that negative charged particles orbiting the atomic nucleus at a considerable distance are the media of the electro-magnetic force. This is the life bearing power and the third force of nature. The electron is a member of the Lepton family. Lepton meaning light one in Greek, and that is born out because electrons being light can travel on their own, and thankfully for us, this ability enables them to act as a binding force. He then said that Ms. Electron is the strangest of all the particles ever know, and if you will pardon the gender comment but it possesses almost feminine traits. You see it is flimsily and elusive and gives but a hint of its presence. It lures one into its depths and then promptly disappears. The class laughed and he continued thus, to tell us that it disappeared because the interference of the observer caused it to alter its position. It just leaves slight evidence of its past. Perhaps for example, if I left here and returned quickly, I might discover cigarette smoke, but no hard evidence because the student will have extinguished it quickly for fear of observance. A voice piped up, "Wouldn't it be a female smoker, Mr Eldron!" On this occasion he accompanied the class in laughter. The lecture went on. He stated that there is one other electron trait that is most peculiar. The electron can take on either of two states. It can be a particle, but it can also appear in wave form! Just imagine the ocean turning into powder and blowing away in the wind! Most of the people had covered this in school but the revision was rewarding. There were other question brewing in my mind. But Eldron quoted, (John E Russell page 176 General chemistry) "Two of the strongest inter-atomic forces are ionic bonds and covalent bonds. The ionic bond is the electrostatic force which attracts particles with opposite electrical charges which in effect means that one or more electrons can transferee from one atom to another thus forming the said ionic bond. The Covalent bond occurs, on the other hand, when two atoms are more nearly alike in their tendencies to gain or lose electrons. Under these conditions outright transferee of an electron does not occur. Instead, electrons are shared between atoms."

Eldron continued saying, "This explains that the force that attracts the atoms also repulses and does so as the atoms become closer together. Using the hydrogen molecule H_2 as an example one finds that at a distance of 0.074 manometers the attractive and repulsive force become just about balanced or at minimum potential energy. The force which pulls the two atoms together is a result of the attraction between each nucleus and the electron of the other atom. The repulsive force is the electrical repulsion of like charges, (i.e.) the two positively charged nuclei and the two negatively charged electrons. When the nuclei are 0.074 nm apart, both nuclei are attracted equally to both electrons. This attraction keeps the hydrogen atoms together and is the before mentioned covalent bond."

IT CAN BE A FORCE

I read more about the electromagnetic force in the library. It told me that James Clerk Maxwell who was born in Edinburgh in 1831 became a professor of natural philosophy in Aberdeen, where he grew deeply interested in a discovery by scientist, Michael Faraday; that a change in magnetism could create an electric current. In 1861 Maxwell stated that electricity and magnetism could be combined in one, and that light is a magnetic field that could transmit itself across space. This was a break from the traditional view; that there is a medium called ether that acts as carrier of the electric and the magnetic fields and their energies despite general disbelief in Maxwell's theory, ten years after his death the idea was generally accepted; heralding a new understanding of this very special force, with its very special purpose; the second force of nature the Electromagnetic! Despite, ether denied in this theory we are still looking at the force that is the principal life-giving agent in matter, a task of unprecedented importance indeed. This is the niche where the characteristics of femininity might again be found – being the life giver of course. This force interacts with electrically charged particles which are mainly electrons and quarks, two of the main constituents of matter. This bridging between leptons and baryons consummates the electromagnetic force's chief cosmic role as unifier, binding atoms and creating magnetism while enabling the natural process of life to flourish. On a small scale, the electromagnetic force causes the electron to orbit the nucleus of the atom in much the same way as gravity causes the planets to orbit. The force is infinite in range like gravity, but it is weak over distances, yet very strong in atoms. Photons (of light) are the means of transport for electromagnetism which in turn propagates universal light as we know it. Light however did not appear in the universe until some 300,000 years after its first moment of reckoning, till then particles were in a state of turbulence and the first electrons had not dropped into place to orbit the first protons thus forming the first atoms of hydrogen. Today the understanding of light also Involves the introduction of the antiparticle. This process is best explained if one describes a particle of light as consisting of an electron and its opposite, an anti-electron. In effect Eldron proposed that a particle of light is created by the annihilation of the electron/anti-electrons, of one another. Nature it has been discovered can allow any particle to be created provided its corresponding anti-particle is produced at the same time. Light has mass energy, and can therefore, if it were energetic enough could break into electrons/anti-electrons while they in turn can emit light. In doing so the electron and ant-electrons cancel out which can if you like, be taken as an unchanged particle of light! The performance happens at the very interface between the universe and the anti-universe, where the creation of particles and anti-particles occur freely; all this of course because of the electromagnetic force. I felt, the delicate balance held in place by the scales of mother nature, reflects an amazing living quality in the electromagnetic force; with its almost uncanny insight and defence against' those who might attempt dangerous liberties, if allowed.

2

The Core

In Eldron's absence a lecturer told us that there is a subatomic particle occurring in all atomic nuclei and carrying a positive electric charge equal in magnitude to that of an electron. It is a tiny particle, smaller than an atom, too small to see, even with an electric microscope, but physicists have managed to photograph them and track its behavior. He felt at this stage he had really got the classes attention, if only out of curiosity. He then, like Eldron, went to the black board and marked a dot saying that if an atom was as big as a rugby pitch, then the dot represents the proton. After the first three second of the universes existence there was loose energy in the form of photons and larger particles called bosons. These early bosons had immense energy, and many broke apart into protons and anti-protons. Most of these protons and anti-protons eventually lost energy and reverted into bosons again. Amazingly some of the anti-protons seem to have disappeared hence the mass we see in the Universe comes from these left-over protons. Different atoms have different numbers of protons; what makes one an atom of helium, gold or oxygen depends on how many protons it has. As said, the Proton shares the nucleus, or center, of an atom with the Neutron. Most atoms have more than one proton, which is matched by another Neutron. Protons are made of even smaller invisible particles, called quarks. He said he knew Mr Eldron had covered this subject, but he wants to add something. This name Quark was picked at random because in Joyce's Finnegan's Wake it descried the seagull with a term, "Three Quarks to a Muster man" This was aptly compared to there being three Quarks to every Proton: three quarks, two up quarks and one down. All this is held together with by the strong nuclear force which has the dual function of supplying the proton with most of its mass rather than the quark. We learned that quarks cannot be dissected. They are the final frontier and must be accepted as they are. They also cannot be dislodged as if you try, they will automatically slip back in position as if held by an invisible boot lace. Up and down quarks make such a difference to the proton for example a proton has two up quarks and only one down, and therefore has a positive charge, like the positive end of a magnet. Two objects with positive charge automatically push away from each and the protons in an atom just do this. In order that the atom can exist, the neutron becomes a necessity. The neutron helps stick the protons together, by using the strong nuclear forces. Then he said he would mention a few words on Neutrons. They are subatomic particles of about the same mass as a proton but without an electric charge, this is called a neutral charge. They are present in all atomic nuclei except those of ordinary hydrogen. So, if an atom has equal numbers of electrons and protons, the charges cancel each other out and the atom has a neutral charge. Neutrons play a major role in the mass and radioactive properties of atoms. I asked if neutrons have quarks inside, to which the lecturer said, "No, yes, no." He then cautioned against people mixing up the neutron with the neutrino. Then he began to talk about the four forces of nature.

THE GRAVITY OF OUR PERDICAMENT

One of my class asked, are these forces of nature primordial the direct bi product of forces that existed before creation? This made me think of Quantum tunnelling where energy from beyond the universe seeped in. As this is a very controversial theory it would be out of place for Eldron. If such were true, then the essence from beyond would have four flavours from four forces not yet in nature but entering the process. These forces above all represent the compartments of the trinity that St Patrick spoke of with great sincerity. However, I knew that the lecturer would not entertain such a debate. Therefore, I for one, had also to lower my sights and laboriously begin continuing my physics adventure with a study of gravitation in serious. This began with the work of Sir Isaac Newton. This amazing person was a world-famous physicist and mathematician who lived in England (1642-1727). Newton invented differential and integral calculus, which turned out to be necessary tools for his composing comprehensive physical laws for the existing theory of planetary motion and time as prescribed by the German Johannes Kepler. Newton formulated three fundamental laws that state in brief. 1. That in the absence of force a body will remain at rest or in its existing state of rectilinear motion. 2. In the presence of force, a body will be accelerated in the direction of that force. 3. To every force there corresponds an equal counterforce, acting in a direction opposite to that of the force.

Newton's concept meant that every two particles in the universe attract each other with a force that depends in a precise and simple manner on their masses and on the distance between them. They are proportional to the product of the two masses divided by the square of the distance between them. This was known as the inverse square law of discrete gravitating masses and was the subject of his famous book "Philosophiae Naturalis Principia Mathematica" (the principles of natural philosophy) published in 1687. The law can be condensed into a brief formula in algebra as follow, $F = ma$. Newton knew that the force that caused an apple's acceleration (gravity) must be dependent upon the mass of the apple. And since the force acting to cause the apple's downward acceleration also causes the earth's upward acceleration (Newton's third law), that force must also depend upon the mass of the earth. So, for Newton, the force of gravity acting between the earth and any other object is directly proportional to the mass of the earth, directly proportional to the mass of the object, and inversely proportional to the square of the distance that separates the centres of the earth and the object.

Newton's law of universal gravitation extends gravity beyond earth, it is about the universality of gravity. [1] Newton's place in the *Gravity Hall of Fame* is not due to his discovery of gravity, but rather due to his discovery that gravitation is universal. All objects attract each other with a force of gravitational attraction. Newton's conclusion about the magnitude of gravitational forces is summarized symbolically as since the gravitational force is directly proportional to the mass of both interacting objects, more massive objects will attract each other with a greater gravitational force. So as the mass of either object increases, the force of gravitational attraction between them also increases. If the mass of one of the objects is doubled, then the force of gravity between them is doubled. If the mass of one of the objects is tripled, then the force of gravity between them is tripled. If the mass of both objects is doubled, then the force of gravity between them is quadrupled; and so on. Since gravitational force is inversely proportional to the square of the separation distance between the two interacting objects, more separation distance will result in weaker gravitational forces. So as two objects are separated from each other, the force of gravitational attraction between them also decreases. If the separation distance between two objects is doubled (increased by a factor of 2), then the force of gravitational attraction is decreased by a factor of 4 (2 raised to the second power). If the separation distance between any two objects is tripled (increased by a factor of 3), then the force of gravitational attraction is decreased by a factor of 9 (3 raised to the second power).

It turned out the professor Eldron was on a break, so as expected a stand-in was to appear. Professor Laura Kovachevich took over. She was tall and very thin and had good taste in her selection of clothes. She was French and her mode of speech made her lectures more interesting. She repeated what we had been told that an object that is twice the size of another is attracted by twice the amount of gravitational force. In reverse of this, acceleration acts on the principle that the smaller the mass, the greater is the acceleration force. Newton's second law therefore held that these two effects will cancel out each other, thus making acceleration constant in all circumstances. Then in easy to comprehend terms he showed that gravity also diminished with distance and was able from

---

[1]   http://www.physicsclassroom.com/class/circles/Lesson-3/Newton-s-Law-of-Universal-Gravitation

there to predict with accuracy the planetary orbits of the solar system. It can therefore be said that mass enters into a relationship between force and acceleration and determines the magnitude of gravitational attractive forces. This dual role of mass is the cornerstone of the principle of equivalence or in other words the equality of mass as a measure of an object's resistance to acceleration and or mass itself when it a source of gravitational attraction.

3

Chateau D'abbadie

D r Kovachevich explained that following Newton's success with the Theory of Universal Gravitation the French mathematician Pierre Simon de Laplace (1749-1827) published his work in a book of five volumes called Celestial Mechanics. His writings demonstrated how the Solar System was in a state of "dynamic equilibrium" based on his view that though most of the planetary orbits change somewhat from time to time the changes are periodic, that is that they eventually return to their original path and in the long run remain constant. One contributor to the plotting of celestial bodies was a Dublin man named Antoine D'Abbadie of French parents who lived in Merrion square. He moved to western France in 1864 and married a local girl. They lived in the Chateau named after him and which is situated on the top of a hill overlooking Hendaye. He had Islamic and Celtic art displayed in the Chateau but more importantly, he built a telescope of high magnitude and plotted the heavens for the French Astrological Society. He was awarded for his contributions. Lest it be forgotten, there was another historic giant of Astro Physics. It was Lord Ross who in 1840 had a giant reflective telescope built by local labour in Birr Castle County Offaly in Ireland. His big achievement was his disclosure of the nature of many spiral nebulae. Soon astronomers and interested people flocked to see his disclosures. His telescope was for seventy years known as the larges reflective telescope in Europe. Larry was abruptly awakened because Laura Kovachevich was staring at him. She had changed the subject saying that with the sun as the nearest object for direct study of a dominant mass, the question therefore was asked, what stopped the planets from falling inwards to its burning centre? To answer this Laplace argued that if the sun were the only source of gravity in the solar system, the planets would respond to this by falling into the sun. As this is not the case, he estimated that each body had a motion which was at right angles or there about to the pull of the sun's gravity, and this he named Angular Momentum. This momentum works hand in hand with that of gravity and is fitting to its name in a galaxy (like many others) that is lens like in shape, somewhat flattened, and with spiralling branches which confirm a mammoth rotation around a central axis. It can be further described as essentially to a circular motion, whether that of an object rotating about its own axis, or of an object revolving around another body. Beyond a certain range of gravitational influence bodies orbit or to put another way, they quite simply fall around, rather than down! They fall that is, without a limit, remaining in almost dynamic equilibrium and resembling the tiny electron orbiting the nucleus of an atom.

Despite these convincing arguments of the success of Newton's inverse square-law there was one problem that emerged in 1900 to baffle astronomers. The planet mercury's orbit was observed to be off course in its perihelion advance as it orbited the sun. In effect every orbit made was a fraction off course with the result of it making different circuits. Even taking the ebb and flow of universal attraction there was still a discrepancy of almost a minute per circuit per hundred years. It took the theory of relativity to solve the problem because it considered the curvature of space which warped mercury's expected route. Einstein's concept held that at a certain point, the geometry of space itself, takes over from gravitation. Matter curves space, and gravitation the acceleration of objects as they slide into the indentations caused by material in the fabric of space. This means that the Sun because of its mass is also guilty of causing indention in space which is the cause of the advance of the mercury by a little over 40 seconds per circuit. Einstein had solved the problem by amalgamating geometry and physics under one heading of Relativity.

Energy it is said, is a fundamental concept which is used commonly but is difficult to define with clarity. Defined In words, energy is the ability or capacity to do work. This means to move an object against an opposing force, which in all cases turns out to be our familiar friend, gravity. If something has a capacity to work, as defined above, then we say it has energy. There are however different forms of energy the first being mechanical energy, which is energy that an object possesses because of either its motion or position. Energy of motion is called Kinetic and is speed (S) and mass (M) related. Kinetic energy is referred to as (EK) and is related to motion and mass in the following formula, EK = MS. Despite the seriousness of the subject, Dr. Kovachevich had a sense of humour and this helped us develop a feeling of belonging. She went on to say that this nasty little statement tells us in so many words that we are trapped; the faster an object is moving, or the greater the mass, the greater is its Kinetic energy. Energy has already been the villain in our previous fruitless effort to travel faster than light and will reappear constantly as the story unwinds. This entrapment gave us some concern. Heroshi and I intended going into space with NASA and nursed the hope of travelling at or beyond the speed of light. We believed that Einstein's alleged curvature of the universe might help us in that ambition or that repulsion might help or that there might be a draw from another dimension not yet discovered. Not knowing our thoughts, Kovachevich went on to explain that energy of position is called-led potential energy and attains this state after it has work done on it, such as being moved to the top of a hill, where it now has more potential energy than an object at sea level. Other forms of energy with a capacity to work are (a) electrical energy, (b) heat energy, (c) radiant or electromagnetic energy, (d) nuclear energy, and (e) chemical energy and finally Quantum Energy. In the laws of conservation of energy, it states that energy can be transformed from one form to another but cannot be created or destroyed in its transformation from one object to another, energy gives off heat which is in fact evidence of energy in transit. The object loosing or gaining this heat is said to be increasing or losing its energy respectively, but they are not gaining or loosing heat as such. In simple terms, it can be stated that material is a sort of frozen energy.

GRAVITATIONAL FIELDS AND RADIATION.

Eldron returned looking refreshed. He said that they should look once again to Einstein's theory of gravitation and to the prediction of gravitational waves. Einstein stated that they would have a property somewhat like those of electromagnetic radiation. They are emitted by massive bodies undergoing acceleration and they propagate at the same speed as electromagnetic waves, at the speed of light, Gravitational waves are polarised; they cause acceleration at right angles to the direction of propagation. According to general relativity, they have properties also like acoustic shear waves and acoustic compression waves as observed in earthquakes. They are not created by a body whose mass merely pulsates in and out without a transverse flow of matter. In other words, there must be a shearing motion that changes its quadrupole moment, which does in turn exist when the source lacks spherical symmetry and sprawls as it were like a double star with its mass distribution stretched almost equally-from a common centre of gravity. The whole notion of this sort of body takes place in a plane, radiating in all directions. The actual motion caused to particles affected by a passing gravitational wave is that they are set in motion relative to each other, rather than all in the one direction as one might expect. For example, four such particles under effect will move as follows; the ones on the left and right away from each other, while the particles- above and below will move towards each other. In the next Instant, the process reverses and continues this alternating motion till the waves are passed. Stephen W. Hawking physicist from Cambridge university and author of "a brief history of tine" compares gravitational waves as like light waves, which are ripples of the electromagnetic field, but harder to detect. Like light, he states, they (gravitational waves) carry energy away from the objects that emit them. He sees any system of massive objects settling down eventually to a stationary state, because as he points out, the energy in any movement would be carried away by the emission of gravitational waves. Hawkins simplifies the text by saying it is rather like dropping a cork into water: at first it bobs up and down a great deal, but as the ripples carry away its energy, it eventually settles down to a stationary state. I got to think deeply about what they had said. Therefore, in an essay that we had to submit I put forward a proposal of there being a golden arc of gravitation holding creation in place. The analogy with water, in this instance I thought very interesting, because if gravity were to flow like water in one direction with time it could well endure being punctured and rippled by the sudden movement or existence come nonexistence of matter. The quadrupole moment of material might be spreading ripples of radiation across the face of an even greater super gravity. This mammoth show of moving gravitation would be entirely undetectable and with peaks and troughs as far apart as both poles of the radius of twice our galaxy. Therefore, we are looking at mass related gravity saying this is where it starts and finishes but neglecting to look far enough beyond the reef, to identify with outside genetic gravitation of the very large kind! Quite unnoticed spherical symmetrical matter might slip into these waves of the arc, synchronising with their frequency and gravitational texture, in a quantum like harmony. To achieve this, I estimated that there must be a double event syndrome; that is to say, to every entry on the face of the gravitational flow, there is a corresponding exit. Having committed my self to this view I had to bear the consequences. I had got in over my head and Eldron said that my assumption was large, and the implications are too far reaching. You are a student and can quote others but do not try and plot your ides in uncharted territory. They are so farfetched that they can be traced to a philosopher of ancient times whose theory was close to the sane. Anaximander and Heraclites, who lived in mellitus and Ephesus, who believed that everything was in a state of flux, in perpetual movement and change. Some basic stuff, which Heraclites took to be fire, was continually exchanged with familiar matter. The observable, apparently durable features of the world were illusory. They compared reality to a river; appearing the same on different days although the water it contained was all the time being renewed. I thanked him for his assessment but regretted I had been so frank. On further consideration. Heroshi came to my aide saying that he reckoned that all this is a first clue to a double event approach. One should look at material with x-ray eyes, looking for sighs to indicate the existence of an incoming and outgoing worlds. Not resting here one can also find another prompt in the twin worlds of anti-matter. Two identical worlds in symmetrical harmony living side by side, not capable of coming together, yet one a mirror image of the other. Two worlds that have demented science and philosophy identify a meaning, yet in this paradox, could be the key to the link between matter and its future destiny! I was relieved by this conversation with Heroshi.

STRONG NUCLEAR FORCE

This is the heart of the matter, the force at the center of the atomic nucleus- the real core. The strong nuclear force is one of the four fundamental forces in nature; the other three are gravity, electromagnetism, and the weak force as mentioned. As its name implies, the strong force is the *strongest* force of the four. It is responsible for binding together the fundamental particles of matter to form larger particles. The reigning theory of particle physics is the standard model, which describes the basic building blocks of matter and how they interact. The theory was developed in the early 1970s; over time and through many experiments, it has become established as a well-tested physics theory, according to CERN, the European Organization for Nuclear Research. Under the Standard Model, one of the smallest, most fundamental particles — that is, one that cannot be split up into smaller parts — is the quark. These particles are the building blocks of a class of massive particles known as hadrons, which includes protons and neutrons. Scientists have not seen any indication that there is anything that is smaller than a quark, except in a quantum field but the search goes on. The strong force was first proposed to explain why atomic nuclei do not fly apart. It seemed that they would do so due to the repulsive electromagnetic force between the positively charged protons located in the nucleus. It was later found that the strong force not only holds nuclei together but is also responsible for binding together the quarks that make up hadrons. Therefore, Strong force interactions are important for holding hadrons together.

According to a physics course from Duke University the fundamental strong interaction holds the constituent quarks of a hadron together, and the residual force holds hadrons together with each other, such as the proton and neutrons in a nucleus. I took a breather, and it was until the following day that I attempted to study the strong nuclear force again. This was to prove a big Kahuna with lots of Manchu activity to its name. I learned that this force speaks for itself when called strong and nuclear, for to act in that part of the atom it just must be strong in every sense of the word. However, the force is very short in range to which the limit is -13 over 10 cm. The force is an attractive force, it emerges through the neutron to act on the quarks also in neutrons and protons that lie within the above-mentioned distance. It overcomes the strange force of repulsion which exists between protons, as stated in Coulomb's law, by doing this it holds proton and neutron together thus saving them the catastrophe of being scattered outwards to oblivion. The strong force is carried by mesons, a name for micro atomic spaceships; particles that transport the strong force around the nucleus. Japanese physicist Hideki Yukawa as far back as 1934 envisaged and named the mason as a short-lived force carrying particle, declaring that they exist from borrowed universal energy permitted by the uncertainty principle. As it turned out he was quite correct, and today nuclear physicists around the world are quite successfully knocking mesons out of quarks through the Process of high-speed impact, in massive proton accelerators.

WEAK NUCLEAR – CLOSE TO HOME

Later Eldron told us that though the Weak Nuclear force is named 'weak' does not do justice. As we will see there is a very special aspect to the weak forces one, two, and possibly three, that makes them more a mystical part of our being than the others. Weak as in a child relative to that of an adult they may be, but their potential is equal. These forces are more local in function and might well come closer to Ernst Mach's principal than that of the other four forces. Therefore, so you and I might understand one another, think therefore of the weak force, as being from your very own neighbourhood, while we proceed! Now he said, 'Let us play some hard ball'. With that he described the force in technical detail saying that the weak force, illustrated by the letter V is carried by W+ and W particles. It acts on quarks and electrons, at a sub-atomic short range of -15centimetres, and is only one billionth the strength of the electric force (yet to be mentioned). It is very versatile and is a carrier of its force via charged current, between an electron and a neutrino thus allowing them interchange one into the other. This happens in much the same way as a particle of light travels between electrons; producing light as we know it, but by a process of annihilation. Because of its role of altering basic particles, it earned it the name of cosmic alchemist. In human terms it might be thought of as, equivalent to the constitution, of the corporate structure.

Despite being spun out and quite weary, I took a look at the second form of weak force; like the weak force one, is a force that works at very close range, deep at the core of exploding stars in the last throws of their existence. The force true to character with its electromagnetic relative, acts like the phoenix, and delivers new life from old, it stripes most of the nuclear material of their electric charges, allowing the nucleons to form fresh configurations hence new atoms, new matter, new growth. The electrons now emptied of charge are neutral, that is to say they are neutrinos which are classed as leptons (the Greek for light ones) that can travel at the speed of light because they are supposed to be mass less. If, however they possess but a tiny shadow of mass, and one is to ponder at the Quadrillions of neutrinos that exist in the universe at any given time; then there would be a considerable pool of matter in the wings, likely to come on stage at any time! If this were to happen then science as already mentioned, could account for perhaps ninety percent of the missing dark matter believed to be yet undetected in the universe. Carried by

W particles our weak force has a strong side when it exerts pressure on a nucleus as opposed to when it tackles the quark alone. By direct pressure on the nucleus, it is estimated that the weak force can devastate a star which is quite good news, if looked at from the phoenix point of view. The weak forces present a unified face that is not like the other forces. It is a special force akin only to the universe and not so directly linked to the un-manifest world.

COLOUR AS THE FORCE – FROM A DIFFERENT PALLET

As we expected, it was Eldron who introduced the class to the Colour Force. He told us that it is easy to be misguided by the term colour in this instance, thinking it to be comparable to a stain glass window or a rainbow as seen by the naked eye! While this could be the case if one were possessed with some extraordinary sight and perception, nevertheless, it is not the reason for the name. To begin the force is strong, and stronger than the strong nuclear force which is its by-product. It is carried by particles called S-Muons that allow the force glue quarks in protons. The colour force holds quarks together in certain rhythms, thus doing for protons what the electromagnetic force does for electrons. The force is the catalyst of mesons while one of its significant properties is that it brings antiparticles into vogue. The quark light interacts with its respective anti colours to form certain permitted patterns sustainable of growth. Colour mixing with paints is different than colours of light. An example of this according to Nigel Calder, Key to the Universe, is that you could say that a proton consisted of three quarks, one to be coloured red, one coloured green and one coloured blue. An antiproton consisted of three anti-quarks with anti-colours; turquoise, mauve and yellow, in either case, the composite particle was white, White is also the natural result of the mixing of the primary colours of light, red, green, and yellow, hence it is quite understandable how the tern colour became used in describing the force. One now finds that where the electromagnetic force is life giving to one part of the atom so is coloured the life organiser of the other, discreetly portraying a magnificent union of purpose for vastly opposite fields!

I scratched some notes about the colour force on a piece of paper. I then perforated the page and clipped in his physics file and turned to gaze out the window. What he saw was a vastly different world then he had previously concluded. I stared at a holograph of nature, something reflective of something beyond, a delicate personal vision sacred to the individual. This chromo dynamic reality is a delicate gift I thought, one that is sustained in balance on a razor between matter and anti-matter. There is incoming and the other outgoing and life is the stress point between the two whiles, still capable of being deeply in a harmonious rotation faster than the eye can see. Yet the eye does see every past bending moment as it turns to leave its impact appears like rain on a lake. The prospects of this heartbeat of time and material left me quiet and subdued now standing at a large paned window gazing out and studying the paved quadrangle below. There were venetian blinds and between each strip it appeared that rain was falling. Was this like the two slit quantum experiment because it was a dry day, yet I could see rain. Surly these were streaks of quantum of light! Putting science aside, I looked beyond, and relished the magnificent scene - beech and oak trees amass with diverse shades of autumnal browns and gold, their branches shaken only by a gentle breeze and the flutter of tiny birds, but now I was satisfied as always with the inherited conditions that the goodness of nature hath provided.

THE NEURTINO – FROM THE INTERIOR

Our professor told us that this illusive object is all around us but cannot be found or tracked unless one is 500 feet below the ground! With eyebrows raised he explained the electron as a member of the Lepton family but that though Lepton meant light in Greek it has further heavy relatives of its own, such as the muon and the tau. These existed in the earliest moments of creation and can still be identified in cosmic rays and are found through the process of particle acceleration such as at the CERN in Switzerland or Stanford California. However somewhat more dramatic is the electron neutrino, known as the phantom of the atomic world. Neutrinos have almost no mass, travel at close to the speed of light and are almost impossible to detect. The burning center of the sun and stars is their source. The earth is bombarded by millions of these invisible blimps every second of the day and night. Experiments in the past have failed to detect many of these products of solar fusion in spite of their calculated large numbers. Experimental evidence taken in deep underground experiments indicates that neutrinos are of three varieties: the electron neutrino, the muon, and the tau. It too a cave below five hundred feet of earth to filter away everything but the Neutrino. In the institute of advanced studies in Princeton, New Jersey and also at Cornell University comes one interesting solution as to the elusiveness of neutrinos. It proposes that Quadrillions of neutrinos are produced by solar fission, with the electron variety being first produced. As they stream towards earth they change into muon or tau versions thus eluding detection. However, at this stage remember that the tau, the heaviest of the three neutrinos is only speculative and has not yet been discovered. To this the class went "Ahh". Eldron continued saying that if the theory is correct the implications are that because of their capability of inter change, these supposedly mass less particles must therefore possess at least a small mass. The implications are quite enormous, because the neutrino is part of what is termed as dark matter, which makes up 90% of the cosmos. The new-found Mass as said, when added to universal density will add to its estimated age and intensify debate on its predictable future! With that Eldron finished his lecture for that day. He distributed handouts to each of the students and asked that they study them.

4

The Tapestry Of Relativity

Professor Kovachivech was back and said, that we will revisit the famous Albert Einstein, who set the world on a new physics footing. He was born in Germany in 1879. As a young man he moved to Switzerland before the second world war where he found peace and a conducive atmosphere to develop his theory of relativity. In later years he moved to the United States where he continued working, contributing to physics until his death in 1955. In 1905 at the age of twenty-six he published his special theory of relativity. It held that notion, time, and distance are not absolute but relative to moving frames of reference. In 1916 he published his second theory of relativity incorporating acceleration and gravitation and going a step further to explain the universe as having curved space and time! By 1919 his theories were well accepted in the scientific world while not long after, in 1921 he was awarded a Nobel Prize. This is Einstein's famous equation, $E = MC^2$. In this he describes; E energy as equal to mass M times the speed of light C squared. This brief formula in its simplicity has been the key to new understanding of the atom, and to a new comprehension of the dual role of mass and energy. To appreciate the interplay between then and link them maternally to the light and the electromagnetic force of nature. Einstein states here that mass and energy are equivalent, and we know that a form of energy is obtained from motion and we can therefore make a calculated deduction. An object in acceleration will experience increased energy which as stated is equal to mass. The increased mass will in like manner require more energy to maintain the increase thus making it impossible for one to travel at or beyond that of light. This once again, was the same bad news and I was saddened. This phenomenon is the limiting factor in terms of the hopes of infinite human travel, it creates a threshold like the curve of an opaque orb if locked at from within. It attaches us with an inflatable ball and chain, that grows as we increase our relative speed, confining us within a grand bowl of stellar activity. All this led to the realisation that Einstein's equations prove that relative time and space as we know it cannot exist alone, only in the presence of matter. In other words, a massive object such as a planet or a star, create the relative time and space in which it dwells. Einstein's Theory of Relativity is based in a universal equivalence of observation of the same event seen from different observers moving at different velocities. The Special Theory dictates the curvature of space by mass, that the speed of light is constant and independent of the observer, (As stated, Energy = mass times the speed of light squared) This mass is such a bully and Einstein knew it and demonstrated it in his theory of general relativity. (New Scientist 08/11/97). It was to take a further fifty five years for astrophysicists in California Institute of Technology, Pasadena to prove that dense bodies such as black holes and neutron stars pull space and time around with them as they spin. This will be called 'frame dragging' by astronomers."

I therefore concluded without validation, that density is derived from an Anaxagoras, or a log jam in any system. For space to be deformed it therefore must be impregnated with some form of density. This density should be diluted with the liquid action of time but if that is not the case then what is the cause? The result most likely is that all mass rotates in and out of existence like traffic being let through on a green light. If the traffic is heavy, then each quantum of traffic travel slower than a quantum of very light traffic yet the space between the lights is the same. In time the road will become damaged and warped from heavy traffic just as space it deformed by mason effect the persons in the slow heavy traffic will experience the painful experience of sensing time to go all to very fast and mass is the cause. Those who travel in light traffic can move at a quicker velocity and experience the joy of slow-moving time, that is they get more value per second there is less mass in their quantum of traffic. Furthermore, traffic between lights A and B have no idea of the experiences of those in section C and D. Time is compartmental, one tick does not know what the other tock is doing therefore it is contiguous but existing in a continuum. If carried to the extreme, one can assume that not all parts of our own body are at the same time. Also, in my view, we only view incidents after they have occurred and not at the same time. No matter how stable things appear they are in different time slots. If one considers whether one end of a crane arm rotates at the same speed as the inner section. Both are one yet they move at different velocities as if not the whole shebang would collapse. Also, if one extended the arm into space it would defiantly have a different time at its extremity than of the inner section still on planet earth. Another analogy might be the builders long armed super crane. When this rotates the extremity cannot be at the same time as the centre, yet they arrive at the end of a swivel at the same moment. To prove this point if one extends the crane arm into space the time difference will then become obvious. Due to gravitational time dilation, the time close to a centre moves slower than one on an extension or simply a clock on a table will be slower than one at floor level though not noticeable at such close quarters.

QUANTUM PHENOMINUM.

Once again Eldron hit us with a very tough subject. He spoke about Quantum mechanics saying that the theory is several decades in existence and contains astonishing insight into the nature of the human mind and reality. This is where Albert Einstein drew a line in the sand because he could not reconcile the idea with his equations, thus he declared, that one should not play dice with God. The theory arose from attempts to describe the behaviour of atoms and their constituents, mainly in the microworld. Because radioactivity seemed among other entities, to be unpredictable in so far as, often and without warning individual radioactive atomic nucleus would decay. The uncertainty as to when this would happen caused curiosity and concern, are the fundamental ingredient of the theory to this day. Neil's Bohr a German nuclear physicist at the turn of the century had devoted his life to address the question of collapsing or not collapsing atom. Quote; (General Chemistry S.B. Russell. P113.) "Eventually he was back to where he started, faced with the same question; either (a) the electron is moving or (b) it is not, and that each alternative is inconsistent with observation. He concluded that something was wrong with classical physics, and in a sense he was correct. Although this model was not completely successful, it introduced new concepts which led ultimately to the development of the modern model of atomic structure. Bohr felt that the clue to the problem, lay in the nature of light emitted by substances of high temperatures or under the influence of electric charge." Bohr firstly assumed that when substances are heated, they emit light because atoms have absorbed energy or flame. He then speculated that it was the electron that absorbed the energy and emitted it as light, then why is radiation limited to certain specific wave lengths each of which produces a line on the elements spectral scale? The answer was discovered in, 1900 by Max Planck another German physicist who experimented and found, energy does not rise in an even flow but that it comes in what he called discrete units. He called these units quanta, symbolised by the letter h, which was soon to become as important a symbol in physics as Einstein's c, denotes the velocity of light in a vacuum, in other words he along with Einstein, showed that electromagnetic radiation behaves as if it were composed of packets of energy called photons. Each photon has an energy proportional to the frequency of light. So why one asks is radiation limited to certain specific lengths, each of which produces a line on the elements spectral scale? In real terms, the energy of an electron in an atom is quantized, or only allowed certain measurable amounts of energy at a time. If one were to visit a game of football, soccer, Gaelic or hurling, baseball or la cross or even watch a game of chess; the enactment of a human analogy of the atom is performed before our very eyes, if we are to call the players the nucleus and the onlookers the electrons. As a result of a score or the prospects of one in evidence the energy is transferred and audible through spectator reaction, the levels of appreciation rise or ebb in quantum like waves of human vibrations directly proportional to the central activity. Indeed, even the forces of nature can fit this picture if the players are assumed to be the strong nuclear/colour force, the spectators the electromagnetic, the force of gravity being the rules of the game, and its connection with the outside world, and the weak forces one and two, being the arena or stadium in which the event is staged. Spectators can become players under certain conditions, players likewise become spectators, the action of one player can excite the whole assembly while their reaction can encourage the whole team, an example of natural interdependency and a thought worthy of our further consideration. I pondered as I did so often, asking myself the same question as before. Are not the forces of nature unquestionably sublime? How could such strong, gentle yet determined forces exist as the result of the first moment of cosmic maelstrom? Are we in its image and likeness – why not! Then in answering my own question, I formulated the following conclusion.

Its existence must be a mirror of the fine structure and condition that exists out and beyond the boundaries of light itself. These pastures will be of far greater magnitude yet magnetic, creative, and surprisingly personal and capable of nurturing a dependent embryonic universe while surrounded by an absolutely hostile external environment until it is time for deliverance. This creation and activation must be the result of a merging between the strong nuclear force and electromagnetic force. A partnership made in a higher dimension and blessed with capability well beyond our present Comprehension." The scenario seemed intriguing and well worth developing, why not! A voice in my mind interrupted my daydream. Pay attention and no more of your ramblings. I was back in college and Eldron was staring at me to the class's amusement. Then, with lectures over for the day people scrambled eagerly to the door as it was time to go.

GOOD VIBRATIONS.

I was blessed with several visits to Trinity College library. The library was built in 1753, designed by the Dublin Surveyor General, Colonel Thomas Burgh. The design incorporates an open ground floor, with a curtain of arcades separating the building from the ground, and was chosen thus, because of the somewhat marshy nature of the site in those days of old. On one occasion which I will never forget, the gentle strains of Mozart's lachrymose were filtering through the ancient walls of the library where I was reading. The four hundred and sixty ninth Michaelmas Concert was taking place at the adjoining college examination hall. With the music's every chord and the ebb and flow of many young voices there was a force, one that reflected more aspects of nature than science in all its volumes could portray. Instinctively I moved to a heavy wooden bookcase, withdrawing another physics manual, and returned to his seat flipping open the chapter required, then focusing his eyes the crisp page displayed before me and I began to read.

"All that is transient, is but reflected. All that is inadequate, here it is perfected. The indescribable, here it is done. The ever-Womanly Leads us anon!"

I read an interesting document that stated a professional called Edward Arthur Milne in 1935 expounded a theory of the universe which has lived to this day and is the basis of many newer cosmological theories. Milne's model is based on the idea of there being continuous creation of matter as opposed to the view that all matter was created in one instant from whence it has since expanded. He furthermore introduced the concept of there being more than one-time scale in the universe and devised an elaborate set of equations to link them together. Now because of the importance of his cosmology in the world of astrophysics, it would be remiss to continue without addressing the next part of his theory as it conflicts somewhat with our view about the role of the forces in nature. Milne unfortunately poses a stumbling block for my theories; this happens very often. The fundamental variance with Milne is found where he re-interprets the principal of Ernst Mach; the local properties of both space and time are believed to be the direct consequence of the existence of surrounding matter, which properties in turn determine the motions of matter. Milne proposed that the laws of nature are a consequence of the contents of the universe. On face value it may seem quite reasonable to claim the natural forces exist as an outcome of matter alone, but this diminishing statement would seem only permissible, if one also acknowledges the possibility of the forces being multidimensional. I interpreted Milne's down grade of the forces as an excusable and natural consequence of one's observation of nature as it appears. At last, Hiroshi and I received our degrees and prepared for the next steps in our adventure. Eldron's last words were congratulations but keep following all your dreams, yes, all those theories that you kept a secret from me. Then he laughed and said I'm sure I will read about both in the not to distant future. We felt almost sad.

Now let us find out where all this leads! To do that one can sit back and enjoy sharing a dream.

PART 3

Making A Dream Come True

Tampa

The phone rang in George Kuhn's office. George had recently discovered a revealing Mayan document about Creation. He reached over a paper strewn desk stubbing out a stogie cigar as he did so,

"Hae'low, Kuhn." he drawled in American fashion though he was originally German. "George its Richard Oppeli, remember me, how you bin'?

"Ah Rich, good to hear from you, how's it in Caltech and where are you calling from?" Rich brought him up to date telling he had recently married a girl named Patty and his physic work to date and then got to the point.

"Look George, or should I call you Jurg?"- he chuckled and continued - "you know that I have been working on anomalies in space, and I know you have done work in the same field, so I wanted to come and see you and talk it over - how'zat?" George responded,

"Rich, it will be a pleasure, but just keep calling me George, I don't enjoy being too much of an old grump. You can come any time nine to five, whenever suits or right now."

"See you in an hour George." The phone went dead.

Tampa University where George was a physics lecturer was quite a beautiful place. The main complex was of typical Spanish Floridian style design, terracotta roof tiles, very open and with Royal Palms fringing the entrance drive. The science building where Richard was going was in a separate block from the main building. He parked his Trans am without difficulty and located George's office on the ground floor.

"Come on in Rich." George's gravelly voice shouted.

George was fifty-six years, thin wiry pale faced and with grey to white hair. He was seated behind a desk with the usual sort of paraphernalia, a computer, printer, and scanner. Along the opposite wall was his more serious equipment, another larger computer and a video, a white board, and a blackboard, flip pads, and a movie projector. Though it was early June he was still in his winter woolies, an old grey jumper, and corduroy slacks. He was in the act of lighting a cigar as Richard entered. The two men were in stark contrast of one another, George an old Jewish mathematician and Richard a corporate looking fellow, with a beige paper-thin seersucker suite, and a pale blue button-down open neck shirt.

George asked about Richard's forth-coming space trip. Richard was glad to be asked and enthusiastically responded, "The object of the mission is to orbit Jupiter, and sling shot towards Andromeda, the Andromeda bit is classified and will not be publicized. There will also be a medical team looking for evidence of hostile viruses tracked towards earth some years ago, serious business. Much or the medical inspiration comes from an earlier report. It was by a Professor J Steele and a colleague, Dr Chandra Wickremasinghe that Covid 19 arrived in China on a meteorite spotted as a bright fireball over the city of Song yuan as far back as October 11th, 2019. It produced a fragile and loosely held carbonaceous unit carrying trillions of virus/bacteria and other source cells. George said he had heard about that report it might not be true, but it did justify serious investigation. He said that also importantly he had been working on a project that would collide bosons and fermions from a different direction than had ever been done before. He had been in constant touch with several universities and also the experimental physics center at UCD and Trinity College Dublin and also NASA where Larry Coughlin and Heroshi Akari were his contacts. George explained that instead of crashing the particles head on, they intend in sending the bosons anti-clockwise around an immense torus and intersect it with another loop, only this time down from above. The collider is small by general standards but necessitates what looks like a tubular metal arch attached to the main colder tunnel. The theory is that the fermions such as protons if bombarded across the path of the bosons, will emit quarks for the very first time in history, and if at the same time the intersection is bracketed in powerful electromagnetic radiation, through a crystal, a plank moment of unity will happen. This in other words matter will form. The alarming possibility is however that as long as the machine runs the matter will keep increasing in mass at a steady pace. He compared it to the great torus of Jupiter that forms a doughnut shaped circle around the planet and at the same time delivers a stream of positively charged particles vertically into its moon Io that then return as negatively charged particles. This flux tube of particles as it is called than sweeps through Io and returns to Jupiter. Then he continued,

"Rich, do you know what I'm at? Well, it is to do with the diffraction of matter if it smacks into bosons from an angle. This will take us to some basic diffraction calculations that are everything to do with incoming and outgoing light rays and I hope they can be used as a blueprint for our plan."

Richard found the office too hot and slowly took off his jacket. George continued amidst a cloud of chalk dust and tobacco smoke, sneezing every now and then as if to demonstrate his unhealth state. He said,

"Richard did you notice I have not mentioned time or the speed of light. Well, I am about to because without it we have a sterile experiment. Time is not what it seems, you know we perceive it as a sort of organizational wave hurtling along with humanity poised always at the wave's summit. Well, this it true to a point but try and think of it another way. Imagine being in a snowstorm where all the flakes are silver instead of white, but that they are swirling down from above and returning, always the same flakes hitting us instant after instant. We are thus each one encased in a time corpus of our very own. Now if we are to join with company or say enter an enclosure, all at once we mesh with other time corpuscles, making a larger one. The result is that this shared time will go more slowly because the mass has increased, and it takes more flakes to sustain it. In the same way our bodies are a combination of smaller time corpuscles, but their limitation is governed by our total mass. Time is absolutely a free agent that becomes organized in such a way to appear as time only because it has entered the three-dimension domain! I am convinced that time is generated primarily by the second force, the strong nuclear! So therefore, envisage that protons are a byproduct of this force and then think about my experiment. Time is the rate at which we send in our stream of protons. They are divided into three streams and they are focused to close together at the boson intersection. They will hit like an incident ray penetrating a crystal. Because of the streaming it is hoped that they will attain a greater speed then could ordinarily be achieved."

Richard smiled and spoke,

"Gee George that's close to what Coughlin and Acari are proposing at the moment." George promptly added,

"Humans live in a time diffraction, that is we cannot experience pure reality but can only grasp it after it has happened, somewhat like traveling ahead of events but looking backwards as we go. This is why we cannot fully grasp what is around us right down to the tiniest granule to the extent that our frustrations are called the quantum effect! When we carry out our horizontal-vertical collision of atoms, we will create a brag effect and the matter we hope to produce will also exist forward in time but be only experienced by us backwards in time, what do yeh' think Rich?"

Richard coughed, to give him time to think and also because of the smoke. George instinctively flipped a switch to the air conditioner, all the time looking at Richard who was about to reply.

"George my old' fellow you are magnificent! This sort of material is revolutionary and may it all come true."

George smiled and handed Richard some papers, saying,

"Here is some of my work, take them with you, there are two envelopes you can open the first marked no.1 and only open no2 when on the space voyage. Now beware of two things firstly because of the time diffraction theory there is a possibility that if you increase velocity and approach the speed of light instead of increasing mass it will be offset by an increase in your magnitude, and you will shift in time and will not travel like we do looking backward; you will jump backwards and exist in real time. Aquinas called that tempus avus, the one that comes just before tempus eternitus. The time, in which we ordinary mortals live, he calls 'tempus'. Now as if that is not enough secondly you should beware that there is with certainty a place in the universe that is very different than we have ever encountered, it is not a black hole but something quite different and that once caught in its draw, one will never break loose, and also your atomic structure could turn inside out, but where it leads, I do not know!

His words were startling to Richard. He stared at George, who was standing very erect and not looking like the nutty professor most people thought that he was, his eyes wide and showing a lot of white. Richard felt almost like a child being scolded or that the trip should be cancelled or that he had provoked some oracle that had best not been disturbed. His throat was dry, he swallowed and said in a thin voice,

"I think I'll have that coffee you offered." He then said, "George do you finally agree that time varies as a result of energy. Everyone has their own time but must operate at the pace of Global time? The latest equation of ours being T=MDC3. Here time equals mass by distance by light to the power of three. The MC is part of Einstein's E=MC2. However, our equation has C to the power of 3 because it rotates in and out of reality. George said that he agrees with that time equation and therefore Richard felt he had achieved something important by his visit. Then he enjoyed the coffee.

"Larry, good luck with the trip and I hope I was of help. No doubt I will receive a full report of the voyage's progress and bye the way here are the document I wrote. Keep no 2. For the trip.

When Larry opened no 1 document later, he was astonished as it was like this,

The Grand Genealogy of most Everything.

Let us look at how metaphysical and physical entities are plotted through the theory of Trinitivity.

Colour	Divinity	Void	Forces in Nature	Atomic level	Gender Traits
Gold	Prime	Pendulum	Gravity	Neutron	Neutrality/Faith
Maroon	Second	Upper Triangle	Strong Nuclear	Proton	Masculinity/Hope
Blue	Third.	Lower Triangle	Electromagnetic	Electron	Feminine/Charity
Green	Fourth!	Universe	Weak Nuclear	(Potential)	(Potential Gender)

Some Common physics and Scientific Denominators of threes and fours;

* There are **three** parts to an atom-Proton, Neutron and Electron.
* There are **three** quarks in Proton and a Neutron.
* Electricity in a domestic plug has **three** wires, positive, negative and earthed
* Christian belief in Faith, Hope and Charity – The **Trinity** and **three** wise Kings.
* There are **three** primary paint colours, red, yellow and blue.
* There are **three** light analogies of colour and three anti colours.
* There are **four** essences of nature, Earth, Fire, Water and Air.
* There are **three** forces of nature plus the weak nuclear, that's **four.**
* There are **three** dimensions in our universe plus time, that's **four.**
* Mathematics has **four** disciplines, Platonism, Conceptualisation, Formalism and Intuitionism.
* There are **four** stages in the fractal generation of a Koch curve.

Time and Time Again;

The theory of "Trinitivity" states that the universe is in a state of continuous destruction and construction. (Much like the philosophy of Anaximander). The destruction is the result of deceleration caused by repulsion and chaos in the void. Construction is the result of a rotation extending from the interior of the strong nuclear force. Every (Fermion) particle rotates in and out of existence. When out it is energized by the nuclear force and returns at infinite velocity three times the speed of light (c3.) Therefore Mass x Distance over c^3 = time. It instantly leaves increasing speed accordingly. In effect each particle has returned before it departs creating a ghost like quantum trail. The universe is thus contiguous and unstable while a true continuum is only found within the two higher stratums. A possible equation for this extravaganza might be as follows:

$$T = \frac{M\,D}{C^3} \text{ (Constant net observable value is just c)}$$

Here Local Time is equal to Mass by Distance (or r) over Light Cubed.
If this equation works you might never know because you just end up with reality!
For time travelled in space substitute "G" for "D" (G =The constant of gravitation).

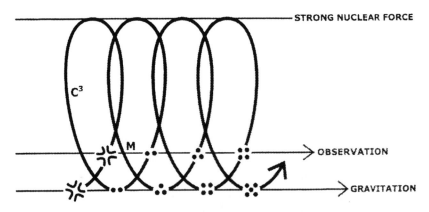

Rotating time propogates mass with every cycle. The explosions are where reality becomes observable to an onlooker within the same system.

2

Up And Away

By coincidence Larry Coughlin and Heroshi Akari would soon meet with Richard. They had completed all the requirements for space travel and had taken a short break before their departure. They had been assembling with others in the University of Miami in Coral Gables. They climbed on board a bus destined to take them and a group of qualified astronauts and physicists to Cape Canaveral, the same destination to which Richard was going. From there they will be delivered to a space platform that encircles the earth. It had been assembled over the past five years and had become a floating launch pad for various space journeys. This was to be the second-deep space trip as the first one ended in controversy. Their findings became government top secret despite the complete team returning. It seems that the Captain and associates lost consciences and it was only regained when they were on the home journey. Though, the prospects of what lay ahead was exciting nevertheless he was impatient to get there. He began drifting into to sleep and awakening in jolts. Hiroshi who was sitting beside him was completely asleep his Japanese eyes looking like small creases in his tanned face. Hiroshi's life had taken him to study in Ireland where he had stayed with Larry's family while attending college. Larry often wondered if Jill his sister had a crush on Hiroshi – they would have made a nice couple. Their children would be cute. With that Larry drifted back into dreamland. He dreamed for the second time about waving goodbye to his Dad and Mom and little Amy and Jill. This was not just a dream it was a nightmare because he might never see them again! However, it was nice to leave earth and worries about terrorism and all that sort of paraphernalia that accumulated in time.

An intercom squeaked into life. Larry was quickly wakened by a voice that repeated a message several times in different languages, "Please prepare to disembark. Enter the terminal through the entrance marked orange. Do not leave any belongings behind. Thank you."

Twenty eager men and women scrambled to their feet and began to collect their baggage much of which was marked with labels from all over the world. As well as astronauts and physicists, there were scientists and military personnel from a host of countries all who intended journeying in the heavens further than humans have almost ever gone before because there had been serious viruses descending on the earth and the origin must be found. Hiroshi bounced to his feet and said,

"Larry here we go after seven years here we go."

Larry brushed his fair hair from his forehead and laughed. Hiroshi's enthusiasm amused him. Though Hiroshi was tallish, Larry was a head higher, so he pulled both their bags from the rack above. Just then he was addressed by a young man with an American accent.

"Excuse me could you pull that one down for me also."

There was an Italian looking fellow with a pleasant smile pointing to a large bag. Larry tugged out an extra-large bag, which was obviously his as it was marked "NASA".

"Thanks so much, my names Richard Opelli, and this guy," He said pointing to a big fellow beside him, "Is Don Travis, Padre to the trip, what's yours?"

"Larry Coughlin, pleased to meet you Don we will need your science most of all." Everyone chuckled and Larry said, "Opelli, why you must know a professor called George Kuhn from the University of Tampa. He told me to look out for you."

Richard said, "Right then you must be from the Irish Section."

Yes, I am, and oh, meet my colleague Hiroshi Meguro from Japan, we're both astrophysicists."

The three shook hands and moved towards the orange door.

They were then quarantined for a week during which time they were hygienically treated and brought up to date about the project, what to do and what to expect. This was a time when people got to know one another but at the end of the time they were happy to be on their way.

On the departure day they were decked in the now familiar space suits and helmets. They were bussed to the ship that was ready and waiting and then in single file they began to enter the gantry. There were supplies being wheeled in and one item caught Larry's attention. It looked like a birdcage – strange he thought. They then entered what was called The SHT – Short Haul Transporter. This was an enormous craft that could take the equivalent weight of thirty people. It had a large payload as its fuel was from pure oxygen and nuclear fission. It gathered oxygen as it went and then as the oxygen thinned it was replenished from the ships supply. The transporters were basically freight elevators and no good for any other purpose. Larry had noticed that it was round, while at its centre great thrusters were beginning to rumble. It was the commercial sector that had developed the idea, as vacations in space were gaining in popularity.

Through a small window Larry glimpsed a bright star, it was undoubtedly the space platform from where they would commence their trip. He felt his heart jump with excitement. The take-off was smooth because it only needed a lower than normal escape velocity. After half an hour, they could make out the shape of a large object docked on the platform. It was their ship. The place they would live for the next twelve months, it was the Callisto named after one of Jupiter's moons. The first impression was of a sleek golden coloured craft with a very large front window. It had no jagged edges but was quite aerodynamic looking with gentle curves. The ship had a nose antenna that protruded quite far in front while the rear half became quite wide. Its propulsion was from a set of large circular outlets lined across the lower side of the stern. There appeared to be a turret on top with a gun like object, which Larry knew, would be a laser gun. Richard was heard to say, "What a beauty!"

Just then another announcement was made, "Thank you for being so patient, we are now approaching the SPLAT – Space Platform and will disembark immediately. To the right that gold object is your ship the Callisto docked and ready for departure. The ship is the property of EUSARUSS – the European USA and Russian agency and your mission reference number is now UMEX – 171. Please indicate that on all correspondences or s-mails etc. From here on your Captain Dave Mc Cluskey of Nasa will take over. Have a safe trip!"

With a hiss the SHT interlocked with the right side of the SPLAT. The group flowed into the reception lobby. It was like being in an airport. There were lots of onlookers watching their arrival. Quite a few were dressed in white and must be space cadets Larry thought. Others were in various types of polo shirts and some in khaki. The group were ushered to an assembly area where they were invited to coffee and sandwiches – earth style. The fellow who served Larry said "Spasibo," when Larry handed back his empty cup. Along the wall there was a series of photos of earlier flight crews, he wondered would their photo be taken! When that was done four officials entered the room while many from outside began to filter in till the room was full. The four consisted of three men and a woman, who paraded to a raised area and turned to face the group. A tall man in his forties and dressed in beige sun tans like a U.S. Naval officer spoke.

"Let me begin by congratulating you all on your tenacity and determination and interest that has delivered you here. To my right is Casper Manz our chief Physicist. He will coordinate the whole science section and medical admin. You probably know of him already. Next is Ernst Kaufman from Zurich, our atomic energy engineer who is permanently attached to the Callisto – it is his baby."

Ernst gave a broad grin.

"Also, beside me here is Laura Bingley my vice-Captain, she or I will be available 24/7 and by the way I'm Dave Mc McCluskey the Captain, just call me Dave or Skipper."

There was a round of applause. The Dave concluded, "Thank you for that, and I want to tell you that your ship the Callisto UMEX (Ultimate Manned Expedition) 171 /10,000 series is named after one of Jupiter's Moons and is driven by eleven Electromagnetic Atomic fired power packs produced at (2) CERN and Oerlikon Switzerland. [2]"

Ernst gave another smile.

"This is the Callisto's second voyage as you know five years ago another voyage was deemed to secrecy after certain discoveries. Now it is up to us to confirm or deny what they found. Does anyone have any questions?"

There were none, so Dave continued,

"The ship will be managed and run by our flight team who are standing around the back of this room."

People looked around at a group of about twenty cadets and crew who responded by nodding.

"Now if you gather in the main arrivals area for a photo, and then you may make your last communications with home and the flight team will take you on board the Callisto."

As Hiroshi turned one of the groups dug him with an elbow but did not apologise. Hiroshi was puzzled. The man slipped away through

---

[2]   CERN – European Laboratory for Practical Physics, Geneva Switzerland.

the crowd as if oblivious to what he had done. Maybe he does not like Japanese people. Hiroshi pondered then, shrugged, and followed Larry to the main hall.

The Cadets began to escort the group into the ship as they came from the communications centre. Hiroshi was now on the phone, so Larry lost in contemplation followed the others into the ship. Then a voice said:

"Sir this way."

Larry looked in disbelief. There in front of him was a most beautiful female. She was a Cadet, with Spanish features, and a soft Mexican or Brazilian voice. Her hair was of medium length and was silky black. Her eyes were hazel coloured, and she was smiling at him. Her golden service badge glinted as she beckoned for the group to follow her. Larry suddenly became alert. The boredom that had haunted him earlier had disappeared. He quickened his step and caught up with the snowy white figure whose magnetism had taken him over. As they walked through the ship, she pointed out various aspects.

"The command area is called the main concourse. It is ringed with computerised controllers and to the front a clear view of where the ship is going. The navigator stands at the EM/SPEC – Electromagnetic Spectrometer. Sometimes it is called the Maggie in haste. He can see things that the naked eye cannot perceive."

She turned around letting her eyes meet with Larry's. Larry recoiled because he felt exposed. Also, he was not anxious to mix emotions with the mission but then what now can he do? Whether she liked him or not did not matter, because ironically, he was already a victim.

They went on past a small galley with a smiling cook. Then a sick bay and an oratory and finally to the sleeping quarters where she turned into an enclosure and said:

"Ladies you are through there, gents you are to the right."

She produced a clipboard and firstly went through with the ladies. After about four minutes she returned and asked the males to give their names and then proceeded to show them to their cubicles. She used the first unit as a demonstration for all to see. Pulling back a curtain she pointed to a bed like object with a Perspex cover.

"This is what we call a Hybo. It is the short for hibernation. One can either take a nap or have a Rip Van Winkle which ever you like."

People chuckled.

"All you do is get in, close the cover, set the alarm and temperature required. In about a minute you will be in dream land with Plato."

Larry was the last on her list so he was prepared to make the best of it, there might not be another opportunity. As she showed him his Hybo he said, "What is your name?"

She pointed to her nametag, but it was not there!

"Oh," she said, Sorry I forgot to wear my name tag. It's Francisca Spazola, from Albuquerque." and then she smiled and added, "Rather than have you guess, my age is twenty-three."

She winked and smiled and asked Larry about himself. He was delighted by her informality after such a stiff beginning and hastily poured out information.

"I'm Larry Coughlin Physicist with the Iropean Space Commission[3] twenty-eight years and still a dreamer. What about you, will you be on this mission or are you staying on the Platform?"

His heart seemed to miss a beat.

She smiled again and said, "Yes, you know I'm a Cadet and this is my life's ambition, I would die rather than miss this experience." The she turned and said as she left, "Nice meeting you Larry I will see you around, there is no doubt about that."

Then in an instant she was gone!

HYBOS

The main concourse became the scene of intense activity. Dave was still dressed like he was commanding a battleship, while Laura was decked out in white blouse and navy pants. Ernst was down in the engine room doing a last-minute check on the atomic power packs. The computer banks were alive with dancing lights. Evita and several other cadets were engaged in collecting information from the banks and delivering it to Lionel the navigator the person who will have to bear responsibility for the ships progress – a very responsible job indeed. He had told Evita that he was from Surrey and she had been quite taken by him, but now that she had seen Larry her feelings had altered. Nevertheless, Lionel was one hell of a guy and he had the job that she would eventually like to achieve.

---

[3]   Iropean – Ireland/European, Space Commission.

Larry and Hiroshi were unpacking the equipment that they would need for their trip, and Richard was taking part in a pre-departure brief in the Captains quarters. At a given time the team emerged, and Dave took position close to the Navigator at the EM/SPEC. A recording began to play issuing standard instructions before departure.

"All crew and visitors complete embarking status and belt in unless part of the navigation crew or engine management. Departure will be at 0.700. All loose objects to be secured."

Larry and Hiroshi found free seats close to the computer banks. Evita was already seated and buckled in place and was talking to another female cadet. She turned as she saw Larry sit down. Her friend looked at Larry and said something to her – they both smiled.

While they were waiting Hiroshi pulled a large envelope from a folder and handed it to Larry.

"Larry we were sent this by Professor George Kuhn, from Tampa University. He told Rich to only open it when in flight. They eagerly opened the envelope. In it was a piece of parchment signed by a Chinese fellow who had been on the trip. What do you make of it?"

It was a sort of Mandala,[1] with a title "Trinitivity". It was marked with various shadings from green to blue through maroon to gold. There were two large triangles and they both connected with an opening that was shaped like horseshoe. There are no markings as a guide, one would have to guess its meaning. Larry looked with curiosity. David Wong signed and called it a multidimension image of what he had experienced.

"Should we ask Dave for an explanation as he skippered the first trip?" "Nope" said Heroshi, "let's wait a bit."

"What do you think it means?"

"I think it is telling us that there something beyond the universe. it's to do with force fields that supports the nature or something like that!"

Then the final countdown began and with a shudder the power packs fired, and the Calisto began to move forward very slowly. Dave gave an order, and the ship began to turn. Then at a given moment the velocity increased so much that they were squeezed back into their seats. This continued till it became almost unbearable. The navigator could be heard reading out coordinates and when he reached a term, Peak velocity 150,000 K par sec, the acceleration stopped. People let out sighs of relief, the sound of the engines reduced.

Back at Larry's Cubicle, Hiroshi spread out the Mandala. He pointed to a small triangle marked in green and said,

"Larry, that is defiantly the universe. It has tiny stars marked on it."

Larry studied the picture and agreed.

"Then my little friend, what the hell are all those triangles doing around it when we know that nothing exists beyond the threshold of light?"

Hiroshi shrugged, "Maybe we should show it Manz!"

Then Hiroshi changed the subject saying,

"Did you ever hear the saying, never in a month of Sundays? Well in space, every month had four Sundays, and in fact four of everything else. The space Calendar for earthlings as devised by EUSARUSS was quite simple. There were thirteen months of twenty-eight days 364 days per year. That left one day short per year and therefore every seven years this was adjusted giving the new month an extra week. In effect Mondays is always the first seventh fourteenth etc. The extra month is called "Newzember" followed by December. Now Larry it's time we hit the hybos!"

His first sleep was memorable. It was quite short just a normal night's sleep and lasted eight hours. Feeling full of curiosity, Larry had climbed inside and set the controls and no sooner had he laid back his head than was asleep. He dreamed of home and of one of his surfing days in west Cork while with his family. They were at a beach called Tramahon and a set of waves from the direction of the Azores had begun to arrive. It had been forecast on magic seaweed and wham reports.

His Dad could be seen on the cliffs preparing to take some action photographs. Larry looked to sea and gaged the swell and rips he might meet. The tide was rising, and the wind was light. Looking at the horizon he could identify moving mountain like waves heading his direction - it seemed they were getting larger. Could waves be alive he wondered? Could they read your mind, and do they have feelings?

Little did he know but the approaching waves were a family ranging from large to small and all equally dangerous. They were a family ranging from small to large, the largest of course being the Father. As he paddled out, Larry feared his predictions might right, but he could not turn back, he must keep going. He expected a set of seven with the final wave being the largest and it will be the bull. Would it have a name he pondered little knowing that the name was Gasper.

Gasper was travelling at twenty-five miles per hour while he and his family had swallowed up many smaller waves thus possessing all their energies. When in sight of land he saw a small surface bug up ahead and planned to devour it. The bug was Larry who was watching the quake waves coming towards him. He thought they were the largest darkest waves he had ever faced. At the rear was the bull wave towering some fifteen feet above the others – Larry had no choice. As he was so far out the lesser waves did not break, but the bull was ripe and ready to tip over and burry him in chaotic foam. Larry was now fully committed and if he did catch this wave, it would land on top of him and push him to the ocean floor and crush his bones. Just then a sea gull swooped bye and quaked. Larry thought about the write "Joyce" and his quote,

"Three quarks to a Munster man."

He turned towards shore and began to paddle furiously. He wished he was being towed behind a jet ski but that was not on the agenda. He must, under his own steam gain lots of speed and can be compensated for any shortfall by dropping with the curl, the place where he would be pushed forward. As expected, he was quickly overtaken and drawn up the face, hovered for a second and still paddling jumped to his feet and began to drop. The wave must feel my board fins cutting his face thought Larry as the updraft sent spray like needled in the air. He was now tearing along to the right and towards the promontory towards his dad and camera. He was below the crest and as he did it so there was an enormous shudder as the wave began to peel off. He bounced down the ragged face keeping traction with the edge of his board. Now he drove upwards and was pivoted high on the top of the shoulder. In a flash, he glimpsed his Dad on the cliff and people scurry back from the beach – this one must be big he thought. Then he repeated his climbing and dropping till the wave curled over him and he was encased in a crystal cylinder that held him for all of three seconds. Then he burst forth in triumph and turned towards shore propelled by Gaspers roaring white water as he began to lose his life and become strewn on the sand. Larry now safe on shore, waved to his Dad and then carried his board up the beach stepping over large lumps of foam littering the expanse. Now he was curious and bend down and scooped up some foam and as he did so he thought he saw many moving eyes then he heard a wail followed by three quarks. He dropped the foam and hurriedly went his way.

Meanwhile, Hiroshi had also been asleep and told us he had dreamed about his lovely Island home in Japan. He heard chimes in the wind, and he dreamed that he was home again in Hokkaido with his family Maguro. From his home he could see Mount Yotei looming above his beloved town. His mother Nasko had prepared tea and Mochi-gashi cakes he was invited to eat them but in the dream never did. Then he was playing with his little brother Jinkichi for what felt like hours, and he felt so very happy. Suddenly he heard more chimes but this time they were different it was his wake-up call.

Larry entered the Galley and poured himself a Coffee. Then he took a Danish from inside a display case and squatted in beside Hiroshi.

Gee Hiroshi there isn't much space in here, it's all outside the ship, did you have a good sleep?"

They both agreed that the Hybos were a success. Just then Richard arrived.

"Hi, you guys, may I join you?"

He took orange juice and toast and said in a low voice,

"There are a couple of strange people on this trip."

He turned his eyes in the direction a fellow who was out in the main concourse intent on computer work.

"See that fellow in the navy shirt." Hiroshi interrupted, "Rich, he is the guy who did me in the ribs!"

"Shush," said Larry, "Want him to hear you?"

Richard continued, "His name is Hamish Cauldron and he has associates called Raphael and a woman called Dalia something or other – I got the info from the Captain's Log. They are here on a project called Lambda Exclusive. It is related to repulsion and the Anti-matter content that lies beyond the Oort Cloud – An area at the extremity of the solar system were Comets evolve.

3

Jumpin' Jupiter

T he Callisto had travelled past Mars and had Jupiter clearly in its sights. Because of their distance from earth, they were out of range for s-mailing purposes. A sense of isolation was felt by most of the crew resulting in people having long faces and resorting to yawning and becoming irritable with one another. Despite this hitch in general, they had all settled down to the tasks on hand and each had adapted daily routines. As Jupiter grew larger and filled the visors many of the team were in hibernation and therefore there were not many people awake to see the spectacle. Then as one of its moons Io, came into view the EM/ SPEC began to generate very interesting pictures. Larry and Richard were among the lucky ones who were on duty at the time. A small group gathered around the flashing table, while the navigator tapped ordinates and computer commands. Ernst, who was there at the time, began to give them the low down on what was happening. Ernst in Swiss German accent began to speak, "Vass, we have here is a close-up of Yupiter. Much closer dan on de last trip. No photographs have ever recorded up so close before, with de exception of the Hubble probe, (1) some years ago."

The screen filled with a breath-taking view of Jupiter and its moons four in all but with two of them hidden. Set against the blackness of space the planet was a luminous colour of coral and white. Ernst spoke, "You see de planet is streaked with four weiss bands off clod,"

He went on to explain that the clouds are stacked in decks of different chemical composition and are interlayer with Hydrogen and Helium Gas to the depth of a hundred Kilometres thick. The layers make up three weather zones, the first being water and ice crystals and the two gasses Hydrogen and Helium. Next comes Ammonium Hydrosulphide crystals, and the last outermost band consists again of Hydrogen and Helium gas, but with traces of Ammonia. Finally, for good measure there is an icing of Ammonia Crystals."

As they watched they observed that near the equator, a row of white horse tail like clouds were broken open to allow masses of Jovian heat to escape from below. The most spectacular of these was a great red spot, which resembles an eye. Larry thought about the foam at Tramahon beach. Was it related to this Jovian world? The heat and redness are supposed to be due to phosphorus organic molecules being transported from below. Ernst told them as if they did not know that Jupiter in Roman mythology was known as King of the Heavens and it does live up to the name.

Just then Hiroshi pushed his way into the group. Larry watched his expression of aught as he gazed at the screen. Ernst continued, "Now look," he said "Zee, here are two of de moons, Io and Callisto – our name sake."

The moon Callisto was now clearly in view sitting there dark and crystal like but distinguishable by its light beige patches – marks made by huge meteorites.

Nigel the navigator now took over. He said,

"These hits caused concentric ridges to spread like ripples in a pond. Its dark slurry crust is reckoned to have formed four and a half billion years ago. The largest Meteorite to have hit the moon, blasted a crater over two hundred kilometres in width and unimaginably deep but this is hidden by the immediate infill of the moon's ice crust that poured into the cavity and froze."

The room glowed pink from Jupiter's light. Then Nigel drew their attention to Io, saying,

"Before we look at Io there is a phenomenon that is not visible to the naked eye and must be electro-magnetically enhanced. It the interchange of energy between Io and Jupiter."

With that he asked punched several coordinates into a keyboard and within a split second the whole picture turned a brilliant blue, splashing its light throughout the chamber. Some of those on the higher levels were distracted and turned to look. At this point Larry noticed a familiar white clad female approach the scene. His heart gave a Jovian jump, for it was that pretty Lieutenant Francisca Spazola who had issued him his billet. She looked so athletic and fit as she bounced towards the group. As she arrived and peered down at the screen her face became bathed in blue light. To Larry she looked like a disco Queen. Her snow-white Naval Academy uniform also glowed blue. In an instant, Larry imagined she and he were sipping tequila in Puerto Vallarta or Acapulco, to the sound of blaring trumpets and guitars. She turned momentarily and looked at Larry and then responded with a knowing smile. The screen now displayed a 'magnetosphere' image of the planet only this time it had altered. It was now completely alive with moving lines that quivered in wide distorted arches radiating left and right of Jupiter. Nigel reminded them, that this activity was the actual magnetic field of the Planet and that it was invisible to the naked eye and could only be seen through their Maggie 500 Sx to which he added was a Swiss invention! He looked at Ernst and smiled.

Just then Hiroshi ambled over to Larry and said,

"Larry do you remember Eldron's paper about the great torus that surrounded Jupiter? Eldron had said that it forms a doughnut shaped circle around the planet and that there was also a great flux of electro-magnetic positively charged particles transferred from Jupiter to Io returning as negatively charged. Here it was now happening right before his very eyes. The sight was mind-boggling. The whole process conveyed by a massive arch that carried the particles one way charged and the other way uncharged. George Kuhn had used this very system as an example of how the whole universe is sustained from a greater dimension and suspended in time. It bears similarity with a great arch in Kuhn's mandala!"

Therefore, he took the paper and mandala to Manz and explained how they came by it. Manz was appreciative but said he would study it late.

4

A Swell Trip

At last, Larry had managed to snatch some time with Francisca. On this rare occasion they were sitting on soft seats in the rest area at the rear of the ship. Despite that the Callisto was hurdling out of control into the unknown, the attraction for each other blotted out the perils and romanticized the setting. It was the first time Larry had had an opportunity to speak privately to Francisca. In fact, this meeting was the closest thing to a date that they could obtain, and Larry was making the most of it. He asked her about her reasons for wanting to become a space cadet. She said she had been fascinated by the idea since she was a child. He then began to ask more personal questions about her family and learned that her father was from Guam and her Mother came from Mexico. She had a brother who was a lawyer, and a younger sister in college. Her parents had raised her in New Mexico but her father he had been killed in military service when she was fourteen. Though Francisco displayed a tough military exterior Larry felt she was tender at heart. Right now, her career was the most important thing in her life, but he wondered would she ever make room for family? He thought that she was the most courageous girl he had ever met and since she was so pretty it was likely her offspring would look superb. Though that would also depend on her partner! For a moment he wondered, would he be that Guy? Then he remembered that before any of that could happen, they would have overcome the nasty predicament that lay ahead. To Larry's delight Francisca had also quizzed him about his family but she had gone a step further and questioned him about girlfriends. This played into Larry theatre and so he invented a few to keep her interested. However, he refrained from asking about her boyfriends, as he knew she would tease him back, but he did ask had she a boyfriend now. To this question she replied,

"That's for me to know and you to wonder!"

They both laughed causing some heads to turn in their direction. Larry felt quite juvenile, but it was the price he would have to pay for having a cosmic crush on the right person at the wrong time.

The ship had now completed its second space month of travel which means eight weeks exactly. Everyone had been busy with experiments and meetings and general application. Every portion of the horizon was being photographed and computerised and analysed. In the evening as they called it most people watched DVDs from the library, or played chess, or read. Larry had little opportunity to mix with Francisco, she seemed to circulate busily in a different world.

The ship's electromagnetic turbo-Atomic charged motors had been turned off, for some while and only used for adjustment to direction. They were being merrily whisked along by gravitation from deep space. They were now close to the Oort cloud and Sirius could be seen straight ahead. The Hamish and his group of Physicists were working hard doing their calculation and peering regularly at the Oort cloud. The Navigator allowed them view also through the Em/spec though they did not show much appreciation.

About an hour later Dave working at his desk and a knock came to the door. It was the Navigator along with two assistants, Rashid from India, and Lisa from Kentucky. The Navigator spoke in an urgent voice,

"Captain Sir, there is a navigational difficulty. We have checked and re checked and reported to Ernst and the Flight officer, but they said to get the information to you immediately."

Dave screwed his eyes and said,

"Okay Lionel, please report."

"Captain, the ship is being drawn 27.5 degrees off course by some object or other. As we speak the ratio is increasing. The source is a mystery it must be very attractive."

Dave responded by asking to see the figures and to know had they been verified. Lionel confirmed and handed Dave a report on the situation.

Dave read a detailed spectrographic survey of the problem area. It had been written by Lionel and Richard. It measured the red shift[3] of receding galaxies and the flow of neutrinos. He focused on the magnetic blurred area up ahead. The area was somewhere beyond Abell 370 a recently discovered cluster. It was an astounding 13 million light years from the Callisto point of departure. That meant that they were being drawn to the threshold of universal expansion. This was indeed a daunting prospect and there was such intense gravitational that area might be laden with dark matter. It confirmed the findings but that the area had both a red shift and a blue shift simultaneously. One side was evidently an inflow and the alternative an out flow. If it is a rotating quasar then one whole side would be moving away but that was not the case. Dr Manz also read a copy and looked at the spectrum and without a word moved over to a talk with some of his colleges. Laura then said they were ready for the next meeting.

Lionel added,

"Some of the crew have drawn our attention to strange phenomena. As the velocity increased oddly some products on the ship have begun to shrink. An example of this was natural fibber wool sweaters, and some food products became noticeably smaller by the day."

Dave did not look surprised

"Lionel are you implying that certain items are shrinking, or are we increasing in size?"

"Sir, I am only now sure about the problem not the answers."

Dave said,

"We have on record that this might happen, it did on the last voyage and to be prepared." Lionel also handed Dave a report on the situation,

Dave asked Lionel to stay and dismissed the other two. Then he called a meeting in the Boardroom and it included Manz, Ernst and Richard who was also versed in Flight Navigation. It was Richards first time in the Boardroom and to his amazement there was a birdcage standing in one corner of the room. Inside was what looked like a canary? It was yellow and as Laura entered the room it let out cheap. Despite the emergency, she immediately went to the cage and dropped some food in through an opening saying at the same time, "There my little Kiki, eat up."

Then she turned to the group and said,

"Kiki, I am glad to say, has not shrunk one centimetre, she is one of us. She will also let us know if our atmosphere becomes any way infected, you know I still do not trust computers."

Then she winked and sat down. Dave looked like he was about to erupt. He wanted to get on with the serious business on hand. One of the Astrophysicists reported

"I'm sorry to say that according to the latest reports something has gone wrong."

There were a hush and people sat upright.

"We believe our size has increased thus causing greater gravitational attraction. In other words, we fear that it is too late, and we have passed the point of no return by at least four hours ago, even reverse thrust is probably too late, sorry for being so blunt."

The group froze; the two Captains stared in disbelief, their eyes showing lots of white.

Dave cleared his throat, but Laura got there first, saying in an over controlled voice,

"We will require an immediate EM/SPEC viewing before we take evasive action, let's move the conference out there."

As it turned out the 'Maggie' showed evidence of their impending doom. It indicated that the gravitation had become so strong that the landscape appeared to warp. This was enough indication that they had defiantly passed the point of no return and up ahead in their path lay the shrouded area still indefinable. Dave finally responded to the crisis saying that they now agree to let Ernst attempt to reverse thrust. He therefore said, "Ernst! Reverse our ships direction with all possible speed."

A debate erupted as to why material was shrinking or as to whether the ship and its contents were growing. Samples were brought to the room for examination and remarkably they were quite shrunken. Manz said that perhaps the ship might be expanding at an inverse square of the Hubble constant. (1) Furthermore, if that is the case, then as we increase, we will be within the equivalent speed of light to our size – but will be many times faster in relation to our prior earth size. This would mean that we would seem to be contravening Einstein's theory Relativity. It would be like we were causing the law to stretch. If the ship reached three times that of light would it become trapped in time like a rubber ball at the base of a waterfall? He stopped for a moment, but no one intervened. Then in a low voice he said,

Larry was asked to come to the board room. He had not been there before. He had heard about the bird cage but when he saw it tried not to look at Richard for fear of laughing. Then Manz addressed the team. "Look Dave and Laura, these pictures are of great interest to us, in the human field we use technique such as obstetrics diagnostic imaging to achieve what you do on a larger scale. I propose that we link up to help one another. Now if our guess is correct, we are now in confirmed danger?"

"Explain?" said Dave.

"Gentlemen, Ladies, in simple terms we are about to be siphoned out of this dimension in one gulp. This zone is a quantum tunnelling field and we do not know what will happen except that on the last trip this is where records broke down."

Dave looked shocked by the frankness of his comment and responded, "Look Casper, sit down and listen for a moment."

Manz scowled. Dave took control.

"Let us not jump to conclusions. First, I accept that we are in some sort of danger, but we need more time to ascertain its extent."

"Heck!" Shouted Manz.

"It will be too late, if not too late already."

Dave asserted himself again saying that Laura had tried to consult with Pensacola, but we are now far out of range. Profiles that she had tried to get earlier on some people were left unanswered. So, in essence they will have to paddle their own canoe?"

"At this hypothetical speed C^3 the Callisto might be catapulted into another dimension."

Laura spoke, "Well Casper, at least the latter is only hypothetical."

Manz scowled at her. Then Ernst again asked if the engines could be turned on to alter their course? Ernst said yes but could he also test fire a reverse thrust to slow the ship "I zee trouble, ahead, trouble."

Dave therefore asked for a show of hands for reverse thrust. Immediately everyone raised their hand. Dave therefore said, "Ernst! Go ahead reverse our ships direction with all possible speed."

People were relieved with that decision.

Richard reminded Larry about an unopened letter from Professor George Kuhn who had given it to him earlier in Tampa. When opened it contained comments about the importance of the forces of nature as a key to the final frontier. It also cautioned about the effects of extreme gravitation. And how anti-matter could harm them if they had any alteration of scale. Then he enclosed another sketch of the Mandala he had got from the Chinese student and ended saying that Thales a Greek Philosopher from Asia Minor said in the fifth century B.C that the earth floats on water that stretched downwards limitlessly. The Egyptians world at the time also held the same belief. Now while we will laugh at the idea in a sense, we will discover that they were correct – no philosopher is ever wrong. Kindest regards. G Kuhn.

"Well, I'll be dog' gone, said Larry, we're up the creek, and old Kuhn face can just sit on his butt and lecture us with theories out of the inferno!"

Down in Ernst's shiny control room, five technicians were on standby. Ernst looked at them and said, "Menche, prepare to ignite. Olivia set one. Karl settings to four zero seven." Then he wiped his forehead and said in a shaky voice, Commence building. With that there was a hum that slowly increased in sound. Soon it became a high-pitched whine. At this point Ernst began moving between the turbines feeling them and observing for idiosyncrasies. Then as all was well, he called out, "Novak, fire all." A copy of this command was re-laid to Lionel.

There was a roar and a shudder, which meant that all motors were now operational. Ernst then called for reverse thrust and his team responded accordingly. Ernst immediately left the area and went up to the EM/SPEC. Dave, Laura and Lionel were there, watching every degree on the spectre. Lionel had learned to be interested in Ernst's moods as the navigation of the ship relied so much on him and his crew. Ernst stood in silence staring at the spectre. Both men said nothing and as the minutes passed a slow realization dawned that the ship was not responding!

5

The Road To Nowhere

Larry hurried towards the main concourse and control area at the front of the ship. A group had already gathered at the EM/SPEC. Their faces were bathed in the blue light emitted from its screen. There was an eerie silence, only broken by the low click, clack, sound from the spectral visor. The ship's motors had been turned off and Ernst had given up his efforts to avert direction. The Callisto was moving at high velocity, perhaps to a rendezvous with the unknown! Then without warning the blurred area cleared to disclose two enormous tunnels. Everyone gasped. The odyssey that lay before them was identifiable as it was punctuated in the space fabric by circles of stars. The navigator spoke hesitantly as he found it difficult to reconcile the whole situation. He described the vista as being tunnels one of which was attracting them inwards and added that at this stage, they could not break the ship from present course. Dave could see the inflow was spilling clouds of very bright matter back into the universe. It seemed that they were witnessing a cosmogenesis of enormous proportions. The universe was being fed with the energy provided by incoming material of high luminosity. Every now and then there were flashes like lightning and rainbows ranged from blue through green ending in shining gold.

Hiroshi asked Larry,

"Is all that activity because of the influence of pure unprecedented levels of background radiation in this locality"?

Larry shrugged, and said, "I guess so!"

The walls of the oncoming tunnel were curved and studded with stars. They were grouped in ribbons and filaments, that began to stretch and cocoon the approaching Callisto. It was like entering a tubular universe, tapering off into the distance! The EM/SPEC was now registering information about particles that were tracking alongside the ship. One identified object was a particle called a 'Tachyon' (Virtual Particle with no mass and travels faster than light). This was most amazing as this is a virtual particle that is supposed only to exist at velocities more than the speed of light.

As if to give some reassurance an aroma of freshly brewed coffee seeped through the ship. A radio in the background began to play a dreary melody, "I'm on the road to nowhere"

Some of the crew made their way to the galley. Manz on the other hand had no time for niceties. He was looking very concerned but was keeping away from the Captain.

By now, he would have expected the Callisto and crew to be emulsified in some time warp, yet amazing that was not to be their fate!

One of the flight officers made a curt announcement, "All crew are to put on RIP kit and strap in, I repeat RIP kit and strap in."

There was a click. Larry reached out and took Francisca's hand, squeezing it gently, before she slipped off to get kitted. As she went, she turned, and smiled as if to say, 'everything is going to be all right'. Then she was gone. Hiroshi sprang into action; he gave Larry a push, saying at the same time,

"Larry common, wake up, she's gone, get going boy."

With that, Larry regained his motivation and strode off at high speed. The task, to be performed was the putting on of a single piece safety gear. Most people were already garbed in part-readiness. The second layer to be worn was an asbestos based, anti-radiation reflective suit. This was designed for in-ship activities, and was not as bulky as a full suite, for prolonged space activity. These lighter suits were called RP gear, (Radiation Protection). They had already been dubbed R.I.P. gear, but the joke ran thin as the situation deteriorated. The suits were packed in compartments under the Hybos for quick deployment. Once dressed Larry, and Hiroshi went to their seats.

The computer banks buzzed, and lights flickered. A steady voice could be heard reading out information,

"Stat. estimated – magnitude now reaching 998 greater than scale of departure. Violation in laws of scaling $Y = a M^{2}$ "

Larry whispered to Hiroshi,

"Are they saying that Y represent the Callisto which has increased more than.75% thus entering a scale of 27 orders of magnitude?"

"Yeh," nodded Heroshi.

"On the plus side someone said we may have a slower metabolism to the point that we may gain longevity. We are told that we will experience less heat loss from the surface of our bodies. This is good news of course, but it poses the deadly question can this process ever be reversed? Then there is the contradiction of physics as it appears we are moving into infinity and infinity does not exist in Quantum mechanics."

Larry added,

"Our size is dictating new phenomena and we are at the forefront of its peculiarities."

Many of the group looked around at the computer reporters in surprise, Larry wondered why they had not already figured it out for themselves! Then as if to answer what was on everyone is mind a Chinese fellow, called Quan Chew, was brought to the EM/SPEC to address the group. He cleared his thought and said,

"Scale is like a one-way street; there is no going back. It is like Mohammed Ali, deciding he was going to join a junior boxing league and start again! He could not! This then also brings us to the question of time! If I may suggest, with respect, that you pack away your watches, because we have already leaped into the future, and from here on our time calculations are irrelevant!"

Some people scowled, and others laughed, Chew continued, "The trick is never to travel to rapidly or you outpace the natural increase of your surroundings. It seems we have done exactly that! Our greater magnitude is altering our overall velocity to the degree that we are over advanced"

Dave said with a stern look, that this is where we blanked out, and lost our memories on the last trip.

"This time we have the equivalent of an aircraft black box for recordings. Let us hope it works."

Manz could not be contained and was allowed have a final word before they hit the proverbial fan. While he spoke, the ship became firmly enclosed in the draw.

"Consider on the good side, that becoming caught in this tunnel may contribute to stabilizing our expansion! Also, there is another startling aspect, a near miss! You see because of our increased size we were becoming alien to our surroundings. Our silicone tracker detected streams of Anti-matter moving towards us. This was just before we reached the entrance tunnel. Luckily, they were deflected because of the intensity of the electro-magnetic field at the entrance. This was the blue effect that you all witnessed. All this estimation was made possible with the assistance of Larry Coughlin's Epona particle detector[9]."

Manz looked at Larry and then went on,

"A clash between anti-matter and the Callisto could have reduced us to a stream of intense Gamma Rays. Thankfully, this did not occur, and it looks like we may escape. Now there are two more peculiarities that are worrying us!"

There was a murmur from the group listening. At the back of the concourse some cooks, still dressed in white, and a female mechanic dressed in green had joined the audience and were listening with intent. They had not yet put on their RP gear; perhaps they were in a state of despair! There was now silence in the spacious enclosure. Captain Dave Mc Cluskey looked at the Doctor in anticipation. Manz coughed, and then continued,

"The first is to identify and track viruses that might be trying to enter the ship. And secondly, hold your breath - in view of all that had happened, we expect next that our atoms, will reverse and turn inside out!"

There was roar of indignation from the listeners. Manz held up his hand, "Now don't panic, hold on a moment, I believe it will happen without causing us any injury whatsoever! What I mean by this is that the nucleus will move out and the electron field will move in. There is hypothesis, by D Coughlan, and G Kuhn physicists, which state that a reversal is quite possible. An inverted atom or molecule is seen as a possible solution to human confinement. You see, also an inverted atom is speculated to have a greater heat loss, than a conventional one! The hot nucleus will not be shrouded by the electron cloud and will lose its heat more rapidly. This will facilitate greater mental activity than possible at present.

Larry immediately went online for the subject of hollow atoms. He recalled that he had read that physicists have already created a hollow atom.[4] What they have done is move the inside electrons out to the outside thus creating a void where they had been. It is very difficult to dislodge these insiders and therefore scientists have tried to

---

[4]   Hollow atoms; (Ref new scientist June 1995 Ian Hughes and Ian Williams Queens University, Belfast. "Scientists take nature's building blocks back to the drawing board; the atom is being rebuilt. In laboratories in the US and the Netherlands, physicists are ripping away the electrons that clad atomic nucleus and rearranging them into a series of hollow shells."

literally rebuild the atom! First, they get a bare nucleus and as it has a natural requirement to have electrons, it is directed towards a metal sheet. Electrons are automatically whipped on board the nucleus, but they remain in the outer regions just as the doctor ordered. Atomic manipulation is something real these days. Efforts are being made in CERN Switzerland to produce an actual anti Hydrogen atom with the intension of producing an efficient fuel for space travel.

Manz had been saying,

"It can be compared to a computer where the very operation, causes heating that in turn can cause damage. If a computer were designed that could function without heat building up, it could function hypothetically forever. In our situation, hopeful that will also be the case! Therefore, this inversion could be our making! You know it has often been said that our world is both upsides down, inside out and backwards! It must be experienced that way to be understood!" Then he attempted to hand out a paper on hollow atom experiments. There was sudden uproar. People were shouting up objections as they felt Manz's scenario was not acceptable.

Just then the dark horse, Hamish Cauldron shouted out,

"I am speaking on behalf of the crew. We propose that volunteers are allowed leave in the four-repair craft in the hold. That way at least some people will be saved. We could draw lots."

Dave immediately sensed serious trouble and called out over the intercom, that that idea was overruled Hamish was not authorised to represent the crew and until further notice he is putting the ship on a state of emergency and silence is now mandatory.

6

Inversion

Now because of their being within a cylindrical world, while travelling at enormous velocity, optically the stars seemed on the move. They looked like thousands of glow-worms travelling in the same direction. Suddenly the Callisto must have come under new influence because all at once, the lights throughout the ship began to blaze. Every electric gadget became activated. Music began to blare, and the emergency siren squealed, of its own accord. The computer banks illuminated, and even the Hybos lit up. The crew of the ship began trying turn things off but could not! The computer operators instantly began to run emergency copies of data, for fear of a shutdown.

The Navigators and both Captains clustered around the electro-flight consul. It was strange, because the EM/SPEC was the only piece of equipment that seemed compatible with the world they were entering. To Larry's surprise, he noticed Hiroshi was doing a pen drawing a sketch of what lay beyond. He looked up at Larry and smiled, saying,

"Larry when I get home, I'm going to sell this and retire a 'zillionaire'.

Did you know that cameras do not work up here? The shutter speeds do not synchronise correctly with the scaled-up situation, I do not know why! Oh, by the way, we never showed the Mandala to Manz."

The Navigator called out, "Peculiar sighting ahead!"

It was in the form of a transparent barrier that resembled a great membrane blocking their path. On the other side there was signs of strange movements from left to right.

Lionel then made a judgment,

"My readings show that the movement is gravitational field of waves not electromagnetic. Why left to right? We can only guess it is related to the arrow in time!"

No one contradicted, the statement, and the ship's 'dire emergency' siren sounded. People instantly pulled up protective hoods and drew oxygen masks from their seats. The ship hurled towards the transparent barrier. It had a surface like a bubble and was so enormous that it blocked their path filling the entire expanse of the cylinder.

"Good heavens,"- Larry blurted, "This must be yet another singularity, a huge, big one, what a bore!"

The transparent barrier was also reflective, as for a fleeting moment the Callisto was in a golden flash on the bubble surface. Just then every clock in the ship began to spin backward and forwards and that included a set of digital atomic clocks in the control area. Then they all stopped completely.

It was at that moment the Callisto hit the membrane. The Captain had yelled, "Impact." Then from the front of the ship a wave of light moved from fore to aft. It was granular and it shimmered. As it went, it warped everything in its path and that included Larry and Hiroshi. Larry heard Hiroshi cry out. Larry was overcome and felt dizziness. He felt like he was intoxicated and about to faint. He opened his mouth to scream but could not utter a single sound. Then he opened his eyes but could not see anything. It was as if he was underwater without a diving mask. Like what had happened to Richard, when he cleared his mask in Crystal River and could only see blurry blue. 'Oh God', – Larry thought "Francisca". He hurriedly looked around for her, but she was not there! He thought, he must rally at the emergency station. He began to feel sick and throughout his body he felt a ghastly vibration.

Then he passed out!

Everyone on board the Callisto, must have shared the same experience. This was evident when Larry regained consciousness because he could see people slumped in their seats, while others groaned in discomfort. He looked down to see if he was intact, and alive! To his utter amazement, not only was he alive, but also his vision was clearer than it had ever been. He could see right across the room and pick out the tiniest detail on the control panels and could hear with incredible sharpness.

He also had inherited a faculty of knowing what was going on behind him, though looking the other way! He thought to himself, "Oh! How strange and wonderful, I feel so sensitive!"

But to Larry's dismay when he looked downwards, he could see partly through his own hands, he had turned semi-transparent! He looked over at Hiroshi who looked to still be unconscious and had a pained look on his face. He looked at the crew and they were also mostly unconscious and partly transparent! Hiroshi's face had altered he had taken on a bluish tinge to his left of his body. To his right side he was pinkish. As Larry stared at his own hands, he found them misty looking and not see through as he had feared. At least his bones and veins would not be on display to the public! Then Hiroshi made a sound and twitched. He turned slowly and looked at Larry. Surprise registered on his hazy face. Larry thought he looked quite ill!

Then perhaps a little overconfident, Larry tried to move, but could not. He tried to speak but could not even form a word. It was like being an infant and having to start the learning process all over again. A feeling of hopelessness took hold. He began to command his fingers to move, and persisted, until they began to respond. He heaved a sigh of relief and began immediately to attempt at forming words. At first, he could only manage to utter a grunt, but within several minutes his voice returned. He then looked across the room at Richard, who was also in the process of self-reconstruction, grunting and trying to form words. Larry then felt the scene was almost comical, and began to laugh exclaiming out loud, "Great Buddha," – Then a pause, and then with great effort he managed to say slowly, – "What have you done with us?"

He unlinked his safety harness, which was also quite transparent, and stood up. The deck below him was soft like lime jello. The walls of the Callisto were just like the deck. The computers blinked, and though they were now 'see through', it looked like they were in working order once again. Larry climbed into a standing position and then extended one hand to Hiroshi, who looked a little afraid to touch him.

"Come on Hiroshi, how do ye' feel? Are you all right?"

Hiroshi responded slowly, stretching out his hand and saying, "Yeh! Larry, how are you?"

The handshake was quite normal, but there was no doubt that if one squeezed too hard the hands would have meshed! There will be new rules of contact to be learned. Larry who was now intrigued with the new state, tried poking his finger through his own hand. To his amazement it sank inwards without causing pain or damage! Then he pushed on his chest but stopped because it began also to give away. He decided to leave well enough alone. Larry then went to where Richard was sitting, and asked, "Are you Ok? Rich?"

Richard replied slowly rubbing his eyes,

"Larry, what the heck has happened to us? Everything is so bright and clear, but are we dead? You know we are inside out according to Laura and Chan. It is a crock of you know what, and none of us are going to make it. Also, I'm never going to see Clearwater and Pat, and the children, ever again, we've had it!"

The words struck terror in Larry's heart. Richard looked terrible underneath the haze, and Larry was worried. He replied,

"Maybe you are right, but it could not be like this to be dead! Everything is way too normal, apart from the transparency!"

At that Richard gave a wail because he had only just discovered his 'see through' hands. Larry tried to pacify him but to no avail. Then, as if to help matters, the intercom crackled, and Laura's voice came through. Larry was not sure whether she was speaking, or just conveying a flow of messages and ideas that everyone naturally received. The message sounded like this,

"Congratulation, we have survived this encounter and I'm glad to say our damage report, is zero, we are intact and are moving ahead. If anyone has any difficulty, press your emergency buzzer and a medic will give immediate assistance. Please remain on full alert, because in five minutes we will be hit on the port side by a series of gravitational waves that are believed to exist at the edge of the sphere of influence of universal gravitation."

Despite the new menace, Richard now seemed more reassured, and some colour began to return to his opaque cheeks.

Larry could not remain still for long his' breaky heart' was thumping he had to find out about Francisca! He knew she was with other Cadets, somewhere over on the vulnerable port side. He shuffled that direction, and ran right into her, as she was coming to see how he had survived. Larry was elated to think she would have considered him. She was smiling as she walked and resembled an intoxicated clown. Larry laughed at the sight. He noticed that, like the others, her garments had taken on a clouded plastic appearance. It meant that the outline of her figure could be seen through the fabric, like she was a super model. Having gone through so much drama, Larry could not resist the releasing of his emotions. He just threw his arms around her and kissed her. He made sure not to press too hard as they might weld together! She did not have a chance to object, nor did she try. The kiss felt perfect, just as good as on earth, but one had to be gentle. Then while she was still in his embrace Larry whispered, "That's because I love you, and I also did it for science."

He let her go, and she responded by giving him a very quick return kiss. The she looked at him sideways with a teasing smile exclaimed,

"A small kiss from Larry, a giant step for mankind."

With that they both burst out laughing. Then from the adjoining area someone shouted, "Shhh, quiet you should be seated."

Francisco whispered,

"We better return to our seats, be good, see you soon, marshmallow man."

Just then on the cook's radio Madonna began to sing, "I am a material girl" Larry rolled his eyes up to heaven and they both shuffled off in different directions. Larry could not help thinking of a 'Richie's mints' commercial that he saw on TV when he was a kid. In the commercial, everything was soft and white and springy, just like now on board the ship.

It was just at that moment that they entered the gravitational quantum field. The Callisto was now hit by the first standing waves. Suddenly the Ship lurched. Larry was hurled along the isle but managed to climb into his seat. Hiroshi turned and said, "Larry where have you been, you must be a bit soft in the head. You could have busted your neck. Do you realise we are hitting the first of those standing waves?"

Larry grunted and strapped himself into the seat, "You forget Hiroshi, these are not ocean waves, and we will probably plough right through them!"

However, Larry was half wrong. With that the ship's nose was twisted upwards and they began to climb at an angle tilted towards the left, their intended route. Then at the top the ship turned and like a roller coaster, it tore down the other side. Then it hit the bottom of the trough it made a wrenching turn, and the procedure up the face of the next wave. This process happened several times till they finally broke loose and got back on course. Their survival was due to the navigators who really knew his job, he did not leave the helm a never letting up for a moment. It was like nautical history being repeated.

"There at the wheel was a lone sailor wrestled with the elements as his stricken craft sailed through the raging torrent." (Self)

Then the waves began to settle down. From where they were sitting, Richard could get a bird's eye view through the front portal of what lay ahead. One of the navigators spotted a bright blue opening where the tunnel widened. It was like an entrance to another world! Above them, the stars disappeared, and the sky opened, and an electric blue ocean formed below. Then in an instant, they vacated the tunnel and glided out into an amazing expanse of open sea. Just then there was a loud exclamation from the Boardroom. The hypnotic moment was shattered. It was Laura, "Help, someone help, Kiki has disappeared. Oh my God, has anyone seen my bird?"

Spread about the Callisto the enormous expanse of liquid seemed to shimmer and radiate light into a misty sky. The Navigator attempted to ascertain their position and the nature of the new environment. He worked feverishly on the EM/SPEC and eventually with a grunt of satisfaction, got a result. He looked around at the anxious faces and stated that they were positioned at the lower central region of an immense triangle. Manz stood beside him slowly nodding his head. Hiroshi pulled out the Mandala. He held it for Larry to see, "Look Larry, this is where we are. Plato's world of ideals."

Right enough the map showed a connecting link or an umbilical between the universe and a large triangle. Maybe the map would prove to be accurate after all.

The EM/SPEC showed that the triangle was generating negative electrical current! The magnetic compass was indicating that north was directly ahead. The Controller said that is where the apex of the triangle may exist. Hiroshi brought up the Mandala to him and quickly explained its logic. Lionel looked on with interest saying, "Thanks, this is the first piece of sensible material I have seen so far. It will be a great help in our navigation."

Hiroshi said, "Keep it safe its precious."

Lionel taped it at the side of the EM/SPEC. Then said,

"According to our estimates which are confirmed by the Mandala, the universe lies to their south in a cut-out section in the lower zone of the triangle. It was amazing that even in this world that there were still linear ups and downs! Then the EM/SPEC confirmed that this triangle was one hundred and fifty times larger than the universe."

With that Richard who by now had regained his old composure, began to draw a parallel between this new-fangled discovery, and Plato's Philosophy of forms,

"In the Timaeus, Plato said quote, that geometrically solids are bounded by planes, and the most elementary plane figure is a triangle. From two types of triangles, he envisaged all solid bodies, unquote. To Plato they were Earth, Fire, Water and Air. Putting it in very simple terms, this triangle is certainly the generator of all water in the universe and it is likely that it is also the generator of air! In fact, it is likely to be the electromagnetic force the third force of nature!"

Hiroshi, commented,

"Plato does not really interest me, but from what we have in our Mandala it looks like we have discovered a truly divine form! We are privileged to gaze upon a perfect 'inelastic collision. There is no doubt that this is the form of all forms and would remain as such even if the universe were to disappear."

No one responded but instead, just gazed out across the expanse. The scene was enchanting with the water altering in colour to take on every tone of blue and turquoise imaginable. Then to add to the excitement there were the flashes of lightning emitted from the many wave crests, whipping past.

The EM/SPEC reports now stated; *Gravitation- zero, replaced by negative electromagnetic gravitational. Landscape Topography —triangular force field. Contents; photons, one only primordial electron. Neutrino abundance and a consistency of newly un-identified particles.*

Despite the absence of gravity, nothing seemed to have changed, people still had their feet on the ground. Perhaps an alternative force had now taken its place! This 'gravitational substitute' would probably be quite local and could not be identified on earth. Richard named it electromagnetic gravity!

As they looked back, they could see a great golden torus that encased the universe and the lower end of the triangle. Its structure looked incomplete. It had a blunt end and seemed cut off where it left the triangle. It was like a swinging pendulum that had not completed its arch! It might be basically a graphical view of gravity from the outside. Hiroshi looked at the Mandala. In it the torus narrowed to a pinhead at the top of the picture. This Hiroshi said, was hyper singularity and where the highest stratum exists. Richard then got involved pointing out as follows,

"Hiroshi, I hope you don't mind my observations but, the torus evidently dictates the arrow in time, and that appears to be anti-clockwise. That is amazing, as it might have been clockwise, and no one would know the difference. At the widest part, the cut off end you can just glimpse the many swirls that resembled quasiperiodic motions of what looks like a mammoth size Kolmogorov Attractor (1). This is found in the mathematics of fractals and chaotic iteration. This means that the large torus was made up on smaller ones. The result of that is that the universe is stretched to resemble a saddle shape. In very simple terms, it looks just like a Pringle potato chip! If one took a bag of Pringles and put them side by side, they would become the inner section of a torus."

He chuckled to himself but regretted telling everyone what he had just proposed.

"The torus is true gravitation as we know it. It bends everything in its path and that includes the universe and this here triangle. The curved universe in turn bends the space it possesses. Then having bent its space, space in turn bends motion, and 'hoop-la' it looks to science that gravity is nothing more than a track in space fabric. That is where people are wrong just look for yourselves it is plain for all to see! It is the most influential force, the first and most important, without it we would have nothing but an otherwise empty world."

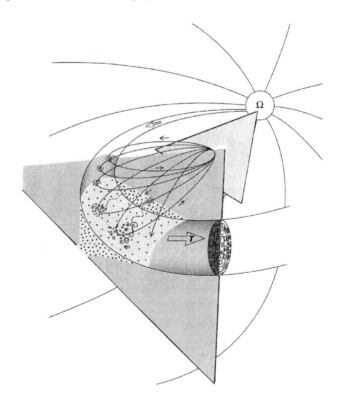

The Assimilation of Force Fields acting in unison. The result is the universe in its image and likeness. The forces of nature shroud the cosmos, giving it substance and life. A Super gravitational field acts as a conical screen in which reality grows. The nucleus of the force beats time while sustaining the universe.

7

Black Flack Attack

The astrophysicists turned their attention to the surrounding void, which was like a great empty vault. However, on closer inspection they noticed that the sky, was alive with activity. Something was not right, there was hostility feeling out there. Every now and then a great swirl of inky substance would move back towards the universe and descend. It was like smoke from a burning oil well polluting everything it met. The effect was just like a meteor burning up on entry to the earth's atmosphere. Then as it crossed the triangle it became vaporised. It did not sit well passing through an electromagnetic field. At that very moment Francisca thought that she saw the source of the venom, a dark object floating in the blackness. She let out a shriek!

"Did you see that?" she said. I saw an object directing an attack on the universe.

Just then Father Travis intervened, "Francisca, you might have just witnessed a cyber-psychological bombardment excuse the big words! From here it looked like a nuclear attack, but it was not. It is no secret that there are dark powers always trying to derail humanity. Some people deny that but here you see it for yourself."

The others tried also to see the object but to no avail. Francisca moved from the window, unprepared to discuss what she had seen! Larry and Lydia who was one of the cadets, followed her trying to provide comfort. Then as they watched the scene altered. The universe faded from sight and began to look like a fractal from the Mandelbrot[5] set and then it disappeared. At least that is what Larry thought.

All this time the ship was moving in a northerly direction of its own accord. Just then one of the crew spotted what looked like a flock of magnificent white dove like creatures, swirling above the sea. A moment later they had disappeared, perhaps they were not supposed to have been seen. Then from somewhere towards the apex of the triangle the sky glowed red in the Apeiron[6] Silver arches of light could be clearly seen leaving the redness and descending back down towards the universe. They noticed that the silver streaks rotated and returned to their source at enormous speed. It was as if the cosmos was a holograph, or part of a three-dimensional film which was being projected onto a curved surface perhaps creating reality! Hiroshi looked disturbed by this feature and said, "Do you know we must have been in that swirl before we got here. What would we do if that machine got turned off? Would we become pillars of salt?"

This did not please Richard, because it gave him pangs of fear reminding him of his state before he had become strengthened. However, on the plus side, Larry said the silver streaks looked as if they were impervious to the fiendish blackness that lashed the universe. Richard looked relieved.

Larry then said, "When I was a kid we went to 'Jack and the Bean Stalk' a Christmas pantomime. In it, young Jack climbed up to the land of the Giant. The Callisto has just performed a similar fête. Why have we not yet met a Giant? Or are we now giants ourselves!"

Richard again looked disturbed.

They remained on the smooth central trail that led towards the apex. The only problem was that things were going too well. The electric equipment was generating more power than ever before and the luminosity in the ship was carnival like. The crew's misty soft textures shone more vividly than before and there was much jibing and joking about their state. Their personal vision had increased enormously, they could see for hundreds of earth miles in this newfound Kodachrome world. It was as if a mystical energy was sweeping the Callisto ever

---

5   The Vague Attractor of Kolmogorov; Also known as KAM and is a mathematical iteration that depicts a torus of concentric sheaths of quasiperiodic motion. A cross section of this consists of a series of smaller sections replicating the outer shell.

6   Apeiron; Both principle and element that steers all things, according to philosopher Anaximenes.

onwards. It was then that they began to hear chimes in the wind and a chant of south sea island like singing. It was what one would expect in Tahiti or Hawaii but was also quite weird.

"Enihi ka hele mai ho'opa.
Mai pulale I ka'ike a ka maka.
Ho'okahi no makamaka 'o ke aloha.
Oka hea mai'okalani a'e kipa." [4]
"Be cautious on your journey, don't be overanxious
Don't be overwhelmed by what you see
There is only one companion of love
When the sovereign bids a visit".[7]

Then the sound abated, and silence descended. Richard turned to Don Travis and said, "Don, what's next? Now you have been through thick and thin and have directed your mind to eschatological questions. Now I, on the other hand, am saturated with physics. However, things are moving so fast that I am confused – screwed up, ye know! In other words, where the hell are we, and what's all this singing?"

Don Travis gave a laugh but could not shed any light.

Then without warning a whispering voice penetrated throughout the ship. It was a female voice and resounded in everyone is understanding simultaneously. It began much like the sound wind. It was ghostly and everyone was startled. It said, "Shalom, Shalom!"

With that some of the group went to their seats and clicked into their safety harnesses. Some pulled the zippers up high in their RP suits; others just stood their ground. The voice spoke in many languages, because later everyone agreed that they heard it in their own native tongues. At this point the white birds re-appeared flying in circles around the ship. To an onlooker, if such could exist, it must have been a pretty sight. The golden coloured Callisto set against a gigantic triangular sea of many shades of blue, under a black sky that had streaks of phosphorous clouds webbed about the horizon. The light provided for this event did not come down from a sun or a moon but was generated from below, by the triangle itself. This entire splendour coupled with the flock of snow-white doves and enhanced with the sound of wind and musical chimes added up to a speckle of magnificent proportions. Then the background sound abated, and the voice spoke clearly,

---

[7] E NIHA KA HELE by Gabby Pahinui

"Little ones, you are the seeds in which we hope. I am Spirinda the Parakeet one who propagates life. You are welcome to my world, but you got here only by a stroke of good fortune. Do you know you have accidentally violated many laws of nature by coming? This would not have happened but nature itself has wavered its laws and permitted your arrival. Nature is indeed your friend. Nature has its genesis in me and springs also from the world of ideal forms, which is also myself! Perhaps your arrival is a sign that the time is right for further evolution."

There was a long pause, which prompted the Vice-Captain to speak. She asked out loud, with respect would the violation cause punishment.

Then there was a further silence. People did not know if a reply was possible from such a voice. After several minutes, just as if all sound were by delayed satellite communications, there was a reply.

"You have suffered enough; we are not beings bent on punishment. We are beings that that take pride in forgiveness and are supportive and eternally curious about all we behold. As you have come this far it would be sad if you did not have an opportunity to experience the fullness of time. Therefore, do you want to continue with this journey? Alternatively, you can be returned unharmed to your original status, so that all these events never happened. The choice is yours, trust me and deliberate amongst yourselves. You may not realise it but you are in a state of prayer by the nature of this very discussion and as a result you will make the right decision, I know. Now take time, relax, discuss, drink, and arrive at a unanimous decision, and then call out to me – I will answer your call."

Then there was a pause during which there was a prolonged silence. Then the voice said,

"Did you realise it is safe for you to open your doors of your craft, and to bath in the ocean? You will come to no harm and will enjoy the experience. Your guardians have much power up here, they are your mentors, shalom!" The sweet fragrance in the ylem was no doubt a testimony to the existence of a being in their vicinity. The Captain went to the EM/SPEC and asked for it to be played back. The replay only showed the triangle, but the dialogue was repeated. While this was happening the waves and the flocks of snow-white doves moved across the great body as if in total defiance of her gravity. Then she went and the triangle returned to its original form.

The first person to speak had other things in mind. They said out loud, "Do you realise that none of us have eaten or drank since coming through the tunnel and the only need I have is to drink, I could not face eating, why is that?"

One of the Doctors named Burnette, approached the Captain,

"In the light of what has happened, it is our intention to do medical check-ups on all the crew. However, two of us have checked each other and analysed some tissue from our hair and nails and can confirm the inversion is in evidence – it really happened. We could not delve as deep as the atomic structure but at molecular level it is there. We have powerful microscopes on board and have been able to see DNA at 1/10,000,000 of an inch in diameter, universal scale related. We have found them to be completely opposite structures to what we know. They are inside out and less compact than before. They are more spaced out, but they are in the same string configuration. We are concerned to know if all the chemical actions 20,000 per cell are taking place, and we would like to have many other questions answered."

Dave nodded in agreement. Burnette continued,

"We intend setting up clinic immediately that is with the Captains permission and proceed with health checks for everyone."

Dave agreed again.

By now people had got busy with the task of refreshment. They began to drink fresh water from the oasis systems. Some went to the canteen and got their water a la carte with ice cubes, while some preferred juice. The cooks were heard to jest, that if word about the situation gets back to base, they would be made redundant. One of them began to suggest that water should be charged for but was booed out of it.

There was concern that the supply would soon diminish but on inspection the level in the tanks just never seemed to go down. The physicists said that they wondered had a new constant been discovered, they might have been correct!

The Captain ordered two of the crew were detailed to test the sea before people tried it. They immediately stripped down to their shorts, as they did not have swim trunks as part of their kit, in fact no one did. On a command from the Dave, one of the computer people taped in a keyboard. There was an immediate hiss, and the door began to roll back. Instantly there was an aroma of perfume accompanied by a musical sound that amazingly came directly from the sea. The interior of the Callisto became bathed in shimmering lights of blue and gold. Francisca thought it was like a most beautiful grotto in a tropical resort. Everyone gasped in delight. Then the two designated crewmembers leaned down and swept their hands in the water. They then cupped their hands and withdrew some of the liquid. They stood up and said,

"Captain Sir, this here water, does not even wet our hand, it is like blue mercury. I feel like I was just baptised in this uisce beatha." Larry saw the joke.

Everyone gathered around and eventually several removed their RP suits and began to swim in their fatigues. Richard and Hiroshi were quick to join in the fun while Larry ploughed in with a big splash. Being a surfer, he could not believe that he was back in the ocean again. He wondered would the waves ever break right in this ocean. He then made a duck dive to see what lay beneath what he might find! It was not unlike the Caribbean – far below he could see the golden expanse of shimmering sand. The effect of rising light was wonderful. Shafts of gold burst from the seabed along with streams of blue bubbles. All this rose and invigorated anything or anyone in its path.

The texture of the water was slippery and grain like, one moment it was flat and placid, while the next moment brought waves. Richard was convinced that they were experiencing first-hand Quantum theory in action. Hiroshi decided to take a sip of the water. He did so and then swallow it. Immediately his eyes opened wide and he called to Richard,

"Hey Rich, try drinking some it's great."

With that he hiccupped, and several golden bubbles popped out of his mouth. Those who were watching roared with laughter. Richard sampled the water and competed sending a shower of bubbles in all directions.

"Gee," He said – "It tastes sweet."

Just then, Francisca pushed into the water and paddled up beside Larry, smiled and pointed downwards. He instinctively made another dive, and she followed. They both met face to face allowing ample time for a gentle kiss and a moment of embrace. For a brief second, they were suspended in a world of blue wonder. It was like midnight in the Caribbean as bright plankton like objects appeared and illuminated the liquid. Time stood still and they slowly drifted to the surface at the speed of the rising bubbles. They were in a trance, and when they broke the surface Larry found himself whispering to Francisca

"Praise to the pneuma, theion, theon, theou pneuma" (Spirit and divine reality in Greek) "Praise to ruah" (Spirit in Hebrew).

As he did not speak Greek or Hebrew, he wondered how he conjured up the words. Francisca looked at him in puzzlement.

"Larry," she said jokingly,

"You speak in tongues, did my kiss cause that?"

As people climbed back on board, to their astonishment they found their cloth were bone dry. Everything about this extra universal discovery was palatable and accommodating and everyone loved the experience.

It was Larry who first noticed that several people had not joined in the fun. That they looked quite miserable and kept away from activities that were not directly related to duties. The more exuberant the crew became the more dejected these people looked. The people were men and women that came from different segments of the operation.

Hamish, Dalia, and Raphael were part of the group. By enlarge these were normal people who for some reason or other did not fit with the new experience. As a result, they seemed to find consolation in each other and therefore began bunching together. Larry discussed the observation with his colleagues and between them some worrying thoughts immerged. Hiroshi thought it was because they were home sick. Richard said it was the lack of food. Francisca suggested that the cause might be that grotesque object that had attacked the universe.

Captain Dave addressed the group.

"My dear fellow explorers, as you know, we have come a long way together. I thank my God, that no one has been killed or injured and there is no need to assume that this will change. Now what do you people want to do? We used to say in situations like this that we are on a mission and must carry on. Now the goal posts have changed. The rules of the game have altered, and we are extended far beyond the call of duty and it's up to you as individuals to say what comes next. It is obvious that this is our last chance to return and rewind the situation. If alternatively, we go on, there will be no turning back and we will have to continue to the end, whatever that may be! There are various options open to us, we can have a show of hands, or a secret ballot or I can say let us try it and see does anyone disagree."

With that a most unexpected person stood up and walked forward. It was Cadet Francisca Spazola. She moved forward in a gliding motion, slowly turned to face the group, and then looked at the Captains. She spoke in slow deliberate words saying boldly,

"You have seen by now the terror that lurks in the void. It is driven by a mysterious dark personality, an agent from the abyss that I do not like. From that ebony inferno comes 'the devil in the machine' the ones that plague the earth. This is what has warped our natures and continuously distorts everything one does in the universe. There is but one force that counters that, and it is the power of this triangle. Already we have been enlightened from the moment we entered the tunnel. As a woman, I for one feel elevated by what we have experienced. I trust and identify with the blue lady, the voice. I feel whole and entire and in better health than ever before. I feel forgiven, washed clean and my spirits are high, and I perceive a very bright future no matter in what form it comes. If we do not proceed, we will erase all that has happened and can never relate it to our universal kin. We will have failed those who we love and above all we will fail those who love us. I vote we continue."

These rallying words coming from a girl and a cadet seemed to tip the scales. There was another thunderous applauds and people spoke out loud saying,

"She is right, let's carry on."

The column of mist had been leading them up the centre of the triangle. Richard thought it was quite biblical. He recalled some text from memory,

(Exodus 13.21) During the day the Lord went in front of them in a pillar of cloud to show them the way, and during the night he went in front of them in a pillar of fire to give them light, so that they could travel night and day.

Up ahead, there was a deep red glow. Was this where the next triangle would be? Manz had read George Kuhn's report and said it would be that. The answer was not long in coming because they began to detect the silver arks that had been shown on the EM/SPEC. Dave said that if they were leaving the electromagnetic field and entering another, to expect some radical changes. True to Dave's word they headed north, the atmosphere became rose tinted and storms began to blow blew towards the apex. The source of the wind seemed to be a ribbon of bulbous mountains running up both sides of the upper one third of the triangle. There were also some intersections in the central spine, which ran off in the direction of these mountains. It was so strange that Lionel produced Hiroshi's Mandala to find a meaning. Hiroshi said he thought it looked like it was all part of a sort of breathing system. The Mandala showed that up ahead there was one more triangle and that this one was a King Pin in the matrix. By now the column of mist began to vaporise, it had completed its task.

8

The Second Force In Nature

Then as the world around them turned a deep rose colour the Callisto slipped off the point of the blue triangle and onto the centre of another. It seems one overlapped the other. In contrast, the new environment consisted of a molten mass of red and maroon eruptions. Every few moments the texture would belch into coloured spheres linked together with strings that vibrated. With the least provocation red bubbles would float in the atmosphere and settle down again to melt into the fabric. At each eruption there was a strange array of anti-colours, turquoise, mauve, green, grey, and mustard.

Lionel gladly introduced a scientist who wanted to bring the group up to date. He was most informative and prepared to give a commentary while examining the screen. He tapped a few commands and statistics began to appear. Then he spoke,

"Most of you know me, I'm Calin Spencer, from Cambridge, a physicist, like most of you. Now look here at the screen, it states that we are receiving images from this new-fangled triangle. It smacks of being the second force in nature because, we are reading that there is a mass of quarks, gluons, and free quark activity. There is evidence of a super strong force with supped up protons, inverted of course and baryons of three different spins. Then there is an anti-world with supped up inverted anti-protons and anti-quarks. There is an amazing sequence in which the triangle is alternating from a blazing rainbow to pure white. One moment there is an earth type rainbow, and the next moment it turns turquoise, mauve, and green as no doubt you have already observed. It seems that white it the eventual outcome of the colours mixing."

They all had a look at the EM/SPEC and then Calin continued,

"Now remember on the scale of things we are quite enormous compared with our original state, that these quarks are larger than anything imaginable. We are in a giant world. Next there is an overwhelming proportion of the strong nuclear force, and the colour force. Remember that everything we experience out there is in a reverse configuration. There is no sign of any atoms only their components. However up-ahead things could be different. Now comes the crunch, temperature! The readings are of temperatures more than (100 million, million degrees Kelvin) x3."

Calin continued,

"You are all no doubt wondering why we are not burned to a crisp. Well, there are three possibilities, one is that we are protected because of inversion, another is that our EM/SPEC is faulty, or that the impossible is occurring and it's a mystery!"

No one asked any questions, and many found the irony of their situation was amusing

Francisca's friend was an Islamic girl called Dr Nadine Bakr. She was eager to talk about their experiences, and naturally got on to the subject of Neurology in relation to the new reality. Sitting on Hiroshi's Hybo with one slender leg on a swivel chair, she began to talk freely. The others squatted wherever they could find space while she spoke.

There is a school of thought promoted by Francis Heighten from the university of Brussels. He says that we are developing a global brain. He sees the Internet and E-mail as its beginning. Since then, we have S-mail (Space) photon boosted communication and magnetic transformed telepathy communications. Should we welcome this Global brain or fear it is one of the questions. Now from what we have seen his theory must be correct as our universe shows every sign of being a living entity. To succeed there will need to be a super organism that can foster vast amounts of information to act as a central brain. There is a process that is called Transitivity, where the Internet begins to look at what it has in the way of information and at where there are information gaps or shortfalls. Then it will begin to question users to make good the missing knowledge. It is thought that humans will be a secondary part of this brain, perhaps a disposable part. Now this is where I come into the picture."

She paused and sipped some water,

"You see, I am convinced from what I have seen that the Human is like the synapse in the neuron. It is the terminal that monitors and controls, rather than the internet. It is part of nature that components and organisms die and are replaced. We as Muslims are perpetually ready to submit and surrender to Allah. We therefore are open to whatever he shows us, no matter how difficult it may be to understand. We are quite sure that he will keep it simple. It is only a reputation of the family on a larger scale and the infusion of intelligence in the form of humans."

Another swig of water,

"The brain of the human has a left and a right side each side controls the opposite side of the body. Information travels through the nervous system at up to the speed of 6.66 km per second. If as we have seen the universe, we estimate to be at least 111101 times greater than the human if our fluid replace light then light would travel in the universe at our estimated speed of 6.66 x 111,101,739,932 km per sec more than twice its known speed (of light 300,000 per second.) This means that each of us is a dynamic universe of our own and combined we will have a synergy value of extra ordinary proportions. Mentally and through the media our combined knowledge can see and understand things that we as individuals could not comprehend. So, the net will be a tool at our disposal, and we must keep it that way. In the Qur'an we are told that the Lord created man from a clot. Now that we are in such an extra-spatial condition, one wonders will we receive enlightenment about his statement? The only comparison that I can find so far is the preoccupation that Christians have with blood and passion. Now we also differ because I like my compatriots do not believe in democracy, as you know it. We believe in obedience to a hierarchical order above, which comes ultimately from God. The Persian poet Rumi wrote, – Oh God do not leave our affairs to us, for if you do, woe to us."

With that there was the sound of voices from the main concourse. Nadine said, "I have said too much, let's see what's happening and Happy Birthday again Hiroshi."

9

Quarks And Colour Up Close

As the ship was now in the new triangle there were results. Around them was an extravaganza of colour that created an atmosphere of strangeness. The EM/SPEC indicated that there were quarks evident in every direction. Some were ups and some were downs,[10] others were even sideways. Then a steady thumping sound developed that grew louder as they travelled into the interior. Larry felt like colonial soldier listening to the vibration of running Zulus on the warpath. Then as the rhythm grew even louder, the gentle scent of a perfume penetrated the ship. Just then the ships bells jangled. The Captain stood wide legged at the EM/SPEC, and the computer banks became very active. Larry looked at the screen and noticed evidence of vapour blowing between the two territories. It may happen because of a temperature difference. It was certainly being absorbed directly into the maroon triangles structure. Perhaps all this was purifying the texture and elixir of life of this strange world! Then it was suggested that it might be a pollinizing process or even an anti-virus purifier.

A range of mountains appeared up ahead, with the now familiar silver streaks both converging and emitting from its epicentre. This consisted of two volcanic type funnels, which as it turned out was the source of the thumping sound! The mountain range was compact and resembled an island. As they listened one of the medical people made some calculations. He determined that it made a thud once every.857 of a second timed on their earth watches. They were struck at the resemblance it bore to the human heartbeat. This vast range amazingly appeared to move up and down with every thump. The crew wondered if it were an optical illusion. The mountains were smooth and round and shaped like an Australian desert rock formation called the Olgas.

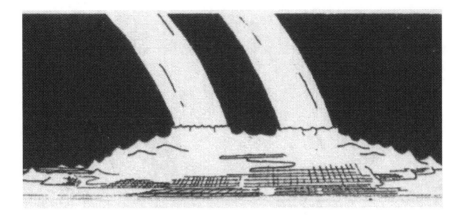

The EM/SPEC showed that twin volcanos were spewing out from one side and receiving on the other. Also, each outgoing pulse was of enormous volume and went skywards disappearing beyond sight. Then the foothills came into view and the twinkle of a lake could be seen to the west. Moving specks in the sky looked like being flying craft circulating and descending to disappear behind the south-west side of the mountains. The volcano was undoubtedly the source of all power and the epicentre for all the silver streaks of light that they had watched for so long. As they became more accustomed to the phenomena, they noticed that the incoming streaks were purple but that the outgoing was a vibrant mixture of blue and gold. One of the crew said out loud,

"Good God, is this the powerhouse of existence?

Another responded,

"Why, yes, it must be, where the heck else would you see a sight like it? It must be a living mountain!" – "Es ist ein herz!" – "Le coeur de universe!" – Another said while adding, "On earth as it is in heaven."

Just then, the navigator compared the Mandala with the image of what lay ahead. He was amazed by continued similarity. Then white patches at the base of the mountain turned out to be dwellings. They were so numerous that it began to look more like a city. There were lights reflected from moving objects giving the impression of a very busy place or maybe because the inhabitants had sighted the Callisto. As it turned out the central communications network had been informing the inhabitants of their every move.

As a result, excitement had mounted prompting a buying spree, the shops had never been busier. No one knew why people were concerned with their appearance, but that was the effect the visitors were having. A reception committee was assembled and given cars to ferry in the visitors.

"City ahoy," yelled one of the Ship's crew. The same crewmember then said, "It looks like Rio de Janeiro, I've been there."

The buildings were of Mediterranean or Californian style and were spread along the foothills amongst canyons and crevices, most were like homes, but some were like apartments. In through the mix there were coliseums and official looking buildings evidently state occasions existed in this society. Then the visitors saw activity in the sky above the city. Small, winged objects could be seen flying in various directions. There were also floating platforms connected to the ground by tubs and an amazing transparent tube extending upwards. This gigantica travelled in a different direction the the volcano's eruption, instead it travelled north and upwards into the mist.

Larry pushed his way up to the navigator and peered down.

Just then as had expected the EM/SPEC gave its first official report; $T = 300,000x3$ T $Avum =.00005$ T $Eternitas$ as $absolute$ $Zero$ $-.00005$. Contents reverse Hadrons Deuterium and Strong Gravitational Force.

Richard arrived and stabbed a finger in the direction of Deuterium saying,

"That is the first time we have had confirmation about this element. No one ever knew from where it came if it ever existed that is. Now look this is where it must originate!"

"Your right," said one of the physicists,

"But look it records Hadrons, and the temperature is much too high for them to exist, could it be like us they are inverted and that is how they exist? Then there is the strong gravitational force, what is that?"

Larry responded,

"It must be that there is a link between the two otherwise we would be floating around by now."

Just then the navigator magnified the imaging of the city. A new feature became apparent. All around the outskirts there were plains of ochre colour that resemble the wheat fields of Manitoba.

"Could that be wheat for bread?" said Francisca.

"Could be!" said Larry "I wonder what else?"

It looked like the Callisto would be delivered into a curved arena that was free from eruptions, quite flat and situated in front of the main part of the city. As they neared, the thumping sound diminished perhaps muffled by the mountains and the buildings. Then the ship came to a stop. At that moment, to the rear of the control room some insensitive card players were dealing a fresh hand. One called Rufus eagerly fanned through his cards laying an Ace, Jack, Queen, and a King on the table face saying at the same time,

"Which of this lot have we met already?" Another said,

"Wait till we meet the Joker".

His comrades laughed and played on with a look of contempt.

Rip, Rest In Purgosia

The Callisto finished its journey and Francisca had been correct, there was wheat growing around the city. A golden pallet of light glowed beneath them as it retracted some of the occupants looked in amazement as it left to become a shimmering line on the horizon before disappearing. Then from out of the town several vehicles made an approach. Above them were four flying objects that turned out to be flying personnel. They made a musical sound as they came. When the entourage drew near it appeared that the cars were quite transparent, to the extent that their interiors and occupants could be clearly seen. They were shaped like two tiered limousines if such ever existed. Their surfaces were smooth and therefore reflected the array of colour from the surroundings. They made absolutely no sound and there were no fumes emitted from exhausts. They arched in a wide turn some of them cruising over wheat without causing any damage. They must have been powered like hovercraft! They then came to a standstill beside the ship. With a thump the four flying people landed alongside the cars and seemed to flick switches to turn off power. They were wearing head visors and when they were opened back, they looked like halos. The flyers were young and had friendly faces portraying white teeth and broad smiles.

Gull type doors opened in the limousines. They were like doors on a DeLorean sports car. The drivers all appeared mainly to be in their mid-twenties and were obviously of both genders. They appeared to also be of the same marshmallow texture that was now part of the visitors make up. They also were subtly coloured pale blue on one side of their faces pink on the other. Some were dark or black skinned but nevertheless the colour tinge was obvious. Despite all this peculiarity, the overall effect was one of beauty. However, on closer inspection, some had quite mature faces and the hair been coloured golden – this might have denoted age. They were dressed in completely contradictory gear, which seemed to indicate a strong element of freedom of choice. There was a girl in a long white dress whose styling was medieval. There was a fellow dressed in a bush shirt and shorts. Another was in combats and a tee shirt and one was in a one-piece flyer jump suit. One of the drivers was quite Islamic looking sporting a dark beard and moustache. The girls wore various hairstyles, ranging from ponytails to long flowing hair. One had a punk style orange coloured haircut and large hoop style earrings while another was dressed in a black linen suite that looked oriental! They were a very individualistic bunch and not quite what one would expect to find so close to the pearly gates. They slowly alighted from their vehicles and walked towards the ship. By now the visitors had gathered outside and were looking quite puzzled and a little shy.

The leader of the host part was a fellow resembled an old-fashioned gardener. He had a straw hat and denim dungarees. He stepped forward and extended his hand to one of the groups and smiled,

"I am Garcia, and this was about to be another historic moment. On behalf of the Son and of Spirinda, I would like to welcome you. You will have an opportunity of meeting them later. We had visitors once before like yourselves and we were sorry to see them depart. Bye the way you have already experienced an encounter with Spirinda when you entered the blue triangle."

Larry drew a breath; his heart was pounding, and he almost felt faint. Francisca gripped Larry's hand again so tight that it almost galvanised together. All at once there was the sound of trumpets from the city, as the significance of the moment had not gone unappreciated. Then they and the visitors began to mingle and carefully shake hands in warm-hearted friendship. There was no language barrier, and the conversation flowed. The flying people were introduced as Jet Packers, from the Angel tribe. They were all quite tall, one girl and three boys. On their back were white twin winged devices. They said that they were powered by sound waves ricocheted from one wing to the other and out the back. They wore pale green suits with arm patches with the word "Cherubim 71st." Someone asked were their saints in the group and were told, "Maybe" – no one is allowed know. One of the groups asked what the name of the city and he was told Purgosia. People turned and said to one another,

"Purgosia, did you hear that, and what is the name of the mountain and does it really move?"

The leader answered,

"Yes, The Olgas, as they move, they propel time and energy throughout existence."

When asked what the triangle was made of, he said 'skrauq,' but everything is alive! No one questioned further but the Captain wrote it down. Then he wrote it in reverse, and it made more sense. When asked if they had ever gone to the edge of the triangle, they said yes, often over the edge and back on the other side. This was performed frequently by Jet Packers doing repairs or who needed a clear view of the occult.

Garcia asked if everyone was now out of the ship. The skipper said no that there were a few who felt shy and unworthy. He asked the Captain's permission to enter the ship. This was agreed and several of them entered the ship and extended gestures of friendship to those within. Hamish, Hiroshi's non-friend, was so shaken by the experience that he clenched a fist and thumped the table. These were the group who could not reconcile to all that was going on and therefore had become more and more isolated as events unfolded. However, after encouragement they reluctantly emerged and joined the others.

Then the visitors were instructed to get into the vehicles and that there was room for twenty passengers in each. People climbed on board and as everything was transparent it was difficult to see the seats. There were small dots that seemed to float in the ether, but as it turned out were attached to the upper corners of the almost invisible seats, they acted as markers. Larry and Francisca sat up front beside the driver who was the girl in the long dress. She had the same spongy texture as Larry and the group, but her skin colour was distinctively blueish to one side and pinkish to the other. Larry thought it was somewhat like Hiroshi after the inversion. Gracefully, she glided into her perch, which was a seat turned sideways and from which she could look up or down or out of the vehicle at ease. On the dashboard the word "Drof/trillinium" was written and there was a tiny, illuminated screen close by on which she could control the vehicle using a device like a computer mouse. She pressed the mouse, the panel lit up to show a map. and with that they moved forward. As they did so a red arrow on the screen depicted vehicle's position. She then turned to the group and spoke, and it sounded to the group like English. Larry and Francisca reckoned that the language was originally Latin, but it was difficult to analyse. She said in a musical voice,

"I am Pepitra Palcevska, when I was a little girl it is recorded that I was sent here by a terrible earthquake. Of course, I do not remember anything, most people say that is how it is! There are some like Russell who is driving the vehicle behind us and he wished he had never been down where you come from. He suffered what you call acute pain before he was released, he never wants to go back; of course, he never will be asked. Some have been asked and I believe a few did!

The incredible truth was beginning to dawn on the visitors, these people had once lived on earth!

Then Pepitra turned and looked at Francisca and said with a smile,

"You are so beautiful, is he the lucky fellow?"

She turned her hazel eyes towards Larry,

"You both look like you have not had any real hardship in your world, I hope you never have, and that you will come here with ease."

Then she winked and turned to the group and pointed ahead. The city now came fully into view. Larry asked Pepitra if there were many accidents. She replied,

"No traffic sweep around each other like your physicist envisage occurring when monopoles collide."

As she spoke, she entered onto the main road where several mobiles touched and slid around each other like they were made of elastic. The occupants let out exclamations and then sighed when they realised all was well.

"This mobile is called a Drof and it is very reliable. It comes in any colour as long as it's transparent."

People knew she was kidding. They were now driving up an incline at the edge of the city. The Jet Packers had followed them and were landing close bye. The city was paved very firmly and without any eruptions like in the plains below. Curious people could be seen milling around while many were looking in their direction. There were strange sidewalks on which people were being propelled along. They were moving at quite a speed but evidently could alight at will. Every now and then a new person would step on and join the moving mass. Both sides of the sidewalks had ribbons of flickering lights that travelled in the same direction as it was going. It looked like a safe efficient way to get about town and also quite some fun. Larry had noticed some of the prominent names. There was Avenue de Chardin, Rue Pythagoras, Place d'Albert Einstein, Rue Nelson Mandela, Avenue Descartes, St Benedict's Pavilion, The Plato Memorial, and many others.

The City population looked young and carefree much like the transport drivers. Jet packs strolled about amongst them. Then Hiroshi spied children, the amazing thing was that they all looked to be about five years of age. Pepitre then explained that people were divided into distinct age categories. Those who came, as infants or embryos or very young children were all rounded up to five years of age but in compensation are given the fully developed intellect. Those who were older were advanced to eighteen, earth years equivalent. Everyone else became twenty-five and the very old become golden-haired and fifty.

"Howzat?" she then said, and everyone nodded in agreement.

The vehicles turned into the entrance forecourt of palatial building ornate with Greek style pillars like the Parthenon at Athens. Pepitra commented,

"You are now arriving at the Euclidian. It is a meeting place and a resting place for travellers. Enjoy your time here your visit is a landmark in history many are anxious to meet you. Oh! By the way, I should have told you things here are very comfortable most of the time but at night the temperature drops, and everyone gets cold. Then by midday, the temperature rises to become uncomfortable. Now the Jet Packers and Saints are not affected, but all others feel the discomfort. However, we must bear this in retribution for being here. You will just have to resign to it, as there is no escape. Adding or shedding cloths will make no difference. However, it is bearable, and the rest of the time here is quite blissful. Oh, but the way, she looked at Nadine, your Islam people will call this Barzakh."[8]

She drove through an opening like a carport. Inside was coated in large terra-cotta flag stoned and the walls around were amber coloured and acted as pallet for murals of magnificent fruit and flowers. Larry was impressed that in spite of this triangle being so rugged yet there was an appreciation of horticultural beauty. They were ushered into a reception area, from which they could look out through broad openings and see the Callisto parked on the plains beyond. Two curious children were in the Lobby. They were evidently intrigued with the visitors. Larry said hello and asked their names. They responded with, Lorette and Rico. They giggled and ran away but kept watching from afar. The ceiling of the Euclidian lobby was very interesting because it had a mural that spread out across a great expanse. Richard pointed it out to Hiroshi, who looked in amazement. It was a Mandala, down to the last detail. However, there

8   Barzakh – The Muslim people believe that all souls go to a patrician or state where they dwell till judgment. In this state even the just will receive some torment because of small offences in the past.

was a second part to it that they had not yet seen. It seemed to show an even greater world beyond. There were three people, one in each segment, while the fourth segment had a geometrical version of the triangular configuration. In the lower corner it said,

"Divine Geometry beckoning us on our weary way By G Kuhn and O Kwang."

Richard grabbed Larry by the arm and pointed to the inscription.

"Would you believe, Old George Kuhn?"

Larry responded, "By golly, he must be up here somewhere, we must be well into the future!"

Behind the Front Desk there were two monitors that gave continuous statistics. One was one called the "Praydaq Daily" and another "Prague Value". Larry was intrigued, but before he could ask Hiroshi interrupted saying,

"Larry, it's your turn next".

Larry stepped forward to sign for his room. Within moments, they were dispersed to their rooms on the various floors. It worked like this; the corridors moved just like the city sidewalks. One only had to step on and state your name, immediately the guest is whisked to their bedroom door. The more curious aspect was that though the rooms appeared to be on the same level in fact they were spread out over seven floors. Everyone was fascinated by the phenomena. Larry, who was on the fifth floor, went in and out of his room trying to discover the split second he and his room were whisked upwards, but there was just no way of finding an answer. It was like trying to open the household refrigerator so fast that the light has not yet turned on! The basis of an explanation was forthcoming, when later Larry was told that each floor transformed into another as they are quark based and quarks can do that regularly. Also, that time did not tick with one event following the other but occurred across a broad front and did not have to pass and could be sustained. Furthermore, events up here can occur simultaneously in the same place without upsetting each other!

Naturally, everyone had a room to themselves but there was a booking mistake made, because the two Captains Dave and Laura were delivered to the same room. Red faced they explained that "Captain" was not their name and they needed separate rooms. Richard said later that they were being tested; had this been Bangkok they might have said nothing. Everyone doubled up with laughter at the thought.

Larry found his room to be quite basic that is, it had a bed and a view. There was nothing else except four objects a computer type screen that almost filled one side of the room and a freshwater dispenser a table with something upon it and a normal type of bed.

There was not any bathroom because neither he nor anyone else had needed such ever since the inversion. On the table there was an envelope and beside it a curious transparent box. Inside the box there was continuous changing aspect of nature. For a while there was a waterfall, then it changed into an ocean then a forest and then curiously it depicted a strange world that Larry did not understand. Larry read the note and it was from the Euclidian,

"Dear Mr Coughlin, you are invited to a reception at 17.00 hrs. Please meet in the Lobby – optional attire. Zahira Ronge Ji (General Manager Euclidan Inns)."

Larry immediately went to the computer and extended his to press a button. However, before he could do so the screen sprung to life. A voice spoke from it and asked, "May I help you?"

Larry said, "Yes I would like to speak to a guest – Francisca Spazola."

With that there was a musical sound and a few moments later Francisca appeared on the screen.

"Oh Larry, you've cut in on me, I was surfing Purgosia, for shops and boutiques. Pepita's sister Agnieszka is here with me showing how to work the system."

Francisca turned and gestured to Agnieszka. Standing behind her was a girl who was very pretty. She had plum coloured hair and a tanned face. Her eyes were greenish and like pools of light. She smiled and said hello in a Latvian accent.

Larry said, "Nice meeting you Agnieszka, I hope Francisca has money! Did you get an invitation to the hotel reception?"

"Yes Larry, no money, but what do you think I have! I have a Euclidian charge card that was in my visitor pack. We are going to browse the stores of Purgosia and I am going to make a purchase or two."

"No, you can't do that. That's not right" – said Larry.

Francisca replied amidst kinks of laughter,

"Never mind, us girls are going to be busy for the next two hours, and by the way Larry, will you come then and collect me at five, I don't want to go down alone."

Larry nodded enthusiastically and signed off in disbelief. Then he checked with the front desk about the charge cards and was told that they were issued only to female guests. He had no further questions.

Gathering Of The Clans

As planned, Larry collected Francisca from her room. She was wearing an eloquent maroon gown. It had been delivered to the Hotel moments after she had placed the order in the shop. Larry was continually in awe. They went to the lobby where some of the group had already gathered. At the appointed time, several vehicles turned into the Euclidian entrance and a large group of people alighted. As the entered the Lobby, Francisca let out a gasp and squealed,

"I cannot believe what I see, Mamma, Papa, Dana, Loraine, Carlos!"

She ran straight into the arms of the approaching figures. She hugged and kissed them and asked them over and over how they got here. Then she tugged Larry over and introduced him. Then they moved away to one side of the lobby and seated themselves. They looked overjoyed yet bewildered. Larry realised that this is what being in the Future really means. It means meeting people who have already passed away. But it was not clear why the crew of the Callisto were not there meeting themselves; perhaps it is because they had gone into the future but had not yet died. Larry watched the goings on with fascination and then suddenly his eyes focused on familiar faces. They were his very own family!

"Is that you Larry? By God it-izz!"

There in front of him were, Maria his Mother, Dan his Father, Jill, and Amy with a fellow holding her hand. Larry was spell bound. He could not move. He felt faint, and then everything went strange. He felt himself falling over and being caught by strong arms. He had no control over his being, he was not unconscious, and such in this world did not exist, but he was the next best thing to being unconscious. Then he slowly came around. He was looking in the blue eyes of his mother. Her very young face beamed down at him with unconditional love and affection, like he had not experienced since he left home. Beside her with tears in his eyes was Dan. The family then introduced Zachary who was Amy's husband back in the 'auld sod'. He was a very friendly fellow and had become one of the families over the years. They drew aside and settled on some seats away from the crowned to talk and reminisce. Then there was an interruption. It was Heroshi, "Jill, Jill, I cannot believe it is you!" Jill jumped to her feet and rushed to embrace Heroshi. "Oh, I too cannot believe you are here." With that Heroshi took her arm and steered her away to the side of the room. Now as they were both overcome with excitement it became easy for Heroshi to blurt out,"

"Jill, I thought I would never see you again and this time I'm not going to let you go, Jill, will you marry me, I will get you a ring soon, but for now just say yes, please say yes."

Jill was crying with joy and in a gurgling voice said, "Yes my dear Heroshi, yes, yes, yes but can we do that up here will be allowed?" "That's not a worry, I'm sure we can fix it with the city or even the ships Captain."

By now the Lobby was awash with family meetings, as more and more of the group assembled. Larry noticed in the distance a beautiful Italian looking girl arrive. She was in the company of three young people who must have been her children. Richard sprang to his feet and rushed across the room and gathered them in his arms. This was Pat his wife and children without a doubt, and Larry hoped that Richard would bear the shock. Richard had been very emotional on the Callisto, and from what Larry could observe he must now be in bits! The Group was then invited to step into the reception room by several of the Euclidian personnel. Doors were rolled back to reveal what looked like a bar and a banquet room. The whole ships company with their loved ones began the celebration. To begin with, there were glasses of wine presented by polite young people dressed in light weight uniforms of material that alternated colour from black to white depending on the reflection of the light. They looked ever so crisp and stood out in the crowd. There were delicious juices and many varieties of wine, ranging from white to amber to pink then blue and various shades of red.

To Larry they tasted like non-alcoholic Alpine 'Trauben-saft' non-alcoholic wine. However, it was not long before the ship's cook and Ernst the engineer had bets on to see how many colours each other could drink. As for the eats, as an appetiser there were platters of very light toasted white uneven bread that was designated for the Callisto group only. It was made from the wheat of Purgosia and the servers told them that it was the bread of life that would sustain them on their travels. There was also a light white substance called manna, and this was another form of bread. Then there was an announcement by Mr Zhu, who was Chinese and one of the directors of the Euclidian. He introduced a guest of honour, the City mayor, and several others. The mayor was an attractive African woman who said she was honoured to be here at such an historic occasion and praised God for his goodness. Larry then got his family aside to have a serious discussion. Larry took up the conversations where he had left off,

BON APPETITE

"Now Mom and Dad, I told you how we got here, and that we will have to leave before we return. This is because we are still in corporality, and that violates the rules of this divine world. An exception has been made but it will only last for a short duration before we must go, just like Cinderella at the ball. If it were not for our body's inversion, we would not have survived and then would stay here indefinitely."

His dad responded,

"Larry are all your group in the same condition, I heard that at least one was killed or injured."

The statement startled Larry, his mind raced, who could that be? Then like a bolt a memory flooded his mind he thought about Hiroshi, and his cry of pain at the moment of inversion. Then he remembered Hiroshi's strange facial colour that seemed now to be permanent. His heart missed a beat. He spoke in a broken voice,

"Dad that might be correct, I'll have to do some checking. Now common you guys tell me about yourselves, and how you got here?"

Meanwhile Heroshi was delighted because he found his parents. Not only was this a great occasion but it was to become greater when Heroshi introduced Jill as his future wife. The Akarie's were a serene group of people. Their lives as a fishing family had made them physically strong and open, and friendly by nature. There was Hiroshi's sister Shohko and his little brother Jinkichi and Nasko his mother. As they strolled into the dining room Larry looked out one of the windows. A large throng had gathered outside hoping to glimpse what was happening within. Larry then realised that unlike the experiences of the blue triangle he now had an appetite. A small orchestra played soft music which included harps.

There was no secret that the food had been imported, as this three-sided island did not produce such products. One strange aspect of the dining was that food is for gratification only. It literally refreshed you but dissolves in one's mouth.

On the menu, there was soup like Gazpacho in a dish chilled on dry ice with an accompaniment called quark cakes. They were like garlic bread on the outside but with a colourful cake texture on the inside. The spread for these tasted like lobster butter.

There was a sorbet of blue water ice and to follow there was magnificent pink fish rather like salmon. It was presented on a triangular plate made of quartz that had been coated in a film of clear ceramic glaze. The slice of salmon was sitting on a bed of blue spinach and topped with lime-flavoured butter.

As an accompaniment there were rose petals of various colours served as a salad or as a hot vegetable substitute for those who did not eat the salmon. There was also a potato type dish that had a sort of hickory perfume like pine smoke.

With all this there was an amazing white wine. It was called "Au bord de Sangrias 80" and was chilled and said to be of grapes and pomes stone. Though this was true, and its aroma was of the hills, nevertheless it tasted like a chardonnay.

After enjoying the meal Maria sat back in her chair and said,

"That was excellent, the food literally melts in your mouth. Your dad and I have always wanted to dine here but never had the opportunity!"

The dessert consisted of ruby coloured berries on dry ice and steeped in a liquid that tasted like white port. There was a hot brew like coffee but was called Dankus and was made from dried broad beans and cinnamon. Lastly there were petite fours baked on rice paper. In their centres there was every flavour imaginable. Some were almond others, angelica, another cinnamon, and many with unfamiliar flavours.

Maria then asked,

"How do you visitors find eating our disappearing food?"

Larry responded, "Mom it is delicious, that salmon was tops but not as good as yours used to be!"

Maria laughed and said,

"That's because mine was the salmon of knowledge."

When the dinner was over, it was arranged that everyone could meet in the morning as there would be an outing to the Olgas mountains. The group then retired to an adjoining room where there was a quartet who played music and seemed to know every ethnic song ever composed. Someone appropriately, sang the 'Auld Triangle and some of the crowd joined the chorus. Then in the wee' hours people retired to rest. Larry said good night to Fancisca and added in that he will call her as soon as he gets to his room. When he got there, he immediately waved his hand across the front of the screen saying to the computer, "Compo, Compo on the wall, find me the finest girl of all!"

He was kidding, but the computer buzzed into life and right as requested Francisca appeared on screen. They both laughed and chatted about the evening, but gradually got cold. However, they had to accept it as the price to be paid for their condition. It was dark outside but there was a red glow coming in the window and filling their rooms, creating a deceivingly snug atmosphere. It was a nice setting and despite the chill they both drifted into their slumbers.

TOUR DE GRACE

Larry and quite a few of the group were taken on the sightseeing tour of the Olgas and Sangria Mountains. The trip was for all visitors and crew, yet some of the group chose to stay behind and that included Hamish and his cronies. A tour guide, whose name was Luka, escorted them. He looked like a man of deep integrity and experience. He greeted them as if he knew them all his life. There were three Limousines. Agnieszka, Pepitra and Garcia were driving each. The trip preceded south westerly along Spazinski Avenue, one of the main thoroughfares. The traffic was varied and consisted of vehicles like their own, or larger, but there were quite a few Angel Brigade transporters. There were also smaller individually manned vehicles, and some were on bikes of various description.

Larry looked at Francisca and said,

"With all the entertainment last night I forgot to ask you about when you went shopping. Did you notice what did other people use for money?"

"Yes Larry," Agnieszka butted in. "They were using Praque; it is a form of currency based on prayer volume and national expansion. In some cases, people use cards that are funded by the success of trade in the stratum." Larry remembered the Praque report in the hotel lobby. She then said that they would learn about it later. Then suddenly Francisca pointed to an elegant looking Boutique and exclaimed,

"Look Larry, that is where I got my gear."

Larry looked at her in dismay. He had not observed what she was wearing. She glared back at him and said, "Larry did you not notice?"

She leaned forward showing her blouse collar had a label that said 'Klaus' in tiny letters. Larry forced a guilty smile said it was nice and waited for response.

She looked relieved.

"Did you buy anything else?"

She rapidly raised her slim foot for Larry to see,

"Yes, these shoes, they can alter texture like the chameleon depending on what I'm wearing."

Larry leaned back in his seat, grinned in admiration. The city had all the trappings of an earth City, an Opera House, several Museums, and a Concert Hall. They drove past a Basilica with a Spanish tile roof, surrounded with tall waving cypress trees. He noticed that architecturally there was a feeling of openness. He then realised it was because all the building were stepped back several meters from the sidewalk but also that each floor was set back from the one below, with the top floor being the smallest. This encouraged plants to flourish on the balconies. This building technique enable bright heavenly light to get down to street level without interruption. When outside the city they passed large road signs and the road widened and turned upwards. It was like an airport runaway. From there on all the traffic became airborne. The driver explained that there are no roads outside the city just route wires in the ground. All Transport have radar connectors to whatever route required. We are now routed for the Olgas.

As they travelled, the ever-continuous background sound of thumping had gotten louder. One interesting feature was that the draft from the blue triangle could be seen filtering across the territory. It caused disturbance that resulted in swirling surface patches that erupted with every colour in the rainbow. It also became apparent that there was an absence of animal life. There was an explanation for this that would later come to fore. Perhaps there is the funny example of Kiki the canary's disappearance. Then as they reached the very high ground, the peaks were capped in pink snow like substance that glowed against the ebony sky. Now for the first time the extremity of the void and the new hemisphere came into view. They could see the heavens above and witnessed a peculiarity they had seen earlier. It took the form of an "X" of monolithic proportions, spreading to the four corners of a vault which in turn encased everything and also the void with its in-built hostility. Like a rose line it divided whatever was behind the vault into three segments. In its centre and directly in line with the point of the triangle the golden torus began its great curve. It looked just like Kuhn's mural on the ceiling in the Euclidean.

L'ARC DE TRIUMPH

They then arrived at the pinnacle of the volcano. The limousine cruised in towards a landing area and gently settled down. There were notices of caution and a safety fence and an entrance to the caverns. The drivers said to wait in their seats. And then said,

"Look one side of this flux resembles Niagara Falls in reverse, all the material going upwards instead of down, but returning through an alternative opening, after completing its fantastic round trip. You have arrived at the fountain of life where one granule of its substance takes three times less than a 'Plank moment' to journey to the universe and back. This is the geezer of reality, the 'be all and the end all of everything.'"

Manz exclaimed that the flux might be a combination of string theory and a Quantum effect over lying an electromagnetic field. People nodded in acknowledgement but not necessary agreement. Luka said that this phenomenon has existed from the beginning of time and that it is time itself, and that it dictates time and "time flies". It is from here that life is delivered to the universe. If one wanted to return to the universe, theoretically all they would have to do is jump into this spray and it would carry them into the matrix of existence. On the way down, they would become potential matter and in an instant their logos would become implanted in some one's embryo. Your reality is balanced on the knife-edge but just a little to one side. Luka then cautioned that they were the only living humans that exist outside the flux temporary though it be. Everyone agreed. Luca added that the cave is called Chasms of Yahweh.

Each driver re-positioned the red arrow on the drive-com screen. Within what seemed like seconds they were whisked downward and through a side entrance on the south side of the mountain. Nearby, Flying Craft could be seen entering and leaving an opening in the cliff face on the south western side. Larry wondered why? They finally parked and all alighted. The sound of thumping was now so overpowering, that they were issued with the devices like the Jet Packers had worn – named sound halos. They fitted on one's shoulders and sat up behind the head. There were control buttons on the collar and by pressing them the sound could be minimised, but it made the wearer look like a trainee saint! They entered the interior of the volcano and found it was like a gigantic cathedral. It had dazzling lights emitting from the walls and floor, thus creating festive atmosphere. The area appeared as large as Lower Manhattan and the vents from the volcano were as high as the top of a skyscraper. The incoming silver arch entered on a bleu tinted entrance and smacking into the nearest of two sub terrarium lakes to re-emerge in the next lake and rocket upwards through the red tinted opening. The lakes were churned from the impact but at the sides it was crystal clear with sandy bottom. There was a sign that said, "Lower Lough Derg," Patrick's Purgosia" Periodically young people, would run in and out of the water evidently enjoying the experience. Luka said that it was quite dangerous as there were tunnels connecting the two lakes. The incoming deluge travelled through this tunnel before rising in the other lake. Some time ago a child was swept away and became born in the universe quite by accident. He had to live a life all over again, what a drag! There were several cascades of liquid flowing into pools by the side of the lakes. To everyone's amazement it turned out to be the very same wine that they had sampled in the Euclidian. Luka then said to the group,

"The triangle generates only two products, wheat and wine, exported all forms of quark like particles and it passes on the logos of life from the Spinal Logo optic canal. I will show you very soon."

Richard popped a question, "Does the triangle get anything in return for the exports?"

Luka looked at him with wide eyes. He slowly stroked his chin and smiled, "Yes, Richard, people!"

When they returned to the city having seen the interior of the mountain, Hiroshi was waiting for them with an anxious look on his pink and blue face. He gathered some of them together took a deep breath and said,

"It is with great sadness that I can answer the question asked. The City hospital confirmed today that I was killed at the moment of impact when we entered the blue triangle."

There was an outburst around the room, Francisca groaned and immediately went and put her arms around Jill. Larry drew a deep breath; his worst fears had been realised.

Heroshi added,

"I was killed with the impact when we hit the membrane in the tunnel. As we had inverted my state was not noticed."

When the gathering was over Larry and Richard stayed back to talk to Hiroshi in private.

Larry asked,

"Hiroshi, when we go back, we will plan to return through the tunnel. Then we will shrink at enormous speed and hopefully fall backwards in time to where we were before trouble began. We must request that it is timed so this can be done. We must insist! If the city permits, then you may be brought back in time to just before the accident occurred. At that point we would not have met the gravitational waves. It will be like we never entered the tunnel in the first place."

"No", Hiroshi said,

"If I stay here, I will not be going back in time with you and when you are back down, I will just not be there."

Larry objected,

"Then we will have to report you as a missing person and Jill will be told. That will make her life a misery."

Hiroshi looked from side to side and said,

"Can we be sure that I won't end up in some time warp by accident?"

Larry said that they would try and get some assurances from the City fathers and come back to him. As further discussion would not be of help, both Larry and Richard left the room to see Dave about the matter. Also, about the intended wedding.

With permission from the city Fathers and despite Heroshi's death, both he and Jill were married in the Euclidian. The families gathered and the occasion was filled emotion. However, as it turned out legislation in Pergosia is lightning quick. Permission was granted on the grounds that it had been a flaw in system that had permitted their entry to the triangles in the first place. Then with the permission Heroshi and Jill were married by Father Travis and a local Buddhist Priest.in the Churtorium nearby. This was an open-air church that was nondenominational. When word got out there was celebrations in the city and at the time of the event a very large crown gathered. The close relatives took seats at the front and nearest to the alter and the occasion was filled emotion yet at the same time it was a happy event. When the ceremony was over bells again sounded in the city and the families returned to the Euclidean for the official wedding meal. This time the meal was just once course, very simple and light. After that the couple were given overnight accommodation close to a well knowm lake Mutnauq and were collected and returned to the hotel that following day.

SHANGRILA

During that interlude Larry brought some friends to visit his parent's home. As it turned out their home was in the south west and close to the same, lake. As anticipated, they became airborne and descended when the driver identified the correct colony of homes, The Coughlin's house was on a hill that looked inwards towards a lake that was in the lower southern regions of the Sangrias. The house was one of ten standard designs that were common in the region. It resembled a very large igloo because of its white dome. Dan and Maria greeted them as they touched down on some gravel. The interior that was quite minimalist. The bedrooms around the parameter, and they too had open arches. Catering was almost non-existent; pluming was not required. There were tables and chairs of art deco design and there were musical instruments everywhere, a Celtic harp, a set of bagpipes a flute, and a recorder. There were many oil paintings hanging on the walls some of dramatic triangle scenery of eruptions, storms and an aura boor ails shrouding a phosphorus ocean. However, there was one that was painted in familiar earth tones. It was a picture of their beloved Tramahon Bay the place where Larry had surfed. Marie had produced it from memory. It was far from being accurate, the proportions were wrong, they were warped and indefinite, rather like that of an impressionist. She assured Larry that the style was not her intension it was just because she had no reference. Larry sketched it out for her and thought it was extraordinary how much she had forgotten. They also had several pictures painted by Monet, Renoir, Turner, and many others. Maria said she got them from people in Purgosia, so she hoped they were originals artists, she was told that they were!

Dan showed Larry some data he had collected for Maria from the Kino graph. He had files with a picture of Monet's garden at Argenteuil (1872), showing a child with a hoop standing in front of Monet's home. There was a well-known Constable painting (1821) showing the Hay Wain crossing a ford. Then there was a Sisley (1897), Lady's Cove, a costal scene of a rocky promontory at Langland Bay. There were many more pictures and lots more on file.

Larry asked Maria how she and Dan had become reunited. She said that he was waiting for her when she arrived in Purgosia. She was grateful to the Grand Central authorities, as they had advised Dan of her immanent arrival.

Up to now, there was no marriage and people were quite happy to live alone or share with their earth mates or spouses or take the opportunity for a break. As there is no reproduction to do so is no threats to people's lives.

Night had now set in and so Maria asked everyone to come to the rear patio window. She flicked a switch on a tiny machine that looked like a camera on a pod, and "hoop la" the back yard transformed into a holograph of already mentioned Monet's garden at Giverny just like one of her paintings. People looked in awe. She then asked the guests to follow her into the garden. She led them through a huge Nymphaea's Studio filled with potted plants and an old straw hat. Then out into blazing sunshine like earth on a bright summer's day. They were walking into an exciting simulation so real that that the flowers had a scent.

There were archways of climbing plants entwined around brilliantly coloured shrubs. To make matters more authentic, there was a water garden that had a magnificent willow pattern style bridge that led to a mass of wisterias and azaleas. Richard dipped his hand in the water and remarked even the water was wet and cold. Lots of questions were fired at Maria. She answered that it is called an Envirolator or Gardex and they can be procured at Bellingham's on Fifth Avenue for twenty-three praque fifty. She began to relate some of the peculiarities of the mirage. She said once she had cut flowers and shrubs, but when the holograph was turned off, they just disappeared. She pointed out that even as they walked along the gravel path for example moved and they reached the end in a few steps. In effect they could traverse the whole garden in several steps where on earth it might take ten minutes. Then she pressed a sound control and the garden filled with the sound of birds singing and the scent of freshly mowed grass. Larry asked would all this disturb the neighbours and was told that it was only short wavelength and could not be seen or heard even from next-door. They came back into the house and gathered on the porch looking out at the view of the mountains and lake.

Larry's dad then said, "Can anyone guess what Mutnauq means?"

"Well, my dear, it means Quantum, Lake Quantum, backwards."

Richard picked up the buzzword and began to listen.

"At certain times, the lake becomes rough. When this happens, the waves can become particles. It all depends on the amount of activity or stress there is on the arch system. When this happens, it is a most eerie experience. One minute you are swimming in water and the next you are swimming in tapioca. There is no danger, but it gives you a fright and if out of your depth you would have to wait till it changed form. Drowning doesn't happen here."

However, he said, "There is another phenomenon, and that is reverse standing waves can also occur and they are also related to cosmic stress." Just then as if by coincidence the tranquillity of the lake was broken, and it began to move. The bright blue liquid suddenly began to produce sets of tiny waves which soon grew larger. These were no ordinary waves because they were generated from the surrounding land by vibrations from the Chasms and travelled towards the centre of the lake. Dan continued,

"These are advanced waves something unknown on earth. (Advanced waves are only known on earth through James Clerk Maxwell's equations on the quantum behaviour of wave time asymmetry.) These waves were very different from earth waves as they were generated from the shore and moved inwards towards the centre where they collided in a chaotic eruption. Then just seconds before the next sets arrived, they dissipate. Wind from the caves on the east side of the lake sweeps some waves into feathering plumes and others into storm rollers. It depended on whether the waves are moving towards, sideways or away from the direction of the caves.".

He thought that if he were a lucky surfer, he could ride a full circle experiencing every shape of wave and ending up in the middle with the fun of being pitched up in the plume.

12

From Here To Eternity

With fun and relaxation over the team checked out of the hotel. They were grateful that there were bills except for one. That was where Hamish and Raphael bought clothing downtown and charged to the Euclidian. This had to paid for but the mortals had no praque so it was transacted by a gift from the Captain donating a picture of the crew smiling before leaving on the mission. Also, some of the clothes had not been worn and were returned. Then the crew gathered in the Calisto. Heroshi and Jill would not be going on the next leg of the journey, but Heroshi would join the Calisto on it return. A few of the younger members of the crew had gathered sweethearts held tightly. This thought Larry is going to be a very sad departure. Then Captains Dave and Laura outlined the group's next intended destination. They pointed upwards towards the misty zone where the seams of the void appeared to come together. Dave displayed a blown-up navigation chart based on Hiroshi's Mandala and Kuhn's mural. The reason for this was because there were no charts in Purgosia. No one travelled upwards any distance without using the tunnels in the Chasms of Yahweh, but this was out of bounds for the visitors. Therefore, City management said they must travel straight up through the void and follow the Logo Optic, tunnels from the outside. Even from Purgosia the path could be seen travelling up the spine of the triangle and trailing to the Omega point just like the North Star as seen from earth. Once they cleared the red triangle their journey would touch on the void and this is where trouble can ensue.

There had been a delay because of a disturbing report that while they were away there had been an accident, and the Callisto had been damaged. Some of the more unsociable crew had attempted to steal the ship. It seems Hamish and Raphael had been the culprits, and in their haste to depart they had caused damage to the delicate motor system. The event had also been observed by the intelligence of the all-seeing triangle which in turn had sounded the alarm. The triangle exerted enormous energy at that time and Larry reckoned that was what caused the storm on Lake Mutnauq. The offenders were then retained in the Callisto for questioning by the ship's officers. Though the ship has been damaged no repairs could be carried out till the Captain received a damage report from Ernst and his team. When the report was received it highlighted the dangers posed by a return trip and re-inversion because the ship's laser gravity-system and rear thrusters were now out of order.

Looking over the engineering report, Dave and Ernst read that on a serious note, the oxygen pumps, needed for the return journey, had also been damaged as well as some of the asbestos plates that formed the outer skin when they tried to force entrance. A few of the town's engineers were sent to assist the visitors but they were not used to the nuts and bolts of earthly mechanics and therefore acted as advisors. Activity began immediately, but it was Ernst and his engineers that finally did the job. While they worked some of the city folk gathered to watch the mortals' toil, a task long forgotten. Eventually the repairs were concluded in a makeshift manner using various pieces of material from other parts of the ship. This was necessary, as the towns engineers advised that any inverted substance of the triangles could not be guaranteed to revert when the ship returned to the universe. Ernst then reported to the Captain that the job was done, but that there was still only a 50% chance of a successful re-entry.

The Captain and officers formed a council, met the hijackers and their representatives. After some deliberation it was decided that the events had been so demanding on the mind and so taxing on the metabolism of individuals, that the laws governing behaviour could not legally be upheld if tested when they return. As a result of this event the Captain ordered that an emergency "pre-inversion code of conduct" be drafted with a view to implementation. This should consider the good of the ship and that it is a sole ambassador of the human race faced with exceptional circumstances. It would also have to encapsulate the moral values and attitudes of the nations from whence they were dispatched. The laws would impose disciplinary action to be taken in the event of any of several offences. These included, hijacking or the causing of deliberate damage to ship or persons on board, or to any of the populations with whom they might visit. The rules were lengthy and finished with a note of caution. It stated that because of the telepathic powers endowed on the host nation it is inadvisable to fantasise or entertain any thoughts that could be construed as being immoral or aggressive. Crew should concentrate on their immediate activities and all strategic discussions are only to take place in structured meetings. It was recognised that all records of offences might become erased as this ship returned through time, therefore any penalties had to be imposed immediate. The penalty for continued breech of the code would include being locked in the ships hold to be released on return. In the case of attempted murder or sabotage one could be simply ejected from the ship in the void and face the consequences.

THE NAVIGATOR

Finally, on the same day and with the ship temporary fixed the departure time arrived. People had been permitted to enter the ship and many said it brought back memories to them. Amongst the crowds were young children and that Lorette and Rico. Then as departure time was nearing the crew announced that everyone should leave the ship immediately. Just then a rather official automobile with a pennant made its way down from the town and headed for the Callisto. The crowd drew back to make way and the transparent vehicle stopped beside the open door. Out from within jumped several military type people. Two of them were familiar Jet Packers, and another was a female in a business type suit but the fourth was a rather odd character. He was a tall fellow with a broad grin and a twinkle in his eye. He sported a bushy beard and wore the cloths of an ancient mariner – this was confirmed by a bundle of charts that he carried in his arms. Around his head was a red bandana that gripped his flowing hair keeping it in some order. Dave the Captain greeted them. The female introduced herself as Zelda Tallings from City Management. Dave remembered seeing her at the welcome function in the Euclidian. Zelda said that she needed a private word. Dave brought her into his conference room and summoned Laura Bingley and offered a seat. Dave introduced his vice-captain to Zelda, who smiled and made a gesture towards the tall man and introduced him,

"This is Paulo originally from Galilee, and when here, he is the official navigator. He keeps sailing boats on Lake Mutnauq and runs a sailing school. You see up to now you have been conveyed everywhere close to land. Now for the first time you will fly in the void and that is sometimes like an angry sea, the sort that only Paulo can navigate."

Dave raised his eyebrows and looked at Paulo who just smiled back, and so Zelda continued,

"Trans-voidular navigation is a tricky business. A wrong move could allow chaos to escalate into vibrational destruction. Also, there is Diva and Thormentus and Zatienne are seen as pirates and are the cause of all our difficulties? You may have observed their antics on you journey here. They are constantly directing trouble in the direction of the universe. Basically, they are enemies of our state and if they choose to become more aggressive one could be in big trouble. Lastly the approach to the entrance that is the omega is perilous and because of all this you will need Paulo, I promise that."

Laura spoke up immediately looking at Dave as she spoke and taking encouragement from his slow nodding in agreement,

"Ms Tallings we will be indebted to you with this offer is Paulo prepared for an early departure, say in half an hour or so?"

Paulo said in a melodious voice,

"As soon as you familiarise me with your navigation system and let me talk you people through some basic rules, I will be ready to depart."

Zelda shook hands with the team and left with the Jet Packers.

Dave called for the navigators and flight team to assemble at the EM/SPEC. Paulo in the meantime was shown over the ship and by the time he returned the group had gathered.

He was shown the Electro Magnetic Spectrum in a fully turned-on position. He saw how it analysed the components in the surrounding fields, how it gave scientific readings and how by diagnostic imaging it could peer in any direction. Then it was Paulo's turn to talk,

"Captain and crew, you have a fine ship here but some of the equipment is obsolete, yet some will be of use. Now your electromagnetic table will be ideal for our purposes and I will tell you why."

Everyone strained to hear. Outside the ship Mexican music was being played and there was loud laughter. He spoke in a steady voice but with the turn of phrase of a sea faring man,

"Me hearties this is what your EM/SPEC will record for us. I'll have ye' know, the void is divided into Latitude and Longitude just like the great oceans of yer' world. I know from sailing in the Aegean Sea and indeed along the coast of Italy and Greece. There I have met storms, but they are nothing' compared to what can blow up in this here void. You met Gravitational waves when you entered this domain, but in the void, you could meet Anti-Gravitational Chaotic Waves. These are the opposite to what you experienced only instead of waves they are shear troughs that are so deep that one might never immerge but vaporise in body and spirit. Now this does not mean death for us as that's impossibility, but it does cause immense inconvenience as one must wait for quite some time to reform. For you lot, however, it would be fatal! This is the sort of backdrop in which your world is dipped and could not survive if it were not for the benevolence of the two triangles and the first force. Until we reach the exterior of the void anything can happen. So, in a nutshell, the void is divided in the old familiar 380- degree circle, thus navigation could be similar that is if we were to hug the perimeter. However, we are not going to do that because we are in the interior where those co-ordinates do not work. We are positioned roughly in the internal central zone at 60 degrees latitude and north zero longitude, which is the polar line through the middle of the sphere. The Logo-optic channel that connects with the omega also matches this polar line. However, it is very flexible and shifts position depending on ebb and flow. However, all this can be combated as I have up to the minute charts that show the danger areas but only, I can read them that are one of the reasons why you need me. Any questions?"

He smiled and raised his shaggy eyebrows. Lionel piped up, "Paulo where did you get your Captain Blue Beard phrases?"

Paulo responded promptly, "From Blue beard who else he lives up here!"

Lionel laughed and then Ernst asked, if the oxygen system will be needed up in the next strata?

"No need," Paulo answered. Dave asked where there would be any other traffic travelling on the same route? To which Paulo replied laughing as he did so,

"I'm glad you asked about that. No, nothing can leave the local atmosphere that is it must cling to the proximity of the triangles. The main shipping lane between the dynasties is in the Logo optic canal that you may have seen in the Chasms. It conveys everything from small angel carriers to large transporters and even some template cruisers on rare occasions. The Template cruisers are used to enlarge our psychological territories up above. They usually are absorbed in outreach duties hacking away at frozen nothingness and filling its place with spirit. Mind you when they return their crews have some great tales to tell. The void is hostile as you now know. If it were not for the Master, Son and Spirinda even creation would not exist. There are also pedestrians, people travelling up or back are what you call saints and have duties in both strata and they also use the optical tunnel system."

Lionel then asked a final question, "Paulo are we vulnerable to the weapons that Thormentus uses?"

Paulo looked thoughtful and then answered in a slow voice,

"Never thought much about that, as I'm a bit out of touch living most of the time back in Mutnauq. In the last great conflict, they used brimstone, but I did hear that they developed a weapon recently that left some Jet Packers incapacitated. "Neg. troughs" are our immediate problem, I'll tell you about them later, you know there could be trouble ahead. However, they are not empowered to kill anyone. If they hit, you with fire you will be incapacitated for several earth hours or knocked into the void and lost for a long time.!"

There were no further questions and the team got down to plotting their route.

Luka their guide, came to the door of the Callisto and wished the group God speed. Then as he walked back into the crowd that had gathered. Larry noticed for the first time that Luka seemed to wear his sound disc, which gave the impression of a halo. He turned Francisca and with wide eyes asked, "Is Luka the Italian for Luke?"

Francisca said, "Yes, you - yoyo?" And giggled.

Then at a given command the doors were closed; names were checked off and people went to their posts awaiting instructions. After what seemed like five minutes, there was sound of slow thumping. It grew louder and was accompanied with the scent of roses, and incense. Outside it seemed that no one had heard the sound and that it was only being directed at the visitors within the ship. This time no one was flustered but felt calm and resigned. Then this time, a male voice spoke on the intercom, "No doubt you have wondered if this land really lives. Well, it does, and it is me. I exist at many levels. It has been great having you with us and to welcome you on the next stage of your journey. Has anyone any questions?"

Dr Manz spoke up in a shaky voice,

"My Lord, is there any truth in the rumour that we have only a limited life span up here and will have to leave soon or face desolation?"

The voice replied, "Yes that is true. If we had not requested one exception, you would have already been evicted. Every moment you spend here is because of our benevolent intervention on your behalf. Therefore, as our guests you may stay till your legitimate curiosity is satisfied! For your added security you will be issued with wrist dials that will indicate when your time is running out but there is flexibility. If there are no other questions, then let the journey begin!"

NEG. TROUGHS

There was a cheer from the crowd outside, good-bye kisses and waving of arms. Then without using engine power the ship rose high in the ether and began to glide forward, gathering speed as it went. Larry looked down and was fascinated to see Purgosia and its vibrant population shrink into distance. In moments, the Sangrias were just red marks on the landscape behind them and below was the line of the central spinal section with the logo optic channel stretching up from the triangle's apex. It was like another umbilical greater than the last and connecting the mid wives of creation with what lies above. It was their navigational reference.

As this Logo optic channel wound its way upward it took on a dazzling array of fractal like colours. Its outer rim was like a million Mandelbrot's, whereas its inner regions were pulsating with every conceivable colour imaginable. Objects could be seen moving both ways perhaps the precious logo for incubation below. Paulo at the helm was intent on fine-tuning the flight path. He was engrossed with conversation with Dave and Lionel. The suddenly he said out loud,

"Look my friends you are about to see the Gates, the Gates to the dynasty, the omega." The mist had now cleared and there like the entrance to Las Vegas was a great glowing horseshoe shaped arch with a smaller 'A' shaped gate within it. The upper area of the omega appeared to be made dark glass. The Logo optic channel and all its transportation tunnels finally linked with the omega through the lower portion of the A. It divided in three with the flight tunnel entering on the left and the pedestrian conveyor to the right. Finally, the torus of gravitation sprung from the base of the "A" to sweep down on creation. Francisca said, "Larry, the canal is like a string of lights on a Christmas tree."

Larry added, "It is the sole lifeline that kept the machinery of creation intact!"

Everyone was absorbed with his or her duties except the team in the engine pit that were redundant for the time being. They were on standby prepared to turn on the engines at an instant. While waiting, Ernst was busy checking and rechecking the oxygen system. The captain told some of the group that while in Purgosia he had met some of the EUSARUSS flight centre team who had been present when the Callisto disappeared. The story had made headlines and several rescue missions had been attempted. It seems they had no idea where to look. Perhaps after the Callisto's penetration the umbilical became concealed!

Just about then Richard noticed a strange phenomenon, he called Larry to one of the rear portals and said, "I've been sitting here watching Purgosia disappear into the distance. Then I noticed something. If you look out the front you see the Omega. It looks almost like a giant dome or a head. Then if you look out here where I am, the triangles seem to line up and form one body under the omega. Look I've sketched it, but it's not as good a Hiroshi's work."

"Quite remarkable,"

Said Larry, "It looks like a full person!"

By now they were much closer to the omega. It loomed large and foreboding – the glass like interior was shimmering with reflection. Travis who was close by mumbled, "This is like the proverbial Pearly Gates -the B-all and End-all of everything."

They turned their backs and walked away, leaving behind them a shimmering festival of lights strung out inside a sphere of blackness.

It was just then that the Lionel called an alert. He pointed to distortions both on the EM/SPEC. They were approaching from starboard. Paulo bellowed, "That's 'em. They are the Neg -Troughs I warned about! Captain Dave let me take command."

Dave nodded and Paulo bellowed once more,

"Sound red alert and action stations. Ernst, standby with team in engine pit. Cadets standby for damage control."

A siren sounded and the ship reduced its lighting. In the glow of emergency lights Larry joined the Navigators at the EM/SPEC. Paulo pointed to the distortions that were closing at a velocity far greater than their own. Pointing at the lines he said in annoyed voice,

"Rats, they are being directed at us from you know who! They are an old weapon used by the dark force of Thormentus and company."

Richard noticed that the black mist had increased considerably. Francisca began to shiver. Paulo called out, "Ignite engines" There was a roar and the ship shuddered. Then in an apologetic voice Paulo said,

"Ernst, one third velocity in reverse."

People looked at each other in dismay. Ernst was startled – what was happening?

The reverse pods were extended and on Ernst's command began to fire. Paulo cried out,

"Turn about 320 degrees to starboard prepare to roll ship. Communication, please issue an immediate distress call and state Neg. Troughs of seven on the Trichter Scale are approaching at five o'clock. Do this as if you were in your own space – it will be picked up."

The Callisto went about and rolled to face the opposite direction. It was heading towards the waves but upside down and moving backwards. Ernst was amazed at the acceleration. It was enormous. He called up to Paulo and Dave, "I cannot believe it we are achieving greater velocity backwards than ever achieved forwards!"

Paulo shouted down the intercom,

Yes Ernst, this void does everything the wrong way around, did you never notice before?"

The first wave warped the bent everything in its path, and the trough behind that was larger and more threatening. As the first wave hit the Callisto was lifted its face stern first. To everyone's amazement they plunged through the surface of the wave and rode it on the inside. Larry froze, he thought of Gasper the wave he had dreamed about. But he had never dreamed of riding the inside of a swell! The world around was now warped in every direction. The interior of the wave was not black and eerie as expected. Instead, it was bright like daytime. Again, Paulo shouted, "Bend the surfaces in the black void and you get the opposite effect."

Within moments, they reached the crest and dangled upside down from the inside of the peak. It was then that Paulo bellowed, "Ernst, engines full throttle forward I repeat, forward."

This time they would ride down the back of the wave nose first. The transition was instantaneous and effortless. Downwards they slid on a roller coaster into an almost bottomless valley. Ernst could not see what was happening and was shivering with fear, yet he maintained control. The ship gathered speed and the G force became unbearable. As they hit the bottom of the trough the Callisto had almost approached the speed of light outside a vacuum's vacuum. Then Paulo shouted, "Roll ships, engines full reverse, attain maximum velocity."

With a roar and a sickening roll the Callisto did a turn that would make a ballet dancer envious. Several computers were wrenched from their fittings and smacked into the ceiling. Some pots and pans hit the walls and Manz who was not strapped down was flung against the EM/SPEC. The nuclear pack exploded into life. The ship under extreme acceleration began a new ascent using all the positive gravitational energy it had attained in the drop plus the energy of the engines.

Once more the ship began riding backwards up the inside. Someone shouted, "Neg. Troughs from Hell!"

Though they had accumulated gravitational energy in their favour it was not sufficient to get the ship to the top. The Callisto rocketed upwards but at ever reducing speed. Everyone gasped as they realised that was happening. The communications operator could be heard calling out,

"Callisto to Omega, May Day Neg Troughs contacted position, Latitude 82.78 north Longitude zero central to 01 east."

Ernst's concern was the fuel supply and the strength of the ship's superstructure; he hoped it could take the stress. If there were many more waves he could be cleaned out of power, or the ship might crack open. Now about two thirds way up the wave, the ship ground to a stop. There was a murmur and it immediately it began to slide down. Several people let out a scream. Francisca thought she heard a child also scream! How could that be there were no children on the ship! Hamish shouted an obscenity, and a sense of horror took over the crew. It was at that critical moment that there was a thunderous crash. A violet light illuminated the ship. It tore a track in the face of the wave and in an instant the complete Neg Trough system evaporated. The Callisto literally fell from its position and landed on "vacuumus firma" or good old black voidular fabric with a bump. People were thrown about once again causing bumps and abrasions.

Through the windows a great piercing light was sweeping around in their vicinity and it had been their salvation. The light was coming from a section of the Omega. It was like the beam from a lighthouse or a beacon at sea showing sailors the way. Then as quick as a blink it disappeared, and the black abyss became calmed. The silence was shattered by Paulo's melodious voice,

"Well, me buccaneers, you are all sea dogs now. Ye' did very well indeed but if it were not for that laser artillery from the omega we would not be here now. Oh, by the way we all owe a word of thanks to the radio operator and to Ernst and to each other."

There was a round of applauds and people heaved a sigh of relief. It was just then that a Cadet burst on the scene with dragging two small figures. It was none other than Lorette and Rico. Francisca let out a gasp. The children rushed towards her crying out, "Please don't be angry, we are sorry, but we just had to come!"

Paulo's eyes widened and he bellowed,

"Now we are in a fine mess, they are forbidden to enter, as they are still Purgosians. We will have to declare them, and I don't know what will happen!"

It was way too late. They could not turn back; they were now obliged to enter the Omega!

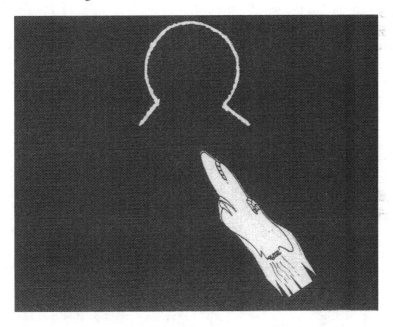

By now the omega was so large it filled the horizon. To an onlooker the ship would be just a dot in the face of the enormous disc. Now at close range Larry could see the glass structure in some detail. It was so enormous that it reflected the panorama of inner creation on its surface. To his bewilderment there were great faces peering down from behind the opening. In the centre of the glass expanse there was a large machine on wheels. From it there was a gun like object pointing downwards in their direction and nearby there were several smaller versions of the same kind. Were these the lasers, the miracle makers?

Suddenly, another shaft of light streamed down from the omega. This time it was not from a laser but emitted from a crack at the top of the A that began to widen. There was a hush within the ship and the EM/SPEC began its usual click. Those at the screen were able to read its recordings.

"Total unification of natural forces. Ultimate singularity. Time 111101.0005x times universal time. Temperature 111101.0005 degrees kelvinity."

Dave and Manz studied the readings evidently puzzled by the last term kelvinity!

Then the crack opened wider and the light became even more intense resulting in the interior of the ship becoming white and more transparent than ever before. The light penetrated every crevice to the extent of making the people become almost invisible. The children put their hand over their eyes and held fast to Fancisca. Then there was the sound of voices from above that echoed about the ship causing the crew to cover their ears. However, Ernst and several of his team were not to be caught unawares and produced some dome halos that they had been given in Purgosia. Several people put on the domes and immediately nodded their heads in satisfaction. The voices could be heard to say,

"Ventilator – Abel, tango, five, niner, diagio, – Okay probe – zero/norez fifty, align.".

Then there was silence followed by a scraping sound and then cough. Then the sound recommenced,

"10 mags – Surfactant – Lower CPAP Anzug betragung – vite chinquo vite."

Then there was another cough, just like a human cough and a tiny laugh. The sound was amplified, and so acute that it vibrated objects in the ship. There was a clank like something had fallen on a floor. Then someone said something in English like "Let it Down Now" A long silver object like forceps descended from above. It was accompanied by another object shaped like a dentist's mirror, which was directed beneath the ship. Then the forceps clamped on both sides of the Callisto, and it was drawn upwards. There was a rush of air cold air, chilling and refreshing. There was an aroma of perfume like lavender. As they ascended, they crossed into the path of the torus of gravitation. For a moment, it penetrated one side of the ship illuminating its interior even more and causing small objects to be drawn to it, just like a magnet. It also caused the crew to go scurrying in all directions but there were no ill effects. Fortunately, it was only a brief encounter and there was no damage.

The Callisto continued to be carried aloft, and people inside the ship crowded the windows while accident and emergency crews remained at their posts on full alert. With a jolt they cleared the entrance but continued upwards. From their perch they could see blackness from whence they had come. The crack began closing below sealing them inside an enormous room. They were lowered onto a smooth "A" shaped floor still facing North. They were looking towards a glass wall. Outside they could see a garden and a large orchard of gigantic magnitude. Beyond it was land sloping upwards and covered in white roses interspersed through golden wheat fields. Beyond the orchard flying craft of all shapes and sizes could be seen evidently arriving, landing, or departing through a transport archery.

VISITING GODOT

The crew gulped in fear as a group of giants suddenly appeared. Some wore facemasks and some wore sound disks on their head's others looked normal. Paulo spoke rapidly to the crew,

"In a moment we will grow in size. Grow to their proportions and they won't be giants anymore. Then and then only will we be ready to exit the ship."

Richard moved to a side portal and observed that the floor they were sitting on was divided into three sections coloured to correspond with the triangles. The lines ran right through other parts of the building like territorial divides. The enclosure and contents were made of fine white material though the walls were filled with holes like a Swiss cheese. These holes were decorative and enabled one to see what lay beyond. The dentists mirror shaped object on which they were perched had been gently removed and the forceps released and withdrawn.

Then there was a jolt, and the Callisto had begun to increase in size. From within the ship there was a sound of groaning metal. The surroundings began to alter as the scale increased. The EM/SPEC was checked for a magnitude report and it began to show sets of numerals adding more zeros than it had ever done before. Most of the crew opened their safety harnesses and for some reason or other clustered in the centre of the ship. No one wanted to be first to alight. Rico and Lorette let out a whimper, which reminded Paulo to insist that they do not leave the ship unless told so. Francisca had now moved close to Larry gripping his arm. Then the expansion concluded. This was their second great growth since leaving the universe, they were fast becoming veterans. There was a flash from someone's camera. However, it was unlikely any picture would result.

Now from their lofty position they could see what lay beyond in more clarity. A river with the colours of a rainbow wound its way down from the territory ahead and descended through an opening. One of the orchard's apple trees stood at the opening with the river flowing through its roots and from there it probably went into the logo optical tunnel.

Dr Nadine pointed out that people were also emerging from the other tunnel to the right and going up steps outside the enclosure. They were carrying briefcases and were chatting excitedly. Richard tried to get a better look. Just then their growing process stopped. The door of the ship opened as if by remote control. There was an amazing freshness from the ether it was a repeat of the perfume that smelt like lilac. In the background there was the sound of changing rhythms and string instruments mixed with the sound of humming machinery. Paulo said to Dave that people may alight now but in pairs. They began to emerge squinting in the brightness with almost no shadows. Larry looked around to survey the area south and directly behind the ship. The expanse of thick glass extended out behind them in a horseshoe shape. The ceiling was smooth and white and very high. All around the perimeter lay a ribbon of computerlike machines with real spongy people working at them. This was evidently the flipside of the glass panel they had seen from below. Mounted in the ceiling was what looked like an enormous laser on tracks? It is pointing downwards at the glass on which there was a great map with co-ordinates. In addition to this there were several vehicles with smaller lasers also pointing downwards. They had large white wheels and were connected to the ceiling with loose power lines. It looked like someone had written a name on side in Arabic writing "The Kahn Opener".

The ceiling though high was filled with information screens that depicted multimedia coverage of every part of creation.

HOWDI PARTNER

Turning back in the opposite direction he noticed some medical equipment. There were facemasks, halo helmets, surgical scalpels while the tweezers and mirror like object that had drawn them up were now hanging on a panel near bye. It was difficult to figure out why this equipment was so prevalent – perhaps this was a sort of cosmos-maternity delivery area!

The group stood still, transfixed with the excitement of the moment. Then the subsistent team came towards them. At first, they had been silhouettes as the light came from behind where they were standing. Then as they approached, they began to look human. The group was overwhelmed by the possibility that they might meet their creators. They all felt lightheaded and inclined towards fainting. Francisca began to shake from head to foot and clung on to Larry for assistance. Several other people were unable to stay standing and were taken back into the ship. Four of the team were now in their midst. They were very tall and dressed in loose cloths like a medical team in theatre. As they moved, their bodies caused a distortion in the surroundings, much like a shimmering road on a sunny day. Their movement caused a sound like chimes in the breeze and there was a perfume like lavender or lilac. The disks behind their heads were shimmering and sometimes flashing as if receiving messages.

The most senior person looked like a male and was taller than the others. He had with bright golden hair and a short beard. It was dressed different from the others as he wore a burgundy cape over white clothing with loose pants tucked into soft black knee boots. As he strode forward the other three followed. He stretched out a hand and spoke in a voice that was mellow yet articulate. The first contact was Dave who instinctively responded by holding out his hand. They both clasped, and as they did so there was applause from around the enclosure. The operational crews were now standing up at their computers to look at the new arrivals, clapping as they did so. It seems that they had a way of cupping their soft hands to the they made the required sound. Then the big man spoke,

"You are very welcome here; my Son has spoken of you. Please realise that you are in a state of mild Ecstasy and Rapture. You are capable of this experience because you have been gently brought through process that prepares you for this visit. What you see approximates what is really here. This is the best we can do for you. However, let me say that you are doing well as no other mortal has trodden this path so far but with one exception, my son and his earth mother!"

The man smiled and quickly continued but only now letting go of Dave's hand.

"Now, who do you think I am? Well, you may not know me, but I know all of you, this is Dave, and Hello Ernst, I was glad to know that your sister's daughter who was ill got better just before your departure on the mission. I could go on, but we do not have eternity entirley at our disposal."

There was a big outburst of laughter and immediately the atmosphere became less tense.

He continued,

"Well, I'll tell you who I am. I am the Father. Your Father, the Father of everything! I am all that is! Up here I am the Father of two, and dwell in territory that is tinted with gold. I stretch out for all eternity. I am so large that I can live in myself and move freely in that territory for example, being here to greet you. I began in the future and therefore know all that is happening at any given time. I had no beginning because the future never comes. I live at the ultimate genetic velocity and can therefore be anywhere at any given moment or everywhere at once. My energy injected into the universe is the elixir permitting time to function. This in harmony with the rotation of flux enables a complete package. Now this is not a boast, but an assurance to you that you have in me the greatest ally you could ever want. All I want in return is recognition of these facts and your good will towards each other."

There was a murmur and several people looked out at the gold coloured territory that dominated the vista outside. He then went on to say,

"I could not remain without shearing the splendour, but I begot a Son. For this to happen it took only my will. To do the same thing you require partners. This is because you are frail, yet it is in your nature to be like me."

Then he swept around his left arm and pointed to a young man saying, "This is the Son of whom I speak"

His Son was also very tall and handsome and had black hair that shone with a tinge of navy blue. He had a swarthy Moorish look. One of the female cadets let out an involuntary sigh. She immediately turned red faced while one of her friends began to giggle. He smiled broadly and stepped forward. His white theatre gear swished as he moved, and the surroundings shimmered in his path. He had a facemask dangling from his neck, and he spoke with the same voice that they had heard in Purgosia.

"You are welcome, I will meet you personally in a few minutes time. I was the one who spoke to you in your ship in Purgosia – remember?"

The Father then gestured in the direction of two females. One was very young, and the other more mature. He pointed to the younger women and spoke about her thus,

"This is Spirinda, the pretty lady who spoke to you in her triangle. She also possesses a territory up here, one that is abundant in oceans and gentle breezes. She is the mother of creation and the electrifying energy that invigorates the genders."

All eyes turned to her she stood tall and slim and resembled a beautiful Polynesian like figure. She had long flowing black hair with a large orchid attached. Her eyes were a bright blue, and her skin was amber. She looked shy because of the attention and appeared to bite her lip and step backwards. It was amazing how one who is alleged to have spawned reality could also be bashful in its presence! Because of her radiant beauty, Larry squeezed Francisca's hand, just to show her that she was still his number one. Her hand went limp and she responded with a kiss to his cheek.

Then he introduced the second female.

"This is Miriam my earth mother and seen by our enemies as a block I their paths of destruction. She is the exception that my Father spoke about. She is whole and entire in every sense and now Queen of this world."

All heads turned to look at the fourth person. There she was a majestic lady with golden hair, and dark brown eyes. She was gentile and graceful while generating the warmth of a real mother. She was dressed in a pale blue wrap that was worn partly over her head.

Underneath the wrap, she wore a straight cut white dress with a thin golden belt that dipped in the centre as it was attached to a golden medallion. She was quite in keeping with the traditional image that many people have had.

Miriam stepped gracefully forward, smiled, and immediately glided into the crowd. She moved from person to person-shaking hands, embracing and addressing everyone by first name. She inquired about private aspects of their lives and demonstrated an intimate knowledge about each member of the crew, and this included the non-believers. Hamish and the fainter hearted people soon got brave and pushed forward to be able to meet this Queen of Eternity. At this point Paulo told the Son about the children in the ship. He froze for a moment and asked where they were now. Paulo assured him that they were confined to the ship. The Son looked relieved but looked towards his mother. She came to him knowing that there was a problem. The Son ushered Paulo, Dave, and Laura to one side. Then he said rapidly,

"This causes a massive violation of our nature, and my tribes could be very angry. However, there is one small possibility. Apart from me Miriam is the only other person here who has corporality. I will make a case that they are her personal guests but if this is not accepted you will all have to leave immediately. Is that okay with you, Miriam?"

Miriam looked as if feeling trapped in the situation. Then she smiled and said, "That is okay, but will there be strict rules and a code to be followed?"

The Son said with an apologetic look, "I'm afraid there will, but I'll explain later."

Then he went to explain to the Father. Paulo said goodbye to the group and that he would catch up later and skipper them back on the return trip. If they had to leave sooner than later, he would be informed. The Father and Son then returned to the group. The Captain and Ernst began a technical conversation about the Callisto with the Son while the father talked to Dr Manz and Nadine discussed the finer details of the logo optic procedure.

KEYS OF THE KINGDOM.

"Let me introduce you to Pedro now not Paulo but Pedro our OMCOM, the omega migration control manager".

The Son pointed to a tall man was standing at a double door chamber with glass walls. The chamber stretched along a large portion of the east side of the enclosure. It commanded an overview of all the activities and written over the door was www. Com/Saint Control

Centre. It was probably written in a very foreign language but that is what the group perceived.

"Pedro and his team administer over all traffic in and out of the deities. He alone holds the codes that facilitated this movement."

Pedro slowly nodded his head in agreement, then he smiled and moved away to perform duties.

Dave asked the son, "How is Praque calculated?"

He replied, "Prayers ascent to Purgosia to the benefit of the inhabitants and a duplicate arrives up here where Praque is produced. The population then can possess Praque or with Praque can buy prayer bonds and even Praque futures. This is a slice of the future an estimate of the volume of prayer at a given space time. This I will explain when we go to the next floor in a few minutes."

He then opened a door to a chamber. Inside was a massive table with a tuning platform on top. It looked like a giant roulette table. It was turning slowly and as it did so gold pieces were falling from an opening at one side. There was some dedicated help who were transporting and counting the material and tapping figures into a terminal.

"This is our mint," said the Son, moving to one side and opening another door. Raphael and his friends stared in disbelief.

The son turned, "Nadine, Dr Manz, this is where we control the inverted biological aspects of the domains. This is where the Hazard Analysis of all Critical Control Points of the system are Monitored. There is Anaesthesia, which is performed by the lasers you saw outside. We monitor the Volcanoes in Purgosia for time pressure per arch revolution known to you as blood pressure. Of recent times we have had to include virus control. This phenomenon is of importance since Diva and his group became aggressive. They regularly send meteorite toward the universe that are loaded with virus. We manage to stop most of them.

There is also occupational therapy and that is related to the triangular alignment and configuration. As you can imagine there are ferocious hauling and tugging at it all the time. If it were to drift something might rip apart. Then there is Orthopaedic Trauma which is psychological support for the cosmos on a continuous basis. Radiology is tied in with the holographs that I showed you and Renal Medicine is rare but necessary. The surgical laser teams have been trying to cut clear blockages that cause the universe to be exposed. It is partly ectopic. So far, we have not succeeded and if not, then the deliverance will prove difficult". Then he said, "Would you like to see the operation theatre?"

Larry looked at Francisca and whispered, "What do you think he means by deliverance?" She raised her eyebrows and shrugged.

Without waiting for a response, he took them into an observation chamber where they could look down on the performance of the surgeons. There was a team of ten who were clustered around a circular operating table on which was a shimmering galaxy. The guests gasped and Larry blurted in confusion, "Sir, is that a Galaxy?"

The Son smiled and said, "Yes, that is a Galaxy extracted from an anaesthetised section of the Universe for repair. You have learned already that through the medium of my arch of time from Purgosia I can halt rotation and thus freeze time temporary."

As he spoke one of the surgeons extended a pointed object close to one side of the substance and directed a beam into its interior. The Son then added,

"Any observer in your cosmos will say that they saw an unidentified flying object and you know they would not be far wrong!"

Some of the group chuckled.

On closer inspection, they noticed that the object was encased in a film of plastic like material or membrane. The surgeons appeared to be reaching inside through the film and that the film stretched down through a gap in the floor. The Son said,

"The film stretches back to the universe from whence the Galaxy has been withdrawn. The reason is that it allows us to work without having to invert its substance. Also, no one can say we broke any natural laws."

As they left the theatre Larry had a last look at the none inverted organic object shimmering like a giant jellyfish glowing and pulsating as it was miraculously undergoing divine surgery by an Unidentified Friendly Organisation. He sighed and put his arm around Francisca and followed the Son on the next stage of the orientation.

THE PRAYDAQ COMPLEX

"There are many mansions in my father's house come and explore!" The doors of the theatre were then thrown back, to reveal what lay beyond. Before them and to the north was the great expanse of the golden coloured territory. It had the hues of autumn with pale green and ochre fields rising for ever upwards disappearing in a blaze of light. It began with a perfusion of white roses, followed by a landscape of hills and dales. The lower end of this mass was like a delta and it was from here that the golden river originated. They could see the layout better from here. The river evidently was the sap emanating from that territory. It flowed towards them and through a fruit orchard intermingled with more white roses and palm trees. Strangely enough there was a large fruit tree growing at the river entrance, so the river flowed right through its roots. The two other tunnels to the left and right of the river, were busy with traffic. The group now could see a large parking lot where evidently many of the flying craft landed. The whole area was steeped in a blue haze that was drifting across from the east. The mist was accompanied by a sound like a humming of bees, but none were to be seen.

One quick look around showed that two other territories encircled them. At the centre of all this immensity lay the enclosure that they had been in. As the group came outside, they realised that there was also a massive building sitting on top of the Omega Centre. The building was suspended by eight enormous, curved legs each leg housing a moving stair, on which people were ascending and descending.

The group ascended by way of the moving stairs. Then to their disbelief they entered an enormous hall that resembled a busy stock market. There were large screens and people were dashing around with strips of paper and talking franticly with each other. Some of them had coloured tabards as if to denote their trade and something was being traded. In one corner there were what looked like a hundred coat hangers on which jet packs and visors were hanging. The people were of both genders but no children, and everyone was focused on texts and numbers that moved on a central screen. There were several columns that looked like they carried up power and information from the theatre below.

The Son spoke, raising his voice above the din,

"This is what we named the Praydaq. It is in fact our Pan-Creational Territorial Telepathies Prayer Market, which to be correct is the PC/TT/PM. Some wise guys call it the Poor Credit Time and Temptation Post-mortem. As I told you earlier, we trade in prayer. The first aspect of all this is as follows; basically, with incoming prayer we produce Praque-using alloys from the golden territory. This in turn can be used as currency but at the same time its mirror image signals more and more expansion into the outreach. The expansion is proportional to the volume of Praque produced multiplied by the quaternal ratio which is running at 4.5% now."

He looked at people's amazement and smiled,

"The second aspect is that with the currency one can also buy bonds which allow a stake in both the expansion in the outreach but also in territories below the omega. Basically, where a population is generated prayer follows and if one knows where to buy the value of their bonds can soar."

He continued, "Lastly, as said, one can buy Praque Futures, based on a guess at what the quaternal ration will be at a given time. This is shaky business, but it is popular. Wealth, however, does not mean that existence changes in any way it is a game of achievement and an opportunity to assist the Deity."

Richard asked what is this outreach that is spoken about so often? The Son replied, "It extends infinitely outwards in three directions above these territories, but it is only a template. The Praque enable it to become 'Paradised' formatted and fertilised."

Just then a bell rang to herald a frantic burst of trading. Though people retained their paradisal dignity, it did wear thin in some instances. A couple of fellows trying to purchase bonds from Calcutta tripped and fell over. Of course, they were unhurt but looked foolish and caused some laughter from other traders. A newcomer to the game was sold a lemon as he bought bonds from Uranus, no population no value! A woman had bonds from Andromeda she had bought ages ago. This was before it became colonised. She had just sold them for enormous profit and was celebrating with her colleagues. In this instance the profit will automatically go towards outreach expansion. One of the traders who was passing was asked by the Son to tell the group what the economic outlook was. He was a small plump fellow with tight cut hair. He said in a flustered voice, "No not good, trade down.8.5% because of a festival in Purgosia, but also because it is the cause of threats from the Pit."

He smiled and went on his way. Just then a gong rang, if it had been a bell it would have been good news, but a gong was bad.

Larry was also looking towards the group at the time and noticed Hamish Caldron known as Ham, a cadet called Cathy Lamont, and a mechanic called Raphael Ullman known as Rap were missing.

Just as they were about to leave Larry asked how does the Com/ saint operate? The Son said that it was made up of people who represent the Deities and that not even he or the Father attends unless invited. They meet daily and administer over all aspects of worldwide affairs. The only zone that is not represented is that belonging to the void. The son explained that they should rest now because tomorrow they will be taken on a tour to visit one of the other two deities. They will visit the territory of Spirinda and her city Of Paradiso.

In an adjoining building there were two dormitories, quite naturally, one female and other for males. The Son recommended that they go there now and rest because this is the time when everyone rests while the sun dims. They will be called at the appropriate time and tomorrow they will be taken to visit the other two territories. So, people laid out on beds and drifted off. Maria saw to the children in the ship which was a very safe haven for them, and she went to her dwelling intending to collect them the following day. Unknown to the group, three people did not remain to rest.

The Scheme

The only dilatory people were the remnants of the Callisto crew who had refused to go on the grand tour. Unknown to Maria they had decided to accommodate themselves in the Callisto. It was still sitting where it had landed on the flight pad facing inwards. Three of the group relaxed in the garden reading and playing cards and enjoying the rays of the fading sun. It was now that they noticed that each territory had a sun of its own. One of the groups called Dalia suggested that they should sample some fruit from the trees, though they had been told it was only for the inhabitants. She plucked one that resembled a wheel with a texture like an orange without skin. Along with two others she sampled the fruit and found it pleasant. The effect was nothing other than it satisfied their curiosity. On the other hand, they all agreed that they shared the same ambition and that they now felt disposed to carry it out. As the suns dimed those who devoured fruit, Raphael Ulleman and Hamish Cauldron were about to turn in when Raphael called out to Hamish, "Ham, don't turn in yet, I have something to say."

Ham who was very tall and thin turned and scowled.

"Common Rap, what is it?"

Rap pulled Ham by the arm and said, "Shush"

Then in a whisper he said,

"Look I've been doing some thinking since today. We could make a name for ourselves because this here utopia is not what it's cracked up to be. It is already out moulded and out of date. I have overheard some of the operators talk and they said that they were under threat from a black triangle. They mentioned Thormentus and we all know that he is the one who shoots psychological fire and brimstone at the universe – we saw that with our own eyes. Those black triangles out there are new age technology. They will overrun here and when they do our lives will be a misery unless we join them here and now. You see when we go back down to earth nothing will go our way unless we show our metal. Are you with me so far?"

Ham replied, with some interest, "Yeh!"

"Okay then listen to this. To begin with the worst-case scenario for doing something wrong up here, and that is we will be sent back to earth so that we can die just to satisfy their system. Then we will either end up in Purgosia or be sent to the Black Triangles. It is a no-lose situation and all we have to do is improve our lot. If we impress Thormentus not only will we improve our lot but also, we will be guaranteed a fortune while on earth. Therefore, lets sabotage the Omega defences and cause an unholy row."

Ham shook his head. Rap cut in quickly,

"Look Ham you miss the point. There is a stash of currency up here called Praque. It is so strong it would make the Dollar and the Yen look like kids' stuff. We will knock off a few million just for ourselves and buy some respect.

Already Ham had changed his mind and began nodding in agreement while a large smile crossed his face. However, he did have a question,

"Rap, you know-like, we are supposed to be inside Utopia, Paradise and all that. Do you think they are reading our minds and watching everything we do, so if we try something, they will jump us?"

Rap said coolly,

"If that were the case, I would have been ejected from here ages ago for the thoughts I have been entertaining. Therefore, I think not, they rely on trust and leave one another to their own devises. However maybe after we have pulled a stroke, they will get wise but then it will be too late."

Ham looked reassured. Rap went on,

"I've been taking stock of things around here and find that when night falls the place dims and empties out. They do not need many to watch what goes on. Also, the void is policed by angel patrols, basis on the blue triangle and also Purgosia. Up here it is mainly Psyco-medical operations and administered by a guys called Pedro and Raphael, my namesake. They seem only to be repairing structures and listening to incoming calls. It is also the main administration centre but most of all it is a trading area that stores large quantities of beautiful P-r-a-q-u-e."

By now Hamish was becoming so excited that he began pulling on his shoes.

Rap had a bit more to add, "Those laser guns on that glass panel are only used on occasions. They are usually unmanned and provide us with an opportunity that should not be missed."

Just then a female voice cut in. It was a cadet called Dalia.

"Okay boys I've heard all you said will you cut me in. If not, I will split on you?"

She was a small fit looking girl, with cropped hair and icy cold eyes. She never smiled but right now was an exception because she was laughing as she spoke. Rap replied,

"Okay Dal, you're in but you better do exactly as I tell you or I'll break every bone in your body when we get back down, that is if I don't toss you into the void before then."

She nodded her head though still laughing to herself.

"So, as I was about to say, all we must do is, nick the loot store it on the ship, find the power switch for the Lasers and fire them at everything we can. That includes shattering the glass screen of the Omega which will be our escape route. Then turn the beam to short range take, out the floor and the whole of their artillery defence will fall into the void and we follow making our escape in the ship."

Ham began to clap his hands in delight. Rap hissed at him to shut up and smacked him over the head with roll of paper that he grabbed from a desk. Rap then said,

"Tonight at 0.300 we will begin our activity. Dal, your assignment is to lock the resting chambers on the ship, and then get down to the engine bay and turn on the main power and follow the manual at the consul. I know it's there I have seen it and the steps are quite simple. However, don't turn the activation key till after we begin shooting. Make sure the main door is wide open and stand by. We will crash out of the hall backwards; it is just as powerful as forwards." Then he said to Ham,

"Your job is to examine the lasers, find the power switch, but don't turn them on. If anyone asks you what you are doing just say you could not sleep and even, ask how the things work! That would be a natural question and we might learn something that way. Understand?"

Ham said "Yeh' Rap, Yes' of course." Rap continued,

"I've been watching the movement around here for quite some time and I've concluded that most of the place is on a sort of automatic system. It is like the very walls are alive but most of the focus is on what is happening below. So that gives us an opportunity and if all goes well the whole place will come apart at the seams. Now just to clarify about this Prayque stuff. It is the substance that Prayers as made from. It is like the way matter it can be turned into energy ($e = mc^2$) in like manner prayer can be turned to Praque ($p = pc^7$) or something like that!"

"Gee Rap" said Dalia,

"I never realized you had it! I'm impressed. How are we going to locate the Praque?

Rap gave a crocket smile and said,

"That's where I come in!" He turned and began to study a map he had already prepared. The few that were on duty were preoccupied concentrating on screens grouped around the perimeter of the enclosure. The silent pair was none other than Raphael and Hamish, both dressed in dark cloths and wearing scarves to cover their pasty white faces. First, they walked cautiously to one of the medical rooms and located two trolleys. Then they tested them for squeaky wheels and were satisfied there was no noise. With map in hand, Rap led the way to Com/Saint and pushed the door, which swung open. The large conference table in the centre was filled with a flat monitor. The tabletop screen was still turned on its screen saver showing lazy pictures from around eternity and intermittingly showing one-liner prayers. One side of the room was lined with cupboards, but there was also a steel door. Rap cautiously turned a handle on the door. To his satisfaction, it opened to reveal hundreds of boxes labelled "Praque – 5,000 Guinsks". At this sight, Ham let out a gasp. Rap reacted in a hissing voice, "Shut up Ham, quiet, you sound like an amateur."

He punched Ham on the arm just to drive home his point. Ham scowled and began to open one of the boxes. Just as anticipated they discovered the contents to be filled coins. They were like crystal, quite transparent like ice but difficult to distinguish. Ham dug his hand into the coins and trickled them through his fingers while reflections danced across his smiling face. Then Rap studied the boxes more closely and found, that it said in many languages one of them English, that the weight was 6.3 Million Gravs. On lifting one of the boxes, Rap reckoned it weighed the equivalent of about 5 kg. Without a word, he returned to the table pressed any button he could see and instantly the screen became active. The void appeared showing what lay below but also it showed three black triangles that had not been there before!

"There's our customers Rap," he said pointing at the triangles.

"Let's get busy."

Rap could not understand the keyboard, but one key had an icon of a bird with a message in its beak. He pressed it and immediately he gained access to s-mail. The address boxes had twenty-three options. He spotted one named that read xxx.thormentus.void666, gave a grunt of satisfaction and typed in the following, "Three disciples in Citadel about to cause major disaster and remove quantities of Praque. Are you interested exploiting the situation? Rewards expected! Reply to raphamdal@uuu. callisto.e/usaruss."

He signed their three names and pressed and pressed the bird button again. The address appeared and several arrows shot towards the text. Then several comments in strange language appeared, almost certainly meaning the message was sent. Then he was given an option of a Bank House icon or an eraser. He chose the eraser, and the message was deleted. They hurriedly loaded twenty boxes on the two trolleys and speedily pushed them towards the Callisto. So far no one had looked up from the task or interrupted, luck was holding. Dalia was waiting and had the entrance lowered. In a few moments they had unloaded the boxes and they were hoisted on board. The two men lowered the boxes into a compartment below a floor section then heaved sighs of relief. Too late and to their horror they heard voices chirp, "'Allo, what are you doing to ze boxes misters?"

It was Lorette and Rico. Dalia immediately fielded the situation, "Janette, why are you not in your Hybos?"

"We are not sleepy. You have fun, can we ride on ze' trolleys?"

"Shush kid!" said Rap, "You better not make noise or tell people what you saw here tonight, or we will have you thrown out into the void."

Janette screamed and began to cry. Rico looked suddenly disillusioned and a fearful expression spread across his innocent face. Rap blurted out loud

"Dal' lock them up in a chamber somewhere – pronto before they blow our cover, also get the quarters locked before more zombies interfere."

Dalia dragged the children to the Cadets locker room and pushed them inside. Then she keyed in a locking command on the digital box by the door.

The two males then headed to the command centre of the ship. To their delight they found a reply to their message from one called

Commander Lucinary 3rd Division AVD (Army of Voidular Dynasties) She or it said, "We are concerned that this might be a trap. Will advance to a strategic proximity and await evidence of your action. If it is favourable, we will exploit, and you will be rewarded."

Rap wrung his hands together in joy. He immediately printed a copy and then deleted the message and removed it from any storage file that might have retained it. Then they both slid into the shadows with combat in mind. They went to where the Lasers were situated, and both climb into the controller's positions, one in a fixed base gun and the other on the mobile gun that stood near the centre of the glass floor. They tuned to short range and without hesitation opened fire. The first shot from Rap on the mobile, sounded like thunder. A streak of red light tore around the perimeter smashing computers and ripping out glass as it went. Rap was shocked by the awesome power he had unleashed. They both let out loud whoops and fired in full circles. This concluded with firing through the glass entrance and out towards the transport tunnels, flight pad and river that looked like honey. They wrecked several flying machines and caused a cascade of golden substance to shoot in every direction. However, being magnetised the particles reformed in an instant and seeped back into the river. Ham let out a roar of anger, and Rap fired again. The second attempt was no better, so they turned the laser upwards at the roof and floor of the Praydaq. The effect was spectacular as a complete section of the trading hall fell down cracking more glass beneath them. Ham, who had been slower to master the controls, was now getting good. He was able to fire his gun in every direction and that included down at the glass floor. Rap followed suit, and in moments there was a massive hole and dangerous cracks. Ham let fly one more time and jumped clear just as his laser begun tumbling into the vacuum diminishing in size as it went. The mobile gun did not fall through but became wedged on a sharp edge with its mechanism, jammed and firing all directions. The side effect of all this violation was a hurricane, like wind at the vacuum sucked at the environment. Everything was now being pulled into the void.

The children heard the noise and felt the ship lurch. Amidst sobs shivers they began to climb up on top of the lockers made possible by a fixed wall bookshelf for literature on cadetship. It acted like a ladder for them to climb. At first Laurette refused, but Rico reminded her about what the men had threatened, so she changed her mind! Then once on top they crawled into an open air-duct that looked inviting.

The two terrorists stopped firing and with beaming grins and looks of guilt on their faces, struggled against the storm back to the ship. Sirens were sounding over the installation and voice recordings issuing automatic instructions could be heard. Dalia was prepared and as planned had the ships motors humming. The power packs were beginning to kick in one by one causing an ever-increasing din. The two threw themselves into the moving ship as it lurched backwards the opening with its hull grinding on the floor. It was about then, that the first Angel defenders came tumbling in from every direction. Flying craft buzzed overhead directing blue powder on to the flames. Ham was last in, and hastily closed the door. The three made their way to Captain Dave's control centre and on the EM/SPEC began to plot the direction of the ship. As the ship lumbered towards the open glass floor escape looked immanent. Rap was at the helm, shouting profanities as he steered towards the opening. Suddenly a buzzer sounded. Rap stared at the consul where a flashing light indicated "Urgent-door A1 releasing." At that very moment, the power automatically reduced and the ship ground to a halt. Rap let out a bellow.

"Ham you idiot, you did not close the door properly!"

To which Ham replied with his eyes wide open in surprise, "Honest Rap, I did close it right, I know I did."

With that they both scurried to the indicated area, where they discovered a dozen Jet Packers and Pedro standing inside the open entrance. To make matters worse Rico was standing with his finger jammed against the door control panel while Laurette was leering at them with a look of revenge on her chubby brown face. The two froze in their tracks and frantically thought about excuses. Dalia saw what was happening and went to unlock the resting area and then slid into her Hybo and closed the lid.

Rap quickly regained composure and exclaimed to Pedro, "Pedro, thank heavens you have come. Whatever is happening, we thought we were lost. We were preparing to fly for our lives."

Pedro snapped back, "Has anyone here been hurt?" – "No" said Rap "Do you know who fired the lasers?"

"We didn't see anything till the flames erupted," explained Ham blinking his eyes in apparent innocence. We think it came from outside."

"Senior Pedro" A tiny voice intervened. It was Janette. "Those men were out and when they came back, they said they would kill us."

She pointed at Ham and Rap who responded with,

"No not at all, we said to mind as they might get killed if they are not careful on the ship."

Laurette had never told a lie and began to cry. Pedro beckoned a kindly female angel to comfort her saying,

"Do you gents realise just how dangerous it was to attempt a departure in the middle of such an attack? This whole event will be investigated, and we are taking charge of the ship till your Captain returns."

"That's great news," said Rap, biting his lip.

Pedro quickly turned and detailed three of his force to take charge and departed.

THE REACTION

There was a sudden high-pitched whine. People stopped in their tracks and turned towards the entrance where a flying craft was descending. The sleek object though mostly transparent had an insignia of a Lamb on its fuselage. Officers in combat gear alighted followed by the Son. He was visibly upset, and his aura shone brighter than usual, while his surroundings warped as he passed. It was obvious that he was in supreme command in this time of crisis. His subjects fully understood the position and watched his reactions and awaited his orders. He firstly looked around and spoke to the nearest hurt person who was been attended by a medic. He gave them his congratulations for being so courageous and immediately went into Com/Saint. There were about fifteen angel officers and saints waiting for his council. Though under enormous pressure he remained calm and spoke in an even voice. He asked Benedict about the Psyco-medical situation and Pedro for a material damage report. Pedro said that there was a doubt that this was an attack from beyond, but it could have been an inside job. People looked amazed. He added that he would confirm all this soon when the cameras are replayed. He reported the damaged floors and lasers but that no one had been lost. However, forty have been disabled so far many of them had been night traders on the upper level. He then asked Gabriel and Michael who had arrived from the Corona, about the battle situation. They told him that there was now a real danger since their defences was reduced the black triangles might take advantage of the situation. If they did not get the vacuum sealed the triangles could penetrate and according to eschatological law would increase in size and become a threat to the whole domain.

A furious effort to shore up defences and seal the damage began. Architects and engineers, some specialists fresh up from Purgosia, began directing operations.

The breeze was still like a tornado in reverse as papers and lighter objects continued to go cascading in downwards spirals.

Gabriel at Com/Saint then surveyed the audio-visual lighted table. It showed the position of the Black Triangles and their dangerous advance.

Just then a voice from Purgosia came through the consul. It was from one of the city Fathers called Alessio. He reported in a calm voice, "Bless you Gabriel, but I am here with the Mayor and several of your angel commanders and we would like to know what's going on? If you have a problem, we get the shudders!" Gabriel smiled. Alessio continued, "Look we know there is a serious threat and are taking measures, but so far we are only guessing."

Gabriel quickly brought him up to date and explained that he would have proper communications restored within thirty minutes (30x100). He said the Son was ready to speak to them through the Chasams. He asked if there was a safety shield along the Logo Optic Canal? Alessio said no, not yet, but he was working on an overall safety shield project. They both agreed that if the Logo-optic flow were damaged it would have a tumorous effect on everything. Gabriel then said that as one of their targets would be Purgosia it might be wise to consider evacuating the population through the subterranean systems to the reverse side of the triangle, just a consideration.

Also, in Pergosia, on the night of the attack, Hiroshi and Jill had been sitting on Dan and Maria's deck looking up at the night sky. They had been watching their triangle change, as usual, from maroon to rainbow and the sky turn opaque. Then in the stillness a gigantic flash came from the Omega. This was followed by red and yellow laser light dancing wildly in the sky with some random shots coming downwards. Then some of the laser beams that had missed their targets came as far as the Sangria Mountains. All this was followed by a loud hissing sound far above. There was an uncanny flow of ether like a wind that disturbed the composure of creation. It was like a tropical storm and as it raged it rocked the two triangles like a Christmas tree in a draft. The family were alarmed. Dan said Heroshi and Jill should return to Pergosia as soon as possible. They agreed and prepared.

Critical Meeting

Dave and Laura were ushered into a meeting room in the Com /Saint area. They knew it was going to an uncomfortable encounter. The Son and senior officials were there with a serious expression on each of their faces. The Son related the events and then said that several billion Praque had been stolen, and that on a replay of the interior monitoring showed it on a trolley and moments later a trolley falling down into the void. Dave and Laura were shocked and asked if any of their people had caused such an accident. They were told that the night people on duty become so traumatised that they could not relate what had happened. Then Paulo arrived and the route back was discussed. It was agreed that they should depart as fast as possible and before the black triangles got closer. There was a frantic scramble as the visitors jumped on board. The crew took up positions and the others seated and closed their safety belts.

Paulo bellowed."

"Here we go and may we not meet any more neg troughs."

The people who were going to act as 'shrinks' (Reduction Controllers) were preparing for the departure. They would deminiturise the Calisto to fit the scaled down domain of mid-creation. One of them a woman had a distinct Russian accent another a man who was Chinese said nothing and another young fellow who sounded south American. Once again there was no need for turning on the power as energy was drawn from the surroundings. Then the south American stood at a consul and called out some numbers, and almost immediately they began to shrink. Francisca could see out a window watching the controllers grow and grow. She turned to Larry and said, "Oh Larry I am getting used this new game of shrink and grow. So sorry it all had to end so quickly." The team were now like great mammoths beaming down from above. Using the same equipment, they were lowered into the opening through which they had arrived. Then just as they were being let go there was the distinct sound of Gregorian chant echoed on their intercom. It was an echo arising from millions of requests for help ascending to the citadel.

Once free of the clamps, Paulo ordered the ship to reverse and face away from the Omega. Then the Callisto and its precious contents began its decent. Several of the group left their seats and went to the stern of the ship to watch the retreating Omega. The forceps had by now been withdrawn and the Alpha opening closed. Sadly, the beauty of the citadel was marred because of the shattered glass and the gaping holes not yet mended. For a fleeting moment, the brightness of the morning sun of the segments shone through the membrane that separated the void from above. The rose lines of the territories could be seen spreading from the Omega and encircling all the way around the void emphasising its container-like shape. This was fundamentally a background lattice of cubes, of which twelve were in the immediate vicinity. Then because of the great distance all colour faded from sight and the blackness of the void prevailed. They were as if inside Adam's apple sliding into its core and looking at its skin from the inside. The time was near for "Le Crunch."

BATTLE ROYALE

Pedro watched the Callisto shrink from sight. He heaved a sigh of relief the whole hospitality undertaking had been a strain and he was characteristically cross. It was at that moment that several of the Com/ Saint Presidium members came running to his side. Their spokesperson a mature lady of fifty said in a quivering voice, "Pedro, our guards did not check the ship for the missing Praque because they did not know about it in time. Also, the monitors now show that two people put it on board the Callisto!"

Pedro froze. He glanced down at the departing speck and then over at the approaching enemy. Then he said in carefully tailored words, "It is too late, yet we create time, now Pedro don't use that as an excuse." Then he snapped, "We will have to bring back the ship. Issue a request immediately and I will explain to the Son."

With that he went to send his report.

On board the Callisto, Paulo and Captain Dave were beginning to sort themselves and the crew into some sort of order. Dave was keen to regain command and deal with Ham and Rap and sort out the whole terrorist debacle. It was then that the ships conventional communications sprang into life. It was Com/Saint,

"This is a confidential report for Captain Dave. Please confirm that we can continue,"

Dave responded with an affirmative and the report proceeded,

"We are now in possession of information about a serious theft. It seems that millions of Praque have disappeared and could be on board the Callisto. We wish for you to return immediately, so we can assist you in searching the ship. Also, there is a danger that you will be caught in the crossfire from an attack by enemy forces that now can be seen rising from the southeast. Therefore, you are requested to return with great haste."

Lionel navigated the Callisto into a pivoted turn. Dave ordered Laura to begin to have the ship searched for the currency and as Manz was nearby he was asked to assist. Dave gathered Paulo and his officers around the EM/SPEC and began to ascertain distances between the approaching enemy and their ship. To the universal scale, it looked as if the dark triangles were at least five hundred kilometres away but because of their high velocity were already moving between the ship and the Omega. Soon the Omega would be in range, but so would the Callisto. Meanwhile, Laura and Manz and all the Cadets began searching the interior of the ship. The task took them down to the engine room and it eventually back up to the Library, where Janette and Rico were reading. It was Laurette, who spoke first, "Allo, Senorita, are you looking for ze' treasure?"

Laura nodded in surprise, while Laurette curtly walked out to the corridor and pointed to the floor, which was in sections. The Cadets quickly removed one section and uncovered the first of the containers. Laura whistled in amazement.

Then the intercom squawked, and Laura reported, in an excited voice, the discovery of the Prayque. This was good news, but it was also confirmation of the frailty and unreliability of the human species. The whole event was quite a mess.

QUASAR LASER

By now the ship was about fifteen-earth minutes from the Omega. A company of Jet Packers came out on Jet Ski to escort them in. Each Jet Ski had two people on board armed with light weapons. No sooner had they began flight, than the pirate Diva's first onslaught began. Her forward command had just got into range, and she demanded quick and decisive action to shock and thaw the enemy defences

The crew of the Callisto could see all that was happening. Not only was the war erupting above, but also below. Paulo said to Lionel, Dave and Larry who had just arrived, "Captain me' thinks we are in a tight spot. It will be only a wing and a Prayer that will get us back inside the citadel."

"You know those guns are based on high sound frequency, that's why it hurts our ears. I cannot look at the flashes either they can blind me. If any of us spirit people get hit by one of those, we become incapacitated for several weeks. That is what can happen to the Jet Packers. In that time the enemy can just walk all over you. It will take our people a long time to locate those incapacitated."

Dave said, "Paulo that is strange! I can see those flashes quite well also, but I can't hear anything." – "Neither can I," said the others, we must be immune.

As most of the divisions of the Omega army were dispersed across the empires of Eternity and the void, it fell on the home guard to defend the citadel. Though the first barrage was devastating, and some shots damaged the gardens and vineyards the home guard were the ones who were attempting to seal the shattered glass and contain the vacuum. The Laser on wheels nearly repaired but some smaller lasers were now beginning to fire. These, however, were not enough to slow Divas advance. The incapacitated and wounded were now numbering hundreds and were being taken back to safer pastures. Diva had fine-tuned her artillery to get maximum results. The Son was in the Com/saint, which was now in the front line of resistance. He was monitoring the activity and being advised on the situation. He said that it was critical that the Praque is not ceased by Diva, as in her hands it could finance a sub creation with incredible complications for all. It was at that moment that the Callisto came under very serious attack.

HEART ATTACK

If things looked bad up on seventh stratum, they were as bad, if not worse, in Purgosia. They were receiving the full brunt of an attack from the forces of Thormentus. It was quite a spectacle the giant black mass filling the sky. All around the insidious object there were streaks of red light raining down on the city. Each streak caused a large explosion of high luminosity and deafening sound. The population was not able to defend, as they were but dwellers in transit. They were relying on the usual garrison along with help from above except that the attack was on such a broad front that no such help was available. The Purgoians therefore contributed as best they could by helping fallen angels' recoup. There was, however, the danger of falling black angels who could be very dangerous. Heavy traffic was now filling the road out of town as special vehicles took the wounded to safety in the Sangrias and into subterranean passages leading to the back of the triangle. The Angel divisions who were providing the city with defence had mounted small lasers on the top of buildings. They were also flying formations to draw fire from the city and prepare for an invading army that would pour from the Thormentus triangle.

However, one frightening aspect was that several battalions had already returned in tatters. By now the Euclidian had taken a bad hit the staff were quelling vibrations that were spreading just as fire spreads on earth. The Chasms of Yahweh had closed their giant doors for safety. Not only had the doors been closed but with a great shudder and the sound of suction the great time flux was reduced. This was the first time in living memory that such a phenomenon had occurred. It was obviously done for safety reasons, but the knock-on effect was miserable. If time was in suppression, then everything was slowed down and would remain so until the flux returned. It was like the world was in an induced coma.

RUSHING ROULETTE

Up at the Omega, things were going badly. Diva had rammed the citadel and her nose was standing like a pyramid in the midst of the ruins. This meant she was partially increased in size in front yet smaller at the back. The Callisto had been forced to stop because of the volume of unfriendly fire. On board the ship, Rap and Ham had been handcuffed and locked in a small storeroom. They were desperate and began tapping a moss code message on a pipe in a random effort to inform the enemy that there was bounty on board. As barrage after barrage exploded all around them, Paulo had to retire to sickbay with his sight impaired and his ears in discomfort. As he went, he was heard to say, "Jude where are you" Then as if Jude had answered, his cry things began to happen but not as Paulo would have liked.

Larry declared, "Captain, I believe we can fight the pirate here and now, because we are immune to demon artillery! Look we have nothing to lose, so let me try."

Dave looked at the Laura and she nodded.

Dave spoke over the intercom,

"Until further notice please take instructions from Dr Larry Coughlin who will be in command along with Laura and myself."

Francisca looked in amazement and pride; of course, her Larry will be well able to sort the problem. Larry spoke to the engine room and requested extra power. He asked Lionel to input his commands, while Ernst dashed to be of assistance. Then he sent cadets to man the upper communications laser and begin shooting at will. Three cadets scrambled up the ladder and swung the gun in the direction of Diva. Then there was a shudder as they fired their first shots. With that there was a high-pitched hum, and the Callisto once again became fully self-motivating. The crew let out a cheer. The cooks turned up the player and a CD played Yellow Submarine. Observers saw the Callisto turn and begin a lightning movement towards the flanks of Diva's fortress. The Callisto was going to attack Diva's flank. Pedro's eyes opened wide in astonishment and the Son smiled.

The effect on Diva was not to her liking. With her triangle facing upwards the rear which was of smaller magnitude was quite exposed. She commanded her lower side guns to fire. Coordinates were barked out and a salvo was instantaneously. A thousand red streaks homed in on the golden hull of the approaching Callisto. There was a shudder and a metallic sound, and, in an instant, it was Diva's guns that exploded. The lasers had rebounded. Every gun that fired was destroyed by the rebound. They were not tuned for meeting inverted substance of the human making. Her lower artillery was destroyed. The Callisto continued course now firing as it went. Diva could not fire for fear of more rebounds. The vacuum began to pull her backwards and, in the confusion, she lost altitude. With a great roar like a sinking ship the triangle began to slide.

Diva, herself, and the gunners at the point, could only look helplessly as they slipped down and back the way they had come. Her army never had a chance to alight. The defenders looked in amusement, waving and hooting as the enemy faded from sight. Then the communications crackled, and Pedro shouted his congratulations and that they should not try to land but head for Pergosia. Larry acknowledged and called for the ship to turn about.

BLACK FACK ATTACK

There were still two black triangles left in action. One of them was that of Zahtienne the third of the pirate group. He was intent on slicing the flow of the optic canal with the razor edge of his triangle. It was a race to the death. If he succeeded and the flow severed it could cause fatal haemorrhage of reality and they would win the day.

On board the Callisto Larry had now got permission to continue advising on evasive action. To achieve this, the Callisto had to make a power dive, perhaps faster than any object has ever travelled before. There would be no more shooting as all energy was needed for the dive. Zahtienne could see them coming and increased his speed. Larry did not know how he could stop such a big mass with such a small ship. Francisca left her post and belted herself near to Larry. Dave looked at her, was about to say something but changed his mind and just winked. She whispered to Larry, "Larry you can do it, I don't know how, but you can do it."

Larry flickered his eyes her direction for a split second and though concentrating on the EM/SPEC. Then he gave a small grin in recognition and called out, "Give me velocity boys – I need mojo!"

There was a hint of increased engine power and a feeling of more speed. The velocity indicator rose one more notch. The point of the black triangle was now extended right below them. The cooks had now been told to turn off their music, but this was replaced by a bellow from the sick bay. It was from Paulo, "Jude, come in Jude, we need your help"

Then a small voice piped up. It was Rico,

"Larry why not get all lights off and down all computers for extra energy?"

Larry shouted,

"Thank you, Rico, all lights out, kill all electro usage, all energy needed for velocity purposes."

The velocity needle rose two points. The controller then began to call out, "Fifty seconds till triangle severs Logo Op."

Larry asked, "Can we close on him before he severs?"

The controller, "Maybe with five seconds spare."

People held their breath. The Callisto might hit Zahtienne at the point. No one could even guess if that would have an effect. The glow of multi colours from the Logo optic filled the Callisto on its starboard side. Below them and closing at great speed was the deadly black point. Just then the enormous power of the Sun Heads poured down from above. The inside of the ship turned luminous and white from the surge of energy. The controller screamed, "Contact"

Then with a thunderous crack the Callisto hit the tip of the Zahtienne's triangle just before it reached the Logo Optic channel. The point severed and shattered in all directions. The whole triangle shuddered, and for some incredible reason began to crumble from the point backwards. It began to swivel off course rise in front and then to sink backwards crumbling as it went. It had vapour pouring out from all sides, and hundreds of its crew were now falling downwards to get away from its collapsing structure. Paulo had now regained his composure and knew what had happened.

"Captain," he said,

"Once again your inverted human material has been of use. This time it has polluted the negative enemy structure just like a vaccine to a virus."

The scene was like the Hindenburg disaster on a larger scale. Angel Jet Skiers had flown up and were already in action shooting at as many of the enemy as they could, rendering them incapacitated and allowing them sink into the depths of the void. Francisca blurted out,

"Oh, this is like a very bad dream. Larry do tell me it is a dream,"

Larry looked at her and with all sincerity said, "Yes, it is a dream I mean it, it is a dream."

She felt better having his assurance and gave a faint smile. Amidst congratulations from the crew Larry then said, "Dave can we now do the same for Purgosia?"

Dave agreed and so the Callisto continued to dive. The decent was at a velocity that the meters could not record. If calculated in the Universe, it would have been three times the speed of light.

Meanwhile far below it was Heroshi looked up to see a golden star sweeping down from the heavens, firing as it came. This was his friends in action!

Pedro ordered that they land in Purgosia immediately. However, before handing back control of the ship Dave and Laura Larry took the liberty of flinging the ship into a roll. Hiroshi could see what was happening and screamed, "Look a victory roll in a spaceship they must be nuts, you could not do that where we come from."

Just then the city resounded to an enormous shudder, as the time flux began once again to increase its rotation. From the top of the Corcovado, the silver deluge correspondingly increased. The familiar pounding recommenced – the heart of reality strengthened once again. Bells began to ring, and the sense of terror abated. Hiroshi asked one of the Angels as to whether the flux could also be reversed. The Angel said, "Yes it has been known to happen, and when it does the Universe begins to contract."

Hiroshi looked around in amazement.

An escort of Jet Packers rose to meet the arrival of the Callisto. One of the escorts who introduced himself as commander spoke. His voice penetrated the ship. He said that they could only be afforded a brief stop. Their time had been almost fully used up and speed was of the essence. He then gave a friendly salute and led them into their landing place. Hiroshi had already decided that he would take his chances and try to return to earth. It was a difficult decision, but he was by now fully reconciled to the choice.

TOUCH AND GO

This time around the Callisto landed without any official reception. However, there was a small ceremony of sorts. A group of singers in flowing gowns that appeared out of nowhere. There also were some military personnel, the city mayor with his entourage and a group of the Callisto people's close relations. As the doors opened, Larry alighted feeling in his heart that he would like to stay. He felt that he was in a dream and was about to wake up. He had no ambition to return to the hassle that the Universe had to offer. The war of the Gods was terrifying, but it did not include the spectre of death and this was a considerable difference. So, despite the war, he felt that he was about to leave pleasure-island after a vacation and did not want to go home. Francisca came out behind Larry holding hands with Rico and Laurette. Just then there was a shout that came from a dark couple. They bounded forward saying "Laurette, Rico we have found you, we have found you at last."

The children were taken by surprise, but after a few tender moments they began to weep and hug their parents, turned, and waved and melted into the crowd. Heroshi and Jill arrived, both looking well and the better of their honeymoon. There were other family members pushing forward to meet the travelers. Richard made his way to Patty who was overcome with joy but sad to think od his departure yet anxious to meet him back on earth.

Then a member of the city management came forward holding a magnificent Excalibur. If shone with a light so bright that people squinted at the sight. Its metal glistened like it was coated in crushed diamonds and the handle appeared to be made of material like ivory. Engraved in small writing, evidently in English, Latin, Hebrew, and Arabic were the words, which he read out,

"In appreciation the gallant action performed in the name of freedom by the Captain and Associates of the good ship Callisto UMEX 171 from – The People of Purgosia and Stratus 7."

Then the list of crew members was engraved in a line down the centre of both sides of the blade. Then he sheathed the sword and handed it to Dave. As an added gift every member of the Callisto got a smaller replica equally attractive.

The Mayor said that he was just here to say thank you and safe trip.

One of the military people approached the Captain and said that they had removed the stolen Praque from the ship and would be transported aloft immediately. Then some of the families gave them food saying that when they arrived in the Universe, they will be very hungry. However, the ship did have dried ration on board to cover such an emergency, but the extra food was welcome. The question was what a reverted Quark Cake would look like in reality. Would it just disappear in a stream of energy?

THE CAVALRY ARRIVE

Suddenly, the either was filled with a very loud buzzing sound. Some of the crew thought it sounded like a blitz from World War II. A monstrous green aircraft with triangles marked on its side appeared. It was as large as the whole of Pursoia and big enough to fight any black triangle. Paulo quickly explained their presence, mainly for Hiroshi's benefit. He added that they have retained their full Omega size as a deterrent to any enemy from down here or anywhere else.

"This is the first of many Template Ships pulled from duty in the outreach and returned to help us. They are as you already know the scouts and the pioneers of deep think. They are the cutting edge between the Word and non-existence. They travel with expanding divine thought cutting through the nothingness, which is as dense as earth rock and looks like grey icy Styrofoam. Now they are being re assembled to knock sense into the pirate mob. Now, enough from me I must not detain you."

Heroshi was now holding Jill in a farewell embrace. His decision had been courageous, and Jill understood while at the same time understanding that she will soon meet him on earth in her past life – also a great understanding and equally courageous. She bade him goodbye, went down the gangway and watched the ship prepare to depart. The news about the supporting Template ships pleased Larry, but he hoped they would hurry. By now the marshal plans were taking effect, and a transparent defensive shield was being drawn over the city and this would guarantee the security. The arch would be unaffected by this cover as it rotated through an opening. Also, if one looked hard and long one could see that the logo optic tunnel was also almost covered in a repellent skin. Just then the singers began a lament. It was soft and alluring and sounded like the Hawaiian wedding song. The words "Sweet Aloha" could be heard. The doors closed the Captains once again became people of prominence, all hands awaiting their command. "Ernst, let it roll," said Dave. With that the ships engines whined, and it began to move. At first their departure was painfully slow. Their friend's relations, and Paulo could be seen waving for what seemed a long time. They then pointed back towards the blue triangle and were gone.

15

Dead Or Alive

T he interior of the ship became buzzing with activity. As planned, they travelled down the red triangle and approached the apex of the blue triangle. They were back in familiar territory and on the road home. The activity within the ship returned to almost normal. Meetings were called to discuss operations. There were maintenance reports and engine tests, and briefings with the crew. Having been so long out of touch with reality, there was a danger that they might not respond effectively on return. Dr Manz was concerned that their muscular strength might have dissipated due to different gravitational circumstances. When possible, gym exercises were performed but all they could do was leave it to chance.

Hiroshi now feeling melancholy returned to his enclosure and sat beside the hybo with head in hands. Richard and Larry knowing his plight followed to make sure that he was not overcome. When they arrived, Hiroshi was meditating evoking Buddha and imploring his return to life when they enter the umbilical. Perspiration gathered on his brow and a tear rolled down his cheek. Richard tried to cheer him up by reminding him that if things go wrong, he will be caught in the flux and whisked back to the Chasms. So, ways he was in a win-win situation. This reminder helped him somewhat.

Thormentus now knew that the Praque had being removed from the Callisto. He also had heard about the Excalibur and realised, as it was made of the same "deterial" and therefore valuable beyond belief. However, he did not know about the replicas. He called his officers to his conference chamber. Diva and Zahtienne also arrived, both in a state of agitation. The atmosphere was tense, and no one spoke waiting for Thormentus's first words. He began quietly,

"Fellow warriors of the cause need I tell you, your performance was disastrous". Then he raised his voice, "Why in the first place did some blithering idiots advise me about the visitors? What did they expect from me? – a miracle!"

He gave a fiendish grin.

"It was better that I slept and never knew about these perpetrators of the void. But ye had decided we will tell the great Thormentus and he will put things right."

Then he roared, "Well you were wrong, I did not put things right and why not? Because of you, and you and you …".

He pointed a crocked finger in various directions, but not directly at the attendance.

Nevertheless, the officers cowed casting their eyes downwards. Then he said in a softer voice, "Now you will methodically re organise, and you will have an opportunity to regain my respect. The plan is as follows."

He sat back and looked at Diva, who promptly spoke in her usual shrill voice,

"As two of our triangular bodies are damaged, we will use them a shield. We will close in behind the Callisto, while I, Thormentus who is intact will lie close to the entrance to the umbilical. We will launch our new hyper stealth fighters that are so slim that they capable of avoiding any rebound from enemy material. Under the command, Commander Wilma Darrel in the Amadeus the attack will penetrate the Callisto stun its crew and collect the Excalibur. Then destroy the navigation and direct the Ship down into the void. All this to be done so fast that their heavy Template ships will not have time to rescue them."

SONG, SONG BLUE

This time things looked quite different as journeyed down the blue triangle. The sea was not so bright as it had been. It had now taken on a midnight blue hue and a great storm was in the making. There were already monstrous waves moving down from its point towards the south and the umbilical entrance. As the sea crashed and rolled, it emitted lightning. The scene was terrifying yet wonderful and as before it caused every piece of machinery on the Callisto to turn on. There was a blaze of light and a roar of machinery from generators to the cook's blenders in the galley. Ernst and the crew feverishly tried to turn thing off, but as before it proved impossible. The EM/SPEC went crazy with lights flashing while it began to blurt out thousands of statistics.

They were now near to three quarters way down the triangle and approaching the great enclosure in which the Cosmos was contained. Hiroshi looked to see if it was still intact. He expected it would still be tethered to the great umbilical. It was into this entrance the whole of the triangles' oceanic power was being channelled. It appeared that all was well!

Then with a strained voice the navigator announced that he had sighted the enemy triangles. Two had risen from the depths and were closing in from behind to port and starboard. Both these enemy objects were in tatters but still active and therefore a formidable enemy not to be underestimated. To make matters worse now they sighted the Thormentus's undamaged triangle trying to cut across their bows obviously to block them off. No sooner than he had made that assumption then a shot was fired hitting them mid-ships. Thormentus was now using a new lower-level anti-human type frequency! The effect was terrifying. The ship shuddered from bow to stern. All power was temporarily lost. They were plunged into blackness and an icy chill swept through the ship. The computers began to make a whining noise as the enemy had launched a screech attack. They then went blank but seemed to recover and spring into life as their astro-virus scans began to work.

Then suddenly the ship became filled with what looked like hail followed by roaring brimstones that tore through the interior knocking the crew over. Richard had been flung against one of the walls receiving a severe bump from a fire extinguisher. In the furore he grabbed it in desperation and punched the release and fired at the whizzing objects. To his surprise with a great hiss the contents shot everywhere causing the hail to dissolve. Then there was a lull, things settled down and the lights came back on. Dave called out, "Chief, any Casualties?"

"Chief Rainer Sir, glad to report no casualties and damaged wall plates that can be mended otherwise, just clean up."

There were none and with a sigh of relief people stood up and looked around. What they saw was Richard standing with an extinguisher and the inside of the ship covered in black spots. Richard looked worried like he had done something wrong but instead he was congratulated and slapped on the back.

A voice was then heard calling out to the crew. It was Nadine, and she was reminding them of a drill.

"I know you have all received messages of doom and despair. This is part of the psycho-virus attack. It may be the first of many. We know the enemy is using its telepathy to scare us so we must be strong. It is probable that in advance of its coming many of you have been prompted to think of your greatest weaknesses or perhaps to despise your colleagues. Isn't that correct? Now to counter this you must think about the strengths that you and your colleagues possess and do this like a mantra even while you are retaliating or using your fire extinguishers."

Richard laughed.

Now in view of the new danger, Dave ordered their atomic engines restarted. With a roar Ernst's turbines and power packs exploded into action. Once again, the ship jolted forward under its-own power and began to gather additional velocity.

Manz told Dave that they should be out of range when they get inside the tunnel? Also, those hits were not a serious as expected.

Dave replied, "Yeh Casper, hopefully we will not try to follow us!"

Then Lionel the navigator spoke, "Captain, I see there are two entrances to the umbilical we must select the one flowing back into the Universe. Which one do you and the committee want us to take?"

Larry joined the group now gathered around the EM/SPEC. It showed that the entrance on the right seemed to be receiving the brunt of the outflow. Waves of electromagnetism were now in evidence colliding sideways with waves of gravitation and disappearing inside. This looked like the way to go.

Dave replied, "Okay Lionel, go for the one on the right."

AMADEAS

On board the flagship, Thormentus estimated that they were too late to stop the Callisto. Therefore because of their extra speed he gave an order. "Prepare to launch the Blades". He went to the launching bay himself and climbed on board one of the sinister looking hyper blades. There was five of them and they, wafer thin and bristling with warheads, antennas, and complex weaponry. It was Francisca who first sighted them and raised the alarm. They were already launched before anyone in the Callisto realised. It was a small glint on one of the visors that alerted her. She yelled, "Captain, bandits at ten o'clock!"

Delia was not under arrest and now it was her turn to try and help Ham and Rap. She had already discovered the door opening code and in moments had liberated the deadly two. She whispered, "This is it boys, you are free, let's take the ship!"

As the ship lurched from the storm and from the manoeuvres, she led him out onto the lighted corridor. She led them to the Captains quarters and there beside his Hybo was a scabbard with the Excalibur in its leather scabbard. She thrust the treasure into Raps hands and said, "Did you know, this is made of Praque."

Raps eyes widened and a wide grim spread across his long bony face. He grunted and said in a menacing voice,

"Are you sure? If that is true it means it can do untold damage if used correctly in every stratum. Let's take the ship.

Dalia smiled; this was just what she wanted to hear. Within a few moments, they entered the engine room and with the blade of the Excalibur pointed at Ernst's throat they took control of the area. His crew submitted for fear he would be hurt. Without hesitation Ham and Rap both threw every switch in the opposite direction. There was a high-pitched screeching noise the immediately the engines shut down. Ernst covered his ears and began to cry saying, "Mein Got, you 'vill destoy everyzing!"

Ham hit him hard and growled, "Shut up old man, soon you won't be needed so look out!"

Then she grabbed the intercom and shouted,

"Captain and crew, this ship is now under the command of the great Thormentus. You are to surrender immediately, if not we will kill, as in cut up, Ernst and his crew, one at a time. You have no choice as we have control of the engine room and the Excalibur that can sever a plasma body in one blow."

DETERMINATION

Back in Stratus 7, there was a meeting for the Committee of the Highest. It would take place high up in the territory of the Father and on a flat plateau adjacent to his great golden orb. The Father stood there waiting on their arrival. He expected, Andrew, Elijah, Mohammed, Abraham, Shirdi-Sai-Baba, Adi Shankar, Jacob, Gabriel, and Michael come. Beside him was a table with a cauldron and a crystal sphere and a map like a horoscope. He invited his Son to speak first.

The Son said that the attack had shaken the very core of their existence. Their old enemy had resurfaced and hit them hard. The questioned was why had they not addressed the problem sooner, rather than letting aggression break out? They must have known that the visitor's arrival had opened old wounds. If we had been vigilant, we could have returned them from perhaps Purgosia as they had seen plenty by then. Now we have inadvertently been our own worst enemy! Now where do we go from here?

One person suggested that they fragment some of their territories into one massive triangle and sweep the void clean – an army that no one could defeat.

Another said this might win the day, but the reformation process would be long and tedious and full of unforeseen difficulties. What would happen if some part of their essence would not re-unite, then a whole new struggle would kindle in our midst?

Another option was to shrug it off and hope it would not re occur again. This was quickly rejected as derelict.

Another option was more deadly. It suggested they withdraw the triangles and severing the Universe and casting it adrift to its demise. The remaining humans would by then have lost their inheritance as blessed offspring which means they could not come into the fold in one body at convergence time. Instead, they could be tolerated entry on an individual basis only. They would all be drawn up immediately and the void closed and crushed out of existence taking with it all the troublemakers. We would then have a secure citadel a fortress Paradise, an island Haven that could not be harmed. We could then consider making a new void and consummating a new creation. Spirinda sprang to the defence.

"How can you think like that, if termination were to happen the further development of humanity would be discontinued, and those who had lived so far would be on the divine welfare? Think of the cost! How much love would we have to pour on them as they would be so individually isolated and out of their depth for all eternity, a burden on one and all. This would also be an act of cowardice and make us no better than our enemies. It was not a solution and it could bring opposition from our own ranks with detrimental consequences."

Then she said that to terminate creation would be immoral and would be the first flaw ever in divine nature. A new creation without a demon in the works would yield a soft child that could never be an AMGOD. Creation could only successfully occur as an antidote to adversity. She said that she loved and believed in the current humanity and would be desolated if latter solution were adapted.

Several others said they agreed with Spirinda and the Father said he was glad they had come to that agreement. Thus, the question of cosmic abortion was eliminated. Then they got down to other immediate needs.

They agreed to attempt special protection for the Callisto until back in the Universe. Then they reviewed a report on Diva's earlier demands. They planned to contain Zahtienne's forces and then to open fresh negotiations. The next intention was to offer psychotherapy assistance to supply them with light and energy like they never had before. Then they decided since the human visit it might also be possible to negotiate some exchange visits to identify how compromises could be established but also to increase security in future and to re-convene after the crisis was over. Then the Father took grey snow-like crystals from the cauldron beside him and rubbed it on the transparent sphere. He gazed into the sphere his face reflecting pixels of light they radiated form its interior. Then he withdrew, looked satisfied and closed the conference.

CLEAN SWEEP

The flotilla of Template ship's commander was named Baptista. He was one who specialised in spreading the word into the unknown, a true pioneer at heart. The Son had spoken to Baptista who agreed to visit with a third of his force. His liners soon emerged through one of the suns and flew straight down through the Omega which was now wide open to allow them passage. Then with a humming sound almost musical they flew down to Purgosia. Baptist stationed several ships as defence of the area and with the others began operation Clean Sweep an effort to cut off the pirates. In moments they had glided over the blue triangle and had caught up with the Callisto. As soon as they ascertained the state of play Baptist reported to Com/saint, and to the Callisto.

The Son came on the intercom, "John we have trouble we have pirates on board." Baptista replied,

"We are blocked by two black triangles with a kamikaze attitude. The Calisto is being buzzed by five Hyper Blades."

Baptist gave some orders to his gunners and in moments all three black triangles were seriously hit. They began to smoke some with flames roaring inside. They fell back immediately. However, the Hyper Blades reached the Callisto which was now under control of the terrorists. began to slow. The blades came along side and suction clamps were shot against the side of the ship. The main entrance was forced open and with a rush of escaping air several black figures stormed inside. The crew of the Callisto were gathered in the navigation area. Rap and Dalia were standing with the Excalibur pointing while Ham had secured a handgun and ammunition and brought up the engine room crew while holding Francisca by the hair saying that Rap would kill her if they did not do as told. At that moment, the intruders joined in. Even Rap and Ham were aghast at the sight of their allies. There was a dozen of them all about six feet high. They were of various build their faces ash white and their eyes were pink and sunken. They had communication helmets with antennas, and some had beards. Then from their midst, the tallest figure stepped forward and bellowed,

"I am Thormentus, the one who defies all that you stand for! Do not dare obstruct me in any way or you will be destroyed in moments. Obey what I tell you, and you or you will spend Eternity in captivity. Who here is your leader?"

Dave stepped forward and nodded. Thormentus shouted,

"I want you to fly back to Purgosia to collect the Praque that was removed. They will hand it over because I will tell them that you will be earth killed if we are not given what we request. They cannot refuse as this is against their modus operandi. Also, if there is any Praque on this ship in addition to the Excalibur, I want it!"

Then he gave a loud laugh and his cronies joined in. At that very moment, a salvo from Baptisat's Cruisers burst among the waiting blades. Larry leapt across the room and knocked Rap to the floor. He grabbed the Excalibur and swung it at Ham, who took the flat of it in the face. He let Francisca go and she in turn flung herself at Dalia and caught her in a vicelike grip. Dalia screamed and kicked but stopped when she saw Larry with the sword pointing at Thormentus. Both he and his group began to retreat. Then he clicked his fingers and three of his troopers came forward drawing swords of their own. Their weapons seemed to be split in two parts and shimmer with fire. Thormentus also produced a sword of his own and shouted,

Burn that infidel, burn him!"

Francisca shouted, "No, Larry, No!"

Too late to stop, Larry sprang into action. Richard remembered the fire extinguishers. He and several of the crew now lunged to the walls and grabbed flare guns and fire extinguishers and began to discharge them at the intruders. The result was that they screamed and seemed to burn from the chemicals. All this turned the scene into one of sheer chaos. Ernst and his team began to work their way back to the engine room to re-start the thrusters. The nearest villain lunged towards Larry. Just then the villain received a flare in the face and fell backwards in disarray. Richard had found another weapon. Larry took a swing at two others knocking them backwards having sliced across both their chests. The sword was well balanced and was easy to wield. One sweep and it cut through any of the flaming weaponry leaving them broken on the floor. The troopers backed off, but Thormentus, seeing Larry's defiance, moved into the fray swinging his own double-bladed flaming sword in deadly circles. Larry's sword seemed to respond on its own. He found himself slashing and thrusting almost out of control. Thormentus got the message that this was not an ordinary adversary or an ordinary weapon. He could not manage to swing his own sword accurately and could only parry in defence. Dave, Francisca, and several Cadets now armed with fire extinguishers began to shoot. The barrage of foam and flare had the desired effect. The black caped enemy began to retreat. Thormentus was soon at the exit beaten back by the dexterity and power of Larry's Sword and with a roar of anger flung his own at Larry. The sword hit Larry pinning him to the wall one section above his shoulder and the other below his armpit. The flames from the sword scorched his face and arms. There was no pain, yet he knew he was burning. He could not move, and the painless sensation was terrifying. Just then Rap, Ham and Delia who had got free followed Thormentus into his Hyper Blade. Rap stopped for a moment turned and looked at Larry's plight laughed and, in a blink, departed. Richard rushed forward and hit the control button closing the door instantly tearing a piece of black material from a trooper's cloak. The blades scattered in all directions. Baptista's ship began to hit them but at least three got away. One of them was Tormentus while two others turned in pursuit of the Callisto.

Francisca and Richard eased the sword from Larry's shoulder and let laid him gently on the floor. A medical team arrived and gave instant treatment. Oddly, his skin was cut but not burned and one good thing was that bleeding did not occur in this environment. He was taken then taken to the sick bay, mumbling as he went that he was fine, fit and well and wanting to continue the fight. With that he passed out. The way was clear for their escape from eternity.

The intercom clicked on, it was Dave, said once again as often before, "Damage report needed." Then "Other than Larry, has anyone else been hurt?"

An officer sprinted to his side saluted and said that the ship was undamaged, and Officer Larry Coughlin was the only casualty but was comfortable. The blades are scattered but dare not follow us into the tunnel." Larry was given permission to leave the infirmary. Francisca got leave from her post to assist him. Their first task was to secure the precious Excalibur back into the nearest Hybo – his own. With that done and the Hybo locked, they headed towards the stern of the ship. She thought how crazy this is. Here I am a simple girl who likes home and family yet here on the edge of eternity with the man of my dreams. Larry also felt romantic. He wanted to grab Francisca and smother her with kisses, but he knew, given the circumstances that it might spoil their very special relationship. So, as it happened, earth etiquette prevailed, and he settled for a good heart to heart conversation. He therefore squinted his eyes and looked at her through a haze. Through blurred vision she looked like an unfinished Mona Lisa. She looked back and did the same and blurting out that he looked like the Hulk without make up. They both giggled and she punched his shoulder, making him yelp!

Then they focused their attentions to the panoramic view out the window, which was amazing. Far to the left, several template ships had arrived and were attacking what remained of the enemy. As Thormentus retreated he radioed Commander Draft, telling him to take the three Hyper Blade and catch the enemy before they enter the umbilical and smash them back eternity. This means they will not have reached the rotation of the arch and therefore will fall back here. Is that clear. Go now."

TUNNEL VISION

The Callisto was now lining up to enter the umbilical. They were flying low and the Triangle and it appeared that their choice of entrance must have been correct. Now there was a strip of golden light pointing as if pointing to the entrance. Then the navigator reported white doves circling, a good omen. With a mighty roar they plunged into a star-studded tunnel.

Larry and Francisca at the stern of the ship watched a black circular canopy closed over their heads. Behind the last glimpse of the bright blue world in which they had lived for several earth days. This was their last look at the future. Then it was also gone obscured by giant waves of both gravitation and electromagnetism. The Gravitational waves were sweeping across from left to right. The electromagnetic waves were coming directly from behind. Where two waves met there was an enormous burst of energy. Just like a "white horse" at sea.

Then suddenly large black dots appeared behind them. They were had the familiar shape of a Hyper Blades! It was remarkable that they had dared follow. Larry excitedly alerted Dave and the Lionel and hurried to the front of the ship.

Dave said loudly, "We hope our black box will have recorded our adventure. Those of you who wish, should pray like heck for a safe delivery of Hiroshi. Both Laura and I wish to say that it has been an honour to share such an enormous experience with you, the finest people I have ever met, and let's keep it that way, God Speed."

Don Travis was already busy, and Nadine Baker was also making offering on Hiroshi's behalf. The EM/SPEC began to hum and click more than usual giving its first physical reading in quite some time.

"Temperature, now registering at infinity. Time-100/sec to Creation. Only Strong interaction – prevalent. Electromagnetic force predominant. W and Z Particles immanent. Higgs Bosons 1%."

Then it began to show an immense radiation reading. The reading was so high that Quan Chow one of the physicists wondered if the ship was about to be destructed. The membrane they will meet was the expanding surface of the original universe's first split second of creation and with it was radiation of considerable intensity.

Then Dave ignored the threat and gave another order, "Maximum Velocity, booster affirmative, steady as she goes."

Francisca whispered, "Goodbye marshmallow man," as she prodded Larry in the ribs.

There was silence except for the steady oxford voice of the controller reading off statistics. Then suddenly he exclaimed, "Strange phenomena appearing – time reversal evident – don't follow, I repeat time – 6000 and rising." At that moment they arrived at the membrane. Once again, Larry felt that eerie feeling, which he was experiencing in Tramahon running the gauntlet from Gasper. There was froth and bubbles splashing all over the windows and Larry thought he heard the sound of laughter from the waves, but he could not be sure!

Then a reminder, the navigator announced, "Achtung, bandits at six o'clock still with us."

Thormentus had not gone away.

The circle of light loomed like the wobbling transparent bubble. Inside it there is a million silver lines showering down from above. This must be the lower end of the infamous arch they had experienced in the Chasms of Yahweh. In a Plank moment they will be back in reality and re-inverted and also homogenised into particles that rotate all the way up to the Chasms and back in an "Augenblick" Larry felt a chill and heard a voice cry out "Blades still at six o'clock" Then he felt a tremendous impact and passed out.

PARADISE LOST

The lights went out, there was a flash and a crack and a jolt, and the Callisto was hurled back to reality. Just as before people had lost consciousness. Hiroshi shouted "Goodbye," and then fainted. That was the moment that they broke through the 15 billion light year of expanding perimeter. Instantaneously a thing bead or brane of light, shot through the ship. It was made up of every colour that light can produce, and it split into hundreds of illuminated shafts that ricochet about the interior. Each particle became hitched to a brane, which was in fact the arch. Then for an undetected moment everything froze and went back to the opposite direction. Larry dreamt that he was swimming in the lake in the Chasms of Yahweh. This was his last memory of the seventh dimension.

Slowly people began to awaken. Hiroshi's mind was in a whirl. He felt like a rag doll being hurdled around in a washing machine. He felt sick and out of control. When eventually he opened his eyes, he thought he would be at grand central nation. He looked for the arrival deck at the arch and for the welcoming crowds and so were the saints and the scholars. He could see figures, but they were huddled in seats in most drab surroundings. Everything was grainy and flickering, and he felt his body had been packed into a press and squeezes. He felt dejected and disappointed. Then he realised he should not be disappointed because he was on the Callisto and was therefore alive! He could feel his pulse beat with enormous rapidity, which meant he was alive! He was alive and human, but he felt like a trapped mammal in a pool. He felt his stomach rumbling and a pain in his head and suddenly he loved it. Then putting all the discomfort aside, he cried out, "I'm alive, I'm alive. Oh, thank you Father Buddha I'm alive!"

He climbed from his seat and moved up to where Larry was at the EM/SPEC. He shook Larry till he groaned and sat up. In a moment they began to celebrate. Larry and Lional read the last report from the EM/SPEC just as they had crashed into reality. To their amazement it clearly showed a reversal of the rotation from the Olgas. Then a moment later when they were back in reality it went back to normal. Larry shouted, "Hear this, Pedro reversed the deluge and saved Heroshi. Thanks be to the Father, the Son and Spirinda."

On the outward journey, people had shed their humanity the opposite was more difficult. They missed the sense of freedom that he had enjoyed with disembodiment and now also must contend with incredibly poor vision compared with the clarity of sight. The ability of being able to see in a complete 360 degrees was now forfeited. This was the restricted world in which they had awakened.

Lionel, now back in control, looked with horror at the EM/SPEC. Hyper-Blades were closing in all around.

There was a sharp crackle on the intercom. It was one of the Italian engineers who yelled, "Bandits still with us, everywhere, Bandits, Devils everywhere!"

Dave called out, "Evasive action – Larry are you well enough to take control again. How the heck did they come this far? By now they should be vaporised!"

As Larry cranked the ship to port he shouted to Dave, "Look they did not revert or diminish, they seem very large and getting bigger. They're not shrinking like us stuck in high magnitude and are turning transparent."

Then the enemy gained speed firing at them as they came. The lead ship now quite enormous looked like it was going to ram them. Inside was a patriotic scoundrel intent on self-sacrifice. He did not know where his shattered remains would go, but he believed that he would find eternal glory in the ultimate world.

Larry tried to change direction, but the Blade was too close. The blade fired point blank. The shot tore through the side of the Callisto and out the other. Just like the Omega there was an immediate draft drawing everything with it. Sirens went off and foam began automatically to pour over the gaping holes. Emergency crew ran to shore up the areas. Manz shouted to Larry, "Look they did not invert, and are too large, anti-matter will annihilate them."

Suddenly just as predicted, a mass of black particles streamed at the Blades from every direction. In a moment, each Blade was covered in seething material obscuring all their vision. The lead ship swerved and hit another further back in the line. Chunks of de-material bounced over the Callisto and a pirate was seen spinning away. Then chaos set in with Blades spinning in every direction as they were systematically crushed out of existence. There was a hideous screech and then silence.

With danger receding, everyone shook hands and embraced. Dr Manz came straight over to Hiroshi and gave him a two second examination. He turned and smiled and pronounced that Hiroshi is alive. Heroshi giggled. It was at that moment that there was a chirp. It was Kiki! He had returned from the perhaps a noosphere by some very strange means. There is no knowing if that was where he had been, but he certainly did not enter the seventh dimension. Laura let her own cry of delight. Kiki was evidently too baffled to fly and so Laura replaced him in the empty cage. He was immediately fed with birdseed while a cook put on an inverted egg to boil.

Francisca moved up to Larry and said, "Well done skipper!"

Larry nodded very slowly looking at the EM/SPEC as he did so, and then a smile crossed his face and he said, "Yes my little Mexican, may I ask you a personnel question?"

No one was listening so he went ahead.

"Will you marry me Lieutenant Francisca Spazola" and IOU a proper engagement ring ASAP. Francisca smiled and said, "Before I answer that Dr Larry Coughlin, what about your Excalibur will it shrink, or kill us as we shrink?

Larry was alarmed. He hurriedly made his way to the sleeping quarters while Francisca came along behind. Had the ship shrunk around his mighty sword? Would it penetrate the sides of the ship and cast them into space? He peeped at his cubicle. The hybo was intact – no damage. He opened the lock and slowly drew the cover. There was the shape of a sword on the bed, but no sword. They both gasped. Larry put down his hand, and he was relieved to feel the contours of a sword. It must have turned invisible at reversion. It was defiantly there so to be sure he pressed to see if it would give away! It turned out to be quite solid.

Larry asked Francisca, "Why had it not stayed at the higher stratum dimension measurements?"

She replied after some thought, "It must be because it is within our ship. It obeyed the environment and shrank with us."

Larry muttered, "The AMGOD is oh so clever – they knew all this would happen."

Then he smiled and closed the hybo and very carefully turned the lock shut.

BACK ON TRACK

The EM/SPEC indicated that they were travelling at a fraction short of the relative speed of light. Then to everyone's joy, it indicated that the time was exactly the same as at their entry over two weeks ago. There was also a concern that when they enter the Cosmos proper, they might get caught in the outflow from the other tunnel just as before. They could be pulled around and keep repeating the circle in a state of eternal return. To combat this, Vice-Captain Laura suggested that they turn to starboard and travel sideways from the draw. In other words, following the contour of the extremity of the expanding universe and then jettisoning all unnecessary items and then applying maximum velocity along with the aid of all boosters available. A brave person who shall remain nameless jested, "There goes Kiki."

All around them, the sky was curved but seemed to be widening. Up ahead they now could see the familiar interior of the universe through the neck of the umbilical. Then seconds later they were fully inside. Ernst gave the turbines everything he could and applied the booster rockets as before. This time they turned sharp to Starboard and travelled along the edge of the light extremity, where there Laura estimated there should be an eddy and less pull. This proved to be correct judgment and for a short time they enjoyed a spectacular velocity and also a view. The surface of light from the dawn of history was like looking at a bubble from the inside, imaginary of course. It also looked like cellophane paper, full of creases and pulls, irregular and ever changing. Then as they were now safe, Dave ordered a change of direction and turned the Callisto in towards the centre of the Cosmos.

It was time for the crew to relax. The cooks had their food products irradiated. They therefore had fresh bacon and eggs. There was consternation when some of the eggs were found to have their yoke on the outside, inversion did not suit them! They turned on some music and began preparing a meal in the galley. Very soon the aroma of grilled bacon and freshly brewed coffee seeped around the ship. Hunger pangs returned and business was brisk.

Travis asked if he could speak on the intercom. Laura nodded permission.

He said the following, "Let us give thanks to the Lord who is both Mohammed the Father and the Son, for they have delivered us through the valley of evil. Also, to the spirit that was given us, so we might succeed."

16

Debrief

The Captain called a meeting of all senior personnel. It was in their conference room, the one with the cage that Kiki now occupied. The meeting proved to be tedious because of the amount of detail that had to be checked. It involved reports by technical services on the fitness of Callisto, damage reports on various parts of the ship, an in-depth study of navigation charts and finally the instructions that all people in the ship were to write reports on events. Not much detail was required, but the main features were to be reported. Qualifying notes were later to be prepared where necessary. It was expected that on earth there would be a suspicion that the crew had hallucinated but if their stories coincided there was a chance that the truth would prevail. If the black box has worked, it should vindicate all our actions. This along with photoreconnaissance and EM/SPEC printouts should suffice. Manz was asked to organise a fitness report on all members of the Calisto with emphasis on mental health. His medical team was asked about their views if the dangers to earth from space viruses. He agreed and then asked, how soon could they begin a sky search for Hydrogen based galaxies, but before he could receive a reply the meeting was interrupted by a petty officer that brought in a report. It stated as follows.

Velocity- 2950,000 k per sec, reducing.
Completion of Global Symmetry Transfer.
Magnitude – normal,
Time – Anti Clockwise Arrow re-established.
Temperature- rising from -273 o Kelvin- Phase Transition now finished.
Force effects – Electromagnetic, (inverse square laws now in effect)
Density – Photon abundance,

Purity of inflow – 100% clarity, Consistent Hydrogen and Neutrinos and Muons
Alternative effects, – Weak Force W+, W-, Z o and Gravitation, – Gravitons.
Background Radiation – 72% active but reducing.
Energy – 10/16 1 TeV

The word EUSARUS sent a chill down Larry's spine. He realised that this was the authority that could prove to be a legal quagmire into which all the crew would fall. It was good that Hiroshi had not remained in Purgosia, as that would have caused immense problems. There was enough of a difficulty created when Ham, Rap and Dalia had disappeared. Dr Manz was asked again to continue his health checks that had already begun. Larry was asked to report on the physics aspect of the events to date. However, he was not in a mood to try and broach such a broad subject in this way. There was just too much knowledge accumulated to be dismissed in one report. He pointed that there was no hard physics in the next dimension. Their reports will be more speculative though based on strong probabilities confirmed by eyewitnesses, but not actual physics. He pointed out that when he and the other physicists would have to read everyone's report because they are contingent to the conclusions that will be drawn. They would be seeking a consensus of the crew's experiences, looking at all the tape recordings and have endless meeting. Then and only then could he comment?

Then Dave opened his log. He read transcripts of the last report they sent to EUSARUSS. It had asked for assistance as they were being drawn towards an unknown source. They had reported much to EUSARUS but received no reply though they had visual confirmation that the authorities received the messages. He said to the meeting,

"There is almost no doubt that they will conclude that we had been destroyed by a Black Hole. Therefore, the story will probably go along the lines that we managed to survive such an encounter. You see if we say next dimension, they will assume it to be a Black Hole and if we report on Omega, they will say singularity. There will be no way that they will either believe or attempt to believe what we report. Unless the black box does its job. So, what I am saying is we must report what we experienced but to be prepared that they will probably say it was a Black Hole experience because that is what they said the last time. I will deal with the loss of the three-crew members and we have plenty of witnesses.

One other thing, I will ask that the Excalibur is used to raise funds for such illnesses as Cystic Fibrosis and others but that it to be donated to the state.

Richard was listening with interest and chanced to look at his watch, the one he had been given in Paradise. It was now completely aglow except for the gold area where they had only had a short visit. He held up his wrist and said, "Captain, it will be difficult to explain where this came from."

Dave looked down at his own wrist, smiled and said is there any other business?"

The Callisto was an object of beauty glowing like a golden nugget as it cruised down into the universe proper. There was no more a blue triangle there was no way back – their experiences were only a memory or even a secret to some. The tip to earth was going to be long and tedious. They would not encounter anything that could match what they had experienced. Therefore, there was nothing more to be achieved, and the only goal was to get back in safety. From here on the trip would consist of simple routine.

Quang Chow reported, Radiation 91% down nine points and dropping, the exit waves must have protected us! Larry was impressed.

HYPER-NATION

Almost everyone who was not on duty went to rest in his or her Hybos. Larry followed suite and slipped into a blissfully slumber. When he awoke, he went to the washroom, shaved, and pulled on a pair of shorts and a dark blue T-shirt with Killiney Bay Surf Club, written in white. As he made his way to the main concourse, he noted that the "Business as Usual" attitude had set in. Orange Juice, Coffee and Danish pastries were provided it was going to be a busy day. Hiroshi joined Larry and told him there was a meeting in fifteen minutes time. At the Captains meeting Dave, Laura, and several of the astrophysicists greeted them and the meeting began.

Dr Quan Chew said that the danger from Radiation had passed, but the meeting was interrupted by the navigator who announced that a strange unidentified object was moving in an erratic course up ahead. A bright disc could now be seen dancing through the stars. As it did so, it seemed to get closer to the ship. There was no time for evasive action.

They were at the mercy of the moment. It looked like a massive UFO was about to ram them. They braced for impact, but the expected collision did not occur. There was no explosion or crash; all that happened was the experience of incredible brightness and the feeling of inertia.

Then the disc stopped and did not move but instead it just turned off! Immediately Dave spoke on the intercom,

"This was not a UFO, it might have been a beam from Omega, a laser searching about our progress and evidently the report was satisfactory."

Just then the navigator interrupted, "Sir, unless I'm wrong, this Spec shows that we are not where we think we are, we have just been pushed within a Galaxy and I suspect it is ours!"

People gathered around the windows. There in front, lay the great sprawling shape the shone so bright that its light began to penetrate the ship. Someone yelled, hip, hip. There was cheer in answered.

It took about two months to accomplish entry to our own solar system. During this time Hiroshi did a lot of paintings that depicted every aspect of the trip; however, he did not have to hide away to perform his artistry. The Captain had no intension of hindering him after all they had gone through. Once inside their Solar System, they slept in shifts. Then as they came near Uranus contact with earth was attempted but without result.

Laura told the group that it was now time to reset the clocks. On estimating the position of the planets and their movement since departure, they estimated that it was now one and a half years and a few days, since they had departed.

The scene outside became filled with light. Jupiter with its moons winked in the distance, as Io and the moon and name sake Callisto came into sight. The Captain arranged for the laser to be fired and all lights out for one minute in recognition.

Soon after that it happened, Richard was awake and pouring over physics notes. He was within earshot of the controller and heard his voice receiver suddenly crack into life. There was a sound of static and then the distinct sound of a human voice. At first, they began to receive numbers and co-ordinate on the EM/SPEC, and then they heard the voice, clearly,

"This is EUSARUSS advance station zero one seven, respond and identify yourself."

Then he began to relay the same message in Arabic, Russian, French and so on.

Dave was called, but it was Laura that arrived first. She cut short the broadcast by saying,

"This is the Callisto UMEX171. We are returning from Extreme Mission code Zero, Zero, Niner, Niner, Zero, Five, One."

In an instant the main concourse filled with people; it was amazing how quickly they had heard about the contact. Richard awakened Larry and the others and was just in time to hear the reply,

"Well, I'll be god' darn, we thought you were goners, now please reconfirm what you said, over."

The Captain emerged and listened to Laura make the official reply with tears streaming down her cheeks. Francisca had her hand over her face and was sitting in a seat with her sides shaking. Larry consoled her but in doing so began to cry himself. He had forgotten that he had a Mom and a Dad or that there was such a place as home.

From that moment onwards, there was no more peace on board the Callisto. Gone was the delicious boredom, with its long periods of contemplation. The ship's crew had become celebrities as the s-mail came back online. The closer they got to earth the more intense it became. At first the Captains had to relate what had happened directly by coded message to the EUSARUSS central command.

He related the bare facts, keeping in mind what could be substantiated from the crews' reports that he had read. In fact, they had included everything down to the last Pirate. However, he said that the explanation of the events would be down to the scientific team who would make their reports when they get back to base. Then he had to explain about the missing crew. This was a difficult situation to iterate. He did so by naming the witnesses who saw their self-chosen departure, and that included Larry. Despite the secrecy of the report, the media got wind of the story, the missing crew and the heroic battles fought in distant places. It began with requests for certain members of the crew to be interviewed by national geographic and every science TV shows on the planet. Some of the wise ones refused interviews and that way were saved gruelling questions. Larry could not refuse because he was instructed to speak in his capacity as a physicist, it was his duty. Francesca and Nadine and several of the other female cadets became icons of their gender. Word had it that women's magazines ran stories about how their supposedly delicate bodies coped with the massive changes. They were asked if they experienced any romantic feelings while in the next dimension. They surprised each other by admitting they did. However,

Hiroshi's experiences were shrouded from the media because his accident was classified information.

The remaining month was filled with photographing planets, making measurements of light refraction, and writing up reports. The intercoms became jammed with earth music news flashes and sports reports. Despite the pressure, Larry found time to sit with Francesca and talk. Then when they were sitting at the rear window gazing at the retreating stars that Larry again asked.

"Francesca, do you remember I asked you to marry me and you did not reply. Do you believe in marriage?"

She turned and looked him with her large brown eyes and replied, "No, Larry not at all."

"Would you agree then to share our lives?" He asked in dismay.

"Larry whatever we do, it's for ever."

Larry mailed and they kissed.

The Captain then announced that non-commercial calls would be permitted. That meant personal call to families only.

This created some real excitement cantered around the STV link up.

Larry got to see his parents on a flickering screen and to speak with them. Of course, he could not disclose that he had met them in Purgosia. The conversation went like this, "Hi mom it's me Larry, alive and well. How are you and Dad, and Amy and Jill, did you think we were lost for ever?"

"Larry oh! Larry" said Maria with tears in her eyes "Thank God your safe and well, we all send our love and look forward to having you. Here is Dan, here Dan says hello."

"Larry my boy, only for your mom's prayers you would not be back safe, so thank her. Now tell me did you have a great experience. We are looking forward to hearing everything when you get back- a big shin dig will be arranged." Maria then added,

"Amy and Jill sent their love, and they will be here to see you on your return. How is Hiroshi, I dreamed he had an accident I hope that's not true."

Larry responded, "No mom, Hiroshi is okay there was no accidents. See you in a about two weeks, Slan!"

With that the name of the next caller came up on the screen and Larry's folks faded from sight.

It was Dr Manz who came to Larry with an idea. He asked to see him in private for a moment. When they were out of earshot he spoke,

"I've been doing my homework and I've come up with ten people, as well as you and I who would be prepared to form committee. I believe there is a strong desire in people to do something because of our experiences. We would be a steering committee for a greater movement that might in time improve world order, climate change, virus control also as a symbol we might use the Excalibur as our motif. What do you think?" Larry was quite taken aback and said,

"Yes, Casper, that's one hell of an idea. The implications are huge so, you can count me in."

BACK TO BASE

When the ship docked at the space platform, they got a muted welcome from crew who did know whether they were heroes or villains. Then they were shuttled to earth in batches, just as they had come up. They were next put into quarantine and taken daily for questioning and debriefing. Viruses it seems were not identified in space and must be earth generated and as this was of public interest it went straight to the news desks globally. The process went on for several weeks, during which time Dave's story was checked and rechecked. Larry had a meeting with the Captain and Manz and said that to quell the storm they would surrender his Excalibur to demonstrate that they did have an extra-universal encounter. On the good side, the black box agreed with the EM/SPEC reports. These were a little vague but the voices in Pergosia came over loud and clear. Unfortunately, there were no images other than the shrouded entrance to the tunnel, but what it recorded was enough to prove the validity of Captains and Associates. The awful consequences of the whole thing were that Ham, Rap and Deli's families pressed claims for damages because of the loss of their relatives. The legal professionals were in a difficult position as there were no bodies as evidence. It became clear that this was a case that would come back, time and time again, to haunt all concerned. However, Dave felt that the administration had enough witness reports to work on and thus got on with his life. When the interrogations were all but over, there was a civic reception that was attended by EUSARUSS representatives, the Callisto personnel, the press, and celebrities from the science world. George Kuhn arrived though uninvited causing a small uproar when refused entry. Richard came to his rescue and the "old braggard" was allowed enter. George, it seems had gathered more information about what had been happening then anyone so far. He said to Richard and a group of the crew,

"Look fellas, I'll put it this way. The confidential reports will remain confidential for a few days, until they are hacked by a kid on the Internet. Then the media and the science journals will take over, and there is enough proof to confirm that the Callisto and crew did move into some other dimension. There is no question of hallucinations or any of that junk."

Directly after that, Hiroshi went to see his parent in Japan, Richard and George Kuhn returned to Florida, Francisca went with them as she had a scheduled stop at Pensacola to visit her Cadet College. Then she intended flying home to Albuquerque to see her parents. Larry then insisted that he book her on a later flight to Ireland so she could spend Christmas with him and meet his family. She had of course met them in Purgosia, but they had not yet met her!

DECEMBER TWENTY-FIRST

Francisca thought it was nice to see the word "Christmas" as opposed to the very commercial "Happy Holidays". She was fed up with a world of so-called equality and insurance laden bureaucracy where it was unfashionable to be human. She detested the efforts that world systems to pasteurise human input and replace it with machine terminology. She therefore took the opportunity to shout out, "Merry Christmas" to as many people as possible. It was now the twenty-first of December and she was meeting Larry in Dublin. He had a long leather case strung over his shoulder and in it was the sword returned earlier than expected. He clutched it so tight that no one would be able to prize it from his possession. It was late afternoon and fashionable Grafton Street was a hive of activity. Though it was already dark, the Christmas lighting now aglow, added an atmosphere of cheer. People were dressed in all sorts of muffled up gear to protect from the cold. It should be noted that they all had face masks to protect from any virus. The two space veterans ambled slowly up the street and wandered into Brown Thomas's department store. Then they visited an art shop and finally went to Weirs intending to buy a wedding ring. Francisca was in a happy frame of mind, enchanted with the warm friendly atmosphere that this city had to offer. She eventually selected a De Beers cut diamond only just in time before the shop closed. Then out of a sense of gratitude Larry took her to St Teresa's Carmelite Church in Clarendon Street which lay close by. Inside there was a crib with the holy family. They both knelt and tried to pray. It was the first time they had reflected on Paradise since leaving the void. Despite their experiences they could not concentrate. The Star of Bethlehem was painted in the background as forecasting a great event. It was amazing to be looking at a statue of Mary that enchanting woman they had met. No one would ever believe where they had been, and that they knew exactly where their prayers would go and who would do the processing. Though she was their friend Mary's face remained intransigent and she just stared straight ahead. Larry knew that Francisca must be sharing similar thoughts and therefore whispered, "Don't worry she can, hear us"

Francisca nodded and held out her hand and the engagement ring for Mary to see. They each put money in the poor box, bowed and departed.

Larry's cell phone jingled, Meli keliki maca. It was home asking what time they would arrive?

OL'SAINT NIC'

Soon after that, they made their way to the suburbs and arrived at Larry's home. His parents and young Amy were overjoyed to meet Francisca. for the first time as they thought. Amy was delighted with the load of brightly wrapped gifts that they brought to put under the tree. She perked up as soon as they arrived to ask if they had seen Santa when they were in heaven? Francisca took the initiative, "We discovered there are at least three Santa's. The first one is clothed in Gold and that is Father Christmas, and the next is in Red and that is the Santa that comes here. Then there is a magnificent one in midnight blue that no one has ever seen and that makes the season so crisp and frosty. She is covered in a haze and wears a crown of silver that sparks. Her smile lifts your spirits no matter how low one feels "Oh they must be so beautiful; I would love to meet the lady in blue."

Maria took Larry and Francisca by the arms and escorted them to the table. She had prepared a welcome dinner over which they talked for hours about all that had happened above and beyond. Now needless to say, Larry did not know how to say that they all had met but as the evening wore on by being pressed for more and more information, he eventually came out with the full story.

As he related what happened in Purgosia, their parent's eyes opened wide. The reports they had got were obviously censored and the story had been quite distorted. They were afraid at first to hear about their own futures because it seemed to be against nature. However, when they were assured that all would end up united in Purgosia they seemed quite relieved.

Traghmahon in County Cork in winter is not quite so pretty as in summer. Nevertheless, it has a rugged winter beauty of its own. The bracken on the headland was now quite brown and the bay looked grey, as did the sky. Christmas was a sort of indoor time of the year; hence the dull weather did not matter in the least. Amy took it on herself to untie the Christmas tree from the top of the car and to drag it in to the living room. Larry erected the tree in a wooden barrel and both Amy and Francisca did the decorating. Francisca then presented Amy with a Piñata all the way from New Mexico. It was so heavy that it almost unbalanced the tree, so they hung it from a fitting near bye. It was not long before they had everything in its designated place, and so, the fun began

PLAYBACK TIME

The following day Hiroshi arrived with Jill. She was ecstatic with his safe return but did not yet hear about his close encounter at inversion. They had rented a car and were now quite tired from the long journey on twisted roads. Despite this Jill suggested,

"Why don't we all go for a drink in Crook haven." Being glad to see more of the countryside they all agreed and so, Larry and Francisca piled into Heroshi's car. They drove to the maritime village and entered a hostelry called O'Sullivan's. It was quiet as there were not so many people as expected. They were greeted and promptly gave their order. As they waited for it to arrive, Jill said life is so natural here, just listen to lanyards clanking on the empty masts and the wail of seagulls in the breeze. All heads turned with curiosity and anticipation. On the next table there was a Cork Examiner newspaper. The headlines caught Larry's attention and he began to read a column of interest. "Hey everyone hear-this, there was a serious car accident yesterday in which a family driving to Clonakilty collided with a truck. Sadly, the parents and their two children lost their lives. They were Lizabeth and Carlo Ryan Valdez and their two children Janette and Rico RIP." Heroshi grabbed the paper and re read the article and breathlessly said, "What a coincidence. This is something we know all about but cannot disclose, except to Jill of course." Jill looked puzzled. Larry folded the paper and paid for it with the drinks bill and with that they left. On the way back Larry related the story about the children to Jill, she was in awe.

On Christmas day itself, there were visits to neighbours and in return others who called to see them. It took till about 5pm before they managed to sit down to celebrate. After dinner they opened some remaining gifts, and then they all went for a long walk across the hills and back by the beach. On their return, Francisca asked Larry to bring in the sword. Reluctantly he brought it and laid the case on a coffee table in front of the fire. He slowly opened it to reveal a lumpy structure under a chammy protective lining. Jill reached forward and let out a squeak as she felt the texture inside. Larry un-sheafed the sword and laid it on the chammy. Its shape could now be easily identified. The family gasped each one in turn running their hands over its contours. Jill squeaked,

"Ouch this is amazing, what is it made of and what is it worth Larry"?

Larry shot back, "Its mad of Praque, a supernatural alloy that is energised by good act of humanity. Also it is not for sale, its priceless and furthermore not mine to sell."

By the embers of the fire the sleek outline of the masterpiece could almost be seen better than in any other light. It seemed to emit a faint glow and seemed also to generate a peaceful feeling. Then Larry sanctimoniously closed the container and put the Excalibur away.

Hiroshi struck up a conversation. The fire was low and as he gazed into the embers of the he looked up at his friends and said, "I wonder where all this will lead us? Apart from marital bliss I see trouble ahead because we have been entrusted with awesome knowledge. What do you all think?" Everyone murmured but no one replied. Then in silence they all stared into the red embers each one immersed in thought!

Printed in the United States
by Baker & Taylor Publisher Services